World's Shadow

Book I of The Quietus of Fate

By Brian C. Kershner

ISBN: 1942082029
ISBN-13: 978-1-942082-02-6

Acknowledgements

Twenty-five years ago, I was enamored with works by Tolkien, Dante, Godwin, and just about every book on King Arthur I could get my hands on. On top of that I read every single one of the Hardy Boys novels, falling in love with the idea of mysteries with unconventional resolutions and fantastical wordplay.

I started simply, a story about a hero and the small band of people he gathered around him. It was all hand-written on yellow legal pads, collected in a binder; a mixture of a child's imagination and a child's writing talent. At the time I was twelve. I always told myself that one day it would be something more.

As a freshman in high school, that something more came in the form of a promise to myself. As much as I loved high fantasy, I was plagued by the fact that it was hard at times to relate to fantasy characters and to see their humanity behind the extraordinary abilities that they often possessed. So I made a promise to myself and anyone who would ever read my works that my characters would be as real as any person they could meet off the street. Whether you loved them or hated them, you could always relate to them, or at least understand their motivations.

It took twenty years for the first of my novels to find its way into publication, and the characters that I dreamt up one summer are still as fresh and vibrant today as the day they came to life in the mind of a child.

Hopefully they will live for you and bring you the same joy.

B.K.

Table of Contents

Chapter 8

Chapter 9

Epilogue

Appendicies

The Dragon shall be loosed by Lightning,
Natural and unnatural element shall impede his journey,
Ancient Wars shall end in his name,
Old animosities will find shelter in his Shadow.

A pretender shall rise beneath a Viper's watchful eye,
Ripples of the past will be seen in the Mirrors of the present,
Fires shall topple the den of the Lioness,
Conspiracies shall litter both the Shadow and Light.

The future is not yet written,
The past never truly dead,
The present favors the driven,
Time is how legends are bred.

-   Aralias Imstra
Prophecies of the Coromor

Prologue

Stepping Into Prophecy

The first rays of sunlight rose over the little town of Lakestone, signaling the beginning of a new day and painting the sky with hues of yellows, oranges and reds. In the new light of the morning, the dense black smoke provided sharp relief to the picturesque sky, rolling off long extinct ashes that lay in strewn piles all over the war-torn corpse of an island. In the distance, the light stretched like spindly fingers over a deep valley. Once, before the war that would nearly rend the world, the valley had been covered completely in ice, a mark of powerful magic that resisted even the harshest summer heat. However, the once great and mystical Valley of Ice had faded into the same mists of legend that had swallowed the memory of its origin, and a more powerful magic had taken root. The thick and ancient ice had melted, the resulting water rushing through the valley into Exeter Lake which surrounded the aptly-named Lakestone. In a matter of hours nearly half of the town had been plunged into the frigid waters. Most of the larger buildings in the city crumbled beneath the rushing tide, but some still stood proud, stretch for the sky like monuments in a submerged graveyard. Beneath Exeter Lake however lay a much different kind of tomb.

On the very bottom of Exeter Lake lay the remains of a palace. This hidden palace was not constructed to match the grandeur of others in the world, it became a nexus from which the most fearsome threat the world had ever seen would emerge. It was a place of evil and hatred, but the power that had once inhabited the palace had been silenced in a war of such proportion that the world still rung with the stories of the heroes and villains. Deep in the heart of the palace had once churned fires that would have melted the strongest stone, but just as powerful forces melted the Valley of Ice, so too did the wards that prevented the water of Exeter Lake from flooding into the palace. When frigid water met smoking magma, the resulting explosion of steam and solidifying rock shook the very foundations, collapsing entrances, filling once vast rooms with porous rock, and fossilizing centuries of hate. No one should have survived the destruction of the palace, but six heroes clawed their way through the maelstrom of fire and stone, cheating death as the palace went through its final convulsions. Their fates had not been tied to the beasts who called the palace their home and they had lived to tell their tale of victory to the world. Though somber, the tale had brought the kingdoms of the world great relief and months of celebration, and Lakestone would be thought of by many as a monument to the thousands lost in a war they would never fully understand. As the celebrations quieted, and the heroes of the War of the Lion faded from view into self-imposed obscurity life seemed to return to some shade of the normalcy that held it before anyone knew such evil could exist. But as the world would soon learn, a single victory, no matter the scale, cannot extinguish evil forever.

Under the rubble of the ruined palace, something moved. Rocks that had been melted into place by primal fire and steam suddenly shifted. More rocks fell away, and as water rushed in to fill the newly created cavity, a form slithered against the tide. It was like a black shadow moving through the water, inching its way through the debris. Suddenly, the form shot toward the surface, exploding through the barrier in a funnel of wind and water. The winds howled against the intruder, but when it extended its wings and caught the breeze with their powerful strokes, the protests waned, and the tumult died down. The midnight-black dragon took one long look back at the remains of its home, and then turned its attention back toward the horizon. The time had come for Shau-ling to live again. He had laid dormant long enough, waiting for his powers to replenish. For an interminable span of time, he had waited in a pit of heat, smoke, and stone, hate fueling every breath. In the first hours and days, it took every trickle of power that remained in his body to stay alive, to reconstruct his body from the husk that had been struck down. For a long time, only the barest powers were available to him, and the hot green flame that was his life-force hung just outside his ability to grasp. But now, he felt the full powers of the Blaze pulsing through him, and as the wind blew across his face, a familiar scent stuck in his nose. He could tell that scent anywhere, and it clawed at his heart and turned his stomach with each breath he took. It was the smell of hope, the smell of the *Coromor*, the only force capable of saving the world from being crushed under the foot of the mighty Shau-ling. The dragon spit a mixture of fire and hatred into the air as the thoughts of the *Coromor* crossed his mind.

Has it been a generation already? The dragon thought to himself. *The time of the Shadows will finally come, and the world will kneel before the might of Shau-ling!*

* * * * * * * * * * * *

Even before the War of the Lion, Marcwell had been the center of the world for culture, economic power, and moral direction. A long line of rulers had forged a kingdom in which the force of ideas rather than the force of arms set the agenda for progress. However, when the darkness of Shau-ling and the phasia descended on the world, it was the young Lord Cedric Binosear that took up the mantle of the warrior and led the fateful strike into the den of evil. Upon his return, Cedric was hailed a hero, and it was thought that a new era of prosperity would dawn under his leadership. However, the great Lord Lion disappeared into the depths of his castle, speaking through intermediaries and through the other heroes of the war. This caused a great deal of confusion, and for some resentment, but the good will generated by the acts of the Lord Lion, even if not heralded by his own voice, lifted Marcwell higher than it had ever been before. But as strange news came out of Lakestone and the frontier kingdoms, it seemed that a pall fell over the royal palace, and decrees from the Lord Lion ceased. Not even the heroes of old were seen acting in their Lord's name. It had been a week since the first puzzling reports had come from Lakestone, and since that day, the nights seemed to pass slower and slower in the city of Marcwell. During the day, the city still bustled with the passing of visitors and tradesmen, and there seemed to be no trouble on the horizon, but when night fell there was a different feeling. It was as if a shroud of dread hung over the world when the sun set and this dread permeated everything, its harshest effects centered in the bedchambers of Cedric Binosear.

If the nights passed slowly for other men, Cedric lived in perpetual darkness. Days passed in the tortured sleepless minutes, and the troubled young man fought hard to push away sleep as much as he longed for the ability to close his eyes and drift off into peaceful slumber. But there was no peace when Cedric closed his eyes. Sleep was plagued with horrible dreams that plunged his heart and mind into horrors that had no name. Each time he tried to sleep, he woke drenched in sweat, his face contorted into a silent scream that none could hear, and as the ragged breaths calmed, he wished he never had to sleep again. It was out of sheer exhaustion that he would succumb to sleep at all, but even then it was broken and tormented.

In his room deep within the royal palace, Cedric lay in his bed tossing and turning. Both he and his sheets were soaked with sweat, and his hands gripped the edges of the bed as though it was trying to throw him to the floor. His eyes were shut tightly, but the expression on his face spoke of pain and suffering. The nightmares had come again to his fragile mind. His face contorted into a scream, but no sound escaped his lips and he remained frozen there for what felt like an eternity in his imprisoned mind. Finally the gates to his private hell burst open and Cedric snapped up to a sitting position. His normally cold and dispassionate eyes were filled with fear and sorrow; his skin crawled and was white with deathly pallor. In his mind he knew that what he had just lived through had been nothing more than a dream, but his heart still felt like it would tear itself from his chest with each labored and aching beat.

Sliding himself slowly to the side of his bed, the still young lord dangled his feet over the side so that they touched the soft rug that lay beneath him. After a long deep breath, he looked up toward the large open window and fixed his eyes on the harvest moon that hung low in the sky over his kingdom. It took a moment for his eyes to adjust, but then he reached for his breeches that hung on a chair near his bed and slid them on. The aches in his body seemed to be magnified with every move, and no matter how he stretched, he could not relieve the pain, so Cedric chose to shut it out. He shouldn't have felt as old as he did. Of course he had suffered wounds during the war, and many of them still ached, but his body nearly constantly felt as though it was being stretched and pulled from every angle, and his joints ached from the exertion. He hadn't even reached the age of forty yet, but sometimes to look at himself in the mirror he felt as though he was twice that age. His hair had already begun to gray at the temples and if he let his beard grow to more than a stubble, it was more white now than black. Lines in his face looked more like cracks in marble than gentle signs of aging, and his joints creaked now more than most of the doors in the palace.

After a strike of the flint, he lit the candle that sat in its golden candlestick on the table by his bed. As light was cast on the table he stopped for a moment to look at the portrait of his sister. It had been a long time since he had seen Anabel, and it was the times when his mind was the most troubled that he missed her sound council and advice. Unlike the rest of the heroes of the War of the Lion, Anabel chose to craft her own identity in the new world that they had helped to create. As he had descended into his own darkness, she seemed farther and farther away from him. Perhaps he had driven her away, or perhaps she had been the first to see that those who chose to stand beside Cedric would only be dragged down by him. Shaking away the fatalistic thoughts, Cedric slowly stood and took the candle from the table and walked over to the hearth on the other side of the room. After a few moments, and much more effort than should have been necessary, he had built a small fire, and he stayed crouched in front of it for a time before he stood and fixed his eyes on the painting over the mantle.

Over the past few years he had spent many nights in this same position, standing by the fire, looking at the painting of his lost bride. It had been years since the forces of Shau-ling had taken her from him, but every day that passed did nothing to dull the pain. He could still see the events of that day playing through his mind as though it were only yesterday, and the horror of her loss still echoed in him every morning when he realized that she was gone. The painting had been done the night before their wedding, and was to be a gift from Cedric to his wife to show her how beautiful everyone saw her to be. But she had been killed before she could see what Cedric saw every time he looked at her. The painter had captured her soul on that canvas, and even as Cedric looked at it, he could see the warm loving glow in her eyes, and he felt the surge of love run through him. Her eyes had always set his soul ablaze, and as he stood there, he felt each tear as they ran down his cheeks. Had it not been for the utter silence in the room, Cedric might not have heard the door open behind him over his sobs. Bright torchlight flooded into the room, casting a young man's shadow on the floor. The young soldier, dressed in full armor had his sword strapped to his side, but yet there was a fear and nervousness in his eyes that should not have been.

"Lord Lion," the soldier said quickly, "the forces of the Shadow have been encountered near Brea and outside Lakestone. Shau-ling lives my lord!"

In that second a change overtook Cedric. The pain and sorrow that held him evaporated, burned away by the suddenly raging fires of hate and vengeance. When he turned to face the young soldier, the boy flinched when Cedric fixed a cold, hateful stare upon him. The tears had disappeared from his cheeks, and the moments of weakness had been erased. The anger and hatred for his mortal enemy burned in his eyes and began to pulse through his veins as the seconds passed. He moved to his bed without a word and drew the Lion Sword from the scabbard that hung on the chair. With the briefest glance down at the polished blade, Cedric turned toward the door, grabbed a wadded up shirt off the table and started toward the door. As he passed the soldier on his way into the hall, he began barking orders in every direction.

"Send word to the troops in Trelon that they will march for Brea as soon as Captain Zerran arrives. Tell Lord Arathorn that he will report to me as soon as his forces are gathered. Rouse Aryx and tell him to prepare to travel at sunrise. Have the armory opened and begin to assemble the militia. The defense of Marcwell and our allies must be our first priority. I will be in the war room. Bring me a piece of parchment, a quill, and some ink there."

"Yes, Lord Lion," the soldier replied.

* * * * * * * * * * * *

Cedric sat at the large table in the center of the war room working diligently on the letter in front of him. Each word had to be carefully planned so that the meaning would be conveyed without using too pointed of a vocabulary. If the contents of the letter were to be read by someone other than the rightful recipient, then Cedric hoped that they would not be able to understand what was being discussed. More than that though, Cedric knew the impact his words would have. He had stumbled upon his destiny without someone to help guide his footsteps. Cedric viewed this as an opportunity to help his successor to avoid some of the mistakes he had made in his ignorance. After he finished, he signed his name and title under the bottom line of the flowing script. After rolling the letter, he held a chunk of sealing wax into the flame of a nearby candle and pressed it onto the letter. He then pressed the ring on his left ring finger, his signet ring, into the wax. He looked absently at the springing Lion; his kingdom's crest, pressed into the golden wax, and then sighed.

As he took a long slow breath, there came the expected knock at the large wooden doors. He closed his eyes and raised his left hand idly toward the doors. For a long moment, nothing happened, but as beads of sweat began to form on the man's forehead, the doors began to tremble a bit, and then they began to open. When they had opened fully, the figure of a young man was revealed. For a quick moment there was a look of concern on the man's face, but it faded quickly, replaced by the sharp face of a warrior. He took three long strides into the room and then went into a long bow as he reached the edge of the table. Cedric opened his eyes and looked up at the new arrival.

Aryx Terian, the man who many called White Lightning, by all rights should have looked more like an old man than Cedric did, but somehow the blond-haired knight still looked as though he were in the best part of his twenties. No lines of time touched his face, and his eyes were as clear and bright as they ever were. Though they had been allies for many years, Cedric had never been able to completely shake the unease that he felt when around the older man. It had been there from the moment they met, like a splinter in his mind's eye. But now, with the threat of another war looming with the Shadow, Cedric didn't have the luxury to humor his paranoia.

"Sit down, Aryx," Cedric said uneasily, "how is your wife?"

"Diana is fine my lord and she sends her regards. I see that you are still not listening to Mailock's advice."

Cedric rolled his eyes at the mention of his old ally's name.

"Mailock may be one of last of the Moridon, and one of the wisest men I've ever met, but I've never been able to trust wizards, Aryx, and I don't think I ever will. And no matter what sources Mailock consults, he can find no proof that the powers that I have gained are causing my weakness. He thinks that it is unnatural that I still have the powers of the *Coromor*, but I believe he is wrong. He does not know the prophecies as well as you and I do, Aryx. And now that Shau-ling has returned, one conclusion has become inevitable."

"Is that why I am to be leaving Marcwell instead of leading a striking force into Brea?" Aryx asked calmly.

"Yes it is. You will leave for the town of Aradon as soon as you are ready. I was there five years ago while you were in Lakestone, so your appearance there should not rouse any suspicions with the townsfolk. There you will find a boy named Logan Ranthall and his father Arin. Arin and I became fast friends, and from some of his stories, I believe that he is the second of the prophecies, Aryx, and therefore is more important than any town Shau-ling has seen fit to assault. Arin was a soldier, he served under Arathorn in the last days of the war, and so he'll understand the gravity of the situation."

"How can you be sure that this boy is the *Coromor*?"

"I can't be completely sure. However, I have been thinking about the prophecies, as well as the riddle that Shau-ling gave in his palace. There is one line that keeps ringing in my mind. From a fallen hero, a Chosen hero, the *Coromor* will arise. We never found the Chosen One of our generation Aryx, and I think that it might have been Logan's father."

"The only way we'll be sure is if Shau-ling attacks Aradon," Aryx commented.

"I agree. We expect Shau-ling to try and take over the large towns like Illimar, Lakestone, and Brea, but if he were to attack a small town, such as Aradon, we know that there is something there he is afraid of. Right now we have the advantage. Shau-ling may know where the *Coromor* is, but he doesn't know who the *Coromor* is. His agents will just have to blindly attack until the Dragon proclaims himself."

"All our hopes rest on a boy, then," Aryx said shaking his head.

"No different than when destiny tapped me on the shoulder, Aryx. Maybe this time though we can avoid the stumbling and uncertainty and take the initiative in the war. Ask some of the townspeople for information on Arin Ranthall; they should be able to direct you to him. He was not well when I was there last, and he did not think that he would make it much through the winter. If he has died, then you will have to deal with Logan directly."

"Yes, my lord."

"You are to keep him alive until the time is right to make him known to the world. Also, you must help him find the Flame. Once he has it in his possession, bring him back to me, and then I will take him the rest of the way. Now, go and find Logan Ranthall."

Aryx bowed, took the letter from Cedric, and started towards the door.

"Aryx," Cedric said in a distant voice, "one more thing."

Aryx turned back to face his lord. There was a different look in Cedric's eyes now. The power seemed to have drained from him, and his eyes stared blankly toward the doors.

"Have you seen my sister lately during your travels?"

"Yes my lord," Aryx replied.

"How is she?"

"She does well Lord Lion. Her daughter is growing into a proud and fine woman."

"Thank you Aryx," Cedric said in a low, pain-rich voice. "You have been a good friend to me over the years, and I wanted to apologize for the way I have acted. I have not truly been myself since Erika died."

"No apologies are necessary, my lord. We stay on because we love you as a friend and a king. If there is nothing more?"

Cedric shook his head. Aryx nodded and set out toward Aradon.

* * * * * * * * * * * *

The Wandering Maiden tavern was another in a long line of inns and taverns that Logan Ranthall had found himself frequenting over the many months since his self-imposed exile. He nursed his drink slowly and chatted with the bar maids as they made their rounds. He was surprised how empty the tavern had been over the past several nights, but people seemed to be staying in their homes at night rather than going out once the soldiers had begun to pass through town. Like Aradon, the little town of Ragihn was nothing more than a stop-over on the way to someplace else, and the appearance of any type of military was enough to make the locals scarce. Logan was about to make his way to his small room above the tavern when several soldiers entered the tavern and took the table next to Logan's in the corner near the fireplace. It was unusually cold for the late summer, and there was talk that the temperatures may force an early harvest. It didn't take long for Logan to begin catching fragments of conversation coming from the soldiers' table, and the more he heard, the more intrigued he became.

"I can't believe they're really sending us out there," one of the men said.

"There's no chance this is for real, is there? I mean, the war was supposed to be over, supposed to be won. How can any of those creatures still be alive?" another responded, very animated in his voice and actions. "Who knows what is really out there? They may have more power than even the Lion and Lord Arathorn. I don't think they care if can survive this."

"I don't want to go fight. We'll probably all get killed."

Logan didn't stay to listen to any more of the conversation, and didn't even finish his drink. There was so much to do, and so little time to do it all. After a quick run to his room, Logan had packed all of his belongings and had retrieved his horse from the stables. It had been too long since he had thought about going back to Aradon, but now there was finally a chance to change his fortunes. The reason he had left Aradon in the first place was to escape the reputation he had fostered as a trouble-maker and a directionless failure. Ever since his father's death, he had been searching for direction, and without that direction he would never be able to take the hand of the woman that he loved. Her father hated Logan, and did everything possible to make the young man's life miserable and deny his access to the woman that he loved. Logan's father had been a soldier once in his life, and Logan when he was a child saw the respect that other's treated his father with. That was the kind of respect that he hoped to win for himself. Life as an adventurer certainly wasn't going to do that, not at the rate things were progressing, but a war, and the opportunity to serve as a soldier on the front lines; that had promise even Logan couldn't resist. But Logan, the faceless nameless, soldier wouldn't get very far on his own, and he knew just a few other restless and reckless youths back in Aradon that were itching for the opportunity to prove themselves as something more than farm boys and blacksmiths. For three days on the ride from Ragihn to Aradon, Logan practiced what he would say, how he would convince his would-be compatriots to join him in his highly risky endeavor. By the time the Old Forest was in site, Logan had the words burned into his mind. It was midnight before he laid his head on the pillow of his own bed in his own little farmhouse on the outskirts of Aradon, but no matter how hard he tried, he couldn't get this eyes to stay shut.

The morning couldn't come soon enough, and no matter how he tried to distract his mind, he couldn't shake the thought that this was the moment; this was the beginning of something that would change his life forever.

Chapter 1

Coming Home

The morning sun shone brightly though the small window opposite the bed where Logan Ranthall reluctantly slept. After a long night of riding, adrenaline still surged through his veins, and though he lay on his bed with his eyes closed, it was impossible for his mind to release the excitement of the coming days, and the opportunities that his imagination was constructing for him. Finally though, exhaustion overtook him, and inevitable sleep found him. The respite was short-lived, and the bright sunlight hit his eyelids, forcing them open with an irritated groan. After a cursory rub of his slightly aching eyes, Logan shambled out of bed, stretching his aching legs. Three straight days on horseback had taken its toll on him, despite his young age, and stiffness had set in not only to his legs but his back. Working through a minor limp, Logan made his way to the window and opened it, letting the warm breeze caress his face. Despite himself, he was glad to be home, and for those few moments was able to banish the thoughts about why he had left in the first place. He was able to forget that this was the home that he was raised in; that this was the place where his mother, and father, and brother had once lived. But they were all gone now. Logan was the only member of his family left, and if he had any chance of finding the opportunity to create a new family with the woman he loved, he was not going to find it in Aradon.

It had been so late when Logan had returned to his boyhood home, the he had not been able to appreciate or process the state that the house was in. He had not been back to the place in almost a year, and yet it looked as though he had not been gone for more than a few nights. Somewhere inside of him, he had expected the place to be overrun with cobwebs and rodents, but as he made his way into the large room that served as the center of the home, he could tell that even the floor had been swept recently. The large table in the center of the room was cleaned and oiled, and the whole house had the feel of being lived in. It hadn't felt like this since his mother had died. Logan's father was a lot of things, but he certainly couldn't be accused of being an adept housekeeper. Those skills also hadn't been imparted on Logan or his brother, and the state of the house never improved beyond livable. It wasn't until after Logan's father had died that Logan, in a moment of strange realization, understood the truth. It wasn't that his father didn't know how to keep the house in the same way that his wife had, it was that he didn't want to. For the place to be spotless and comforting as it had been when she was alive would have been too much for Arin to take.

Shaking away thoughts of the past and of his parents, Logan returned to his small bedroom and pulled a relatively clean pair of pants and shirt from his pack and threw them on. He slicked his longer than normal black hair back with his hands, and tried to keep it from looking too unkempt. Exiting the bedroom, Logan found himself looking at the dark entryway that led to his father's bedroom. The growl that came from his stomach was enough to prevent him from reminiscing more than he already had, and the lateness of the hour added urgency to his steps as he made his way through the farmhouse's door and started the long walk toward the town of Aradon.

Aradon was not very important of a town in the grand scheme of things, and had been one of the few towns in the area that had been largely untouched by the ravages of the War of the Lion, or any of the wars for ascension that had preceded it. The town itself was on the farthest borders of the Kingdom of Trelon, and though the town paid its annual duty to the Queen, the people of Aradon often considered themselves to be in their own quiet corner of the world. It was rare that any visitors from the larger cities came through, except during harvest season. Aradon's claim to fame was its market that took up most of the center of the city, and traders from all over the countryside would set up shop in order to sell their wares, and acquire enough of the regional crops to take to the larger cities. And while there were many other little farm towns scattering the countryside, Aradon was able to offer the most diverse array of produce, including the increasingly rare Seluiyn fruit. However, once upon a time, Aradon apparently had been more than just a farm town, and the threats of the world had required construction of a great wall that surrounded the town proper culminating in a single wide entrance that could be closed off by a massive thick iron gate. The Gate, as it was called by the residents of the town, hadn't been closed in the memory of even the oldest of Aradon, and was a holdover from a long-dead age. For many years, the town council had debated as to whether or not the Gate and the Wall should be torn down. While there was a sense of tradition and history surrounding the Gate, some felt that it was an unnecessary display of aggression to those visitors who passed through. Logan's father had been one of those members of the council who opposed tearing down the wall. Though outwardly he always held that keeping traditions and antiquities was the reason for his opposition, privately he was comforted by the presence of the Wall. He had been a soldier for a portion of his life, and security in those days, he had once said, was in short supply.

As Logan made his way through the Gate, he noted that there were two guards, one on each side of the Gate greeting visitors as they entered Aradon. He didn't remember there having ever been guards there before. Maybe the paranoia caused by the appearance of soldiers in Ragihn had spread to Aradon. He shrugged away those thoughts and was greeted by the sight of the largest building in Aradon. Unlike most of the major towns that Logan had had the good fortune to travel to with his father and during his own adventures Aradon had only one inn and tavern. The *Traveling Bard Inn* was the first building that anyone saw when they entered Aradon, and looked as though it was built in an age very different from the rest of the town. Aradon as a whole was common, understated, and decidedly rural. However, the *Traveling Bard* was patterned after the more modern and regal inns from Trelon and Illimar. As such, it was a three story brown brick manor, and was by far the largest building in the town. It had taken the masons and stone smiths quite a while to finish the structure, not only because the materials were hard to come by, but also because the ground proved to be ill-suited for a building the size of the *Traveling Bard*. Sinkholes were discovered constantly, causing the foundation to crack and at one point it looked like the project would be abandoned. But in true Aradonian fashion, practically the whole town rallied together and finished construction. Logan had been only a baby when the last brick was put into place, but now the *Traveling Bard*, stood proudly; a focus of civic pride for all who had a hand in its construction.

As a way to show his appreciation to the town, the innkeeper and his wife began a tradition in Aradon, serving breakfast to all of the working men and apprentices in town before they started work for the day. Most of the workmen paid for this service, while others bartered services in exchange. Every morning at six bells, the smells of fresh baked bread and seared breakfast meats would begin wafting from the open windows of the large kitchen, and it would be minutes later that prepared plates of food would start emerging from the kitchen to be placed on tables in the common room. Breakfast every morning varied, but everyone got served and there was never a complaint about the quality of the food. Most of Logan's friends were apprentices in one form or another when he had left on his journey, so breakfast at the *Traveling Bard* was as good a place as any to start his recruitment.

Most of the seats were filled by the time Logan walked into the common room, and despite his slightly haggard appearance no one seemed to take notice of him. After a quick scan of the room, a sly smile came to Logan's lips that he quickly suppressed. A moment later he was sliding into a seat across from a blond haired young man only about a year younger than Logan. His hair was shorter than Logan had seen it the last time they were together, and it looked like he had just started shaving and wasn't very good at it yet. David Tamerlane had also filled out in the last year, his shoulders starting to become laced with heavy muscle and his chest becoming broad and powerful. Such was the fate of those who worked under Torris Sandar. Torris was the town's blacksmith and had the reputation of being a hard man who demanded every ounce of sweat and exertion he could wring from his apprentices. Logan's best friend Pike Rhuiden had been an apprentice for Torris as long as he could hold a hammer and swing it without falling over, much like Torris' own son Gwydeon. But Gwydeon's calling was not in blacksmithing, and though he still helped out around the forge when he was needed, Torris had known that Gwydeon's heart was elsewhere. David had only started on as an apprentice for Torris in the year before Logan's departure. But in two years, the change in David's physique was striking to say the least. The four of them, Logan, Pike, Gwydeon, and David had been thick as thieves since they were children, and if there were anyone he could convince to join him in his plans, it would be those three.

It took David a moment to look up from his quickly vanishing plate of food to acknowledge the new arrival to the table, but when he did, he nearly choked. After taking a minute to recover, a wide smile came to David's face, and he could not help but laugh. Before saying anything, he signaled one of the bar maids to bring over a plate of food to Logan, and as she sat it in front of him, David began speaking.

"Did you ride the horse in, or did he ride you?"

Logan flashed his best smile and could not contain the laughter.

"I thought I was going to have to drag him the last few miles, but what can you expect from a horse that was bred in Illimar?"

"Sailors don't know anything about horses," David answered, picking up the old joke. "They would have a better chance teaching the horses how to swim."

"How have you been David?" Logan said, bringing the first fork-full of food to his lips.

"Busy as always. You know Torris; he's never one to let a minute go by without getting the most out of you he can. It's probably why Pike quit."

This time it was Logan who nearly choked.

"I thought Pike loved working at the forge."

"He did," David answered. "It was just working for Torris he couldn't stand any more. You remembered when Pike missed that day before you left? He couldn't sit down for a week after the beating Torris gave him. Pike always said that it was your fault he got so drunk that night."

Logan laughed again, this time putting his fork back on the table.

"Bella Sandar was the reason Pike got so drunk that night. And if Torris didn't tan Pike's hide, it would have been Eldar."

There was a long silence that held for the next few moments, the unspoken question hanging in the air. Though he knew better than to ask, Logan let the question find the air.

"How is Elwyne?"

David looked at Logan for a long moment, and then nodded.

"She's fine."

Again the silence descended upon the two young men. David took the opportunity to finish his breakfast, and after wiping his mouth he pushed his plate forward and sat back into his chair eyeing his old friend.

"So," he said trying to keep his tone even, "to what do we owe the pleasure of your return to Aradon?"

The implication was clear in his barely restrained tone. Logan knew David long enough to know that he was upset and the old friends' reunited levity would not take them much farther.

"I just came in from Ragihn…"

David put his hand up and looked around to see if anyone else was listening.

"There's been strange news coming in from Ragihn and some of the other small towns between here and Trelon. Father and the City Council have been keeping things quiet to keep people from being alarmed, but Torris has had Gwydeon and I working almost double shifts for a month now. Even Pike came back and helped out a few nights. Things have been strange since the first notices came in. And no matter how hard my father has tried to keep a lid on things, rumors are flying about monsters and soldiers on the move. I'm sure you saw the guards at the Gate."

Logan nodded, then lowered his voice to a conspiratorial tone and leaned in.

"I ran into a few soldiers in Ragihn. They're being deployed somewhere to fight, and believe me when I say that morale is not high."

Suddenly the light of understanding flooded into David's eyes.

"No."

Logan rubbed the start of the beard on his chin with the back of his right hand.

"Not even going to hear me out?"

"What's to hear out? When was the last time that any of your schemes worked out? When was the last time that you didn't get us all into trouble? And I seem to remember that you were the one who left us all."

Logan felt as though he had been struck.

"And you know exactly why I left."

David hesitated for a moment. Seeing the look in Logan's eyes, he knew he went too far. Sensing David's uncertainty at what to do next, Logan pushed the momentary anger and hurt to the side and pressed forward.

"It won't hurt to listen."

The momentarily impassive face cracked into a smile the next moment, and suddenly David nodded his concession.

"And I suppose you came all this way just to talk to me."

Logan smiled and shook his head.

"Alright. I'll get Talon, Pike, and Lane. No doubt they'll be at the merchants. Talon's been sweet on one of the new traveling merchant's daughters. And you know as well as I do, that never ends well. We'll meet at your house at lunch. I may want to hear what you have to say, but I'm not going to risk Torris' wrath on one of you schemes. At least not yet."

"You really think he's lay a hand on the mayor's son?"

David stood up and cocked a smile.

"You really think I'm willing to find out?"

* * * * * * * * * * * *

With David gathering some of the troops to hear Logan's pitch, that left Logan with only one destination. The training grounds stood on the far side of the town, nestled up against the Wall. It was a place where all of the aspiring warriors went to practice with a sword, lance, or whatever other type of weapon they chose. The instructors, almost all of them former soldiers that fought during the War of the Lion who had returned home to Aradon, worked hard to make sure that everyone who wanted to know how to fight was trained and ready for whatever endeavor they set out upon. Though a town comprised mostly of farmers and their families, the people of Aradon were not weak-willed. If a threat came, the people of Aradon would defend their families and friends with their lives if need be. Logan himself had been in the training grounds for many months before he set out on his adventures, supplementing the skills taught to him by his father. Despite whatever natural talent and inherited skills he had, Logan was not considered very prepared for the path he chose to walk by those who instructed him. Gwydeon Sandar on the other hand was very accomplished with his training, probably because he spent more time in the training grounds than most of the instructors. The training grounds themselves were no more than a large field segmented off into smaller areas by a large log fence. The six fenced-in areas radiated like spokes on a wheel from a central building complex that served as armory and changing rooms. In the far corner of one of the areas were a man and a woman embroiled in a playful yet intense duel. Another woman sat just beyond the fence, watching intently.

Logan began moving slowly toward the dueling pair, his intention not to distract the pair or their audience. Gwydeon Sandar moved through a long series of well-practiced attacks and parries, keeping the counter-attack options of his opponent as minimal as possible. The woman, Eldar Merin, was fighting totally defensively, but her defense could only be described as perfect. Every attack was blocked or harmlessly parried away, and the feints Gwydeon threw to elicit a response were ignored; the trap clear to her practiced blue eyes. Their clashing styles on the field of battle were mirrors of their clash of backgrounds and attitudes. Gwydeon was commonly born; the middle child sandwiched between two sisters, and destined to inherit the family business as the town blacksmith. Like his father, Gwydeon was broad through the shoulders, and his arms were layered with thick muscles. However, his many years of training with the sword had helped to lengthen his frame so that his thick musculature would not slow his speed with the blade. His shoulder-length brown hair was caked with sweat, but still flowed about his head and face as he moved from attack to attack. It was slightly longer than the last time that Logan set eyes on his childhood friend, a trend that he was sure upset Torris Sandar to no end, but kept the attention of Gwydeon's many female admirers. To say that Gwydeon was a darling of the town was an understatement. But his martial prowess was only exceeded by his dry wit and his discomfort with social niceties.

Eldar Merin's hair was far shorter than Gwydeon's, and blond, and her frame could only be described as short and lithe. And where their physical presence were certainly polar opposites, so too were their attitudes. Where Gwydeon was reserved, Eldar was abrupt, almost caustic. Eldar was the daughter of a wealthy family from Trelon, but when her parents separated, she and her mother came to Aradon. Her new father was a man named Joseph, and he treated her like she was his own. But Eldar was raised as a member of the court of Trelon, and so had far better manners and was better spoken than any of her peers in town and took it upon herself to be big sister, mother, and tutor to all of the backward farm boys whom she deemed worthy of her attention. Initially she thought that learning the sword was beneath her station, but Gwydeon skillfully bartered sword lessons for etiquette lessons. However, that deal turned out to benefit Eldar on both sides of the coin. Eldar turned out to be a savant with the blade and before too long, Eldar was getting the better of Gwydeon in training. Their duels became less about training and more about experimentation, the two fighting a full speed without fear for the other's safety. They were the two best swordsmen in the town, and perhaps in the whole of the Kingdom of Trelon.

The two circled each other, hard exertion mixed with playfulness. To the untrained eye, the two would have looked as though they were playing at a duel, and anyone with ears would have come to the same conclusion. While Eldar was a lady in every sense of the word outside the training grounds, while in its confines, she had all of the poise of a drunken sailor. Gwydeon took on a different posture while dueling Eldar. He seemed freer than at any other time, as though he was truly himself. But the trained eye saw something more, even in the playfulness; the two were exerting themselves as though they were running at top speed every moment. Gwydeon's muscles were tight and his movements as nimble as a cat's. Sweat streamed down his chest like a river. Eldar's exertion matched his, her simple shirt soaked with sweat and clinging to her as though it were skin. Logan remembered one incident where Pike got into a fight with a travelling merchant for some explicit descriptions of Eldar's training attire and the little it left to the imagination.

As Logan approached, the playful taunts and laughter gave way to a final serious exchange where Eldar disarmed Gwydeon, and he sank to his knees, laughing despite yet another defeat at the hands of his protégé.

"I see things haven't changed very much," Logan said as he entered that section of the training grounds. "Still letting the high and mighty lady win?"

Gwydeon turned his head to look in the direction of the new arrival while Eldar spun around and glared in Logan's direction, her lips curling into a scowl. Gwydeon laughed out loud again and then made his way back to his feet, pulling his shirt off of the fence post nearby and wiping his brow. It was no secret to anyone that Gwydeon dreamed of leaving the little farm town of Aradon behind and joining the Lion's Mane, one of the most renown armies in the world. The woman sitting on the ground also looked up, but her expression did not change. Logan tried hard not to look in her direction, but it was a battle that he could not win. Elwyne Tamerlane was the most beautiful woman that he had ever laid eyes on, no matter where he had traveled across the country side. Her beautiful auburn hair and soft brown eyes as well as her soft features and slightly pale skin were burned into his memory. Eldar had been teaching her to be a proper lady, and the two were practically joined at the hip. They may not have been sisters by blood, but they were by deed.

"Perhaps the famous adventurer would be more of a challenge for her then," Gwydeon said, drawing Logan's attention away from Elwyne, "I'm sure she wouldn't mind seeing what new techniques you've acquired on your travels."

"Yes Logan," Eldar sneered. "I'm sure it's been too long since someone put you in your place."

"I'm afraid I'm still not in your league, Eldar," Logan said putting his hands up in mock surrender. "But if you could spare your sparring partner for a bit, I would appreciate it."

Gwydeon arched an eyebrow and Eldar's scowl deepened, but before either of them could utter a word, it was Elwyne who was on her feet rounding on Logan.

"You went to see David before you came here, didn't you? You've got some scheme that you're planning on involving him and Gwydeon in, don't you?"

Logan knew that Elwyne would immediately have that response as she was very protective of David, and with good reason. Logan had a knack for getting people in trouble, though most often he took most of the blame for himself.

"I suppose you've got Pike and Talon already?"

Gwydeon's question brought a different look to Eldar's face. This one was of marked irritation, but there was a hint of sadness in her eyes that was quickly hidden. She and Pike had once been a very happy couple, but the explosion of a fight that ended their relationship still was sending shockwaves through those who counted themselves as friends of one or the other. They avoided each other as often as they could, and any room they were in together found the temperature dropping several degrees. Talon once tried to make peace between them, but ended up getting his ears boxed and a bloody nose for his trouble. As if his nearly sibling-like relationship with Pike wasn't enough to sour his relationship with Eldar, that incident pushed him over the edge.

"David said he would get them over to my house at lunchtime. And no, Elwyne, I didn't ask him to miss work, not that he would anyway, considering how much he's afraid of what Torris would do to him."

"At least one member of that family has some intelligence when it comes to dealing with you, Logan."

Eldar's jibe brought a scowl to Elwyne's face, but she didn't turn to regard Eldar.

"Lunch time should give me enough time to finish my practice and clean up," Gwydeon said, cutting through the tension as though he didn't even know it was there. "I'll be there."

Logan did his best to suppress a smile. Gwydeon would listen to his proposal; there was no doubt about that. He was the most level headed of the group, in all things, but his thirst for adventure made Logan's look amateurish. Had it not been for the circumstances that forced Logan to look for opportunities outside of Aradon, it would have been Gwydeon who was the first to set out for new horizons. Nothing anchored Gwydeon but his own doubts, but contrary to his beliefs, no amount of practice could ever make those demons disappear.

"Then we'll be there too," Eldar asserted following a long exhale and a shake of the head, "even if it means I have to be in the same room with that arrogant bastard."

Elwyne barely suppressed a smile, but she couldn't stop it from glittering in her eyes. Despite himself, Logan felt one corner of his mouth raise slightly, but he too did his best to cover his pleasure. With a nod, the four said their goodbyes and headed off in different directions; Logan toward his home, Eldar and Elwyne toward the changing rooms, and Gwydeon back to his practice.

On his way back to his home, Logan could not keep the smile from coming to his face. He had been away from home far too long, and even more pressing, he had been away from Elwyne for what seemed like a lifetime. There were many nights that thoughts of the beautiful young woman had been the only way the he could fall asleep, and now she was even more radiant than she had been in his fragmented memories. Whatever lay before them, whatever challenges would rise to meet them, Logan knew in his heart that once his childhood friends were by his side, there was nothing that they could not accomplish. Of course, as always, they would have to navigate their own internal strife. Logan could not help but laugh at the thought that the monsters of the world were not nearly as frightening as Eldar's temper. If he could keep Eldar and Pike from each other's throats, he could accomplish anything.

The Stranger

Upon returning to his home, Logan began to prepare for the meeting that would occur in a few short hours. Though confident in the plan, the additions of Eldar and Elwyne to the mix would complicate the explanation and make the whole proposition that much more difficult. He was sure he could sway Pike and Talon, probably Gwydeon too, but now David and Lane were questionable, and Eldar and Elwyne together could probably bring the whole thing crashing down. But Logan had already committed to his course of action. Regardless of what happened in the meeting to come, he would be leaving Aradon again, probably for the last time. After clearing off the table in the main room of the house, he moved to the back bedroom, the one that had been his mother and father's. At the foot of the bed was a chest that looked as though it had been through several lifetimes of storms. Parts of the wood on the lid had been scratched in many different places by the ropes that had been used to tie it down on bumpy wagon rides. Whatever paint or lacquer that had once been on the wood had faded away to a ghostly quality, and the metal was tarnished and spotty. The hinges creaked loudly when Logan forced open the lid. It took only a moment to retrieve the long parcel that lay tightly packed in blankets and sheets. The ancient blade was carefully wrapped and tied with twine that took some effort to remove. It was a long blade that had a slight curve about half-way up its length, with a soldier's hilt that showed some wear and use on the pommel and cross. It was not an ornamental weapon by any stretch of imagination, this weapon was meant for warfare, and had seen use in that regard. The polished silver blade shone in the sunlight streaming through the window high in the east wall, and was only outshone by the golden hilt. Carved in the blade of the sword was the figure of a springing lion, the symbol of the great protector, the Lord Lion. In the chest was also a jeweled scabbard and leather sheath made for the sword. The scabbard had been presented to Logan's father by the Lord Lion, Cedric Binosear on the occasion his visit to Aradon. It would never be worn, and that winter, as Logan's father lay on his death bed, both scabbard and the sword had been entrusted to his care, the only possessions that Logan's father had of any value. On the sheath was an inscription written in the Old Tongue. This ancient inscription read: *Tar' em aer rahsan belican harrim ae*; all fear he who wields the power of the Lion in battle.

Though he had never used the sword, with the exception of some sessions with Gwydeon in the training grounds, it felt as though it belonged on his hip once he had strapped it into place. Logan was still adjusting the scabbard's belt that looped around his thigh when he walked back into the front room of his home, and upon looking up was frozen by the sight of a stranger standing just inside the front door. He appeared to be a man about twenty or so, but his eyes told Logan that he was much older. There was an edge to him that spoke of danger and that he was not a man to be trifled with, but the contrast of his features to his clothing complicated any attempt to get a clear impression. The man had the look of war and battle about him, that much was apparent. He had a small black beard and tattered dirty blond hair which hung in a loose conglomeration around his neck. This stranger obviously didn't care that he looked like a vagrant, but that appearance was shattered by the clothing that he wore under the commoner's cloak. Wrapped in the cloak, this man could have walked down the main streets in any town and no one would have thought him anything other than a beggar. Under the cloak, the strange man was dressed in rich garments with a single round ornament on each shoulder of his light armor. It was difficult to see the sword that he wore on his right hip, but as the cloak furled back once, Logan got a good look at the sword, and instantly recognized it. It was the same design as the sword that Logan now wore on his own hip, a soldier's weapon, and now this ragged man was standing in front of him with an almost identical sword. Somewhere in Logan's head a familiar voice began its tirade. He knew the voice and the words all too well. His father had taught him to size up any opponent before a prospective battle, almost to the point that the little voice in had become Logan's own. By the way that the stranger wore his sword, it was obvious that he was left handed, either that, or he had a very strange way of drawing his sword. Also, he wore a golden gauntlet on his right hand that had a brilliant aura around it. More than anything, that single piece of ornate armor seemed completely out of place. He could have been anything from a lord to a beggar and everything in-between. The fact that he had no qualms about entering a person's house without permission made me start to believe that he was nothing more than a thief who had cobbled together his outfit from whatever he had been able to steal. When he opened his mouth to speak, the words rolled from his tongue in a rich baritone that was almost melodic but filled with strength and confidence.

"Are you Logan Ranthall?" he asked tensely.

The man's rich baritone voice still echoed in Logan's ears as the long seconds crept by. The man's voice under other circumstances could have been called soothing, but now it was simply another factor that kept Logan on edge. Whatever peaceful tone was conveyed by the man's voice, it was belied by his eyes, which were in constant motion, scanning the room as though invisible attackers would jump from the shadows at any moment. Speechless, Logan stood frozen in his tracks, the silence holding him. It was the stranger who seemed to sense Logan's trepidation and slowly eased his hand off the hilt of his sword.

"Easy, my friend. There is no need to be alarmed. I'm a friend."

"Friends usually don't arrive unannounced," Logan said finally finding his voice. "Nor do they arrive armed."

The man straightened, a look of irritation passing over his features for only a moment before a calm smile came to his lips. The smile actually made the man look younger, as though he could be Logan's contemporary.

"A fair assessment," the man said finally, "but you have to ask yourself, if I had really wanted to do you harm, would you have been alive long enough for us to have this conversation?"

CHAPTER 1

There was a rumble in the pit of Logan's stomach, possibly from his heart hitting bottom. He had been so focused on strapping the scabbard of his sword into place when he emerged from the bedroom that the stranger could have killed him a dozen times over, and Logan wouldn't have been aware of the man's presence until it was far too late. In fact, the stranger had somehow managed to open and close the notoriously loud creaking door of Logan's home without Logan hearing anything. Before Logan could answer the obviously rhetorical question, the stranger spoke again.

"Perhaps we should sit and talk."

Logan nodded absently, and the stranger moved deftly past the young man after a curt nod in his direction. After allowing the stranger to pass, Logan waited a handful of steps before following. While the stranger may have been able to surprise him by his entrance into the Ranthall home, Logan would ensure that he would not be caught off guard again. When Logan entered the main room, the stranger had already taken a chair near the interior wall that separated the main room Logan's father's bedroom, away from the windows as well as directly opposite the hall that lead to the front door. Logan sat in the chair directly opposite the stranger. After a moment, the stranger threw his cloak off his shoulders, allowing it to fall onto the back of the chair. Logan was finally able to make out the figures on the ornaments on the man's shoulders. The one on his left shoulder was the same springing lion that was engraved onto the blade of the sword that Logan now wore on his hip. The other appeared to be a lioness sitting on a golden glade that stretched before a great palace. Anyone living in the area knew that was the symbol of the Kingdom of Trelon, the kingdom that Aradon ideally would have been a part of had it not been for the historic stubbornness and self-reliant quality of its people. Laying his gauntlet on the table, the stranger reached into a pocket of the cloak, retrieved a letter, and then placed it on the table. Before Logan could acknowledge either action, the man began to speak again.

"Five years ago, Lord Cedric Binosear passed through this town during his tour of the countryside after the conclusion of the War of the Lion and the victory over the forces of the Shadow. He and your father became friends, and now in his time of need, Lord Cedric sent me to find your father Arin and to call upon him to come to the Lord Lion's aid. However,

I learned quickly after my arrival in Aradon that your father had died the winter following the Lord Lion's visit to Aradon, and that not long after you had left town to seek your own fortunes. I thought that I would not be able to deliver this message, but it seems that fate has decided to assist me in my errand, as you had returned only last night."

"How did you…"

Logan's question trailed off into nothingness. The answer was immaterial. However it was that this man knew about Logan's father or Logan's travels didn't matter; there were too many coincidences to be explained away. There was something greater at work than Logan could explain, and now that the name of the world's savior, Cedric Binosear had been invoked, these pieces of the puzzle were thrown into greater relief. Nothing was explained, nor did it make any more sense, but somehow the coincidences were more palatable.

"I remember Lord Cedric's visit," Logan said absently, "everyone in town does. None of us had seen royalty before, I mean except for the Merins. All the banners and the armor, it made an impression. No one from Aradon actually fought in the war, so our only exposure was from stories that the merchants would tell, and occasionally a letter from a far-away family member would contain snatches of news. I didn't know that my father and the Lord Lion became friends."

The man nodded silently.

"Apparently there is much about your father that you didn't know. Not only did your father fight in the War of the Lion, he was awarded the sword that you wear on your hip by Arathorn Geoffrey after your father showed incredible bravery in the face of overwhelming and nearly impossible odds. When Lord Cedric dispatched me here, I did some research on your father, and spoke to Arathorn. He had fond recollections of your father, and says that many men owe your father a debt that they can never repay."

Logan sat stunned, and could not keep from looking down at the sword. But then his thoughts and his eyes drifted back to the man across the table. What kind of man could be summoned by Lord Cedric Binosear for a mission in a time of great need? What kind of man could casually meet with Lord Arathorn Geoffrey?

"Who are you?"

The stranger pulled his shoulders back and drew his back straight. Even seated Logan felt as though the blond man towered over him.

"My name is Aryx Terian; I am a Knight in the service of Lord Cedric Binosear, the Lord Lion, and the ruler of the Kingdom of Marcwell. I hold the rank of General in the Lion's Mane, and am second in command to Lord Arathorn Geoffry."

Logan's whole body felt like it was vibrating in time with his heartbeat. The man sitting before him, the man who had invaded his home was not a common criminal or an assassin, he was a knight. More than a knight, he was one of the elite, the best of the best, one of the few that stood at the Lord Lion's side at the height of the war. To be a member of the Lion's Mane took a level of dedication and skill that surpassed the elite from other militaries. Gwydeon has been training his whole life just to get noticed by this elite force.

After a moment of letting his declaration sink in, Aryx reached down and picked up the letter from the table and extended it to Logan.

"Lord Cedric tasked me with delivering this letter, and I was to place it in your hand if your father was no longer living. Everything that you need to know about the purpose of this visit is contained within, but it is up to you whether or not you will have the courage to accept the words you will read. What the Lord Lion did not say but I know from my years with him is that no one man can dictate the fate of another. Whatever you find upon breaking the seal of this letter, you must be the one to act or not act upon it."

For a long moment, Logan hesitated. His hand finally extended and touched the rolled parchment. After retrieving it, Logan held it in his hands for a very long time, turning it over and over in his hands until finally stopping to look at the golden seal holding the parchment closed. The seal held the same springing lion that was on the blade of Logan's father Arin's sword, as well as the on the ornament on Sir Terian's shoulder. No matter what words were waiting to be read, Logan knew that they had to be of incredible weight and importance, otherwise they would not have been entrusted to someone the caliber of Aryx Terian. Nearly holding his breath, Logan broke the seal on the letter and slowly unrolled it. The letter was in a fine golden flowing text, and after a quick uncertain glance up at Aryx, Logan began to read the letter aloud.

'Hello, dear friend. Just as my life was changed by the words and actions of another, now I unfortunately must change your life. The world called upon me in its hour of need, and now, I must call upon you in my hour of need. It has been a long time since I have been in your fine town, and I wish that circumstances would have allowed me to return, and it is unfortunate that in this instance I can only send my words and not present this to you myself. I truly enjoyed my time there among your people. What I tell you now is of the utmost importance, and all other things in this life that you hold dear pale in comparison to what I am about to say. Though to your ears that must sound fatalistic and laughable, I assure you, I would not use those words were they not the truth.

My hard fought enemy, the Lord of the Shadows, Shau-ling, has reemerged from the depths that I consigned him to in order to threaten the world once again. In order to face him, I need your help. Believe me when I say that you are the only one capable of carrying out this quest. I need you to find a great weapon that I lost after my duel with Shau-ling. This is the only possession in the world that I would value above my life and the life of my subjects. I cannot describe the value of this weapon or exactly what it is. This is the reason that I sent Aryx. His first purpose is to help you in your quest, and second to help you identify the weapon when you find it. He is a man of great power and skill and can help you in ways that you would never dream possible. Once you find this great weapon, bring it back to me and then we will journey the rest of the way together.

I am not a well man, my friend, and for that reason I am asking you for your assistance. There is another reason that I am making this request, and I believe that I owe you that explanation. After my battle with Shau-ling, and during our escape, I heard a voice resonating though the palace. It was Shau-ling. What he said at the time was nothing more than a riddle and I perceived it as an evil taunt, but now I know it had a deeper meaning than that. He said in a great and horrifying voice, "You are not powerful enough to defeat me yourself, Lion. It would take seven of you to equal my power. This has merely been the first act in an on-going play. The next act will feature the Dragon, a son of your future friend, and he will only try to prolong the play for the people of your world. This is a war that you can never win Lion, but I will see you again. When the seventh of your kind is brought before me, and the last battle begins, I will have my revenge for all time." Then the palace started to crumble around me.'

'What Shau-ling said never started to make any sense until now. I am the first of seven, and you, the son of my friend, or as Shau-ling referred to you, the Dragon, are the second link in the chain. Five more like us will come and fight Shau-ling, and when the seventh has reached his palace, we shall all live again to fight and finally vanquish Shau-ling. Please, I beg of you to follow your destiny and find the weapon of which I spoke. Good luck, Lord Dragon. I hope to see you in Marcwell soon. Be careful. Shau-ling's minions are aware of your existence already, and they will stop at nothing until they see your dead body at the feet of their lord. More than your life rests on the completion of this mission. The lives of five generations to come rest on your success, and your failure could mean the death of the world as we know it. Please, for the sake of us all, find the weapon and bring it back to me here in Marcwell. From here I will lead you to Shau-ling, and then the battle really begins.'

Logan held the scroll in his hands for a long moment after the last words crossed his lips, but the words felt sour in his mouth. Finally he let the parchment slip from his fingers and fall to the table, his heart sinking along with the paper. His mind was spinning from the revelations in the words from the sainted Lord Cedric, and no matter how he tried to make sense of it all, he could not. He was to be a savior of the world in the same way as Cedric Binosear had been? He was the one who would stand up against Shau-ling and protect everyone's lives from that darkness? The fate of seven generations of people, most of which had not even been born yet, rested on his shoulders? It was ridiculous. It was beyond laughable. But the longer Logan stared at the golden words, the more that he knew he could not ignore them. It didn't matter if he believed, it mattered that Cedric believed. Who was he to argue with the judgment of the savior of the world? He could not live the rest of his days if what Cedric detailed came to pass and he had not lifted a finger to prevent it. Suddenly something came to his mind, as though strange disparate pieces suddenly clicked together.

"I was in Ragihn, and overheard some soldiers talking. They were talking about creatures and being sent somewhere to fight."

Aryx held up his hand and looked over his left shoulder for a moment, his eyes closed as though he was intently listening for something. After several long moments he turned back and lowered his hand.

"You'll forgive my paranoia," the knight said, his voice slightly lowered. "The shadows have been my enemy for many years, and as careful as I have been in approaching you, the stakes are incredibly high, and even the faintest whisper on the wind can find its way into the wrong ears."

Logan nodded and waited for the knight to continue speaking. The longer the silence remained, the more Logan began to feel the phantom weight that Aryx must have been feeling. Finally, Aryx reached into a small interior pocket of his cloak and produced what looked like a very old parchment that was bound with a simple golden ribbon. With a gently pull, the ribbon came loose and the knight laid it gently on the table before unrolling the parchment and sliding it halfway across the table where both he and Logan could clearly see the contents. As soon as Logan's eyes came to the contents of the parchment, he saw that it was a map of the continent that housed the kingdoms of Marcwell and Trelon, as well as many other major cities. The continent itself was called Mithacarthia, and was the most densely populated of the three continents on the world of Onea. Mithacarthia was shaped like a boot laid on its side, with Aradon roughly half way up the body of the boot near the center off the landmass. Marcwell was closer to the toe of the boot, right on the northern coastline. Sitting at the very tip of the toe was a city called Askronilka, a city renowned for its mercenary armies, as well as its mysterious history that few knew the truth of. Aryx let the contents sink in for a moment before moving his finger across the map to a point near the heel of the continent.

"During the first war, Shau-ling's forces were first spotted in the town of Lakestone. At least, that is what we believed. We found out much later that the servants of Shau-ling had infiltrated other kingdoms long before the monsters appeared. Before I was dispatched to Aradon to bring you into the fold, Lord Cedric received word that once again Lakestone appears to be the tip of the spear. Creatures that are known to serve Shau-ling were spotted just outside the town, and there are signs that they are massing for an assault."

He moved his finger from Lakestone deeper into the body of the continent to a larger city.

"Before the war, relations between the major kingdoms were strained at best. While technically Brea should have been the one to come to the defense of Lakestone, the distrust that held between Brea and Marcwell would not allow such neighborly concessions to be made. Lakestone had always been a tributary of Marcwell, and so Brea left it to Marcwell to come to the small town's defense. After the war, Lord Cedric took great pains to unite the world. Though there were still many banners, many kingdoms, and all had their own interests to attend to, there was a great understanding that larger threats had to transcend such petty differences. Mutual defense pacts were signed among all of the major kingdoms, and if it was discovered that the forces of Shau-ling had returned from the shadows, then each kingdom that was able would mobilize forces."

Again Aryx paused and began pointing to several different points on the map, some major kingdoms, while others were small, almost insignificant towns, including Ragihn.

"Marcwell's military ranks swelled during and after the war. In order to keep watch for the return of Shau-ling's forces, Lord Cedric authorized the creation of Watchtowers. These small detachments would be able to be mobilized quickly to combat threats no matter where they appeared, and would be used to bolster the ranks of the armies sent by the larger kingdoms. When the creatures of Shau-ling were spotted near Lakestone, the mutual defense pacts would have required Brea to mobilize their army immediately. Unfortunately, Brea did not fare well after the last war, and there had been significant internal strife that has decimated their ability to defend not only themselves, but their neighbors. To that end, Lord Cedric authorized Arathorn Geoffry to recall many of our Watchtowers from all over Mithacarthia in an effort to mount as much of a defense as possible. Though there is not much left of Lakestone to save, the thought is that if the united army can halt the advance of Shau-ling's forces, much of the carnage that was seen in the last war could be prevented. I assume that the soldiers that you encountered in Ragihn were members of one of the Watchtower detachments."

Logan nodded absently with his eyes scanning the map.

"My friends will be here soon," Logan said finally, "and suddenly the plan I had to sell them on had become infinitely more complicated."

Aryx nodded.

"Lord Cedric would say that the best course would be to tell the truth, and do not disguise the danger. During the last war he was able to gather those to him that would prove to be invaluable in facing the darkness, and that was done simply by being honest and genuine."

Logan chuckled to himself.

"I'm not exactly known for being honest and genuine, Aryx," he said with a slight chuckle in his voice. "But maybe that will be a refreshing enough change that they'll listen."

It was then that there was a knock at the door. Logan took a deep breath and pushed away from the table, steeling himself for what was to come.

The Gathering Light

Logan had crossed the room and was standing in front of the door when the second knock came. A quick look over his shoulder revealed that Aryx too had retreated away from the table, and he was nowhere to be seen. Most likely he didn't want to shock any of Logan's soon-to-be compatriots before the time was right. Taking another deep breath, Logan opened the door, and before his eyes could even focus on what was outside, a blur of motion pushed the door back toward him, and two figures came barreling into the house. By the time his senses had adjusted, Logan saw the massive form of his oldest friend, Pike Rhuiden standing in front of him. Pike raised both of his huge hands and put them on Logan's shoulders, pushing him roughly against the wall as they had done when they were children; the difference was that this time the gesture of familiarity hurt. Just over Pike's shoulder, Logan could see Pike's other-half in mischief-making, Talon Aielin.

Pike Rhuiden was best known as a troublemaker first, a warbling troubadour to any woman who could stand to listen second, and a student blacksmith a distant third. He had already spent three years at the forge under Torris Sandar before David started working, and after two more had decided that he didn't need to live under Torris' yoke any longer. Though Logan was quite sure that wasn't the only reason that Pike left Torris' service. Torris was a member of the City Council, and had long been very friendly with the Tamerlane family. Because of his relationship with the

Mayor's daughter, Logan had drawn the ire of many of the families of the City Council, including the Sandars and the Merins. So naturally, the long-standing friendship that existed between the Rhuiden and Ranthall families made for interesting infighting within the Council. Pike and Logan were cousins, as Pike's father and Logan's mother were brother and sister, but the two had always done everything together, and were more like brothers.

Once he had left the forge, Pike had returned to the family business working for his father Tam and with his friend Talon in carpentry. Pike and Talon did most of the work chopping trees and building the houses and other such jobs while Tam handled all of the money and smaller scale jobs. Once Pike and Talon even traveled to Illimar to learn from some of the shipwrights there. Unfortunately the trip ended in disaster. After the first day with the shipwrights, Pike and Talon went out with some of the apprentices to the local taverns and drank and caroused all night. Talon ended up passed out in a hog pen at the edge of town, and Pike woke up in bed with the wife of one of the shipwrights. The five day trip became two, and aside from some amusing stories, Pike and Talon returned with very little to show from their journey. Though the truth of the matter was that it was foolish to expect any other result when the two were together for any length of time. Where Pike was often the brawn of the pair, Talon was placed in the often unenviable position of the brains. While he excelled at getting the pair into trouble, his faults often lay in getting them out again. Talon had the reputation of being more of a trouble-maker than Pike, and the two had known each other since they were born. In fact, they were born on the very same day. Talon and Pike spent most of their days working in the forest chopping trees, and most of their nights drinking and singing at the *Traveling Bard* where they would make fools of themselves until they were thrown out on their ears. For most it made for an entertaining night, at least until the wine and ale began flowing too freely, and then the patrons would suffer from the sour notes and bawdy lyrics. It wasn't that Pike and Talon were bad singers, in fact many had commented at how talented they were. The issue was that they were often much better at drinking than they were at singing.

Pike pulled Logan away from the wall for just a moment before slamming him back again.

"Good to see you, Logan," Pike said smiling. "Hope you have some ale. It's been a busy day and I could use a drink."

"Aye," Talon added as he pulled Pike toward the kitchen, "it's terribly thirsty work to be so irresistible to the ladies of the marketplace."

Logan laughed and pulled himself away from the wall in time to see David walk through the door trailed by Lane Toridon. Lane was the enigma of the group, and one of only two members of the childhood friends that had been born outside of Aradon. His parents were from a wealthy southern town, but moved to Aradon to get away from courtly life. Strangely enough they would not speak much about where they were from, but the pieces often pointed to either Brea or Scalla. Lane's father was something of an alchemist, and for some time made a living as an apothecary. Lane's parents had invested in his studies from the time he could read, and the young Lane's passions quickly became ignited by the study of the arcane arts that were most often practiced by the Moridon. While the often shadowy sect of sages known as the Moridon had been predominantly myths and legends prior to Lord Cedric's war against the forces of Shau-ling, the war had changed all of that. One of Lord Cedric's closest advisors had been from the leadership of the Moridon, a man named Mailock, and he had mobilized the sect in support of the Lion. Somehow, Lane's parents had been able to procure some texts from the Moridon, and those were used to train the young Lane on his path. However, the best application of his abilities was often seen at children's birthday parties where he would dazzle them for hours with small bursts of light and birds that would appear out of thin air. He knew, as most did, that they were simple tricks and that he was capable of much more, but he did it because it made the children happy, and ultimately that was all he wanted. Lane's parents had died not long after their arrival in Aradon, and Lane was raised by most of the families in the town in one form or another. In fact Logan remembered a time when Lane lived with Logan and his father for almost an entire year. Lane had never considered himself an orphan and often remarked that he was lucky to have such a large family to depend on. Lane quickly shook Logan's hand and followed the other three into the kitchen, where Logan could already hear the glasses and bottles being broken out.

Logan closed the door and turned away, but he was barely half-way to the kitchen when another series of knocks came from the door. Knowing that it was most likely Gwydeon, Elwyne, and Eldar, Logan steeled himself and returned to the door. He could not help the reflexive swallow before pulling the door open. Thankfully it was Gwydeon's face that Logan saw first, and he was able to turn away before the assuredly disapproving looks of Eldar and Elwyne came into view. As soon as Pike saw Gwydeon, he started to offer his friend a glass, but as soon as there was unsteady eye contact between Pike and Eldar, the whole room went cold. Any possibility of small talk died that moment, and almost silently the group found their way to seats around the dining table. Logan's house had practically been built around the concept of a large dining table in the center off the house. Logan's mother had come from a large family, and while the Ranthall clan had been very small, Arin had wanted Victoria to have the ability to host her extended family and friends in comfort whenever she wanted. Unfortunately events conspired that would never allow that to happen the way that the couple had intended. After Victoria's death, the table found itself most often used for City Council meetings, most of which often devolved into shouting matches of one form or another.

"Shall we get this over with so the responsible members of this group can actually get some work done today?" Eldar asked her impatience and discomfort barely hidden behind her hostility.

"What is this important matter you wished to discuss with us, Logan?" Lane asked.

Lane was always the mediator of the group, and had the most level head during the times of strife. As with all close-knit groups, there were problems that flared from time to time. More than once, Pike and Talon's nights of debauchery ended with a fist fight between the two, and Lane would be called to patch up both their wounds and their friendship. Lane had also been called on to work out issues between Pike and Logan, Elwyne and Gwydeon, Gwydeon and Pike, and Talon and just about everyone.

"David told us you ran into something interesting in Ragihn," Pike said leaning back with his arms folded across his very broad chest, "but he wouldn't tell us much more than that. So what's the big mystery?"

Logan braced and then began.

"My time as an adventurer couldn't exactly be called a success. I've spent most of my time floating from place to place, doing odd jobs, mostly as a messenger or guard for merchant shipments. My last job brought me to Ragihn, and after being on the road for almost five days, I was just going to go lie down and sleep, but I thought I would go to the tavern and just have one drink to help me unwind. I was surprised that the tavern was full, even more surprised that most of the patrons were soldiers. Ragihn doesn't have a reputation for being very friendly to outsiders, and even less friendly to the military. There is still a lot of bad blood from the last war, and the border tensions that once existed between Trelon and Marcwell. I caught some snatches of conversation about the fact that the soldiers were being deployed and weren't happy about it. My thought was that we could catch on with these soldiers on the way to their destination, either as mercenaries or something similar. I would have just gone myself, but I need someone to watch my back, and there is no one that I trust more than all of you."

"Still trying to be a hero, Logan?" Elwyne asked.

"He's not the only one," Pike said. "Is the Lion's Mane knocking down your door yet, Gwydeon?"

"At least he has ambition beyond getting drunk every night and finding your way into some stupid girl's bed," Eldar retorted.

"You didn't have a problem when it was your bed," Talon countered.

Eldar balled her fists but Elwyne's gentle hand on her wrist seemed to ease the anger slightly. Lane's apologetic look found Logan's eyes.

"It's amazing you got us all in the same room, and this little example of our current level or relations is a small taste of the everyday life you left behind."

Pike snorted.

"Which is exactly why this little journey of Logan's sounds like the right plan. I don't need to be here anymore, there is nothing here for me. I'm not going to be like my father who grew up and died within a mile of where he was born without doing anything more than inheriting the family business. Even if I don't accomplish more than catching on as a blacksmith in some town somewhere along the way, then I'll still have done more than he did."

"Besides," Talon added. "There are more bars and more women to be found. The company here has gotten a little stale."

Talon pointed his chin in Eldar's direction and smiled and evil smile before continuing.

"I'm in," Talon concluded.

Eldar folded her arms and shook her head. She had been the collective conscience of the group as well as a type of surrogate mother or older sister. Logan's mother had died giving birth to him; Lane's mother had been dead for a long time. Elwyne and David's mother had been dead for three years, and Pike's mother had died just the winter passed. Talon's mother was gone most of the year working as a merchant, and Gwydeon's mother was most often embroiled in some business related to the City Council. If Eldar disapproved of the plan, she could sway David and maybe even Gwydeon. Elwyne almost always agreed with what Eldar said, and a lot of the time it seemed that she argued with Logan just for the sake of arguing.

"Just when I think that you are starting to grow up and get some sense into those puny brains of yours, you fall for Logan's cheap talk." Eldar countered. "He has no idea what it is that he is talking about, and he is probably making it seem like there is no danger. There is a chance that if you go out there and fight, that you will die. Nothing that Logan dreams up is ever simple, and it is usually extremely dangerous. Most of the time, it's those people that follow him that end up getting hurt the worst. David, do you remember the time he told you that you could jump from house to house in Aradon with no problem, that he had done it a hundred times?"

David nodded.

"And what happened?"

"I fell through Tam Rhuiden's roof."

Eldar nodded and turned to Pike.

"Pike, do you remember the time Logan found that old still behind old man Fadrin's barn?"

Pike nodded and laughed.

"Yeah, Talon and I passed out drunk, and when our father's found us, we couldn't sit for a week they beat us so hard. But I'd do it again in an instant."

Eldar frowned.

"So follow him if you want," she said with venom, "but just remember that you are putting your lives at risk for a foolish boy's childhood dreams."

"Don't you have dreams, Eldar?" Logan retorted. "Don't you ever want to do anything else with your life other than just stay here forever? Isn't there something you want to do, or someplace you want to go? My father always taught me that there is nothing in life that just comes to you, and it is our way to fight for what we want. He fought all his life to get what he wanted and he ended up happy. My father lived by fighting and by chasing his dreams. I want to chase my silly childish dreams and make something of myself. I'm not going to settle for just being a backwards farm boy. If you want to stay here for the rest of your lives, then stay here where it's safe. But if you want to chase the dreams in your heart, come with me. Take a chance, and live for once in your lives."

"I'm in," Gwydeon replied. "I have nothing here in Aradon but my friends and my dreams. I'll follow them with you, Logan."

"I already told you I'm in," Pike answered. "The safer you try to live your life, to closer you get to dying."

"You couldn't keep me away from this," Talon added quickly. "Sounds like fun."

"Where my friends go," Lane said, "I follow."

"We might as well chase our dreams while we still can," David said looking right at Elwyne. "I'm going."

Elwyne grimaced to herself and then nodded. She wouldn't give anyone the satisfaction of letting her decision be given voice, but as long as David was going, she would be right there with him. All eyes shifted to Eldar, and there was a look that was a mixture of shock and resignation on her face. Finally it was Elwyne who broke the silence.

"You have to follow your heart, Eldar."

Eldar closed her eyes for a brief moment and nodded.

"My heart is with my friends, it always has been. I'll go."

There were cheers from Talon and David and a call for a round of drinks from Pike, but when Logan leaned forward and put his elbows on the table, a dark cloud coming to his features, Gwydeon silenced the group and everyone turned their attention to their leader.

"There's more," Logan said finally. "I'm sorry I didn't give you the whole story to begin with, but I needed to know that you were in at least as far as my original plan before the rest came to light. In fact, I didn't even know the depths of what I was proposing meant until an hour ago. The soldiers that I came upon in Ragihn were part of a Watchtower group from Marcwell. There had been sightings of monsters, like those that the Lion fought against in the last war in the town of Lakestone. The soldiers were being dispatched there to form a perimeter to keep the evil from advancing further."

"Ok," Pike said, trying to make sense of the news, "so instead of fighting pirates or mercenaries or revolutionaries, we're fighting monsters. This whole thing had fighting written all over it, so what makes a difference what we're fighting?"

"It makes all the difference in the world," a voice came from the darkness of my father's bedroom. "Men have patterns; men feel fear of their opponent. The creatures that you will be fighting against fear only failure and that will make them fight harder than ten men."

There was a slight grumbling around the table when Aryx emerged from the shadows and came to stand at the table. There was a chair that he could have sat down in, but instead he chose to stand, giving a different gravity to his words.

"This is Sir Aryx Terian," Logan said after a moment, "a knight to the Kingdom of Marcwell, here on a mission from the Lord Lion, Cedric Binosear himself."

There were shocked and disbelieving looks, and for a moment Pike and Talon even laughed as though it were some grand joke, however Aryx's stern and disapproving looks put an end to the laughter quickly. Logan brought his voice back up quickly, before the shock ran out of control.

"Listen," he started softly, "I know it will be hard for you to believe, in fact I'm having a hard time believing it myself, but the Lord Lion sent Aryx here to find me. He needs my help, and I need yours. I can't do what's being asked of me alone."

"Why you?" Elwyne asked. "You said yourself that you've been doing odd jobs and nothing of importance since you left Aradon. What would have brought you to the attention of Lord Cedric?"

"Logan," Aryx said after a moment. "I think you should tell them everything. Read them the letter."

He reached into the pocket of his cloak and produced the parchment with the flowing golden script. After handing it to Logan, he leaned back against the wall and waited as Logan unrolled the parchment and began to read. Logan felt his mouth going dry many times during the reading of the letter, and though he had already read the letter once, the words still sounded unbelievable to his ears. It was as though a spell was wafting through the air, capturing everyone through the recitation of the words, demanding silence and complete attention. When the last part of the letter had been read, Logan lay the parchment down on the table and looked around the faces of his friends. The looks were varied, mixtures of disbelief, horror, and shock. The room remained silent for a long time before Lane cleared his throat and stood.

"Friends, I have not been doubtful for a moment from when the first hint of a journey had been given to us by Logan, however, I cannot help but to doubt this. We're not soldiers, and we're not heroes, and that letter details a quest so much bigger and preposterous than anything we could have ever imagined. How can a group of farmers and, if you'll forgive me, troublemakers who would rather spend their time drinking and whoring, possibly succeed in something larger even than the Lord Lion can handle? This whole thing frightens me to the core."

Aryx bowed his head for a moment and then spoke.

"I was there from nearly the beginning with Lord Cedric," Aryx said slowly. "He wasn't much older than you, and yet not only was he expected to lead one of the most powerful kingdoms of Mithacarthia, but he was to do it without a standing army, and with a hostile city government. He left, with only Lady Erika Belnosian at his side. Along the way, Lord Cedric was able to gather those to him willing to risk their lives for the betterment of all without fully understanding the risk or knowing what they were up against. When the true evil revealed itself, and the fate of the world rested upon one man's shoulders, none of those who swore to defend him abandoned his cause. They rose above their former lives as pirates, thieves, wanderers, and commoners, dedicating themselves to something bigger than whom and what they had been."

Here Aryx paused, letting his words sink in before continuing.

"You're scared. You should be. The creatures you are about to face are some of the most fearsome to ever walk this world. But you are not the first to face them. And you will not be facing them alone and unarmed. Every bit of information that we were able to gather during the first war, as well as every tool and weapon that was at our disposal or discovered after the war will be yours for the asking. You are only common farmers if that is what you choose to be. Your fear can only harm you if you let it. This is your opportunity to walk through the door that destiny has opened for you. Lord Cedric and everyone who once followed him were willing to give their lives for this, and so was I. Will you be as brave now that the choice is yours?"

Logan cleared his throat.

"With or without you," he said after a moment, "I'm going. No matter what the prophecies say, and no matter what Shau-ling may have intended with his revenge, the right thing to do is fight. It's what my father would have done."

Silence held around the table until Gwydeon's voice pierced it.

"Since we were children, all we wanted to do was make a difference. We didn't know enough to say it like that. We dreamed about being great heroes and slaying dragons, and doing great things. We've been responsible, taking jobs as soon as we could. We've helped those in our community who were sick and injured. There isn't anything that we wouldn't do for one another. If we would have been this age during the last war, is there anyone here who doesn't think we would have fought? If this is the return of Shau-ling and his Shadows, is there anyone here who doesn't think we would go off to fight when the call came? Well this is our call. This is our opportunity. Maybe if we do everything we can now, then we'll save lives. Maybe cities won't have to suffer this time around like they did in the last war. Maybe we can make the difference we have always wanted to make."

He then stood.

"I'm going."

Elwyne was the next to add her voice, something that surprised Logan.

"Logan's father always said that there are no heroes, there are only men and women of conscience who know to do the right thing when the right thing is necessary, not when it is convenient. Convenience makes alliances with cowards. I'm not a coward, and so, I'm going with Logan, and with my friends."

One by one all added their voices, and so they were a strong party of eight friends and a powerful guide. The next words came from Aryx.

"We should leave within two days. Take the time to put your affairs in order, but do it as quietly as possible. Our disappearance should be quiet and unexpected. We will leave at midnight tomorrow through the Mithacarthian Woods."

Logan nodded.

"Good idea, Aryx. I'll take care of transportation. It'll look less suspicious if I do it. We'll meet at the stables, its close enough for all of us."

There was brief conversation before the group broke up, and Aryx mentioned that he was going to scout around the town for more information. There was so little time, but now there seemed to be so much to do. The bells of the local church rang to announce that it was one in the afternoon. Everyone would be headed back to work, and it would give Logan the opportunity to gather what they would need for their journey. The time for their great adventure would be upon them soon, and no matter what, Logan would see it through to the end. Perhaps this would be the first time he actually did.

CHAPTER 1

Chapter II

Bitter Greetings

Logan closed the door after the last of his friends left and returned to the dining table where their journey saw its beginnings take root. He sat down in the closest chair and put his head in his hands. There was still so much he didn't know and didn't understand, and the whole course of his life had just been permanently and irrevocably changed. He wouldn't want to show his uncertainty or his fear in front of the others, least of all Pike. As close as Logan and Pike were, they were also incredibly different, and to a degree that most would think would drive a wedge between them. However, it always seemed that Logan's strengths complimented Pike's weaknesses and vice versa. People in Aradon looked at Pike and Talon as the dangerous combination, but in truth no one caused more trouble than Logan and Pike when they were together. Logan was a plotter, a thinker, and he understood the sly way to accomplish things that Pike usually accomplished with brute force. Pike was filled with rage and constant feelings of thwarted ambition, but sometimes his quickness to action absolved Logan of thinking too much about the moment. Now that Logan found himself embroiled in this quest, this path to either saving the world or damning it forever, he needed the sometime single-mindedness that Pike often represented. Though it was sometimes misguided, Pike had clarity of purpose, usually because he didn't fully understand what he was getting himself into. Talon had that clarity too, but where Pike's bents were usually either rage or alcohol induced, Talon prided himself on his clear thinking recklessness. Yes, he enjoyed the drink; enjoyed being out of control when it suited him, but his love of alcohol was dwarfed by Pike's. Talon loved playing with people's perceptions, loved making them wrong, and loved knowing that he knew more than everyone about every situation. Any time he was surprised, that is what truly fueled his anger. All of those characteristics and all of those brought by the other members of the group would be invaluable in the days and weeks to come, and there was no doubting that the trials and tribulations ahead of them would tax each of them to their breaking point.

Shaking away the thoughts of what was to come, Logan tried his best to focus on the here and now, knowing that his primary responsibility was to secure horses for their travels and see that they were fed and groomed before the day was out. He would have them moved to the far stables closest to the forest, that way their leaving would draw less attention. Logan made his way as quickly as he could from his house back to town proper, and found his way to the marketplace. As it was harvest season, the oversized tent that housed every type of merchant imaginable was filled to overflowing. The livestock merchants were on the far side of the marketplace, and the horse merchant was the farthest among them all. Logan spent several minutes going through the selection of horses and then spent much longer haggling with the merchant to get a lower price. The merchant unfortunately was at a disadvantage in the negotiations because some of the richer families had begun their own horse breeding, led by the Tamerlanes. Within a matter of three to four seasons, the horse merchant would stop bringing his stock to Aradon; there would be no profit once Mayor Tamerlane had his way. The merchant would arrange for the horses to be transferred to the stables, and Logan then made arrangements with the stable boys to ensure everything would be taken care of. By the time all of the necessary preparations had been made, Logan was exhausted and headed back to his home for some sleep. Despite how tired he was, it took a long time for the excitement and anxiety to flee from his body enough to let sleep take him.

When the sunlight hit Logan's face the next morning, he wasn't sure if he had even slept. His body felt rested, but his mind was still jumbled with the hangover of fear and expectation. To keep up appearances, Logan threw on a shirt and made the short trip from his home to the *Traveling Bard* and met David for breakfast with the rest of the apprentices. For once, Logan was actually early, and found a seat several minutes before David made his way into the inn. He looked like he hadn't slept much, and when he sat down he could not help but rub his eyes. The two friends talked for a little while, small talk mostly, in order to not bring attention to themselves and the journey that was only hours away from truly beginning. Eventually the small talk moved to conversations about families and the happenings while Logan had been away. The largest topic turned out to be the situation between Eldar and Pike. Their hostility had very nearly ended the conversation before it really had gotten started the day before.

"They haven't spoken a single word to one another in over a month, at least until yesterday," David started. "It seems like there is something more to this than a simple argument. They were always difficult with each other, but this is bordering on hate. Nobody wants to get involved. But nobody wants this to keep going the way it is. Elwyne is closer to Eldar than any of us, but she doesn't even want to ask."

"I wouldn't want to either David," I replied, "after what Eldar did to Talon, I would be a little too afraid to confront her with it."

"I'm not brave enough to get in the middle of it either," he added. "The only person who has anything to say about this other than Eldar and Pike is Gwydeon. He keeps telling everyone that it is none of our concern and that it is something that Pike and Eldar will have to come to terms with."

"What's so odd about that?" I asked. "Gwydeon has always been the peacemaker of the group."

"It's the way he says it, Logan. It's almost like he knows exactly what is going on."

The bells rang marking the end of breakfast and the beginning of the working day. While David headed to work, Logan decided that he would get in some practice time with the sword. Gwydeon had been at the training grounds since nearly dawn, as was his ritual. Logan hadn't used his father's sword in a very long time, and he couldn't think of anyone better to help him get a feel for the sword than Gwydeon. Arin's sword was far heavier than the sword that Logan was used to. Gwydeon was helping

Logan to shorten his defenses to compensate for the increased weight when Logan began peppering his old friend with questions.

"I hear Eldar and Pike are still having problems," Logan said as the two were slowly dueling.

Gwydeon countered a hard thrust and then backed away, parrying another with the flat of his blade.

"Nothing more than usual," he replied, "but it's none of our concern. They'll work it out for themselves."

"So," Logan said pushing him, both mentally and physically, "you do know what's going on between them?"

That apparently incited Gwydeon's temper. He spun underneath Logan's slash, and brought his sword up so that it hit the flat of Logan's blade just above the guard, sending the sword flying out of Logan's hands.

"Yes," he said looking dead in Logan's eyes, "but it is not my place to discuss it. I would think that you would be more concerned about Elwyne than any problems that Pike and Eldar are having."

The bells rang out again, signaling the start of lunch, and he excused himself. Logan watched Gwydeon go, his pride a little bruised by his friend's words, but Logan recovered his sword and walked back towards his house. His pride wounded and his heart heavy, he decided to try to get some sleep before the journey, so that he would be well rested for the long ride ahead. As he walked down the path toward his house, he could not resist a feeling of cold and desolation that began to fill the air. At first he thought he was just being overcome with a feeling of self-pity, but the stronger it became, the more it seemed to be coming from outside of him and not from his heavy heart. With a look down at the ground, Logan saw that the shadows were getting longer, and everything was becoming dark. When he looked up at the sky, he was shocked to see huge dark clouds rolling in above the town. These clouds were like none that he had ever seen before, and their ominous black shapes looked as if they were destined to loose a storm of such power and fury that they would destroy the entire world. Fear beginning to fill him, Logan quickened his pace, and though he did not want to get caught in the rain, there was something deeper and more primal driving his haste. Every time he looked over his shoulder, it seemed that the clouds were right above him, and they seemed even darker and more menacing. The cold feeling of death began to rage over Logan with every step, and it was as if the clouds themselves were giving off the wave of horror. Suddenly, there was a sound like thunder, and when Logan spun around he saw a sight that had been pulled directly from his worst nightmares.

In his childhood Logan had been told stories about terrible monsters that came down from the clouds to snatch away young children that did not obey their parents. It was the same kind of stories that all parents told their children in some form or another. Of course, those stories never really worked on Logan or his friends, otherwise Pike and Talon would have had entirely different personalities after they had grown up. The first time Logan had heard the stories, it wasn't even from his father. It was from Gwydeon's mother. He had gotten into something he wasn't supposed to, the memory of which had faded after time. Now though, as he looked up at the sky, all he could hear was his voice in her head telling him that one day the monsters would come to hold him accountable for the things he had done in his life. The nightmares were coming to life, and like the stories that Aryx had told them the morning before, the whole world looked as though it were about to come raining down on top of him. A glimpse of one of the creatures had caused his blood to run cold, but now that his eyes had locked on one of the monstrous forms, he didn't know if he was going to pass out from fright or laugh at the absurdity of it all.

The size of the beasts was amazing. Even at great distance they would dwarf a man. They were a color of black that made one think of death, and their bat-like wings flapped against the ever increasing wind, keeping them high above Aradon. Bone spike protruded from the creatures' knees and elbows, and razor-sharp white nails could be seen on the creatures' hands and feet. A wide flat tail flapped behind the monsters, helping them to glide effortlessly and hover menacingly. There were seven or eight of them, but Logan couldn't get a clear count because of the clouds and the speed at which they were moving. High above the city, the mass of creatures began to circle around the whole perimeter of Aradon. Once they had formed a circle, their speed increased, and after several moments they began to circle lower and lower in the sky, as if they were preparing for some kind of attack. Logan drew his father's sword from the scabbard on his hip, more out of reflex than anything else. After several moments he started running toward Aradon. Out of the corner of his eye, Logan saw someone running toward him. It was Aryx, but it took quite a few moments for Logan to be sure that his eyes weren't playing tricks on him. The man was moving faster than any man Logan had ever seen in his life, a blur of color that could have easily bested the fasted runners in the town, and probably in the whole of Mithacarthia. Aryx was upon Logan in seconds, grabbing the much younger man by the arm and dragging him to a complete stop.

"Wait, Lord Dragon," he said firmly, "we have to get you to safety."

There was an edge to his voice, a force that demanded attention and obedience. But there was something more, something very close to fear.

"What are those things Aryx?"

Aryx looked back over his shoulder and pointed at the creatures with his sword.

"Those are Shadowwalkers," he said with the hint of fear in his voice turning to anger. "You can call them Shau-ling's way of saying hello. All they know is how to inflict destruction and death. They'll kill as many people as necessary in Aradon as they can in order to get to you."

A shudder of panic shook Logan to the core. Whatever was about to happen, it was all because of him. These creatures that now circled the only home he had ever known were there to destroy him, and they and they master didn't care about the collateral damage. In fact, Logan was sure that the more collateral damage they caused, the more successful their mission would be considered. They wanted to draw Logan out into the open, and if Aryx hadn't been there, they would have succeeded easily. Aryx was protecting Logan more from himself than from the creatures. He bit his lower lips and stopped pulling against the knight's grasp.

"What can we do to stop them?"

"While they are in the air, there is nothing we can do to stop them. They're going to attack from the air to start the slaughter, but they have to come down eventually. Once they do, we'll take them on the ground.

Believe it or not we have the advantage there. Until then, all we can do is watch."

"Watch what?" Logan asked.

"That," Aryx said pointing back toward Aradon.

The circling pattern that the Shadowwalkers were flying in now widened so that the entire town and even some of the outlying farms was between them. Lower and lower they circled until they were just a few feet from the tops of the largest buildings. One of the huge beasts opened its mouth, and then suddenly a beam of white flames erupted from its open jaws and sprayed down upon the helpless people. Logan clenched his fist in rage and tried to pull away from Aryx to run toward the town, but Aryx just tightened his grip, holding him back, and all Logan could do was watch helplessly as each one of the Shadowwalkers in turn sprayed death down upon Aradon. Even from where he stood, Logan could hear the screams and cries of pain coming from the city, and the smoke billowed high into the sky mixing with the dark and foreboding clouds. A second circuit around the city brought another deluge of death down upon it, the sound of glass and wood breaking under the strain of the assault joining the cacophony of death. The onslaught stopped after a few streams of fire, and then the Shadowwalkers began diving down into the city and to slowly and methodically snatch up the townspeople that were running from their flaming homes. It was as if it were a game to the massive beasts, burning the houses to flush out the prey, and then seeing who could gobble up the most villagers. It was apparent that the Shadowwalkers were not going to stop with the village. They returned to the circling pattern after only a few minutes into their diving attacks until it slowly and methodically straightened, setting a direct course to Logan's house.

By this time, Aryx had begun to pull Logan away from the scene of unspeakable carnage and was leading him toward his house. Logan was absently aware of being dragged away, his jaw slack, and his eyes beginning to water from a combination of smoke and unbearable sadness. The monsters were gaining ground, and by the time Aryx flung the door to Logan's house open, pushed him inside and slammed the door shut behind him, they were practically on top of him. Aryx stood straight outside the house, his glowing golden gauntlet on his right hand, and the hilt of his sword clutched tightly in his left. Logan heard a muffled shout from Aryx through the door, and decided it was better to fight for his life than hide from the battle. By the time Logan forced the door back open; Aryx had already engaged the Shadowwalkers in combat. Three of them were circling while the other four seemed to be waiting on something. The strange thing was that the Shadowwalkers would look right at Logan and not do anything. So, instead of making some rash move, Logan waited, hoping that Aryx was as good as he claimed to be.

Aryx didn't seem to be rattled by the disadvantage of his being outnumbered and surrounded. He slowly eased into a defensive stance, wheeling his sword over his head. The gauntlet on his right hand pulsed with a darker, eerie glow, much different than the rich full color that it had only a few moments earlier. Slowly, he maneuvered his sword back down in front of him, as if he were ready to parry an attack. Suddenly, a whirlwind of wings and claws came at Aryx from behind. As if anticipating the attack, he turned reflexively and let the advancing Shadowwalker fly right by in its useless attack. The beast stopped, screeching and cursing in some incomprehensible language, and flew back to the circle of Shadowwalkers that still surrounded Aryx. The glow in Aryx's gauntlet started to gain a more reddish tint as the battle progressed, almost as if it were being stained with blood from the inside of the metal. The circling ceased, and Aryx tightened his grip on the hilt of his sword and he prepared for the next attack. A Shadowwalker touched down in front of Aryx with its claws bared and folded back its wings to prepare for battle on the ground. Aryx took the opportunity that this second of hesitation had afforded him, and buried his sword in the gut of the massive beast. The Shadowwalker screamed in pain as Aryx withdrew his blade. Pasty blue blood oozed from the wound in its stomach, but even as it recoiled in pain, it prepared to retaliate with a strike of its own. A hand with four-inch claws sprang forward, only to be met by the raised now crimson gauntlet. The sound of claws ripping at the metal was painful. The beast roared and pushed against Aryx's defenses, but the knight flashed a quick smile and then there was a flash of light from the gauntlet as a pulse of lightning shot from somewhere inside the gauntlet and raced into the body of the monster. It thrashed about in pain as the bolt burned its body from the inside out, reducing it to a crisp black figure of its former self. Aryx pulled back his gauntlet, ripping the brunt clawed hand from the now dead body of the monstrosity. As he flung the charred extremity to the ground, he turned to the others with fire in his eyes and the powers of a vengeful god in his hands. Lashing out with the powers in his gauntlet, he decimated the remaining Shadowwalkers. One however was spared the quick and painful death. Aryx turned to see that one of the cowardly beasts had escaped the fate of his brethren and was flying back into the clouds at an astonishing alacrity. Aryx raised his eyes to the heavens and called out to the beast in the Old Tongue.

"Erieal tarnsde ita ol'jah Halicin!"

When he turned back around and saw Logan, he frowned. After sheathing his sword, he wiped the sweat from his brow and walked up to the younger man.

"I thought I told you that we needed to keep you safe."

He sighed and then shook his head.

"Never mind," he said suddenly, "Lord Cedric used to do the same things, and so I guess I should be used to it by now."

Logan didn't know if he was more shocked by Aryx's reaction to him or by the display of power that he had exhibited, and could not find the voice to put to my questions.

"How did you do that?" Logan finally muttered.

"I have powers that you are not yet ready to understand, but I will explain them to you in time. We were lucky that the Shadowwalkers were only interested in me this time."

"Why did they only attack you Aryx?" Logan asked cautiously. "I was standing here the whole time, and they looked right at me but didn't do anything."

"The Shadowwalkers are blind in the daylight. Unless you engage them, or they are able to get close enough to smell power, or human flesh, then they will fly around burning random targets, or complete whatever mission that their master has assigned to them."

"The damage was too ordered to have been made by blind creatures, Aryx. How could the damage be that precise?"

"The targets had to be put in their minds by Shau-ling himself. They didn't need to see with their eyes to hit those targets because they were seeing them in their minds. Well, what little minds they have anyway. If Shau-ling is sending Shadowwalkers here, he must know that you exist and that you are here in Aradon. Not only that, there must have been agents loyal to Shau-ling here in Aradon at some point, most likely after the last war. He doesn't know who you are yet, at least, not by name. That fact is our only advantage right now. For the time being he will only be able to use random attacks and won't be able to track your movements with his human agents."

That cold feeling deepened inside of Logan. There would be more death, more destruction, and inevitably more creatures hunting for him, just because he existed. Aryx turned away from Logan for a moment, looking at the burning cinder that used to be the town of Aradon, and then he turned back and walked to the front door.

"Find your friends," he said opening the door, "if any of them are still alive, and bring them back here. I think it is about time that I tell you all exactly what we are up against and your role in this whole affair. Now that this war is more than a theory, they have the right to change their minds. I wouldn't fault any of them if they did."

With that, he turned away from Logan and walked into the house. Aryx's face was contorted into a frown, and his eyes were dark and full of barely-contained rage. He had the look of a man who had seen death on this scale many times before. Logan stared after him for several long moments, wondering what it could be that Aryx was going to share with them, and it was clear that none of it was going to be pleasant or easy to hear. Then, suddenly, the realization of Aryx's words hit Logan between the eyes like a hard punch. Some of Logan's friends could have died during that attack. He turned back to face the smoldering ruin, and the muscles in his hands throbbed. His father's sword slipped out of his grip and fell to the ground, all of his thoughts turning to his friends. All of Logan's other cares faded away and there was nothing more that he wanted to know but finding out if they were alive and well. His legs ached as he ran faster than he ever had before, trying to get back to the town proper as quickly as possible. As he ran through the town, he was surprised how many of the smaller houses were still standing. They seemed to only suffer superficial damage from smoke and proximity to heat. Some escaped damage all together. As he surveyed the destruction, it was obvious that it had been planned to bring the most kills in the shortest amount of time. The *Traveling Bard* had been burnt to the ground, and the marketplace along with it. They were probably the first targets hit. Logan ran from alley to alley looking for some sign of his friends. After a few minutes of searching, he spotted Gwydeon by what used to be a church near the town square. The church itself had been decimated, and only bits of the foundation were still intact. As Logan got closer, he noticed that the entire group that had agreed to join him on the quest was huddled together by the graveyard behind the church. His arrival was greeted by Elwyne running toward him, her face stained with tears. For a moment he thought that she was going to envelop him in a hug, but instead she slammed both her fists in to his chest. She pounded on him repeatedly, cursing and sobbing.

"All of this is your doing isn't it, Logan? You brought these monsters down on top of us didn't you?" Elwyne's words were harsh and venomous. "They killed my brother, Logan. They killed David!"

Fate

The events of the ill-planned battle ran through the Shadowwalker's mind over and over as it flew away from the site of its latest defeat. Slowly, its tiny mind began to piece together the fragmented events recorded by its different senses. After years of not having daytime sight, the Shadowwalkers had learned to perceive events without the use of eyes. Losing their daytime sight had been a punishment inflicted by the master long ago. Why Shau-ling had punished its ancestors was no longer remembered, but the lesson taught was still felt every day. The Shadowwalkers had been lucky. Punishment was a welcome event after failure because it meant you were still alive to serve another day. Other races had not been fortunate enough to escape with only punishment. The point made after a punishment was very evident; never fail the master again. The Shadowwalker knew that failure was now going to be a harder cross to bear.

As it made its way slowly through the thick white clouds, a single horrifying thought entered the minute brain of the Shadowwalker again and again. What punishment for this latest failure would be awaiting him? Failure had meant the death of many breeds over the years, and almost all of those failures had been blamed upon one of the breed. To Shau-ling, the failure of one was the failure of all. How many sister and brother races were now extinct because of past failures? The master had eliminated the Kalbraks because of a failure to eliminate White Lightning in the master's last lifetime. And now, the squad of Shadowwalkers sent to Aradon had failed in that same fated mission. Though, how could it or its master have known that White Lightning was involved with the new *Coromor*? Surely this failure was not the fault of the Shadowwalkers.

Maybe Master will show pity on us due to the circumstances, it thought to itself.

Darkness began to fall in the skies. The sun was just beginning its descent behind the tall mountain peaks to the west, painting a beautiful picture of reds, oranges, and yellows in the western sky. As the sun sank lower, the Shadowwalker began to regain its lost eyesight. Only at night was it able to open its large yellow eyes and peer out into the world of men. The pain that the sunlight brought it was now relieved by the glowing moonlight. With its eyesight now fully restored, the Shadowwalker immediately recognized the skies that surrounded it. The clouds, water, and the islands that it flew near brought a new thought to its troubled mind. Home.

Many hours it had been flying over the distance between Aradon and its new home. It had seen lands and seas still untouched by human hands before it reached the island where Shau-ling had built his palace. After a few more minutes in the beautiful nighttime sky, the Shadowwalker had reached its destination. No island was visible to the sky-bound observer, but the Shadowwalker knew where it was. In the air, the watery mist was becoming thicker making the mist more palpable. The light mist became so dense that the Shadowwalker felt like it was swimming in the ocean rather than flying through the clouds. It knew that the time for meeting its master was drawing closer.

The island, called the Island of Mist by most men, was not very large, but size had not been a factor when Shau-ling chose the site for his new palace. What did matter were what made the Island of Mist special and unique. Under the high waterline of the raging ocean sat the foundation of the Island, a stone called berionite. Berionite was said to be indestructible by any means, natural or man-made. Berionite was rarer than diamond in small quantities, and to have an island's foundation made out of the special stone was beyond calculation in rarity. Because of this Shau-ling was instantly attracted to the island. But this was not the only feature that made the Island of Mist a desirable site. The thick hanging mist that perpetually shrouded the island was more impressive than the foundation, and the legends behind the mist kept almost all foolish travelers away. It was believed that the mist was inhabited by the souls of the fallen warriors from the War of the Lion. This legend gained credibility as that it had only formed after the War of the First *Coromor* had ended. The truth was much less grand and fear-inducing. Groups of Jeresei chanted endlessly, using their abilities to keep the mist hanging in the air. Due to this, Shau-ling knew he could operate nearly totally undisturbed for as long as this generation would last. And safety was perhaps the most valuable commodity in a war of this magnitude.

Before the large winged beast banked through the rolling boundary of mist, it took one last troubled breath of fresh sea air and then started its descent. After only a few seconds into the deep clinging mists, the Shadowwalker began to make out some of the landforms of the island below it. Finally under the protective veil of the mist, the breathtaking scenery of the island came into full view. The sea beat wildly against the white sandy shores, and some white peaks of water crashed against the heavily sloped face of the ring of mountains that surrounded the island. Near the center of the island was another ring of mountains, and this was where the Shadowwalker sped toward. This was one of four entrances to Shau-ling's palace, but the only one that was accessible to the flying breed. Shadowwalkers detested water, therefore the other three entrances, which lay deep at the ocean floor, were not viable options. After completing a dive near the ground, the Shadowwalker slowed its approach, creeping toward the foot of the interior mountain range. Each of the high mountain peaks glowed with the crystal-like water droplets from the veil of mist, and in the moonlight, the intensity of the light was greater to the sensitive eyes of the Shadowwalker. Within a matter of moments it had reached the crest of the range. Increasing speed a bit, it clung close to the face of the mountain before soaring over the peaks and then diving down into the dense jungle that lay below. Holding the increased speed from the dive, the Shadowwalker skillfully maneuvered its way through the tightly packed trees and dense underbrush until it glided over the huge blood-red lake in the center of the jungle. The lake, called Blood Lake by all that served Shau-ling, had an ominous and eerie glow in the mist filtered moonlight, and the sight of the placid waters sent a shiver to the very core of the leathery-skinned beast. Again the Shadowwalker plunged into the thick jungle, dodging low hanging vines and dense foliage. Suddenly the inner wall of the ring of mountains was upon the Shadowwalker, and it dove deeper into the underbrush, barely in time to enter the cave at the base of the rock face. The cave narrowed quickly into what resembled a lava tube. The sides were as smooth as glass and reflected the dim glow of the mist that was still collected on the body of the Shadowwalker. Because of the slippery appearance of the cave, the beast had the feeling of moving faster than it really was. The tunnel continued straight on for a few yards and then shot downward suddenly, in a matter of moments the tube began to open, until finally the Shadowwalker had entered a large well-lit cavern.

Hovering just above the floor of the cavern, the massive creature looked around slowly. There was nothing but a few torches hanging on the wall to light the different passages out of the chamber, but the Shadowwalker still had the feeling as though it was being watched. After being satisfied with the solitude of the chamber, the beast touched down lightly on the soft floor. The chamber was a massive receiving area for the airborne creatures under Shau-ling's control. The Shadowwalker had been inside the palace many times in the past, but within the natural winding caverns, it was easy to get lost. The center tunnel was the path that the Shadowwalker knew it had to choose, and it would only be a few more moments before it would be face to face with its master.

As it made its way through the center tunnel, the Shadowwalker folded its wings back nervously. Fear crawled along its leathery skin with the creature's cold sweat. A shiver ran through it as it made its way closer and closer to meeting its fate. The thought of running away began to become more prevalent in the beast's mind, but something seemed to be pulling it toward the presence of its master. There was no escape from the will of Shau-ling. If the Shadowwalker had a god that it could pray to, it surely would have, but it knew deep in the pit of its heart that no amount of praying to even the greatest of gods would save it from punishment.

The tunnel soon came to an end into yet another massive chamber. Unlike the large receiving chamber, this new cavern was not at all empty. The room was filled, nearly to capacity, with other beasts that served the mighty Shau-ling. Many of them would never see the light of day, because they were merely servants. Others though were warriors that had seen combat in the greatest wars ever fought for the shadows. The name of the room was the Pen, and it had been called that for thousands of years. Calmly scanning the room, the Shadowwalker looked for others of its kind, perhaps in an effort to hide, but there were none of the large leathery beasts to be found. Hiding was only prolonging the inevitable anyway. But it was still more time that blue blood would be pumping from the Shadowwalker's heart, and more time that it would go on living. However, time was not to be an ally to the Shadowwalker on this occasion. Fear began to enter the Shadowwalker's mind once again, a fear that began to manifest itself in the cold sweat that rolled from it pores. It knew that time was growing short.

Escape.

The thought in the creature's mind grew louder with every second that passed. It could fly away and never return, escaping the punishment that lay ahead. Never again would it have to live in fear of failure, awaiting punishment around every turn. Casually, it turned back toward the receiving area tunnel. After several steps toward the passageway, the fear began to lift from the Shadowwalker's heart. It was going to make it out of the palace alive. Suddenly there was the feel of a clawed hand resting on the massive beast's shoulder. The Shadowwalker muttered a curse in its native language and then turned to face its assailant.

Being over eight feet in height, the Shadowwalker was used to looking down on the other creatures that served Shau-ling. This usually gave the Shadowwalkers and advantage, creating an air of intimidation and fearful respect. This time, however, was different. The Shadowwalker still towered over the creature it was facing, but looking down on the beast sent a shiver of fear through the larger creature's body. The smaller beast was the size of a human, and was very much like a human in form and appearance but with several very noticeable differences. First and most striking was the red skin, which was a deep crimson. The second and possibly more disturbing physical feature had become the tell-tale identification of the breed. The features of the face, while human in form and orientation, were impossibly sharp, looking like they had been chipped from marble rather than being formed with skin and bone. The cruel features had a more demonic feel with pointed ears and the thick black hair that coated the top of the creature's head. Two small round horns protruded through the hair on the top of the beast's head, and completed the demonic aura of the creature. The haughty smile on the face practically extended from ear to ear, the trademark of the beasts known as the Jeresei.

The Jeresei had long served as the personal guard and errand boys for Shau-ling. They were hated and despised by all other breeds that served the master because of their preferential treatment and gloating disposition. This hatred brought rise to curses and foul nicknames that followed the Jeresei in each and every lifetime. In the Shadowwalker tongue the name given to the Jeresei was *Valtamine*. Loosely translated, it meant impotent lap dog. For many lifetimes the competition for favor between the Shadowwalkers and the Jeresei had been heated, but the difference was that while the Shadowwalkers were punished and mocked for their failures, master never seemed to notice the faults of the Jeresei. As the hatred boiled in the Shadowwalker's veins, it knew that this time would be no different.

"Let me pass *Valtamine*," the Shadowwalker growled in a deep, hate-filled voice, "I should not like to spill your imitation human blood on the floor. There are those creatures that dine on the spilled blood of master's fallen victims that would choke on the foul meal that your poisoned blood would be."

"I was not aware that your breed was capable of such wondrous articulation," the Jeresei replied mocking its larger opponent. "In fact, I am surprised that that puny brain of yours has the capacity to support more than a three word vocabulary."

"I have no time to deal with the likes of you," the Shadowwalker rumbled. "Why don't you go to see if master has any special errands for you to run? Or perhaps one of the phasia needs his boots licked."

For a long moment the Jeresei stood looking at the Shadowwalker, the smile never leaving its face. It was almost as if it was trying not to lash out after the comment and was desperately biting back its anger.

"The master did have and errand for me. He wants to see you now."

Suddenly the desire for escape entered the Shadowwalker's heart stronger than it had ever been before. It turned its massive head and looked down the passage that led to escape, freedom, and life. However, to its dismay, two more of the Jeresei had taken up positions behind it, urging it toward the master's presence. Inwardly, the Shadowwalker sighed and bade the Jeresei to lead the way. Again, the haughty deceitful smile sat on the face of the Jeresei. It was obvious that the beast was taking great pleasure in the Shadowwalker's misery. After a moment, the Jeresei turned and erupted with a ear piercing laughter that resounded through the Pen. The two Jeresei in the path behind the Shadowwalker echoed the laugh and then began to lead the way through the palace.

The path that the Shadowwalker was led down was a familiar one. Every beast that served Shau-ling had been down this path at least once during its life. The Jeresei led his captive though the winding tunnels, past another small receiving area, right up to a large set of golden doors with markings of a language so ancient that even the oldest and wisest of the world could not remember the language that had followed this one. The two trailing Jeresei moved forward and began to open the large golden doors. Once the doors shifted an inch, the warm red glow and heat of the next chamber flooded past the Jeresei and Shadowwalker. Memory of this new passage stirred inside the Shadowwalker.

"*Lyunsia,*" the lead Jeresei said proudly.

The Jeresei word for the Hall of Terrors rang out true in the ears of the Shadowwalker. This was the place all of the beasts under Shau-ling's control feared the most. Any punishment that could be envisioned was considered a better option than being sent to the Hall of Terrors to have your failures dealt with. There were beasts that lived in the Hall of Terrors that had far better imaginations when it came to inflicting pain and suffering than Shau-ling ever would. Their power was nowhere near as great, but their innovations and imagination easily made up for what they lost in sheer power.

Without the knowledge of the beasts that dwelled there, the Hall of Terrors itself was enough to strike fear into the heart of any sane being. First off, the Hall itself was nothing more than a path of pure black berionite stone suspended in the air by great pillars. Underneath the walkway was an ocean of fire and light. The ocean was in constant motion, with jets of flame and geysers of lava shooting up in an angry convulsion.

Some of the geysers reached the level of the walkway, spilling liquid fire onto the perfect black stone. This ocean was the source of the soft eerie light which filled the room with dancing shadows that looked almost alive. At ten foot intervals, smaller walkways split off from the main path to the left and the right. This divergence occurred ten times down the length of the Hall. The Shadowwalker knew that these paths were truly the most potentially treacherous portion of the Hall of Terrors, as that the paths led to cells located in the walls of the chamber. In each of these cells lived one of Shau-ling's special creations, fiend of such horror that they defied a collective description. The closet the Shadowwalker would come to a classification was pure evil.

As the quartet of beasts reached the end of the path, the Shadowwalker found itself staring at a large black door. The door had the shape of a stylized dragon carved in the upper three quarters of the massive doors, but in the lower quarter of the door were inscribed the words, "*Talois perima chena ta lota kai mesha eria chi Shau-louing*". The words were from the Old Tongue, mostly referred to as the language of the gods. The inscription struck fear into all who heard it spoken. Roughly translated, it inscription read, "Heart of Terror, Seat of Despair, Throne of Power, enter the presence of the mighty Shau-ling." The words sent shivers through the heart of the Shadowwalker. The Heart of Terror was commonly referred to as the Council. That was the secret place where the phasia had been born and met in every lifetime under the direction of Shau-ling himself. The Seat of Despair was the throne in Shau-ling's personal torture room. It was called the Seat of Despair because all who laid eyes on it suffered greatly before being put to death at Shau-ling's hands. The last was the Throne of Power, the golden throne that was the seat of power for the entire empire of the shadows.

The Jeresei raised its hand and laid it upon the symbol of the Dragon. It then closed its eyes and bowed its head. The Shadowwalker could hear an incantation in the Old Tongue being spoken, but the words did not have enough volume to be understood by anyone. After the Jeresei had finished speaking, it removed its hand from the symbol and took a step back. Suddenly, two surges of flame burst up from the fiery depths below and forced the four creatures to step away from the door. The flames remained intense for a moment, and then seemed to recede revealing a creature beneath. The beast had no true form, other than the ever changing movements of the flame, but the greenish glow in the fires set it apart. The Shadowwalker and the Jeresei bowed deeply and waited for the ancient guardian to speak.

"State your business," the voice rolled like thunder, "or face the wrath of the Flame."

"This beast has been summoned to the presence of Shau-ling by the master himself," the Jeresei replied in as bold a voice as it could manage.

"Enter."

The Flame vanished, and the door began to creak open. The slow speed of the doors movements began to break the will of the Shadowwalker as it only prolonged the inevitable. Once the door had opened fully, the Jeresei led the Shadowwalker into the throne room. At first glance, the room seemed no different than any other that the Shadowwalker had been through, with the rock walls and a cavernous expanse lit by torchlight. The major exceptions were the dragon carved into the floor of the chamber and the golden throne that stood a few feet ahead. The Shadowwalker had been in the throne room once before, every beast had. Shau-ling at one time or another had sent for every beast that served him and Bonded them into his service. The process was not understood, but Shau-ling, in effect, leashed every beast to his whim. Now, the Shadowwalker was back in the presence of its master, fearing that its life was about to end.

One of the Jeresei shoved the Shadowwalker hard. The large beast took the hint and made its way toward the throne. It walked slowly, its eyes never leaving the glowing golden throne, until it stopped in the very center of the dragon carving. The light in the chamber began to dim, and in a matter of seconds it had disappeared completely. A moment later a ball of green fire erupted from the throne and extended to nearly touch the ceiling of the cavern. Out of the ball of flame, a huge black clawed foot emerged. Seconds later, another foot came into view followed by the cruel head of a black dragon. In a matter of moments, it had appeared fully.

The creature stood upright on its back legs, the golden talons reflecting the green light of the ball of flame, giving the dragon a more ominous appearance. Its body was huge, over ten times the size of the largest Shadowwalker, with a muscular frame that looked as though it could move a mountain. Huge bat-like wings extended from joints just behind the massive upper shoulders of the Dragon, folded back proudly. The black scales of the beast, looking as though they were the size of a large shield, also reflected the eerie green light of the flames. The dragon's mouth was open, showing the sets of sharp teeth and fangs that gleamed white with tips like daggers. The Shadowwalker tried hard not to look into the glaring eyes of the monster, but it could not resist. Slowly, the two beasts locked their eyes on one another's, the Dragon's brilliant crimson eyes beaming down at the smaller beast. Fear entered the heart of the Shadowwalker more than ever, and it quickly broke eye contact. The dragon roared in intimidating laughter, and then the beast looked back to the golden throne and watched as the flames receded. After a moment, a man dressed in black emerged from the shadows behind the throne. As soon as the Shadowwalker saw the man, it took a step back. The man was not a man at all; he was one of Shau-ling's greatest creations, a being known as a phase, and the children of Shau-ling. However, this was not just a member of the phasia, it was the first born of the phasia, a man named Jeroch.

Jeroch stood for a long moment, one hand on his hip, and the other perched against the throne of Shau-ling. Few creatures were brazen enough to touch the Seat of Power, even among the Phasia, but Jeroch knew no limitation to his entitlement. His dark brown hair stopped just above his shoulders and flowed back away from his face allowing his cold grey eyes to smolder in the light without impediment. His face was expressionless, but the Shadowwalker felt as though every iota of the phase bespoke malice and disgust.

"Jeresei, you are excused."

The Jeresei all bowed and the hurriedly left the room.

"You know why you have been summoned," the phase said in a proud and stern voice, "give your report."

"As ordered," the Shadowwalker said after a slow bow of ascent to the powerful member of the phasia, "my detachment was dispatched to the city of Aradon. The targets that Shau-ling placed in our minds were all easily destroyed, inflicting many casualties. However, as we were told before the mission, there might be some resistance, and indeed there was."

"Continue," Jeroch said impatiently.

"We felt a familiar power outside the city, so we investigated. Our initial thought was that it was the Dragon. However, we were surprised to meet White Lightning."

The dragon shifted uncomfortably, the name striking a chord of anger within it.

"We engaged White Lightning," the Shadowwalker continued visibly shaken by the dragon's reaction, "but because of his skill and out limited daylight sight, he was able to defeat us, but I managed to escape to bring you the report."

The Shadowwalker waited for a response. The reward for its wait came in the form of a giant clawed hand scooping down and grasping the shocked form of the smaller creature. The dragon glared at the Shadowwalker for a moment, the anger surging inside of it. Then, the dragon roared loudly, squeezing its massive clawed hand tightly around the body of the Shadowwalker. The pain was intense, and in a matter of moment, the pain erupted from the chest of the Shadowwalker in the form of a scream seconds before it was crushed to a pulp in the palm of the dragon's hand. After another angry roar, the dragon threw the dead carcass of the Shadowwalker violently to the ground. Then, the dragon disappeared. Suddenly, a voice thundered from everywhere in the chamber. The voice seemed to ring from the walls and the ceiling, as well as the floor.

"Jeroch," the voice said to the phase, "bring the Tarnae and the Jeresei to me."

"Yes, master," Jeroch replied.

The phase bowed to the throne and hurried out of the room in the most dignified way possible. Minutes later, Jeroch returned with several Jeresei and one of the beasts known as the Tarnae. The Tarnae was a large yellow ball followed by a trail of dense mist. As it rolled into the chamber, it changed shape and color many times. However, it always retained a ball-like quality and the thick mist trail. Once the group had reached the throne, the Tarnae slowly changed its shape to a form like that of the Jeresei. Within a few moments, the imitation was complete, and there stood seven Jeresei, Jeroch, and the Tarnae in the mocking shape of a bright yellow Jeresei. They all bowed to the throne in the next moment, and waited for their lord and master to address them.

"The Shadowwalkers have failed me for the last time. Their inadequacy in dealing with White Lightning and the band that will undoubtedly follow the Dragon has proved them unworthy," Shau-ling's voice boomed. "They will not have the opportunity to fail me again. I have placed my faith in you now. You, Tarnae, you will wait in the forest that lies between Illimar and Aradon. There you will await a party of adventurers. None of your games this time, Tarnae. Trap them and kill them. Now, go."

"As you wish," the Tarnae laughed. After reassuming the form of a ball, it rolled hurriedly out of the room.

"Fool," the voice boomed, "it will surely fail. The Tarnae will never simply kill anything; it is too dependent on its games. That is the reason I have summoned you, my loyal Jeresei. I place great faith in your abilities. Once the *Coromor* reaches Illimar, White Lightning will no doubt steer him towards Falke and then to Marcwell. I want you to use your special talents to make sure that the pathetic rabble does not make it to Falke."

"Yes, Master," the Jeresei replied. They left the room quickly, leaving Jeroch alone with his master and father.

"What of me, master?" Jeroch replied. "The Jeresei will also surely fail."

"Of course they will fail. They aren't going to be able to kill my own flesh and blood alone. But, they will be able to deal with the *Erieal* and whoever else is foolish enough to enter this war. Jeroch, my mission for you is a simple one. Go to Marcwell and keep a close eye on your friend the Lion. Have Erdric help you. He has been in Marcwell a long time sowing the seeds of disruption. Sooner or later the Dragon will make his way to see the Lion, White Lightning will see to that. When he does, the Lion will no doubt proclaim him for what he is. Once that is done, they are all ours. There will most assuredly be a banquet in the Dragon's honor.

There you will deliver my greetings and your dagger through the Dragon's heart. Death to the *Coromor*!"

"Death to the *Coromor*!" Jeroch repeated, "Glory to the Shadow!"

Jeroch left the room and shut the heavy door behind him. The letter to the *Coromor* that Shau-ling had given him laid sealed in his human-like hand. He longed to plunge his dagger into the heart of the Dragon. Revenge pulsed through his veins. How long had it been since the Lion had ended his life in the last generation. The memory of his death at Cedric Binosear's hands ran through his head every day of his new life.

"Your time is now, Dragon," Jeroch said to himself. "After I kill you, I think I shall exact some revenge upon your predecessor. Cedric Binosear has only just begun to know suffering at my hands."

Struggling Forward

Logan stood his body completely numb as Elwyne continued to pound on his chest, tears streaming down her face and a mixture of sobs and curses coming in fits and starts from her lips. All he wanted to do was stop her tears, to wrap her up in his arms and make everything alright, but his hands would not move, and there was no power in his throat and tongue to make any sound. When finally he was able to force his arms to cede to his will, he tried to hold Elwyne and console her. She struggled against his grip, first pushing away at him and then finally slapping him across the face with all the force she could manage. Logan's arms went slack, but he did not release her. She raised her hand to slap him again, but Gwydeon swooped in, taking hold of her wrist and pulling her away. Logan vaguely heard Gwydeon say something both to Elwyne and to him as Gwydeon pulled her away, but his mind could not process the words. The numbness had spread from his body to his mind, and it hurt to think. Elwyne's words kept ringing in his ears, drowning out all other sound, and they clogged up the passages of his mind slowing and blocking all other thoughts. At that moment he could do nothing more than try to form a picture of David's face in his mind. It was vague, cloudy, and the more he grasped at the details the quicker they fled. Frustration gripped his heart. He had just seen David a few minutes before and already Logan's mind rebelled at the demands of memory. Pike was the next to approach Logan, and Logan could see the remnants of tears in his friend's eyes. There were no words, there didn't need to be. As strong and as stubborn as Pike was, Logan knew that his friend's heart was broken. Pike's arms were around Logan before he knew what was happening, and then were gone a moment later, but in that moment, there was something communicated that transcended words. David was gone. Once Pike pulled away and walked passed Logan after another clap on the shoulder, it was Lane's voice that finally seemed to pierce through the veil of shock.

"When everyone scattered, David ran to the forge to make sure that Torris and the other apprentice blacksmiths got to safety. He had just gotten them to the catacombs under the church and was coming back out to gather more survivors when the church itself got hit. We're not sure whether it was the blast from those things or the falling debris that got him."

Logan tried to take solace in Lane's words, but there was none to be found. Of course David would have sacrificed himself to save others. Logan would have expected nothing less, and the more he turned over Lane's description of David's final moments in his mind he began to wonder if that kind of selflessness was within him. The fate of the world may have rested on his shoulders, but in the end would he have the bravery needed to sacrifice everything he knew and held dear.

"Gather everyone at the house," Logan heard himself say. "Aryx wants to talk to us. Wants to explain how this could have happened. Though I don't know how any of this could ever make sense."

Logan's voice trailed off, the words sounding hollow. Lane put his hand once more on Logan's shoulder and nodded absently before walking past. After several moments, standing alone in the remnants of the church courtyard, a wave of revulsion surged through Logan's body. It pounded through his temples like hammers striking the sides and back of his head repeatedly without rhythm. His heart felt as though it was being squeezed by a vice, and his guts were being twisted. His stomach lurched and fell seemingly at the same time, and all strength melted from him. Vaguely aware of the first tears that began to roll down his face, Logan's legs went weak, and his knees buckled. No matter how much her wanted to stop the tears, he couldn't and then the first hard sob shook his chest, and destroyed what balance he had left, and he fell to his knees in the ash and rubble. He didn't know how long he knelt there. His mind tried to fight back the emption, tried to rationalize that no amount of tears would change anything, but the senselessness of the loss destroyed any chance of controlling the emotions of the moment. How many had died trying to get to him? How many would not survive the night from the injuries sustained in just a few minutes. Finally the sorrow began to ebb, but it was replaced by something deeper, something far more primal. Hatred. The hate surged through his body like fire, strengthening his legs, strengthening his heart. Putting one hand down into the dust and ash, Logan supported himself and pushed off the ground. That moment the strength failed, and he remained on his knees. But the thoughts of the dead, people that he had known all of his life surged through him and he was able to find his way back to his feet. For the first time, he didn't see the destruction around him. A red haze had descended over his vision, and all he could see was the path before him. Before he knew it, he was standing at the front door to his house. He reached for the door handle, and the haze of red snapped as soon as he saw that his hand was covered in ash and dried blood. Logan wasn't sure how long he stood there turning his hand over and back, examining the tracks of blood that were nearly black from the soot embedded in it. He vowed at that moment that this would be the last time he stood by and watched people die.

By the time Logan entered the dining room; the rest of the group had gathered and were seated. Most had small cuts and scrapes from the attack, with Pike and Talon seeming to have the most visible wounds. No doubt they had put their strength to use freeing those trapped in the collapsed buildings. Elwyne had moved past tears, at least for the moment, and Eldar was sitting close with her arm around the younger woman. Logan leaned against the wall just outside the dining room, wiping the sweat from his brow and smearing some of the soot. Aryx emerged a moment later from the room that had once been Logan's father's, with bundles of papers, scrolls, and parchments in his arms. Without a word he laid them on the table and then put both hands on the table. He seemed to brace himself for what he was about to say, and then he raised his head and began to speak.

"My friends, I am sorry to hear about the death of your friend David. I did not know him, but there is no doubt that character he showed in his last hours has earned my respect, and that he shall be remembered once this war is over as a hero. I had hoped that this conversation would have been had under better circumstances, but the attack on Aradon has created a necessity that could not have been foreseen. I have no choice but to tell you the grim truth of what it is you find yourself embroiled in. I hope that after you hear my words you will be able to find some meaning for the death of your compatriot. However, after I finish my tale, you will have to make up your minds as to whether or not you wish withdraw your support for this quest. It would be a noble decision on your part if you stayed here to rebuild your home. There is no shame in defending your home, especially with what is coming."

Aryx paused for another long moment, waiting for his words to resonate in the young men and women before he continued.

"What was told to you by Lord Cedric's letter was the truth, but there were some very important omissions made for fear that the letter would be intercepted by one of my lord's enemies. Even with me acting as the courier, there was still a chance of interception. There are fearsome creatures that owe allegiance to Shau-ling, and their power dwarfs even mine. The weapon that you were asked to find is called the Jeweled Dragon's Flame. It is a very powerful weapon, and to our knowledge cannot be destroyed by any force. But once it is used for its destined purpose, it disappears, only to reappear in a new location when it is needed once more. A weapon like the Jeweled Dragon's Flame is neither of light nor dark, and its power can be held by either side. If this weapon were to fall into Shau-ling's hands, he would have enough power to rule to world unopposed, and there is nothing that anyone, not even Lord Cedric, could do to stop him."

Aryx swallowed hard, and it was obvious that what he was about to say was difficult.

"Lord Cedric is not a well man, as he alluded to in his letter, but there is nothing ordinary about his affliction. He is very weak and at times very frail, but the ills of his body pale in comparison to the ills of his mind. Often he seems distracted, as though his thoughts are far away. He cannot pay attention to any one thing for a long period of time, and he is equally absent-minded and paranoid. After the battle with Shau-ling, a wave of force struck Lord Cedric. It seems to have warped the power within him, and it continues to manifest itself in ways that we had never seen before. He now has certain powers that are unnatural and frightening. He can move huge objects with just a motion from his fingers, or even just a thought. Shortly after his returned from the battle with Shau-ling, Cedric tried to work within Marcwell's government to restructure the way the kingdom was ruled, to ensure that the right people were making the decisions. Cedric never wanted to be the one to make those decisions. He was satisfied simply with being involved, and I think in a way he knew that he wasn't the same as he was before the war. His dealings with the Mayor of Marcwell, his dead bride's father, had always been civil and productive. But shortly after Cedric's return, Artur Belnosian was murdered. When the Mayor's son Erdric accused Cedric of conspiring to assassinate his father, Cedric raged and threatened to kill Erdric. Erdric had been commencing a campaign of misinformation and distrust and the threats made by Cedric made him lose the support of the people, even after his actions in the world. In an effort to escape the false accusations, he used his new powers to move his entire palace into the depths of the Mithacarthian woods. After a time it was found that the mayor died in his sleep, and that the assassination talk had been engineered by Erdric in an effort to seize power. Lord Cedric was cleared of the charges against him."

Aryx breathed deeply and shook his head.

"We, the four who survived the palace of Shau-ling: Lord Arathorn Geoffrey, Mailock the wizard, my wife Lady Diana, and myself; convinced Lord Cedric that he was needed in Marcwell and helped him to move the palace back where it belonged. Within a year or two, his condition had worsened, and he stopped traveling to the towns that had supported him during the war. He stays in the palace nearly all the time now, talking only to the four of us. Sometimes though I wouldn't call what he does talking."

"What do you mean, Aryx?" Eldar asked.

"Lord Cedric either orders us on some quest or tells us to leave him alone. He has always been a solitary man, and he only opens up when times necessitate it. The night that he sent me to bring the letter to Lord Logan was one of those nights."

"Go on, Aryx," Elwyne said in a wavering voice. "What did he say to you?"

"He told me, but not in words, that I was to help someone avoid the same web of death and destruction that he was trapped in. By him sending me to help you, he was trying to keep you from stumbling on your destiny the same way he did. He asked about my wife and apologized for his conduct over the last few months. Then he asked me if I had seen his sister. That in itself shocked me because he never talks about her anymore. Sometimes his random thoughts are hard to keep up with, and though we were in the middle of a crisis, he still seemed to be concerned with things that should not have been clouding his mind."

"His sister?" Logan asked slowly. "But I thought that Lady Anabel Binosear died in Shau-ling's throne room while trying to save Lord Cedric's life."

"That is the story that the bards are singing because that is the story that Lord Cedric wants them to sing," Aryx answered, a sly grin coming to his lips. "In truth, that is not what really happened. You see, once we had reached the throne room, Lord Cedric was the only one who could duel with Shau-ling. So, Mailock used his powers and created a sphere which would protect us from Shau-ling's evil powers. However, if anyone on the inside of the sphere broke through the sphere's boundary, they would be outside Mailock's protection. From the moment the duel started, it looked as if Lord Cedric would not survive. Cedric was off-balance and had lost the grip on his sword. Shau-ling was about the strike the final blow and sent a bolt of black energy streaking down toward Cedric's limp body. Lady Anne leapt from the bubble of protection and shielded Cedric's body with her own, buying him some time to recover. Thinking that his sister was dead, Lord Cedric eventually overcame Shau-ling and freed the world from his evil. After the battle was over, we were able to revive Lady Anne, but upon our return to Marcwell she left our company under a new name to pursue her life as a normal person again. Many of us however believe that she left because she saw what Cedric was becoming before any of the rest of us did. The events of the war had strained the relationship between the two, and though Anabel would support her brother to the end, at times she felt that the best way to support him was from a distance. She has not been known as Anabel Binosear since the day she left Marcwell for the last time."

"So for all intents and purposes, Lady Anabel Binosear is dead," Lane added flatly.

"Exactly," Aryx responded. "She has recently taken control of a kingdom, and is ruling under an assumed name, even though the leadership knows who she is. Lord Cedric wonders about her at times, mostly at night when he walks through the halls of the palace talking to people who aren't even there. To my knowledge, Cedric hasn't slept in just over six months."

The assertion was so absurd that no one at the table could even muster a reaction.

"So," Eldar said shaking her head, "our only hope for survival is totally insane."

"Not insane," Aryx chided. "But Lord Cedric is not the man who walked into the mouth of evil all those years ago. However, he is still a powerful ally."

"What do we do now?" Pike asked brushing aside Aryx's comments.

"Ultimately, the decision in yours," Aryx replied, "but let me tell you all this. One thing is for certain, the attack on Aradon proves that Shau-ling already knows of Logan's existence. Let me tell you from personal experience that once Shau-ling has the scent of the *Coromor*'s blood, he will not stop until he has eliminated the *Coromor* and all that follow him. As I told Logan earlier, Shau-ling can sense his presence, but until he knows the identity of the *Coromor* his realms of attack are limited. However, that will not stop the phasia from wreaking havoc on the world."

"The phasia?" Talon questioned.

"The phasia are the children of Shau-ling. They are creatures of such evil that it permeates their being and becomes their only focus in life. Mostly, they will focus on finding and killing the *Coromor*, but their evil will not stop there. They love to create terror and confusion in their enemies and have been known to strike one another down to get what they want.

Make no mistake, they are some of the most dangerous opponents that you could ever face, and they are almost as dangerous as Shau-ling himself."

"What is this *Coromor* you keep talking about?" Gwydeon asked.

"Loosely translated from the Old Tongue, *Coromor* means the one who brings change. Actually, when the word was first used, it supposedly meant the one who brings destruction. Either way you translate it, the fact remains that the *Coromor* is the only being who has the power to defeat Shau-ling. Cedric was the first *Coromor* of the prophecies, a fact he didn't discover until he was well upon his destined path. Logan is the second. It seems though that the knowledge has done little to insulate him from danger. No matter what happens on this quest, Logan, the *Coromor*, must survive to fight Shau-ling in his throne room, or our world is doomed to the rule of the Lord of the Shadows."

Logan stood straight from where he leaned against the wall and looked around the table before finally turning his gaze toward Aryx. The two men's gazes met, and after a long moment, Logan faltered and looked away. There was shame on his heart, shame that he could not put into words. He had run away from every real responsibility he had ever known, and now, the fate of everything rested upon him. Logan opened his mouth to speak, but Aryx put his hand up and shook his head.

"I know your question. You want to know about Shau-ling."

"It would be nice to know exactly what it was that we were going up against. The stories that I've heard have all probably been exaggerated to the point that there is little truth left in them, and besides, I had a hard time believing in an army of monsters and demons anyway. But after seeing the Shadowwalkers, I'm almost ready to believe anything. I would still like to get the story from someone who witnessed it first-hand though," Logan responded.

"Surprisingly enough," Aryx began, "the stories being circulated are remarkable accurate. Perhaps in this case the truth seems more fantastic than the best poet's lies."

After a shake of his head and running his fingers through his dark blond hair, he scanned the table once more and continued speaking.

"Cedric was to marry the love of his life, the lovely Erika Belnosian. At the wedding, an agent of Shau-ling, without a doubt a member of the phasia, appeared and killed Lady Erika. Cedric, grief-stricken and nearly out of his mind with rage began scouring the countryside in an attempt to find the assassin. However the criminal disappeared without a trace and Cedric was never able to exact his revenge. So, Cedric began to do research on the evil that plagued the land and he was able to find old writings by a man named Aralias Imstra, the leader of a group called the Hand of the Light. In these texts he discovered the existence of the creature we know as Shau-ling and the legend of the *Coromor*. This research also made him aware of the Jeweled Dragon's Flame. After we retrieved the Flame, Lord Cedric led us deep into the bowels of Shau-ling's palace, to the very heart of its evil, a place called the Hall of Terrors. We lost some good men in that den of hell, but we were successful in our quest, and some of us made it out alive."

"But that doesn't explain what Shau-ling is," Eldar remarked shortly.

"I was just getting to that," he relied evenly. "Shau-ling is a creature of pure evil with the ability to control the very fabrics of time and reality. He does so under the charter of the Creator's Laws, but he is still very much bent on the destruction of every living human soul on this world. He has the ability to change into whatever form he wishes, but he seems to prefer that of a large black dragon. Shau-ling can use any weapon that is open to him in any form that he takes, but he prefers to use brilliant green flames that he calls the Blaze. He draws this power of the Blaze directly from his palace, and from what I have seen, his creatures do as well. It seemed as though everything we fought was more powerful in his palace than it had been in the outside world."

Logan could see the stress and uncertainty on the faces of his friends.

"What do you think we should do now, Aryx? We're all rattled, and we need a direction."

"The sooner that we leave, the better," Aryx answered. "Those of you who are still dedicated to this journey, gathered what you need, and meet us at the stables at the edge of town. We'll leave within two hours."

They all nodded to him and stood up to leave. There was a lot of uneasiness in the room, but that much was understandable. Aryx was the last to leave. Just as the day before, Logan shut the door behind him and then sat down in the seat at the head of the table. Suddenly there was a pair of hands on his shoulders, and he jerked away from the hands and turned with his hand dropping down to the hilt of his sword. Elwyne's shocked face stared at him, and he exhaled sharply and brought his hands up in the most unthreatening gesture he could manage.

"I didn't mean to startle you," she said apologetically, "I only wanted to try and help you relax, as well as apologize for the way I acted earlier."

"I understand and I forgive you, what else could I do?"

She bit her bottom lip and looked down at the floor.

"Logan, I've missed you," she replied in almost a whisper.

"And I've missed being here with you. I almost can't bear being away from you," he said lifting her chin to look into her eyes.

Logan moved the chair out of the way and took her into his arms, holding her tightly. After a moment she looked up and let her lips slowly meet his, but just as quickly she pulled away from him and walked to the window wiping away the tears that had started falling from her eyes.

"Then why were you gone so long?" she said through her tears.

"You know what your father said, Elwyne. There was no way that I could come back until I had enough money to show him that I could take care of you the way that he wanted me to. You know that he wouldn't accept less."

She looked over at him and nodded before turning her gaze back out the window.

"Stay here where it's safe," Logan said finally, "I don't want you put in danger where there might be a possibility of losing you."

"Logan, David died because he believed in what you and Aryx were telling us. He knew that there was a chance he could die, and so do I," she said walking toward him.

"No, you don't, Elwyne. I don't want to lose you."

The frustration was thick in his voice, but she simply smiled and brushed her hand across his face and forehead.

"You will never lose me Logan Ranthall. My father may be able to send you away for a while, but there is no way that I will ever let you leave me behind ever again."

Logan finally forced a smile and she kissed him lightly on the cheek before moving past him. She stopped and squeezed his arm briefly and then left. Logan quickly gathered his belongings, most of which had already been packed and slung his pack over his shoulder. As he closed the door behind him, it seemed strange to be leaving Aradon again so soon. But within a matter of minutes he was standing with Aryx at the edge of town. Logan saw Aryx stiffen slightly and turned his gaze back towards town. Gwydeon came over the hill, and Logan could feel a slight sigh of relief escape his lips and some of the tension ease from his shoulders. Next to appear were Talon and Pike, with Lane trailing slightly behind them. Only a few minutes before the deadline both Eldar and Elwyne appeared, and the party was complete. As they were mounting their horses, Logan spoke.

"I just wanted to say thank you, to all of you. I know what we're leaving behind, and if it weren't for the weight of this on my shoulders, I think I would want to stay in Aradon and help rebuild. As Aryx said, we don't know who is watching and we don't know who is in league with the Shadows. The name of Sir Aryx Terian floating around with a party of young people is bound to raise suspicion, so in towns and around strangers, we should address him as Lan. There's no telling how long this disguise will last, but we'll play it as long as we can. Does everyone understand?"

There were nods all-around, and the group quickly started toward Illimar. Aryx and Gwydeon took the lead, and Logan found himself bringing up the rear of the group. Though she often looked back in his direction, Elwyne stayed with Eldar. Hours passed on the road, and the travel was quiet and required little attention. The low stress journey was exactly what the group needed, and it gave them time to try to process all of the horrors they had been through. As evening approached, Pike and Talon began singing and joking which infused the group with a new life. The evening breeze swept across Logan's face as he surveyed their surroundings. The hooves of the horses kicked up so much dust that it obscured the exact edges of the path. Logan felt as though the forest were watching them with unseen eyes as they made their way deeper into it. Ducking a branch, Logan pulled his horse to a stop to take a drink of water. As he looked around something appeared in front of him.

A ring of smoke came out from under one of the trees and manifested itself around Logan's horse. There was no sound, smell, or feel to the smoke, and he struggled to be sure that what he was seeing there in front of him was real at all. The smoke parted to his right and seemed to form a path. Taking a deep breath, Logan felt as though he had no choice and turned his horse down the smoke-lined path.

CHAPTER 2

Chapter III

Dreamscape

Riding down the forest path, Aryx looked around aimlessly, his training imploring him to know what was going on all around him at all times. But he knew that he was traveling with a group that did not have experience enough for a quickened pace, no matter the danger they had just left behind. It was like the first days with Cedric Binosear all those years ago. They would need rest and encouragement, but the shock of the horror left behind and the horror that lay ahead would prevent them from truly feeling the loss of their homes. Finally, he put his hand up and signaled to stop and make camp for the night. He had just begun to start a small fire when Gwydeon rode up to him.

"Aryx," Gwydeon asked calmly, "have you seen Logan anywhere?"

Shaking his head Aryx answered, "Not since we left Aradon. You might check with Elwyne or Pike, they were nearer to the back of the pack."

"I already have. Aryx, I'm worried. No one else has seen anything of him for some time now."

Aryx grimaced. Logan's position as the leader of the second generation of the prophecies made him a valuable commodity, but if he felt that he was being smothered or coddled, he might not be ready to do what was necessary when the time came. He had just lost everything he had ever known, and that would be weighing on him, probably more heavily than the rest because of his feelings of responsibility.

"The road to Illimar holds no threats, Gwydeon. It is patrolled constantly. Logan is taking his time and space to think about what has happened and to prepare himself for what is to come. He deserves time, as you all do, to come to terms with this in your own time and in your own way. He'll come soon, and if he has not returned by morning, I will search for him. There is no better tracker in this part of the world, and he could not get far."

"If you think that is best."

Aryx forced a smile despite the concern that was blooming inside of him.

"Logan will not run from his responsibilities, Gwydeon."

Gwydeon stopped and turned back to face Aryx.

"A year ago, I might have taken more comfort in that statement."

Gwydeon rode back toward where the rest of the party had set up camp and dismounted. The rest of the group was sitting around a fire, most trying to recover for the long ride. None of them were used to such traveling. Aryx was several feet away near his own small fire, the glow barely enough to illuminate his eyes and the steel of his sword that he was slowly sharpening. Gwydeon sat down by the fire and took a drink from his water skin.

"Why are you drinking water, Gwydeon?" Talon asked.

"What else do you expect me to drink, Talon? Dirt?" Gwydeon replied laughing.

"Well, I did happen to bring a few bottles of my father's finest ale along. I'm sure that it would help us to pass the time a lot better than the water would," Talon replied.

"I'll drink to that!" Pike exclaimed taking a bottle and raising it to his lips.

They passed around the bottles until they were empty, and after an hour of drinking and attempts at small talk, they all sat back relaxed, and some more drunk than others. As usual Pike and Talon were the ones who had imbibed the most, with Elwyne, Gwydeon, and Lane drinking only enough to be social. It was Eldar that did her best to keep up with the troublemakers.

"I never really noticed it before," Eldar said, her words slurring slightly.

"You've never really noticed what before?" Lane asked.

"I've never really noticed that Pike and Talon both have scars from their elbow to their wrist, but on different arms," Eldar replied.

Pike and Talon both offered up their arms to the group, letting the firelight fall on the scars.

"I'm not sure how I got this," Pike said lounging back against his pack. "I think my father said it was an accident when I was still in diapers."

"Drinking and getting in fights even then?" Elwyne teased.

"Probably fighting with Talon," Lane commented.

"It's just a coincidence," Talon said laughing.

"It's not a coincidence."

The voice seemed to come from everywhere. The party looked around, trying to find the mysterious voice that had spoken to them. However, there was nothing to be found. All that was there was the quiet calm of the surrounding forest.

"Who said that?" Gwydeon asked grasping the hilt of his sword tightly.

"Find me if you can!" the voice shot back.

Suddenly both fires were blown out by a gust of wind leaving the group in darkness. Gwydeon drew his sword and moved into a defensive position with his back close to a nearby tree. Lane pulled the hood of his cloak over his head and grabbed his quarterstaff off the ground.

"Is everybody still with us?" Lane asked.

"I'm still here," Gwydeon replied.

"Talon and Pike are over here with me," Eldar replied.

"Aryx and I are over here," Elwyne answered.

"Stay together, we'll have light back in a minute," Lane said.

Lane rubbed his fingers together, and muttered a few words under his breath and a ball of flame burst into existence and floated there above his open palm. It wasn't very much of a source of light, but it was enough to see by. Lane focused his eyes on a pile of tinder where the fire had been, and blew the flame in his hand onto the awaiting pile. The fire burst back into existence, and the light in the woods grew. The wind began to blow again, but the fire remained.

"No need to worry about the flame being blown out friends, it is a magical flame and it cannot be extinguished by any form of wind or water," Lane said.

"Good," Aryx said coldly, "let's concentrate on finding that voice. I doubt it will be content to simply taunt us for long."

Aryx drew his sword and walked back over to where his fire had been. He picked up a rock and walked over to the magical fire. From there he walked to the edge of the light, and Gwydeon walked over to him. Abruptly, Aryx turned around and motioned for Gwydeon to stop.

"Lane, is it normal for a magical fire like this to cast light that ends so abruptly and in such a perfectly round pattern?"

Lane walked over to where Aryx stood and looked down at the ground to see what Aryx was talking about. Sure enough, the light from the magical fire came to an end about two feet in front of them. Not only did it just end, it came to a stop in a perfectly round circle, in all directions.

"No, it isn't normal. I have a theory. Stick your hand outside of the boundary of the light."

Aryx nodded and turned back toward the darkness. He took a deep breath and then reached into the blackness. Suddenly, Aryx disappeared. Everyone standing there reacted in shock and terror. Everyone that is, except for Lane.

"Aryx," Lane said calmly, as though the man was still standing right beside him, "pull your hand back through."

A moment passed and nothing happened. Then, without warning, Aryx reappeared in the same place he was when he disappeared. Aryx took a step back, and then reset himself. He then sheathed his sword and straightened himself.

"That was the oddest place I have ever seen," Aryx said shaking his head.

"Describe it," Lane pressed, "in detail if you will."

"It was a smoke-lined path. There was no light, but I could make out everything so clearly that I was sure I was seeing it," Aryx replied slowly.

"That's what I was afraid of," Lane said shaking his head. "If what I believe is true, we are in a great deal of trouble. What Aryx just experienced can best be called Dreamscape. It is a rip in the fabric of normal existence and can be used to hide people, towns, and even the stars in the sky. Dreamscape itself has no limits to its size, but it is controlled by those who live inside it."

"What could be powerful enough to hide stars?" Pike asked.

"If Lane is correct, then we have encountered yet another of Shau-ling's favorite weapons," Aryx said with disgust. "And if I am correct, the reason that we have not seen Logan for quite some time is because he has been captured by a Tarnae."

"A what?" Pike asked.

"Tarnae," Aryx replied.

"And just what the hell is a Tarnae?" Talon asked frustration thick in his voice.

"The Tarnae are what you might call a master of riddles. It survives by trapping unknowing travelers in Dreamscape and giving them a challenge. Usually, the challenge is to solve a series of riddles and make their way out of Dreamscape before the Tarnae finds them and kills them. As you can probably guess, the Tarnae cheats," Aryx answered.

"How so?" Elwyne asked concerned.

"The smoke-lined path that I described is not any ordinary path; it's more like a maze that is in reality a part of the Tarnae itself. Therefore, as the prey advances in the challenge, the Tarnae changes the appearance of its maze form and eventually traps its opponent in an endless loop. Then, after letting its opponent run around for a while, solving useless riddles the Tarnae kills and eats its prey," Aryx replied.

"So, Logan doesn't stand a chance," Pike commented.

"Not unless we help him," Talon replied.

"Then we don't have a choice," Eldar concluded.

"We're going into Dreamscape," Gwydeon agreed.

"If we are going into Dreamscape, we had better stay together and concentrate on finding Logan. However, I find it very strange that the Tarnae revealed itself to us," Aryx replied.

"Yes, what were we talking about when the fires were blown out and the voice spoke to us?" Elwyne asked.

"The coincidence of the scars on Pike and Talon," Eldar answered.

"Yeah, that's right," Talon commented, the displeasure thickening in his voice. "We were just sitting here having a few drinks talking about the scars and how much of a coincidence it was that we both had the same scar but on different arms. Then this Tarnae thing butts into our conversation babbling that it wasn't a coincidence."

"And I was telling the truth."

The voice shocked the party. Several of the friends jumped to their feet and drew their weapons. Looking around all the time, Gwydeon slowly began to speak.

"There it is again," Gwydeon said, "the scars must be important after all."

"That they are weakling," the Tarnae replied. "After all of these years, who would have imagined that I would find you here in this dismal wood?"

"Me?" Gwydeon asked.

"Pathetic creatures such as you are beneath my notice," the Tarnae scoffed. "No, I am only interested in those with power, and how could I resist the smell of power coming from the three of you."

Aryx spun around, looking in all directions for the Tarnae. All that he saw, no matter where he looked, was the forest. The darkness outside of the magical flame seemed to grow deeper and more menacing with every passing minute.

"Three of whom?" Aryx asked.

"Aryx Terian, the self-styled White Lightning and hero. I've been watching you ever since you left Marcwell. It's bad comedy that Cedric still allows you to lick his boots, pretender."

"So, why didn't you strike when you had the chance?" Aryx replied. "Were you afraid that I would be too much of a match for a ball of slime like you? Or was it perhaps that Shau-ling was holding your leash a little too tight that day. Which was it?"

"You are no concern of mine White Lightning, your time is passed. The *Erieal* are what concern me now."

"Shau-ling must be desperate if he has you chancing legends," Aryx asked buying time and pushing the point.

"Come now, White Lightning. Playing dumb does not become you, especially when you aren't smart enough to do it properly. Yourself, Diana, Mailock, Arathorn; you all assisted the *Coromor* in his conquest of Shau-ling last generation. You may not have known what you were, but you fulfilled your roles nevertheless. Now, I must stop this new generation of *Erieal* from helping the Dragon defeat my lord in this time," it replied in a hateful voice.

"So the *Erieal* are here?" Aryx asked slyly.

"I sense the presence of two who bear the mark of the *Erieal*, however, I have never before encountered more than one of them without the presence of the *Coromor*. But no matter, one of the *Erieal* is already in my trap, and now I intend to add two more to my collection of fallen legends."

Suddenly, a great burst of wind blasted through the darkened forest and surrounded the party, casting them into the void only known as Dreamscape. The transition was not an easy one. The sleepless dream that was Dreamscape demanded that only souls would be allowed to enter. The force of the wind that the Tarnae created was powerful enough to rip the souls from the bodies of the party bit by bit. After the seemingly unending transition, the adventurers woke up on a dark, smoke-lined path with no light and no way out. Slowly, they could make out one of the ends of the path opening and they all walked toward the opening, ready to face whatever they had to in order to make it out alive. Every one of them had two things in common. They were all clutching their weapons tightly, and they were all more frightened than they had ever been in their lives. Even the battle tested Aryx Terian had fear in his heart as he walked down the seemingly endless smoke-lined path. The ground below them was softer than it should have been. It felt more like flesh than good solid dirt. After what seemed like hours of walking, they came to a split in the path. The path that they were following diverged into three separate paths, and each of these paths was marked with a different colored smoke. The path to the right had a bluish tint, the path to the left was red, and the path that stretched ever forward retained the same eerie yellow color. Without a word, the party broke up and followed separate paths. Eldar and Elwyne continued down the yellow path. Aryx, Lane and Gwydeon followed the path to the right, and Pike and Talon went down the path to the left. Somewhere in the darkness of Dreamscape, the Tarnae laughed in pleasure.

"The right path has been chosen, some will survive. You will all find me, dead or alive."

CHAPTER 3

* * * * * * * * * * * *

Pike and Talon walked side by side down the path, waiting for some sign that they were going to find Logan, or at least a way out of Dreamscape. Talon clutched his spear tightly, and Pike took the ax out of the loop in his belt. Walking forward, they came to a wall of clouds. The clouds were much different than the smoke that lined the path. The clouds seemed to have an inner light, and were extremely large. However, the clouds didn't seem to have any definite shape or form, they were just there.

I wonder what it going on here. First we started out fine, now Logan's got us into some damn place that we can't get out of. I wonder what Shau-ling is doing right now. He's probably sitting back in his palace having a good laugh about all of this. This cloud is too thick to see through. Well, here goes nothing.

"Well," Pike said, "here goes nothing."

Pike took a slow step forward and entered the cloud directly in front of him. There was a rush of wind and Pike began to slowly fade out of existence. Talon kept his eyes trained on Pike until he was into the opaque mass that constituted the bulk of the cloud. A few minutes passed and Pike made no sign to Talon. No indication that he was alive or dead. Talon became increasingly worried.

"Pike," Talon said.

Nothing.

"Pike."

Again, nothing.

"Pike!" Talon yelled at the top of his voice.

"Your friend is with me now," the Tarnae's voice echoed back, "and soon you shall be joining him."

A gust of wind hit Talon hard and started to pull him toward the mass of the cloud. Talon quickly turned away and started running into the force of the wind. He quickly turned his head and looked back toward the cloud. The light in the cloud seemed to pulsate the closer he came to its boundary.

No matter how hard he tried and no matter how fast he ran, he was being edged closer and closer to the edge of the cloud. Suddenly, Talon's foot hit a rock, and he fell to the ground just in front of the cloud. He dug his fingers into the ground below him and tried to pull himself away from the mass of white. The gusts became stronger and Talon soon became aware of the fact that he was being suspended over the ground and that his feet were beginning to penetrate the boundary. Only one thought entered his mind from that point on.

I'm going to die.

And then everything went black.

* * * * * * * * * * * *

Lane, Aryx and Gwydeon walked cautiously down the path that they had chosen for themselves. The further they walked the redder and more blood-like the color of the smoke became. It had been almost two hours since the party had split up.

"Two friends, both deep in fear. Death came to them swiftly, bliss most dear. The party is down to five. It's up to you to stay alive."

The Tarnae's last words lingered in the air for a long time it seemed, and then were no more. The three adventurers looked to each other and then shook their heads.

"Do you think he really killed two of us?" Gwydeon asked.

"It's more than likely that he did," Aryx answered. "Tarnae are known for, or all things, telling the truth about its kills."

"Who do you think he got to?" Gwydeon asked slowly.

"Try not to think about it," Lane scolded. "What's important is that we are alive, and we have to try and find Logan. If we don't, we'll all end up dead."

Gwydeon nodded and kept walking down the path. No one else spoke. The path seemed to twist and turn many times, and soon the path came to an end, and in the very center of the path stood a well.

"Each of you can see what I am," a voice said from inside the well, "and you will face your test here. You will each be asked a question. The answers to these questions will determine your fate."

Lane looked back over his shoulder and noticed that a wall of smoke had appeared behind them. They were trapped. Lane swallowed roughly and looked back at the well. It was very large and as he peered over the edge, Lane could not tell if there was a bottom to the well or not.

"The first question," the well said after a moment, "is to you Gwydeon Sandar. In battle, you are challenged by the leader of an opposing force. You know the leader well, and know that he is of far superior skill. You have three choices as to your reply. The first choice is to fight the duel. The second is to decline the battle. The third is to run and hide. Weigh your decision carefully, Gwydeon Sandar, for your life hangs in the balance."

"I have no need to weigh my decision; I choose to fight the battle."

"So shall it be."

Aryx and Lane watched as Gwydeon slowly disappeared from view. They both knew that Gwydeon was brave, but inwardly they prayed that his bravery had not just gotten him killed.

"Aryx Terian, you are well known here. We respect you and give you a choice. You may leave this place now and go back to Marcwell, or you will die. It should be a simple choice. What will be your decision?"

What should I do? I can't just leave the Coromor here. I can't leave Logan here to die. What if he's dead already? How can I help a dead man? What should I do? Live to fight another day?

"The choice is made."

Suddenly, Aryx began to disappear in front of Lane's eyes. Slowly he faded more and more out of the reality that Dreamscape had created for them. Now only Lane remained, left to decide his own fate.

"Lane Toridon, the final question is yours. What is your answer?"

"I cannot answer," Lane replied puzzled, "I don't know the question."

"That is not what you should be worrying about weakling," the Tarnae laughed. "The problem is whether or not you will survive. Or more appropriately, how long will you fall before you hit bottom?"

The wind began to rise in intensity all around Lane. Soon his robe was being lifted by the strengthening breeze. Suddenly, Lane realized that it wasn't just his robe that was being lifted by the wind. He looked down and found that he was suspended three feet above the ground. Lane tried to remain perfectly calm, but eventually the fear overtook him, and he began to move forward. The more afraid he became, the closer the wind took him to the well. Minutes later, Lane was falling. Then the darkness fell.

* * * * * * * * * * * *

Eldar and Elwyne both kept watchful eyes as they made their way down the yellow path. Nothing had happened since the last time that the Tarnae had spoken. They didn't know who was left alive, but they had to continue on. They were sure that Logan was still alive and it was up to them to find him. And then the voice rang out again.

"Three more down, two to go. You may be the lucky one, or maybe no. It's up to you, the choice has been made. Your life hangs in the balance, be very afraid."

The words rang out so clearly in each of their ears, and the volume was almost deafening. Undaunted, Elwyne and Eldar walked down the path ready and waiting for whatever came. They didn't have to wait long.

The path soon came to another split and they decided to follow separate paths. Elwyne took the path to the right, and Eldar went to the left. They wished each other luck and went their separate ways. Within seconds, they were each alone.

Eldar felt the fear creep in on her as she walked slowly down the path. She looked around aimlessly trying to find some break in the monotonous walls of yellow smoke. Without warning, there was a flash of light. The light momentarily blinded Eldar, and she was unaware of what was happening. The light faded away, and she was trapped in a whirlwind of fire and smoke. She screamed in pain and horror, and closed her eyes trying hard not to acknowledge what was happening around her. The heat of the circling flames began to increase slowly, subjecting her to the pain of burning flesh. She tried to scream, but no sound came out of her throat. Eventually the pain gave way to the sensation of sleep, and she faded into the dreamless sleep that was her death. Dreamscape shuddered as it welcomed another into is collection of souls. Only the Tarnae laughed in pleasure.

* * * * * * * * * * * *

Elwyne walked calmly through the maze of twist and turns of the path that she had chosen for herself. Nothing had happened for hours it seemed.

I wonder how Eldar is. It's been so long since I've seen anybody. Where's Logan? I never realized how much I missed him until now. Why did he leave? That's a stupid question. You know father said that he couldn't marry you until he had enough money. Father is so protective of me. I know I'm his only daughter and he has to take care of me, but I want to be with Logan.

"You're my only daughter, and I have to take care of you," a voice said from behind her.

Elwyne spun around to face what had spoken to her. Expecting to see something there, she found nothing but the same yellow smoke.

"Who said that?"

"I did my daughter. I have missed you since you left. I had no idea if you were dead or alive," the voice replied.

"Where are you?" Elwyne asked spinning around looking for the voice that called to her.

"Right behind you my dear."

Elwyne turned around sharply, and again found nothing. Then, something appeared before her. The form took shape slowly, but after a moment, Elwyne recognized the form as her father. His hair was the same dark brown that she remembered, and his eyes were as caring as ever. She didn't recognize the clothes that he was wearing, but the man inside the clothes was her father. He walked over to her and pulled her into his arms. He kissed her lightly on the forehead and then hugged her tightly. She rested her head on his shoulder and felt his chest rise and fall with his breath. She took a deep breath and then started to say something, but he was gone.

She spun around, looking for some sigh of where her father had disappeared to, but no sign could be found, just the same yellow smoke. The loneliness took her, and she began to hate Logan for drawing her away from her father. In her mind's eye, she envisioned Logan standing in front of her. Suddenly, as if she were in a dream, Logan appeared before her. And, just as in her vision, a sword was in her hand. Without warning, Logan stepped toward her and impaled himself on her sword. He slid off the cold steel blade and fell to the ground. His clothes were soon soaked with his blood and she cried in pain and anguish. She soon found herself wishing that she were dead. In a matter of minutes, she had lost both her father and the man that she loved, and it was all her fault. She swallowed hard and made her decision. The time had come. Her grip on the hilt of the sword tightened, and she took a deep breath. Then came the blissful darkness.

Of Time and Riddles

Logan found his mind wandering as his horse navigated down the smoke-lined path that he had encountered after dropping back from the rest of the group. The further that he traveled down the path, the more substantial the faint yellow smoke became, and seemed to form a more solid border around the bases of trees and lacing its way through the underbrush. It seemed that the whole character of the forest changed because of the smoke. The trees seemed more menacing, and the wind that rustled not only the leaves but also the long blades of grass and small bushes would blow hard for several moments and then die away to nothing. Everything felt confused, like the forest was trying to understand the new additions. Logan's horse itself seemed to sense the menace that was growing in the forest. On two separate occasions, the horse stopped, its head craning, smelling the wind. The second time, the horse's eyes went wide and it started to bolt in the opposite direction. Logan dug his heels into the horse's flank and pulled up hard on the reins trying his best to keep control. As he was trying to keep himself in the saddle, Logan only partially noticed the dark clouds begin to gather overhead. When finally the horse settled, Logan looked up and could see only darkness. The wind flared up again, this time with a cold chill that shook Logan to the bone. There was also a smell woven into the hard breeze, a smell like rotting meat. When the horse reared and bucked underneath Logan again, he wasn't able to get a good grip on the reins, and they were pulled free from his hands. He couldn't help but fall forward, and he grabbed hard onto the saddle. He tried to push his heels into the horse's flanks, tried to regain control, but he couldn't get the leverage that he needed. Another buck from the horse sent Logan flying through the air. Two large bushes broke his fall, but his head struck the ground hard. Everything went black, and by the time Logan was able to force his way back to his feet, there was no sign what direction his horse had gone in, and because of the darkness, there was no telling how long he had been lying there. Though he was now on foot, he took some solace in the fact that his sword belt had been strapped around his waist and not lashed to his saddle. He knelt down and looked at the tracks that were dug into the ground, and tried to make sense of them. It was clear which direction he had come from, but then the tracks got confused. It was as though the horse spun around in circles several times and then was simply gone.

Logan cursed to himself and then closed his eyes. When he opened them again, he forced calm through his body and set his mind to work on the problem. Many times during his childhood, he and his father had made the journey from Aradon to Illimar through the forest. One of them would walk beside the over-laden cart while the other made sure that the oxen stayed on the path. However, in all the times that they had made the journey, the road had never been as smooth as the path Logan was examining, and they had never seen anything like the yellow smoke. Finally Logan stood and resigned himself to walking, and continued down the path instead of going back the way he came. Though he was trying to concentrate on everything around him, Logan could not keep his mind from wandering as he walked down the smoke-lined path. His wandering mind made it impossible to keep track of time, and when he finally stopped and looked around, he wasn't sure if he had been walking for several hours or only a few minutes. One thing was for certain; his legs ached, probably more from the fall than from the walking. After wiping his brow, he looked down the path and was surprised to see that there was a three-way fork ahead of him. He was sure that that fork had not been there the moment before. The fork, while offering three choices, did so in a most unexpected manner. The path that led to the left was lined with a reddish smoke, the center continued with the eerie yellowish smoke, and the path to the right wound out of sight with a lining of blue smoke.

So, what's it going to be? I actually wish that Aryx were here so that I could rely on his experience with strange occurrences, especially considering my track record with making the right choice when it really matters. My decisions usually fall into one of two categories, either incredibly brave, or incredibly stupid.

"You look like the incredibly stupid type."

The voice echoed for some time before it stopped ringing in Logan's ears. It was as though someone had been standing beside him and shouting as loud as possible in both ears at the same time. His hands went to his ears reflexively, and he closed his eyes to shut out the pain. When his eyes finally opened again, Logan looked all around and could see only the smoke. He put his hand on the hilt of his sword and contemplated drawing it for a moment, and then let his hand fall away.

"Alright Logan," he said out loud in an attempt to shake the eerie silence that had come after the mysterious voice. "Either you're hearing things, or you're starting to go crazy."

Your imagination is starting to get the better of you, Logan. I know this path is getting on your nerves, but you can't let it rattle you. Ok, let's get moving. Which path is it going to be? Red? Too much bloodshed left in my future I'm sure, so I'll pass on that. Blue? Lots of water. Drowning doesn't sound like a good way to go. Well, looks like I stay with yellow for a little while longer.

He tried to laugh to himself to break the nerves and uneasiness that were building inside of him, but the eerie silence was too much to ignore. Again his mind started to wander, and he could not keep his mind focused on the path ahead. The trees along the path all looked the same, with the same spacing between them. There wasn't so much as a large rock, or a broken branch that he could use as a landmark to be sure that he wasn't walking in circles. Finally there was a change in the scenery in the form of another form in the road. This time there were only two possible choices, but no colors to differentiate them. Reaching into his pocket, Logan pulled out a coin and quickly flipped it. Heads came up, so that meant he took the right fork.

Again monotony set in, but this time it was accompanied by exhaustion. It was as though the yellow smoke was sapping every ounce of strength from his body. His legs ached, and his body felt as though it weighed twice what it should. However, he knew he could not stop, could no surrender to fatigue. He had to go on. Just then there was a rumbling sound from the path ahead and there appeared to be a shape materializing. The form began to move in his direction and once it reached the edge of his vision, he began to be able to make out more of the thing's shape. It seemed more or less human in shape, and Logan instinctively took hold of the hilt of his sword, but did not draw it from the sheath. Then, just before the form was fully in sight, it seemed to blink out of existence for just a fraction of a second and then reform. The shape was clearly visible, and one that Logan would have recognized anywhere. It was Elwyne's father.

As he took in the features of the man, Logan recognized that there were significant differences from the man he had known since he was a child. His eyes held such intense sadness but at the same time incredible rage. The man stopped in front of Logan and held his gaze, sending a shudder through Logan's body. The power and the force of the stare caught Logan by surprise and caused him to flinch. When Logan recovered and looked at the man's face again, the face had changed. A cruel smile had replaced the angry frown, and the smile twisted his face, warping it so that the edges of his mouth rose far higher than they should have been able to, almost to the level of the tops of his ears. The man laughed an evil high-pitched keening laugh, and the color in his eyes shifted from brilliant blue to a dark glowing red. Again the man laughed and then began to speak in a high-pitched voice.

"So you are the impudent fly who has found his way into my web. Welcome to my domain you pathetic whelp. I had hoped for much more of a challenge when Shau-ling sent me to deal with you and your little friends."

Anger boiled in Logan. He had fallen into a trap. He cursed himself for not expecting it after the attack on Aradon. The Shadowwalkers had succeeded in flushing them out of the larger population of the town into the forest where they were easy prey for this new creature. Before Logan could respond to the jibe, the creature spoke again.

"I must say that I had expected more of the *Coromor* and his companions. I could have easily killed all of you by now, but I had hoped that you would have given me at least a little more amusement. But like your guide White Lightning, you are all boring. Perhaps you will be able to show a little more spirit."

Logan clenched his teeth, trying to hold back his wrath.

"What have you done with them?"

The thing laughed again, only louder this time. It was meant to inflame Logan's senses, make him lash out, but Logan continued to control his rage. All Logan really wanted to do was to draw his sword and lop the creature's head off, but he knew that he had to find out what had happened to his friends, and if what the creature was saying was true, they were being allowed to live as long as they were amusing.

"They have not been harmed, permanently. At least not yet. Their pain and sorrow are amusing me, just barely, for now. Your kind always tastes better when they are marinated for a time in fear. But I assure you that they will not keep my attention for much longer. So, you'll have to keep me amused. I will make a wager with you, child. You will be given the opportunity to save your little companions, but you have to play my game. If you succeed, then they will be saved, and you will be able to leave here without further incident. However, if you fail even one test, if you make even one wrong choice, your lives will be forfeit, and I will feast on your souls for as long as they will last."

Logan clenched his fists, but nodded slowly.

"Name your terms, monster."

The creature's wide smile disappeared and was replaced by an equally deep frown.

"Monster? You dare to insult me when I have been nothing but generous to you and your friends? I allow them to live and you disparage me? For that I should kill you all now and be done with it."

The creature folded its arms and turned its back to Logan. It was almost as if the thing was sulking like a spoiled child who wasn't getting its way. Logan waited, not sure what he should do in the situation, but he was not going to apologize to the monster. This was most likely just another part of the creature's game; another attempt to keep Logan off-balance. Finally the creature turned back slightly toward Logan, enough that he could see half of the monster's face.

"But, as I so enjoy my little game, I shall forgive you your transgression, just this once. Now, the game I offer you is quite simple. Your companions have fallen into my traps, and I shall give you clues to their whereabouts as well as clues to save them from the lethal situations they have found themselves in."

"Then give me the first clue, and I'll save them. You won't derive any further amusement from us, and I assure that when this is all over, I'll come back for you."

The creature laughed loudly again, the smile twisting its face even further.

"My, aren't we confident? Your town is slaughtered by Shadowwalkers. You get separated from your companions by a simple misdirection, and now you stand before me boasting about your abilities. Your stupidity must truly know no bounds. Very well then, since you are so sure that you will be able to win my little game, let us make the stakes more interesting."

The creature's smile seemed to grow even larger as it lifted one hand over its head and then began to mutter words in a language that Logan could barely hear let alone understand. After several moments, something began to appear above the creatures head, and over the next few moments slowly took shape. As soon as Logan recognized the item, his heart sank. The object consisted of two bell-shaped glass pieces that were joined at the slim open ends. The glass pieces were encased in a black wooden casing that allowed for the viewing of the contents of the glass from all sides. In the bottom bell, sand filled about three-quarters of the volume. After the form of the hourglass had materialized fully, the creature's eyes glowed brightly and it laughed once more.

"Perhaps a time limit will make the game more interesting for both of us. I will give you one hour to find and save your friends, one hour only. But here is the trick, my young and impudent friend. Time works differently here, and depending upon where you are in my domain, time may flow faster or slower. Take too much time, and the game is over and you all will be mine to feast upon. Not that it matters much. You have already proven that you are not a match for me or for my riddles. I shall enjoy sucking the marrow from your bones."

Logan grimaced, but tried his best to find the depths of his courage and resolve. No matter the taunts of the creature, no matter the power that it obviously had at hand, as long as he was still alive and willing to fight, there was a chance for salvation. The hourglass was a prop, nothing more. The creature was obviously in control of every aspect of its domain, so it could change the flow of time as it saw fit. As long as Logan continued to entertain the creature, it would allow the game to go on. He took a long deep breath, and then let his voice find the air again.

"I'm ready."

The next moment, the creature was gone. The hourglass remained, and it bobbed in the air for another moment before turning over to start the sand falling. The creature's voice seemed to boom from everywhere all at once as it had before, but the sound was not deafening as it had been the first time Logan had encountered it. The high-pitched voice doled out the first of the clues, a mixture of lyrical words and laughter.

"Just ahead is a lonely little girl. She is lost in longing and in sorrow. Around cold death her fingers will curl. Alone she does not wish to see tomorrow."

When the voice faded, Logan swallowed and continued down the path that forked to the right. He knew that either Eldar or Elwyne lie at the end of the path, and he hoped that the creature's riddle would indeed give him the tools that he needed to save his friend's life.

* * * * * * * * * * * *

Elwyne walked calmly through the maze of twist and turns of the path that she had chosen for herself. Nothing had happened for hours it seemed.

I wonder how Eldar is. It's been so long since I've seen anybody. Where's Logan? I never realized how much I missed him until now. Why did he leave? That's a stupid question. You know father said that he couldn't marry you until he had enough money. Father is so protective of me. I know I'm his only daughter and he has to take care of me, but I want to be with Logan.

"You're my only daughter, and I have to take care of you," a voice said from behind her.

Elwyne spun around to face what had spoken to her. Expecting to see something there, she found nothing but the same yellow smoke.

"Who said that?"

"I did my daughter. I have missed you since you left. I had no idea if you were dead or alive," the voice replied.

"Where are you?" Elwyne asked spinning around looking for the voice that called to her.

"Right behind you my dear."

Elwyne turned around sharply, and again found nothing. Then, something appeared before her. The form took shape slowly, but after a moment, Elwyne recognized the form as her father. His hair was the same dark brown that she remembered, and his eyes were as caring as ever. She didn't recognize the clothes that he was wearing, but the man inside the clothes was her father. He walked over to her and pulled her into his arms. He kissed her lightly on the forehead and then hugged her tightly. She rested her head on his shoulder and felt his chest rise and fall with his breath. She took a deep breath and then started to say something, but he was gone.

She spun around, looking for some sigh of where her father had disappeared to, but no sign could be found, just the same yellow smoke. The loneliness took her, and she began to hate Logan for drawing her away from her father. In her mind's eye, she envisioned Logan standing in front of her. Suddenly, as if she were in a dream, Logan appeared before her. And, just as in her vision, a sword was in her hand. Without warning, Logan stepped toward her...

…and grabbed the sword. She could not believe what was happening. In her vision she had killed Logan and then killed herself. She didn't know how many times the perverse and painful scene had played itself out, but no matter what she tried, no matter what she thought, she could not stop the wave of sorrow from overwhelming her, could not stop Logan from impaling himself on the blade, and could not stop herself from falling on the blade herself. Her hands went limp and the hilt of the sword fell away. Logan put both of his hands on her shoulders, and the wave of pain overwhelmed her. She started sobbing uncontrollably, tears streaming down her face. Logan pulled her into his arms and held her tightly.

"You're safe now, Elwyne. It's over."

She pulled away and looked up at him, her eyes filled with a combination of shock and horror. Her mouth opened as though she wanted to speak, but no words came out. Finally her jaw worked again and her words came out strained and scratchy.

"It was my father," she said, "he was here. And then…"

Logan pulled her to him again, and gently ran his fingers through her hair trying to comfort her.

"It wasn't your father, Elwyne. There is something living here that can take any form it wants. It's been torturing you, trying to break you for its amusement. Luckily I was able to find you and figure out its riddle. But the others are being tormented too, and we have to help them."

Elwyne put both of her hands on Logan's chest and pushed hard. Logan almost fell because he was unprepared for her violent reaction, but she continued to walk backwards, her hands up, and her voice shaking. Tears streamed harder down her face.

"No, Logan, I killed you. I killed you over and over again, and I couldn't make it stop. Each time it was the same. My father would come to me, and then he would disappear. Then you would appear and walk into a sword that I held. Then, I just couldn't go on without out, and I turned the blade on myself. I have to be dead, and the Great Dark One has to be punishing me for everything wrong that I've done. Now he's going to torment me by letting me see you and then taking you away from me again."

She turned away and shielded her face. Logan could hear her crying, and it did not seem as though she could stop the tears that flooded from her red and swollen eyes. She really believed that she was dead and she was doomed to live out the eternity of death facing her guilt day after dreary day. Finally Logan grabbed her from behind and pulled her back into his arms.

"You're not dead Elwyne, and neither am I. We're just trapped in this damn place and I've got to get us all out of here."

For a long time they stood there together, and Logan held her as tightly as he could. Her tears and sobs began to slow until finally she turned back to face him and pressed her head against his chest. Her breathing was still erratic, but Logan could tell that she was starting to get a hold on the emotions that had previously been raging out of control.

"Just stay with me Logan, promise me you'll stay with me."

Logan continued to hold her close, as tightly as he could, and resting his chin on the crown of her head. Finally, Elwyne looked up and a weak smile graced her tear stained face. The smile was short-lived and faded into a look of confusion, her eyes finding something over Logan's shoulder. He turned his head and hanging in mid-air was the object of Elwyne's confusion. The creature's hourglass had reappeared.

"There is a monster here; one that has trapped all of our friends and is torturing them like her tortured you. It wants me to play its game, and it put a time-limit on me, and that is its way of letting me know how much time I have left."

The confusion in Elwyne's eyes did not diminish for a moment, and then he tried his best to more fully explain what had occurred, and the game that the creature was playing with their lives. They walked together back in the direction of the fork in path, and by the time they had returned to the location of Logan's first meeting with the creature, he had recounted nearly everything.

"So that's how you got into Dreamscape," Elwyne commented absently.

"Into what?"

"Dreamscape, you puny minded fool," the creature's voice boomed. "I see that you have found your little playmate. How touching. Such a sweet little girl she is, and her fear tasted very sweet indeed. I could have made a meal of her for many years. It's a pity that such strength and beauty were wasted on a pathetic human. But no matter, she shall be back in my clutches soon, considering she has placed such faith in a failure."

Anger boiled in the pit of Logan's stomach and the torture of the woman that he loved caused his emotions to burn brighter than they ever had. He could not remember a time when he had felt so much rage, never a time when he had hated anything so completely. He was nearly seeing red when the creature spoke again.

"So you managed to save one of them. Even the most pitiful creature is occasionally blessed with luck. But you are too simple to grasp the truth of this situation, whelp, and soon all my hungers will be sated by your flesh. Are you ready for your next clue, or would you rather give up now and admit that you are not strong enough?"

Logan's answer came in the form of silence.

"Day and night to me are but the passage of time. There is no dark, there is no light. They say that the eyes are to the windows to the soul sublime. If it be true then how can they see wrong and still feel right?"

The voice was gone again leaving only the riddle in its wake. Logan turned to Elwyne and put his hands on her shoulders.

"I know you're scared, and so am I, but we can do this. Just hold my hand and we'll get our friends out of this, together."

Elwyne nodded and took hold of Logan's hand as they walked down the yellow smoke-lined path on a collision course with the chamber of horrors known as Dreamscape.

To Kill the Sandman

Eldar felt the fear creep in on her as she walked slowly down the path. She looked around aimlessly trying to find some break in the monotonous walls of yellow smoke. She heard something rustling behind her and spun around on her heels. The next moment, as if emerging from the yellow smoke, two figures were just there. Her hand went to her sword, but there was something familiar about the figures. Finally the shorter of the figures came into focus, and she recognized Elwyne's features immediately.

"Eldar!" Elwyne called.

Eldar started toward the two figures, moving her hand from her sword and waiving. Suddenly, the wind began to gust and there was a light that started to appear all around them. Something clicked in Logan's mind, the solution to the creature's riddle coming into sharp relief in his mind's eye. He put up both of his hands.

"Close your eyes!" he yelled. "Don't open them for any reason!"

Without warning, the light flashed brighter, and Logan shielded his eyes with my arm as he held them shut tightly. Blindly Logan groped about and found Elwyne's arm pulling her toward him, and pushing her face into his chest to shield her. All around us the wind began to swirl faster and faster. I could tell that the light had faded away, so I chanced a look. What I saw around me was a swirling torrent of fire and smoke. Logan and Elwyne could feel the heat against their exposed skin. Eldar heard the warning just before the light flared, and she dropped to her knees without question, throwing her arms over her head to shield herself. The wind whipped around the trio, ruffling clothing and gusting hard in an attempt to knock them over and expose their eyes to the tumult. Gradually the flames began to subside and the wind relented in its assault. Then, just as suddenly as the wind had appeared, it was gone, punctuated with one last bright flash of light that could be perceived even through their shielded eyes. Eldar stood from her crouched position and then ran towards her two friends. She hugged Elwyne tightly and after a long moment nodded in Logan's direction and gave him a half-smile.

"Thank you Logan," she said relieved. "If you hadn't come along when you did, I would probably have to go through that again."

"How many times have you been through that?" Elwyne asked swallowing hard, her own memories close to the surface.

"I don't know. Each time I knew what was happening, but I didn't know how to stop it. It just kept happening over and over again, and each time it was the same. The burning and the pain were all so real. And then it just stopped and I was back on the path again. I tried turning around and walking the other way, but the light found me no matter what I did. I even tried standing still."

As much as she may have been hurting inside, Eldar would never let that pain show on her face. She was too proud to let anyone see her cry. It was then that the creature laughed again, and the keening laughter rolled through the air like thunder.

"How touching, and how nauseating. You humans and your need for platitudes and sniveling emotionalism. How do you creatures believe for a moment that you can defeat Shau-ling when you cannot even defeat your own emotions? Unlike the phasia, I am not flawed with such tripe. So you've managed to save two, I would applaud, but you are too pathetic for praise. There are still five more of your friends that need to be saved, and more opportunities for you to prove the failure that you truly are. I will give you the next clue, if there is enough bravery left in you."

"We aren't afraid of you, Tarnae," Eldar yelled back defiantly.

So that's the creature's name, Logan thought to himself. *Always nice to know the name of the thing you want to kill.*

"We're ready for your next riddle, beast."

The Tarnae grumbled something unintelligible, before laughing loudly once more.

"The ancients await prey in their cloudy slumber. Can you stop what you cannot see? Their unseen arms too many to number. Can you stop what you cannot see? They'll wrap you up with aim to encumber. Can you stop what you cannot see?"

Once more the Tarnae laughed, the sound echoing and reverberating everywhere. The volume increased and all three members of the group had to cover their ears to keep from being overwhelmed by it. When finally the sound subsided, Eldar frowned.

"I look forward to ripping out that thing's tongue."

"If it even has a tongue," Logan commented absently.

Eldar gave him a withering glare.

"It has something I can rip out so that it can't make that sound ever again."

Despite herself, Elwyne giggled, and the three began walking down the path. Eldar had drawn her sword, and though Logan was sure such a gesture was made to make her feel better, he too drew his sword knowing from the Tarnae's riddle that there was a hunter waiting for them. After some walking, the color of the smoke faded from the bright yellow and gradually became a crimson red. Again the Tarnae was intervening in the configuration of Dreamscape to ensure that Logan and his friends ended up exactly where it wanted them. Logan knew in the back of his mind that if the Tarnae had truly wanted to, it could have had them walking in circles until his arbitrary time limit expired. But that was the creature's weakness. Of course it needed its prey to survive, but more than that it needed the entertainment of its game. Logan had seen through the ruse, and knew that he could concentrate on the riddles and ensure that all of his friends were safe. As he turned the riddle over and over again in his mind, they pressed on, waiting for the so-called ancients to appear.

* * * * * * * * * * * *

A gust of wind hit Talon hard and started to pull him toward the mass of the cloud. Talon quickly turned away and started running into the force of the wind. He quickly turned his head and looked back toward the cloud. The light in the cloud seemed to pulsate the closer he came to its boundary. No matter how hard he tried and no matter how fast he ran, he was being edged closer and closer to the edge of the cloud. Suddenly, Talon's foot hit a rock, and he fell to the ground just in front of the cloud. He dug his fingers into the ground below him and tried to pull himself away from the mass of white. The gusts became stronger and Talon soon became aware of the fact that he was being suspended over the ground and that his feet were beginning to penetrate the boundary. Only one thought entered his mind from that point on.

I'm going to die.

"Hold on Talon," Logan yelled. "I'm coming."

Logan ran quickly toward the wall of lighted clouds and was standing beside Talon in a matter of seconds. All he could do was draw his sword, but the riddle still had no solution in his mind. There seemed to be nothing other than the wind pulling Talon into the clouds. Eldar too was there at Talon's side, with Elwyne hanging back from the trio her eyes scanning the wall of clouds looking for clues to the solution to the riddle. Logan put his arms around Talon's waist and tried to pull him away from the clouds. It was no use, the force, whatever it was continued to drag Talon forward. Eldar quickly added her force to the effort, but it was no use. They both dug their heels into the ground, but they were all still being dragged forward by some impossible strength. Finally, without any other option, Logan released Talon and took hold of his sword, wildly chopping at the air.

Several times his blade connected with nothing but solid ground, and frustration began to slowly overwhelm him. Taking her cue from Logan,

Eldar too took hold of her blade and began attacking the space around where Talon hovered. Though disheartened, the two had no other option but to continue, the riddle still whirling in their minds. Suddenly Logan's blade struck something solid, something other than soil and rock. There was a loud sharp screech from inside the cloud, and Talon's slow progress into the cloud was halted, and he hung there motionless in mid-air. For a long few moments, Talon hung there motionless, but then the pull resumed and the inevitable collision with the wall of clouds began anew.

"You have to hit it three times Logan," Elwyne called out. "That was part of the Tarnae's riddle. Find it again and hit it three times."

This time Logan and Eldar's swords began moving with purpose. Logan's blade struck true again, and just as before a screech echoed out, and Talon hung motionless. Eldar too found something solid, and her stroke brought a louder scream, and whatever was holding Talon released him and he fell to the ground. Logan's final strike brought what could only be described as a blood curdling wail from inside the cloud boundary. Where their strikes had connected, a white tendril appeared, part of it still wrapped around Talon's foot. Whatever the beast was, it was invisible to the naked eye while alive.

"Where's Pike?"

"That thing already got him, Logan," Talon replied, trying to get to his feet.

The words weren't even out of Talon's mouth, and Logan was running toward the clouds. The creature that lived within the clouds appeared to be retreating from the threat that had just taken its prey from it; however it was not moving with any rapidity. Logan was easily keeping up with the retreat, and within a matter of moments was leaping into the clouds. Whatever he thought he would find beyond the cloud barrier could not have prepared him for what was on the other side.

The creatures could barely be distinguished from the clouds themselves and Logan only could perceive them like a blur caught by the corner of the eye. They were easily three times the size of a human and had at least twenty tendrils extending around a central body. In one of the outstretched tendrils, Pike was fighting against one of the creature's impossibly strong grip. Several of the tendrils flew at the new invader at once, but Logan quickly dodged them as best I could and made his way as quickly as possible while parrying the strikes toward Pike. Logan felt as though he was dodging his way through a forest of thinly trunked trees at full speed during a hurricane. As soon as he was close enough, Logan lashed out with his sword, and after a few quick yet precise strokes from his blade, Pike was free. Though he was putting up a valiant fight, Pike had expended all of his energy and slumped to the ground. Using the momentary distraction of the beast's pain, Logan helped Pike to his feet and draped the exhausted man's arm over Logan's shoulder, and started moving as quickly as he could back toward the cloud boundary. A jungle of white tendrils sprang up to bare our path, but a new flash of steel carved a path. Eldar had followed Logan into the den of the ancients, and was using her superior sword skill to help clear the path for the retreating men. In a matter of moments the three were able to burst through the tangled mess and fell back through the boundary. Covered from head to toe with blood, the trio was able to make their way back to their feet, finally safe, at least from the threat within the clouds.

When Logan looked back toward the clouds, he saw that they were retreating at a faster rate now. Within a few seconds, they were out of sight completely. Elwyne and Talon approached Logan and the others as they sat on the ground panting. While there were no visible wounds on Pike or Talon, both Eldar and Logan showed several visible wounds from the confrontation with the ancients. Elwyne did her best to patch the wounds, but the best she could do was stop the blood from flowing freely. While four of their company was out of danger, The Tarnae still had Gwydeon, Aryx, and Lane under its control. Despite the pain and exhaustion, Logan forced himself to his feet, unwilling to let anything get the better of him until he knew everyone was safe. The meaningless hourglass reappeared, this time accompanied by the face of the Tarnae. The face was the same on that had been on the figure that served as Elwyne's father when the challenge had first been made, only this time his smile was not as wide.

"My poor ancients. They are not used to their meals biting back. You are all proving to be more troublesome than entertaining. It is time to bring our game to its conclusion. Answer one last riddle and you shall be victorious, but fail and all of you, even the ones you think you saved shall be my meals for many weeks and months to come. Perhaps this trouble you have caused me shall allow me to savor the meal you shall provide."

The Tarnae paused, its smile widening. When it spoke again, its tone was shrill and condescending.

"At my heart I hear the ocean; at my head I touch the sky. Drink from me and you shall live forever, ignore me and you shall wither and die. Can you answer my questions? Can you fathom my depths?"

Laughing again, the Tarnae disappeared. Pike hurled a few curses at the now empty space where the Tarnae's bloated smiling face had been. It took several moments, but the group of friends gathered themselves and began again down the smoke-lined path. It took only a few minutes of walking before the color of the smoke began to change once again, this time from a deep crimson to an ocean blue. Before too long, the path opened into what appeared to be a sculpture garden, and as Logan took in the faces of the sculptures, he knew that it was not a place he wanted to be, and it certainly was not safe. There were representations of each member of their group, but the faces were horribly contorted into looks of pain, shock, and horror. Each sculpture's mouth was opened into a scream, eyes wide. The statue of Eldar was on its knees, deep furrows cratering its face as though it had been badly burned. Elwyne's statue had a sword plunged into its chest, emerging from its back. Both Pike and Talon's statues had thick tentacles wrapped around their necks and limbs, each missing a limb and large portions of their torsos ripped out and lying at their feet. Gwydeon's statue had dozens of arrows sticking out of his body and a sword buried in his stomach. Lane's statue had its legs broken off, and the rest of the body was lying on the statue's base, beside the broken legs. Only Aryx's statue appeared to be unmarred, and Logan's statue was conspicuous by its absence. A moment later, Logan turned and a large black well was suddenly standing in the center of the sculpture garden. It took only a few moments for the rest of the group to notice the well, and all gathered around it. Logan's mind immediately went back to the Tarnae's riddle, and knew that the well had something to do with the solution. Once everyone had gathered, a voice echoed from somewhere within the black structure. The voice seemed pained and disturbed, but there was still a strange power there.

CHAPTER 3

"Welcome Dragon. Welcome Water Brother. Welcome Wind Brother. It is good to see those of you who have lived almost as long as we have, and it's good to see that those who are still willing to fight against the darkness. We will not, and frankly cannot explain who we are, but we will say that we have served the *Coromor* before and now are trapped by Shau-ling and tortured into doing his bidding. Thus the Tarnae are using us and our power to help enhance its control over Dreamscape. However, though the Tarnae can demand actions of us, it cannot truly dominate our will. Our allegiance is to the *Coromor*, and to the forces of the Light. So we have done what we can. The Fire Brother's predecessor, White Lightning has been here and was placed somewhere safe. He will appear to you shortly. However, our will does not enable us to simply give your friends, the ones you call Gwydeon and Lane, back. If you wish to save your friends, you must answer us a question. If you answer correctly, your friends shall be returned as unharmed as possible. But if you were to answer incorrectly, we would have no choice but to exercise the Tarnae's will. Do you accept our terms?"

Logan steeled himself. How could so much depend on the answer to a single question? There was an absurdity to the fact that the fate of the world rested on Logan's shoulders, and yet all of it could end if he was not intelligent enough to answer correctly. Finally Logan closed his eyes, took a long deep breath, and then answered.

"There is no choice. I accept your terms."

There was a cold wind that burst forth from the well, and then the voice returned.

"The question is this: During a battle long ago, during the Lord Lion's reign, a creature challenged the Lord Lion to combat. This creature was quickly destroyed, a victim of its own arrogance and pride. Because of the hubris of the creature, Shau-ling punished its entire breed. What was this breed, and what was the punishment?"

Logan could not suppress the smile. Even though he did not know as much as he wished he knew about Shau-ling and the forces at his disposal, the small morsel that Aryx had shared with him was going to be the difference between their life and death. But perhaps the strange creatures in the well knew that Logan would know the answer, knew that Aryx had informed him about the Shadowwalkers. No matter what the truth was, they would be saved by Logan's next words.

"The breed was the Shadowwalkers, and the punishment was the loss of their daylight sight."

There was a billowing laughter, one filled with relief that came from deep inside the well.

"That is correct Lord Dragon, and it is good that you have learned the lessons from your past. Your friends are now safe, and we have repaid our debt to the ancestors of your line, and perhaps have gained a measure of revenge against our captors."

That moment, Gwydeon, Lane, and Aryx appeared. There were no visible wounds to either Aryx or Lane, but Gwydeon was bleeding badly from a multitude of wounds. The wounds all appeared to be from a sword or dagger, though there were also shafts of arrows emerging from his back and shoulders. Many of the sword wounds were very deep. Elwyne and Eldar were immediately at his side, doing their best to treat his injuries.

"By the Light, Gwydeon," Pike remarked, "what happened to you?"

"The well asked me a question, about whether I would fight a man with greater skill. The question was if I were challenged to personal combat during a battle by a foe I knew had greater skill, would I fight the duel. No matter what the situation would have been, you know that I could not refuse the challenge, no matter who the opponent was. It's not arrogance, you know that. But to protect my friends, to do what was right, I could never refuse. If it would end a battle, killing the general of an opposing army before too many lost their lives; I could never live with myself if I did not try. Before I knew what was happening, I was standing off against this man with a sword in my hand. Of course, the scales were more than out of balance as I was already seriously wounded. I never dreamed that someone could have the skills this man possessed. He carved me up even through my best defense, and even if I would have been at full strength, I doubt anything would have changed. The battle seemed to go on forever, and no matter how deep he cut, I never fell. Then I was here."

The well bellowed again.

"There is no need to fear his injuries. If the wounds are inflicted in Dreamscape, they will be healed when you leave. Good journey, and may the light carry you."

After those final words came from the well, it disappeared. Then, the Tarnae began to take shape where the well had been seconds earlier. Its body no longer took human shape; it was more like a yellow blob. It rolled around, shifting colors and shapes. Eventually it stopped and took human form again. This time the face was pouting, and instead of a smile, its lips were drawn into an incredible frown. It stood there proud and tall, the king and ruler of its massive domain. It was in full control of everything that dwelled within, and that power had made the Tarnae wicked and cruel. It raised its arm high above its head, and the arm began to change. It shifted back to the yellow amalgam for a moment and then began to extend outward, solidifying and drawing out to a point. After a few seconds, it returned the arm to its side, and the imitation human hand was now holding a sword.

"I'm impressed, Dragon. Though I must say I had hoped you would have faltered at least once. Dining upon you would have been preferable to admitting defeat. But I must congratulate you upon your victory. It was well earned. I shall open a portal back to your world, and you may leave as soon as you wish."

"So," Talon asked warily, "we're just free to go? Just like that? Why would you do that?"

The Tarnae ignored Talon and kept its eyes trained on Logan.

"I am magnanimous in defeat Dragon, but only to a point. You have solved all my riddles and saved your friends. The game has been won, and I have been defeated for the first time. Do not test my patience or insult my good intentions."

After all of the threats the Tarnae had made about its ability to kill them all on a whim, it was just letting them walk away as if nothing happened. It was too easy. But, the escape seemed real, and the main thing was that they would all be alive and safe. Logan's quest to vanquish Shau-ling would still be attainable.

"Well, I guess it's time to go home," Logan said with a sigh.

"No. Wait," Aryx said quickly.

"What is it?" Elwyne asked.

"We can't leave," he said hatefully, "there is someone still trapped in here."

Pike rounded on the Tarnae.

"Is that true?"

"White Lightning, meddling in affairs he does not understand as always, is correct," the Tarnae said looking past Pike and still at Logan. "There is another of your kind here in my world, but he is mine, our agreement and our game does not relieve his fate. You may not save him unless one of you would like to take his place."

"How about I take your head instead," Pike countered.

The Tarnae laughed loudly, for the first time acknowledging someone other than Logan.

"Do you honestly believe that a pathetic creature like yourself could be a match for me? It would be an insult to lower myself to fighting something like you. Perhaps you could provide me more entertainment than your painfully disappointing savior did."

Suddenly the smoke disappeared and they were standing in a void. The blackness was countered by the appearance of a bright yellow sun rising from the east. Slowly, the light started to reveal a grassy glade and a very familiar setting. In the distance, there was a small building and a very large field. The field was separated into five or six parts by a large log fence. In each of the sections was equipment that would be used to train men who wanted to become swordsmen. This was the very field that the childhood friends had all spent so much time in when they were younger. Off in the distance the spires off the old church and the gray stone wall that surrounded the main part of town could clearly be seen. They were all back home, in Aradon as it had been only a day earlier.

Pike walked quickly to one of the areas laid aside for sparring, and the Tarnae followed without hesitation. As soon as Pike drew the ax from the loop on his belt he charged the larger opponent. The two combatant's weapons locked together with a loud crash. Pike fought hard against the power of the Tarnae, but was eventually shoved away and sent sprawling to the ground. The Tarnae did not advance and allowed Pike to get back up to his feet. Again Pike charged, but instead of allowing his ax to crash against the Tarnae's sword, Pike ducked low and buried his shoulder into the gut of the Tarnae, sending him flying backwards and crashing to the ground. As it hit the ground, the Tarnae lost the concentration that allowed it to retain its form, and it split apart into thousands of little yellow balls. Not knowing exactly what to do, Pike stood and watched as the little balls rolled back together and reformed the Tarnae's body. As soon as the Tarnae returned to its human guise it lashed out, but Pike was a step quicker, his ax connecting with the Tarnae's shoulder. The blade of the ax severed the arm from the rest of the Tarnae's body, sending the appendage falling toward the ground. A moment before it hit, the arm decomposed into its native form and upon impact dispersed into thousands of useless particles. The Tarnae's reaction was to strike again, but Pike had smelled blood, and with a single long hard stroke of his ax, the Tarnae's sword shattered, and the follow-through sent the Tarnae's head flying. When the head and body came to rest on the ground, they disintegrated.

That next moment, everything around them, the glade and other creations of the Tarnae began to disappear. Then, just as before, they stood in a void. The blackness was staggering, but it lasted for only a moment. Dreamscape simply shattered. Parts of the void hung in mid-air, showing the true size of Dreamscape as it compared to the real world. Pieces could be seen as far as the eye could see. Eventually, like stars at dawn, the pieces began to fade from view. They were all safe once again in their own world, and standing with them in the forest clearing was a new addition to the band of friends, a stranger who called himself Gideon Viruci.

Chapter IV

Fire and Earth

The road through the forest had returned to its natural form once the Tarnae and its wicked warped reality had been banished. The trees no longer looked sinister and forbidding, and the fire that the group had built seemed not to be a source of comfort and relaxation rather than a desperate lifeline that held a group of scared adventurers barely from the brink of death. Almost an hour had passed since Pike had delivered them from the clutches of the Tarnae, and in that time the priority had been getting to know the other prison of the Tarnae's vile intentions. The first thing Gideon Viruci said about himself was that he was a thief from Alimidar, and very little else. In Alimidar, thievery was an acknowledged and accepted career, just like being a blacksmith or carpenter anywhere else in the civilized world. Thieving and scavenging were valuable skills, and it was widely held that those who survived the initiations into the thief's guilds in Alimidar were the very best. There was no lock they could not pick, no trap they could not detect and subvert, and no danger they would not brave if the pay was sufficient. Gideon had been traveling from Illimar on his way to Kandor when he was snatched up by the yellowish smoke in a way similar to Logan's experience. Much more than that Gideon would not reveal, and he seemed much more rattled by his experience with Dreamscape. He wasn't cold, but considering the circumstances, some healthy distance was to be expected. Some of the members of the group had lived through horrible nightmares again and again, and any trauma like that would give one pause to speak at length. The rest of the group was understandably tight-lipped as well, and though he had had the least traumatic experience, Logan himself was glad that little was discussed about the actual horrors of Dreamscape. The thought of Elwyne being tortured was bad enough, but knowing the details would have made it all too real.

The next morning as camp was breaking up; Gideon began gathering his belongings to continue on his way to Kandor. When Aryx saw this, he moved to the man and began to speak to him in a very calm and measured voice. However, Gideon's reply was anything but; his thick Alimidarian accent sounding hostile and resentful.

"Would by any chance you consider traveling with us a little longer," Aryx asked. "I know you have just recently come from Illimar, and perhaps you could act as a guide and update us on the state of affairs there. It has been far too long since I was in Illimar, and any information you could provide would be invaluable."

Gideon regarded the taller man for a moment and then chuckled.

"And jus' why da 'ell would dat interest me? Got business in Kandor, done me business in Illimar. Pay me, or let me go me own way."

Aryx frowned.

"You were held captive by the Tarnae, and we saved you. You have no idea what it is that you have become embroiled in, and you owe it to us to repay us for your salvation."

Gideon dropped his bag on the ground and moved toe to toe with Aryx. He was easily head and shoulders shorter than the knight, but he did not appear to be intimidated in the least.

"So ye save me, now ye want me to be yer flintin' slave? So the great and powerful White Lightning is really just a flintin thief like me. Heard 'bout ye, Aryx. Heard yer 'savior of da world" bit was all jus' an act. Why don't ye jus' go back to Marcwell an' bed down dat little wife o' yers? Better yet, maybe dat's what me payment should be."

Aryx seized Gideon by the collars of his shirt, but before the confrontation could escalate any further, Pike and Talon were breaking them up, and Logan interjected himself between them as well. Instead of dealing with Aryx, Logan turned his full attention to Gideon.

"I know you don't know us," he said as strongly as he could manage, "but Aryx is right. We need all the help we can get, especially after the ordeal with the Tarnae and what happened to our hometown of Aradon. But if you need to be paid, I can arrange it."

Gideon looked Logan up and down and scoffed.

"And jus' who're ye? Ye want me ta jus' trust ye?"

Logan reached into his pocket and produced a small coin pouch. He held it out in his palm and locked his eyes on the smaller man.

"This is just a start. There is plenty more that you can be provided with. You may not believe this, but I have a title; a fact that Aryx can confirm. Aryx will be able to arrange for payment for you once we get to Illimar. Right, Aryx?"

The knight frowned.

"There are funds at my disposal that can be made available. If that is what it takes for this thief to allow us to use his services, then so be it."

Logan nodded and looked back to Gideon.

"Is that sufficient for you?"

Gideon looked first to Aryx and then to Logan before smiling.

"As long as yer coin keep flowin', den we 'ave no problem."

Gideon returned to his packing while Aryx stood and stared for a long moment before also returning to breaking down the camp. Elwyne moved to Logan and put her hand on his shoulder reassuringly and gave him a warm smile. Everyone focused their energy on the task at hand, cleaning up the camp and ensuring that as few signs of their passing remained as possible. Gideon proved to be the most adept at covering their presence, and now that he was assured of his payment he seemed totally dedicated to ensuring the safety of the group, as well as his continued employment. Only an hour after dawn, the group was back on the road to Illimar.

While the Mithacarthian wood was never kind to travelers, those who knew the paths never had much trouble with bandits. The safest path was the path from Aradon to Illimar, mostly because no one cared about the traffic from Aradon. However, the trail from Illimar to Trelon was always populated with highwaymen and thieves of all kinds, looking to hijack the shipments that ran between the two powerful kingdoms. There were darker and longer paths that ran out of Illimar, many that wound to the south in the direction of Kandor and Sador, but few from Aradon ever journeyed farther than Trelon with any frequency. The fact of the matter was that Illimar was the destination for traders of all kinds, because of their massive ports, and because of the frequency of ships from the larger cities that berthed there. Illimar to Falke to Marcwell was the most well-known of the shipping lanes, but there were many others that emerged from Illimar. This was the reason that Aryx was leading the group to Illimar; it was the quickest way to Marcwell and thus to Lord Cedric.

The morning travel was long, but it was made longer by the fact that no conversation flowed. There was still a great deal of residual uneasiness from the confrontation with the Tarnae, and many in the group were afraid to bring attention to themselves with their normal jokes and singing. After they had stopped for a mid-day break and had some food and wine in their systems though, the conversation was a little more free and jovial. Pike and Talon led the conversations, as usual, comparing bawdy stories with the newest member. To his credit, Gideon was able to keep up with the pair of troublemakers, and even bested them with some truly questionable stories, which were all met with either a groan or a roll of the eyes from our female companions. Once the laughter from the stories ebbed, it was Gideon who surprised everyone by launching into a song, one that had been heard in the *Traveling Bard* on many nights. Pike and Talon joined in immediately, and after the first verse, both Logan and Gwydeon joined in at the chorus. Eldar and Elwyne joining in at the second verse shocked everyone and once the song was ended, all that was left were light spirits and laughter. When night finally began to fall, the group had finally reached the edge of the forest. The remainder of the journey would only take a half a day at the slowest. A small winding stream would lead the rest of the way to Illimar, the source of the stream nothing more than a pool of water that probably wasn't large enough to deserve the title of a lake. The group set up camp on the bank of the tiny lake on its outer edge at the tree line. It appeared that some of the shipwrights from Illimar had been harvesting trees around the lake, and there were some loose timber left from their work. Pike was the first to comment how happy he was that the group didn't have to rely on his sometime clumsy axe work to feed a fire. As the group set up camp, Aryx and Gideon quickly organized a hunt, and within a matter of minutes they had downed a deer for their evening meal.

Aryx seemed to watch Gideon through the entirety of the evening meal and only Lane's conversations with Pike and Talon ever seemed to jar his attention. Lane was the inquisitive one of the group and was trying hard to make some sense out of the words of the Tarnae and the tests that had been devised.

"He kept talking about the *Erieal*," Lane kept repeating. "And just before the last fight, Pike, the creatures in the well called you Water Brother. Even though I was still falling, I could hear everything that the well was saying."

Pike just shrugged and continued eating. Lane turned to Aryx and continued his line of questioning.

"Does this make any sense to you?" Lane asked.

Aryx sat silently for a moment, obviously keeping his own council, and then slowly nodded. But instead of elaborating on the point, he simply raised the chunk of meat back to his lips and continued eating. After another long moment, Aryx looked back up at Lane and saw the incredulous look on the younger man's face. The older knight's attempt to stifle his smile was unsuccessful, and finally Aryx relented.

"Like you Lane, I was cognizant of everything that the well was saying, but I was also privy to a conversation that you were not. I have had contact with the creatures of the well before, and thus, the information they provided you can be trust. As for the *Erieal*, from a certain prospective, the story starts when I first met Lord Cedric."

Many relaxed back feeling that a long story was about to begin. Gideon didn't react at all to Aryx's mention of Lord Cedric, and their earlier confrontation proved that Gideon knew who Aryx was. However, there was something more to the way that Gideon reacted to Aryx, a distrust and borderline disgust that could only come from familiarity.

"I was a young hunter living out in the badlands outside of Askronilka," Aryx continued. "Not too many people ever traveled the route from Marcwell to Askronilka then, and it could be months between seeing people. Before that I had been living in Alimidar."

Gideon's eyes widened slightly at the mention of his hometown, but the reaction was brief and barely noticeable.

"Relations between the Alimidar and the rest of the world had nearly dissolved after assassins appeared, murdering all three royal families and stealing the Sacred Swords that marked the families' right to rule. It had caused the whole of the city to fall into chaos. So, I thought that I would find safer lodgings and perhaps work as a mercenary in the one place that wanderers of all kind are welcome, Askronilka. One night I was out trapping game and heard a woman's scream from a few hundred yards away. By the time I found the source of the scream, I saw a very young woman armed with a spear facing off against five Jeresei. At the time I wasn't nearly as familiar with the Jeresei or their tactics as I am now, but there was no doubting the lethality of the creatures and the fact that the young woman stood little chance of successfully defending herself. Because of my value for all human life, I did my best to assist the young woman, and it took only a few moments to dispatch the beasts. As it turned out, the young woman was none other than Erika Belnosian. The name only held vague weight in my mind and memories, but I agreed to accompany her on her journey to Askronilka to meet with a man that she simply referred to as her patron. That next morning I was face to face with Cedric Binosear, the Lord of the Kingdom of Marcwell, and on Lady Erika's suggestion I was given the rank of knight for my bravery and dedication to the protection of life. Lord Cedric also requested that I act in the role of protector of Lady Belnosian, a decision that she vehemently opposed."

Aryx paused, his jaw tightening, the memories obviously impacting him. However, he paused for only a moment before continuing.

"By the time I had reached adulthood, I learned that I had the power to channel and control lightning. The power also could be used to manipulate other types of fire, but my control was always better with lightning. For most of my life I thought my ability was simply a fluke of nature until I started traveling with the Lord Lion and his companions. After a while, I started to realize that I had been given these powers for a reason."

His gaze dropped down toward the fire that crackled in front of him. The light given off by the small leaping peaks of red and orange was not bright, but it was enough to make out the facial expressions of everyone there. Aryx's gaze was sorrowful, almost as if the memories that were flooding though him brought him pain and sorrow. The look of anguish lasted only a moment before he continued his tale.

"As the journey progressed, I began to spend more and more time with Mailock the wizard. Mailock had been one of the main sources of information to Lord Cedric about the coming of the *Coromor* and the *Erieal*. As a member of the Moridon tribe, Mailock seemed to information about the subject that only the Moridon were in possession of. The more I questioned Mailock about the *Erieal*, the more information I was able to pry out of him until I was able to piece together an answer to the rather disjointed riddle."

Finally, the part everyone had been waiting to hear. The Tarnae talked about the *Erieal* and was willing to kill because of it. Somehow, Pike and Talon were involved, and I was sure that they wanted to know as much as Lane and I did, if not more so. Though they hid their concern about it, I could almost feel their nervousness. Aryx had everyone's full attention, and when he spoke again, his voice was filled with a mystical energy, almost as if something else were talking through him.

"The legend of the *Erieal* dates back to the infancy of the war against the forces of Shau-ling. The *Erieal* were four brothers gifted with the powers of the Creator, and given the ability to channel the most primal forces of nature in an effort to aid the *Coromor*. Once united with the *Coromor* the *Erieal* were supposed to be the lynchpin by which the *Coromor* would be able to gather his strength and topple his foe. However, much of the legend was lost to the ravages of time. Some stories were passed down from generation to generation of those who served alongside the *Erieal* from that time of antiquity. Aralias Imstra reunited many of those descendants into a group he called the Hand of the Light. The Hand of the Light would go on to become the Moridon. When Mailock would tell the stories, I had a hard time believing him, but once we reached Shau-ling's palace, that all changed. Once we entered the Hall of Terrors, every creature that Shau-ling had at his disposal came at us with only one thought in mind, killing us. Obviously though, they focused most of their energy on cutting down Lord Cedric. Lord Arathorn, Mailock, my wife Diana, and I formed a protective ring around the Lord Lion and defended him. We knew we had no chance, but Cedric had to survive in order to fight Shau-ling and bring an end to the nightmare. It was during this last stand that the true nature of our little group was revealed. While I had always been able to channel lightning, and I used that ability to defend Cedric, the ground rumbled and bucked under Arathorn's command, shards of ice erupted from Mailock's fingertips, and Diana held off the on rushing attackers with walls of wind."

"I hate to interrupt such a wonderful story," Eldar said trying not to sound facetious in her annoyance, "but how does the story go from having four brothers to your wife, Lady Diana, having such powers?"

"Too much has been lost, too much of the truth that can never be recovered," Aryx answered. "Mailock was always very vague about how the powers passed on, but he was sure that from generation to generation, the powers of the *Erieal* would be passed on, and it's obvious now that the four recipients do not need to be related, nor do they have to be male. The Moridon demanded that some secrets could not be shared, and not even the Lord Lion could order them to betray their secrets."

"Wonderful," Eldar continued, "not only are they legendary, but they are completely random and may not even know that they have any powers at all."

Eldar's comments hit Logan like a punch in the gut but he couldn't understand why. On some level Aryx's words seemed like they made sense, that they were undoubtedly true. It was a legend that could greatly aid in the task to defeat Shau-ling, and the Tarnae's insistence on destroying the *Erieal* made far more sense now that these facts had come to light.

"There is one way to determine the members of the *Erieal* regardless of the random nature of the gift. Some information had been left out of the original legend, most likely in an effort to protect those gifted with power from generation to generation. Thanks to Mailock and Arathorn, we were able to fill in some of these intentional blanks. Each of the *Erieal* bears a special mark, something that sets them apart from the rest of the population. All of the *Erieal* of that generation bear the same mark but on different places of their body. In my generation, the mark was a scar in the shape of a long dagger. As you can see, it is located here on my left wrist."

Aryx turned over his left hand and revealed the special mark. As he had said, there was a long scar that resembled a dagger. At first glance, it appeared to be nothing different from any of the other scars on his arm, and there were many of them for comparison. But at a closer examination, the difference became more apparent. With normal scars, the redness soon disappears and all that is left is a white streak on the skin. In the case of the *Erieal* scar, the redness was very bright, and it seemed to cast a glowing effect on the scar in the dim light of the fire.

"Arathorn, Mailock, and Diana all have the same mark on them. However, Arathorn's is on his left ankle, Mailock's is on his right ankle, and Diana's is on her right wrist. Hopefully this information will assist us in locating the *Erieal* of this generation."

Pike seemed upset at the vague and seemingly foolish lead.

"The only time we've heard about these damn *Erieal* is from that laughing fool Tarnae. He interrupted our nice drinking session when Eldar started rambling on about the scars on Talon and me. Then the Tarnae starts babbling about *Erieal* this and the *Coromor* that. Then of course we all take that lovely ride to Dreamscape."

"In Pike's own backward and thick-headed way," Eldar said and received a look of defiance from Pike in return, "I think he's saying that the scars he and Talon have were important enough for the Tarnae to reveal himself and attack."

"So it's safe to assume that the scar is the mark of the *Erieal* in this generation," Elwyne concluded.

Gwydeon seemed to be lost in his own thoughts, mumbling to himself, as if he were trying to put pieces of a verbal puzzle together.

"One of the *Erieal* is already in my trap," he said absently.

"And I will add two more to my collection of fallen legends," Lane finished.

"That's what the Tarnae said before he snatched us up," Talon commented. "So that means he already had a member of the *Erieal* and he was going to trap me and Pike. So who did he have? Was he talking about you, Aryx?"

The older man shook his head and locked his eyes on Gideon.

"No, at the time the only two people in the Tarnae's clutches were Logan and Gideon. The Tarnae said himself that he didn't feel the presence of the *Coromor* and because Logan has yet to touch his powers, I'm sure they are still dormant within him, and undetectable to any of Shauling's minions. In my mind, that only leaves one possibility."

Gideon looked back and forth at the other members of the group, finding all eyes looking at him. The trained thief found the attention disturbing but stood his ground and stared back into the accusing eyes of Aryx Terian. One of Gideon's hands had slipped down to the hilt of his dagger, probably more of a reflex to the shock, but Logan moved between the two men anyway.

"Relax Gideon," Logan said calmly.

"What the hell do ye mean relax, Logan?" Gideon said in his thick accent. "I ain't no damn Eril...or eel...or whatever the hell ya want ta call it. I'm Gideon Viruci, best damn thief from the guilds in Alimidar, and I ain't no legend, and I ain't gonna be told otherwise."

"Roll up your pant leg, thief," Aryx said sternly.

"What?"

"I said, roll up your pant leg."

Gideon took a step back.

"What are ye, Terian, some kinda flintin' fairy who likes lookin' at another man's legs?"

Talon barely stifled his laugh at the incredulous comment, but Aryx stormed forward grabbing Gideon by the collar of his shirt and pulling him up to where the two men's faces were only inches apart.

"I said pull them up," Aryx said again, this time in a quiet yet intensely violent voice.

A split second later, the point of a dagger slid under Aryx's chin, and the smaller thief smiled and added voice to the initial silent threat.

"Ye better be watchin' who ye be grabbin' there, White Lightning. Wouldn't want ya ta loose anythin' precious, like yer head, now would we?"

There were several tense seconds that passed before Aryx released his hold on Gideon and the thief backed away. Not lowering his dagger, Gideon reached down with his off hand and rolled up his left pant leg, and displayed the bare flesh to everyone.

"Are ye satisfied now, Terian? No scar, no mythic mark. Just one hundred percent pure thief."

With a cocky smile Gideon dropped the pant leg and then tugged the dagger into his belt line before turning his back on the taller man.

"What about the other leg, thief?" Aryx asked firmly.

Gideon turned back and shot an angry stare at Aryx before lifting the other pant leg, revealing a long scar that ran from his ankle up to the back of his knee.

"What was that about mythic marks?"

"A guy got lucky in a bar fight," Gideon replied.

Aryx stood resolute.

"Alright, ya flintin' fairy. Don't know how da damn t'ing got dere, and don't really care. Ye say Gideon Viruci be one a dese *Erieal* t'ings, den so be it."

"Well I guess that solves the mystery," Logan said, thinking out loud.

"Except for one thing," Lane commented, "who is the fourth *Erieal?*"

"That will wait," Aryx said still glaring at Gideon. "It's starting to get late and if we're going to make it to Illimar at a good time tomorrow we need to get an early start. Everyone try to get some sleep."

Many members of the group fell asleep almost immediately, most of which was still due to the exhaustion of the stressful ordeal in Dreamscape. The first night after that nightmare had not been restful, and adding on a full day's travel did not help the situation. Most had tossed and turned through much of that first night, and Logan felt somewhat guilty that he most likely got more sleep than the rest of the group combined. On this night however Logan found it difficult to relax his thoughts and let slumber take him. Most of the night he lay there thinking about Illimar and what lay ahead. In his mind, he ran through the whole journey, the results of which were never too gratifying. As soon as it began, it seemed the night was over. The golden sun was just beginning to rise over the crest of the hills to the east, lighting the sky in a slowly spreading red and orange haze. Within few minutes, the rest of the party had been roused, and they prepared for the next leg of our young journey.

"Aryx," Logan asked mounting his horse, "when do you think we'll reach Illimar?"

"By mid-day if we keep a good pace, though with two horses carrying two people, it will slow us a bit. Once there I will make arrangements for a ship to take us to Falke. Don't worry Logan, Lord Cedric and I have friends there. We will easily be able to find a ship that will leave tomorrow. In the meantime, you can take some time to relax in one of the local bars."

Though Logan was beginning to trust Aryx more and more, he still was not reassured by Aryx's detachment and absolute confidence. Regardless of what Logan thought about Aryx personally, he had far more experience than any of them, and the plan as he laid it out was the most logical. Much like the morning journey after Dreamscape very little was spoken on the last leg of the journey to Illimar.

The City of Lights

Following the small stream, Logan and the rest of the group followed Aryx and Gideon's lead out of the Mithacarthian Woods across the wet lands. While the ground was solid, the vast majority had the feel of a swamp, marked by its long-bladed grass and tall reaching reeds. The only trees that grew in the area were tall and broad weeping willow trees that constantly looked as though they were laden with water. Illimar was known not only for its shipyards and vast warehouses, but also for its consistently wet weather. It was said that it rained daily in Illimar with the severity varying wildly depending upon the season. By the time the sun had reached its zenith in the sky, the group finally was in sight of the city of Illimar. The glorious city had gain its apt moniker the City of Lights because of the way the sunlight reflected off of the glass towers that formed the city's skyline. As they approached the outskirts of the city, the four large buildings in the city's central square dominated the view. The buildings themselves were made of nothing but glass and wood, and as the sun reflected off the glass towers, streams of light poured forth in all directions. Most of the time, the sunlight reflected off of the glass and hit the water, making it sparkle like the finest gems in the entire world, a truly awe-inspiring sight. Aryx slowed the pace as soon as the guards at the city's entrances came into view. Obviously the news about the creatures appearing in Lakestone had reached the City of Lights, and thus the military had been mobilized. Illimar was one of the most defensible cities in the whole of Mithacarthia, predominantly because the city itself was surrounded by water on three sides, and because the ports were always manned by several military vessels whose artillery was dedicated to the defense of the city. To the east of Illimar was the Great Sea, and to the west was the Gulf of Illimar. North of Illimar the two large bodies of water met. The only entry into Illimar was the bridge to the south, which forded the Illimar River. The Illimar River connected the Gulf of Illimar to the Great Sea at the foot of the city.

Upon reaching the foot of the Great Bridge, one of the sets of guards that stood on either side of the bridge approached. The guards were dressed in gray mail from head to toe and wore large war helmets that had the shine of the sun reflecting off their polished silver exteriors. They each carried a shield in their left hands and a spear in their right. On the shield was painted the crest of Illimar, which consisted of a springing white lion on a field of gold. In the background of the crest was a rising golden sun that was deeply etched into the metal of the shield itself. The guard approached Aryx's horse and stopped about arm's length from Aryx. He quickly took the measure of the mounted man while his companion remained a pace behind, his spear ready.

"State your business here in Illimar," the guard said gruffly.

"We are here to charter a ship to Falke," Aryx replied.

The two guards looked at one another, and then the lead guard looked back at Aryx.

"Very well then, you may enter. But let me warn you friend, we in Illimar do not take well to strangers, especially in these troubling times. If you cause any trouble while you are here, I assure you that the maximum penalty available will be inflicted upon you. And that, of course, is public execution. We had three yesterday, all outsiders."

Pike scowled, and Gideon seemed to be disturbed by the information as well. As usual, however, nothing seemed to faze Aryx.

"As I said," the guard continued, not knowing what to make of Aryx's cold response, "we do not like strangers in Lionstown."

For the first time, Aryx grimaced. The look passed over his features quickly, and as soon as the guard stepped back, Aryx spurred his horse quickly into the city. At the entrance of the city, a public stables stood for traveler's horses to be cared for while within the city's walls. Aryx dismounted quickly and remanded control of the reigns to a stable boy. Quickly the knight pressed several coins into the stable boy's hand. Pike dismounted near the older man, and asked the obvious question.

"What did he call this place, Lan?"

The alias sounded odd to Pike's ears even as he used it, but after the twin confrontations on the road to Illimar, it was wise to try and avoid any further complications. Logan doubted that the ruse would last long, but perhaps Aryx would be as adept at not drawing attention to himself as he had been in Aradon.

"Lionstown," Aryx replied coldly. "It was a pseudonym taken by the people of Illimar after the final battle with Shau-ling was won."

"Well," Elwyne commented smiling at the stable boy who led her horse away, "that's a nice tribute by one of Lord Cedric's allies."

Aryx's scowl deepened.

"Illimar never took a position in the war. They were cowards who were too busy protecting themselves and their extensive trade investments to worry about sending troops to assist with the siege. We have never forgiven Illimar for its false patronage. We, meaning those who took a stand and fought, of course."

Gideon leaned against one of the posts of the stables, cleaning his nails with one of his many daggers.

"Taking a stand and fightin' is for 'dose dat 'ave nothin' ta lose. Alimidar never took a position either. 'Ave a grudge 'gainst dem too?"

Aryx scowled in Gideon's direction.

"I have a grudge against all cowards. Those who act only out of their self-interest are no better than the creatures trying to tear down everything they built."

Two men who had been within earshot of Aryx's remarks hurried away and Aryx's eyes followed them until they disappeared into a nearby tavern.

"If it wasn't for the fact that Illimar still recognizes Lord Cedric as the savior of this accursed city, the Lion's Mane wouldn't have stopped with Lakestone. I'm not sure I would try to stop the forces of the Shadow if they decided to level this place."

"Not holdin' a grudge are ye?" Gideon asked.

"All life is valuable," Elwyne added. "Even those who will not fight for the greater good."

Aryx spun on his heels and was about to chide Elwyne for naivety, but instead of finding the young woman's eyes, he found Gwydeon's staring at him.

"Defending life, in all its forms, is the only thing that matters. Whether a people be self-interested, self-destructive, or have no sense of self at all, they all deserve to make those choices, and not have those choices dictated to them. That's why I'm here. Remember, Aradon didn't fight in the last war either, except for a precious few brave men of principle. Did you welcome the destruction there as you would welcome it here?"

Gwydeon's voice was full of barely restrained anger. Aryx's posture changed, his shoulders slumped slightly, and there was a darkness that filled his eyes. But after another moment, the stoic demeanor returned.

"You're correct of course, Gwydeon. The wounds from the last war are still very deep, and there are times that I forget that few have the perspective that I do. Innocents should never be made to suffer, but those few who make the decisions for the many must be held accountable for their actions."

For a long moment the two men stared at one another, the silent battle of will and moral raging in ways that defied the spoken word. Finally Aryx turned and started walking toward the docks.

"Enough of that. Let us make our arrangements for passage out of this cesspool."

It took fifteen minutes to traverse the town and enter the dockside district. All of the docks were situated on the northwest side of town, and seemed to be very busy. By the time Aryx led the group to the dock master's office; the door was closed and locked. Obviously, the dock master had more pressing business to attend to. Aryx apparently did not feel like waiting for the dock master to return, and pulled aside a man who was simply carrying items from one building onto one of the large ships that had docked at the port. Within a matter of moments, the man hurried over to us and bowed.

"Lord Merric," he said coming up from his bow with his eyes locked on Logan, "I had no idea that you would be coming to town today. I will have the dock master meet with you as soon as he gets back into town. It shouldn't be more than fifteen or twenty minutes. Please, grace my humble household with your presence while you wait. I'm sure my wife will be more than happy to fix you a meal; that is if your lordship is not in too much of a hurry."

For a quick second Logan stood there, not knowing what to say or do. Sensing several groups of eyes focused on him after the man's display, Logan simply cocked his head and nodded.

"I gladly accept your hospitality sir, but there is no need to trouble your wife. We will be sailing as soon as arrangements are made with the dock master."

"Of course Lord Merric," the man replied.

The man bowed deeply again and bid the assemblage to follow him to his home. He led them a little ways from the docks, down to the southwest side of Illimar. This was considered to be one of the poorer parts of the city, home for most of the dockworkers and sailors who spent little time upon the land. When the man finally stopped in front of a small red house,

Logan began to feel a wave of relief. The house appeared to be a little smaller than Logan's home in Aradon, but there was something that would not allow him to relax completely. There was a palpable feel of danger around them, and though Logan wasn't sure if it was real or simply understandable paranoia. The man opened the door and entered, calling out his wife's name several times. There was no answer to his calls, and finally the man gave up trying. He then hurried back toward the docks, giving his guests full use of his home. He bowed three more time before shutting the door, leaving all more than a little bewildered.

"What, exactly, did you tell him, Lan?" Logan asked as soon as the man had disappeared, but keeping up the ruse in case there were ears poised outside the obviously thin walls.

"Well," he said with a hint of comedy in his voice, "I told him that you were in fact Lord Merric of Baldazar, on an urgent mission to meet with the King of Falke. Also, I mentioned that if you were not delivered to Flake within ten days, that Illimar would be blamed for your murder, and the King of Falke would authorize a full invasion."

"No wonder he was so accommodating," Pike commented.

"Well," Talon added, "I say we take the full measure of what this man has offered us."

"Agreed," Eldar said smiling.

While the house was not large, there were plenty of places for us to sit and relax. A half-hour after their arrival, the door opened revealing the man and another gentlemen who Logan assumed was the dock master. Before the door opened they could hear loud cursing coming from outside, but most of the words and the context were lost. Only the curses were clear. The dock master was on the rotund side, a large belly hanging over his belt, the oil and grease stained shirt barely containing the girth. He held a pipe between his teeth, the smoke from which tangled in his hair. The fat man was obviously the one who had been cursing, but after the door had opened, he very quickly bit his tongue mid-curse.

"Good day to you my lord," he said making a wide, fake smile, "my name is Seelious Monk. I'm the dock master in these parts. What can I do for you?"

Logan stood quickly and started to take on the role that Aryx had planned out for him.

"Mister Monk, you've kept us waiting. First of all. . ." Logan started.

"First of all," Aryx interrupted, "we should make sure that there are no prying ears."

Aryx looked over his shoulder and nodded at Lane. Logan looked over to his friend wide-eyed, and Lane smiled before closing his eyes and muttering a few words under his breath. Apparently Aryx and Lane had conspired a course of action that they chose not to share with the rest of the group. Once Lane opened his eyes, he nodded back to Aryx.

"No one will hear us, so long as we speak in normal tones."

Aryx turned his attention back to the dock master.

"No need to keep up the ruse now," he said before standing and quickly embracing the rotund man. "It's good to see you again old friend."

The dock master took a step back from Aryx and put his hand on the knight's shoulder smiling brightly.

"By the Light! Aryx Terian, you old bastard you! How are you?"

"Just fine Ren, but its Lan this trip."

The dock master smiled wider and laughed. With a wink he closed the door and then turned back toward Aryx, the smile still wide and bright.

"So, what brings an old war-horse like you to Illimar without his royal Lion highness's entourage and fanfare?"

"Well Ren, it's one of Lord Cedric's little clandestine missions, so I'm not at liberty to say too much."

Ren nodded quickly, as though he had heard the same excuse before.

"Give me the short version."

"We need a ship," Aryx replied.

"To speed the wayward Lord Merric to Falke to seal and alliance no doubt. That boy is as much a lord as I am the King of Trelon."

Aryx laughed.

"The queen hasn't been married for some time my old friend, but I doubt her standards have dropped that low. Our young friend here is indeed a lord. May I introduce you to Lord Logan Ranthall, future Lord of Aradon, heir to the throne of Marcwell, also the Lord Dragon."

"You brought the bloody *Coromor* to Illimar!" Ren shouted.

"Keep your voice down you old fool," Aryx countered. "Lane may have talent at concealing us, but there could still be one of Shau-ling's faithful standing outside the door doing his best to listen to every word we say. And I wouldn't have brought him except that we are in a bit of a rush, and this is the fastest way."

Ren nodded.

"So that's why you came here. Makes sense. If the boy is what you say he is, then no doubt our evil friends will have every direct route in and out of Marcwell and every other major city well-guarded. But, indirect routes, like the one from Illimar to Falke to Marcwell will have a lot less security."

"Maybe there is a brain in that ale filled body of yours," Aryx prodded.

"Not much of one, old friend," the larger man answered. "Aye, I do have a ship that can take you from here to Falke, but she's not quite ready yet. She got into a bit of a rough patch to the south and lost half her crew. They should be seaworthy by tonight though. If you get a good wind, you should be on the docks at Falke in five days, six, if the weather isn't too kind. The ship's the Raging Storm, just look for the tallest mast, and that'll be her."

"I thank you old friend. Lord Cedric I am sure will be grateful as well for your assistance. I do however have a question about the crew, considering the circumstances."

"Don't worry, Lan," Ren said winking with the name, "the captain is one of the Lion's Faithful from the war, so there's nothing to worry about."

Aryx turned back to face the group and put his arm around the broad shoulders of the dock master.

"Everyone, this is Ren Manderis. He was a valuable asset during the last days of the war to the Lion's Mane. If it weren't for his ships, our travels wouldn't have been as effective as they were. I've never seen a more daring ship captain. He was willing to tackle shallow water and narrow passages that most would not consider."

Logan shook Ren's hand, and it was Pike who asked the obvious question.

"Seelious Monk?"

Ren laughed.

"What Aryx failed to mention is that Ren Manderis is a wanted criminal in most of the ports of Mithacarthia on charges of piracy. Charges I add that are absolutely untrue."

Aryx laughed.

"Only because they don't cover half of the things you actually did."

Ren shrugged off Aryx's arm and frowned.

"And would it have been too much for the bloody Lion to give me a pardon for all of the good things I did during the war?"

Aryx gave a wry smile.

"Lord Cedric did pardon you for everything you did before the war. It was the crimes you committed after the war that you are wanted for."

Ren and Aryx stared at each other for a moment before Ren broke out in a bellowing laughter. Ren clapped Aryx on the shoulder, and Ren excused himself so that he could make arrangements at the docks for the Raging Storm to sail as soon as she was able. Aryx chose to accompany Ren, and advised that the group should remain in the cottage until nightfall when everyone would meet at the docks. Pike and Talon by this time had gotten quite sick of the little cottage, and were agitating for a more festive place to spend the last few hours in Illimar. Despite Aryx's warnings, the agitation was successful, and Gideon suggested a small and not very heavily frequented tavern not far from the cottage. It took only a few minutes to cover the distance between the cottage and the tavern, an establishment known as the Calm Sea.

The Calm Sea was not a very large building when compared to some of those that surrounded it. However, the bar itself would have taken up much of the ground floor of the *Traveling Bard* back in Aradon. As soon as Pike made it through the door, his eyes locked on the scantily clad girls making the rounds at all the tables. Fearing Pike and Talon making too much of a scene, Logan urged his compatriots to sit down at a table near the back wall of the bar. Soon enough, one of the barmaids stopped at the table to take orders. Through Pike's staring and Talon's pawing, orders were taken with Eldar and Elwyne looking appalled throughout. Within a few minutes the young woman returned with a full tray. Though she nearly spilled the drinks because of Pike's playful grabbing, she continued to smile and laugh, though Logan was sure he could heard her cursing under her breath as she walked away. Gideon, Pike, and Talon began telling tales and jokes. Of course the more they drank, the more off-color the stories became. Barmaids would stop to be ogled on occasion; completely diverting Pike or Talon's attention from the joke or story they were attempting to tell. Unfortunately things started to get ugly just before sundown.

The six men that walked through the door just before sundown were clad in black clothes, covered in mud and soot, and looked as though they hated the world. Not even the flies had enough tolerance for filth to stay with these utterly disgusting men. Each one was fat and their beards looked as though they had collected nearly as much food as the men had shoveled into their mouths. Swords hung on their hips, and their half-open sweat-drenched shirts revealed the coat of chain mail that lay underneath. As they walked through the center of the bar, they found a table in the middle of the room and each took a seat. Wood creaked with every move that the men made, and the smell coming from the men at the table forced more than one of the patrons to leave the bar. Not surprisingly, it did not take the men long to being making obscene advances at the barmaids, and not in the same good humor as those made by Pike and some of the other men in the bar. One of the men grabbed a girl by the arm and forced her to sit on his lap. The girl was struggling against the powerful grip, and though she slapped and punched at him, she was no match for the much larger individual. She was able to resist most of his attempts to roughly fondle her, and the girl was clearly a fighter. The disgust for the man's actions became palpable in the room, however none of the bar patrons looked as though they were going to lift a finger to help the bar maid. Pike however was not one who was a stranger to instigating fights in a bar when it became necessary.

"Is this how you fat pigs get your company?" Pike said, his speech partially slurring. "Don't think that one is too interested."

The fat man grinned and laughed loudly. His voice bellowed and bounced off the walls, giving his laughter much more volume than it really had. After passing the girl to one of his companions, he stood up and drew his sword.

"You think you can take her from me? Because if you do, you better be the best swordsman in the world, cause if you aren't, you're not gonna last more than three seconds."

Again the man laughed, but his laughter was cut short as a dagger flew between his legs and embedded itself in the solid wooden chair he had been seated on only a moment earlier. The man holding the girl threw her to the floor and stood up, sword drawn. Two more of the men stood, taking the defensive, ready for a fight. Looking over his shoulder Pike could see Gideon stand up from the table and circle around close to the bar, his hand holding yet another of his seemingly endless supply of daggers. Gwydeon also had left the table his sword still sheathed.

CHAPTER 4

"It seems the odds are evening up," Pike said, his lips twisting into a cruel smile. "You've let the girl go, but if you still want to fight."

"I'm not going anywhere, runt."

"I was hoping you would say that," Pike taunted.

The man closed his fist tightly around the hilt of his sword, his eyes filled with anger and hate. The back-swing of his sword very nearly cleaved the skull of one of his companions, but when the blade came crashing down Pike's axe was up and ready, meeting his blade with a thunderous sound. Pike was overmatched by the man's strength, and as he brought his height and weight to bear on the cross of their blades, Pike could feel his knees buckle under the strain. With one single burst of strength and speed, Pike disengaged from the cross, letting the fat man's blow fall well wide of his intended target. When their blades met again, the combat started to get out of hand. There was a flash of light that came out of the corner of Pike's eye mere seconds before the steel of one of the other men's blades ripped through his flesh. Blood flowed freely down Pike's right arm, and he could feel his hand twitch involuntarily. The sharp blade had cut deeply into the muscles of his arm, leaving it nearly useless in a fight. Gideon was quicker than Pike's adversary pulling his free from the combat while in the same instant burying a dagger into the interjecting man's skull. The man's eyes crossed and he fell to the floor, blood flowing down his face. Suddenly the sound of a bowstring being drawn and released filled the room. Two arrows flew from somewhere behind the bar, striking two of the men that remained at the table. Another dagger and an arrow later, the only man that remained was my initial challenger. Gwydeon was on the man in a second, vaulting over Pike's downed form, and Gwydeon wasted no time in striking at the man. The strike was not a strong one, but it was true enough to draw first blood. The slash landed across the free arm of the fat man, almost instantly soaking his sleeve in hot blood. Barely flinching, the fat man returned the strike. His sword thrust missed, and Gwydeon's counterstroke cut deeply into the flesh of the fat man's stomach. As the moments passed, the man's anger grew, and it seemed to make him more reckless in his attacks. His next three strikes were nowhere near being effective, but Gwydeon was not able to capitalize on the opportunities to counter. Then the fat man drew Gwydeon's blood. The tip of his sword pierced Gwydeon's left leg, and sensing the opportunity, the fat man pressed his advantage, digging and twisting the blade deeper into the tortured flesh. The force of the blow staggered Gwydeon, sending him toppling over one of the wooden chairs. The chair broke his fall and supported most of his weight. The fat man looked at the rest of the group and laughed.

"You see what happens when you challenge me! Now watch as I finish him!"

The fat man turned his attention back to Gwydeon, and raised his sword high over his head. The fatal blow was close at hand. Suddenly, Gwydeon grabbed the dagger that was still lodged in the chair and hurled it at the heart of his adversary. The shining metal point struck home, easily piercing the flimsy chain mail, digging deep into the putrid heart. Blood flowed and spurted in all directions, in for a few seconds, the man stood in utter disbelief until finally the sword clattered to the ground and the fat man fell. Death hung heavy in the air.

"Good shot Gwydeon!" Talon yelled.

"Couldn't 've done better me own self, lad," Gideon commented proudly.

Elwyne was quick to tend to Pike's wounds while Eldar helped Talon and Lane bandage up Gwydeon's badly wounded leg. As they worked on the wounded, Logan approached the bar where the bar maid who had been accosted now stood, a bow held tightly in her hand. She looked much more like a warrior, weapon in hand and a quiver hanging off her shoulder. On her hip she wore a sword, but from the look of it, it didn't see much use.

"I suppose that I should thank you," Logan said smiling.

"Not necessary," the woman replied dismissing his advance, "it was the smell that was getting to me. Otherwise I would be finishing off your friend there for pawing at me too."

Pike laughed and put up his hand.

"Would it help if I apologize?"

Any reply the woman had was cut off by a pounding at the tavern's door.

"Surrender yourself in the name of the Army of Illimar. You have assaulted members of our ranks, and the penalty for this crime is death. If you surrender peacefully, our lord may be merciful. Fail to comply, and we shall be forced to take you by force, and your ends will be swift and bloody. You have one minute to decide."

For the first time, Logan noticed that all of the patrons had left the bar. One of them must have informed the army about the brawl and the death of their people. Now the only hope was to make it to the Raging Storm before the Army of Illimar could catch them.

Encounters

The knock on the door now became louder and more insistent. The Army of Illimar was serious about gaining retribution for their lost men, no matter how foul they may have been in life.

"Hold please," Logan said as calmly as he could manage, "I don't think you understand the situation here. I think that if you would listen to exactly what occurred and spoke to all of the parties involved you would see that this is nothing more than an act of self-defense."

"The circumstances are irrelevant," the voice from the other side of the door responded. "In less than a minute this door will no longer protect you. Your only rational plan of action is clear. The lord will hear any appeals that you might wish to make. Make your decision quickly. Surrender or be destroyed."

Logan's attempt at a reasonable and peaceful solution had failed. He didn't want to have to fight, but they could also not surrender, when surrender would eventually involve an axe, a wooden block, and a little bucket. Time was growing short, and there weren't very many options left open. Glancing around the room, there were no places to hide that wouldn't be immediately searched once the door was broken down. Suddenly Logan realized that the bartender was gone. Ducking back behind the bar, the path the smart man had taken was clear. Every smart bartender had a secret way out of his establishment just in case the wrong element, such as bill collectors or the authorities, came calling at inopportune times. Pike and Talon finished stacking tables and chairs in front of the door to buy the group a few more minutes. They knew that it wouldn't last very long under the pressure of a battering ram, but every extra second would gain more ground.

The back exit was nothing more than a small crawlway that led under the building to a small grate on the far side, away from the prying eyes of normal citizens. It looked as if hardly anyone used the alley with the amount of refuse strewn about. The grate was hanging away from the passage, obviously because of the bartender's hasty exit. As soon as Logan was through and into the alley, he turned back and helped the rest of the group through the narrow opening. From the shouts coming from the other side of the building, and the crash of shattering wood, it was obvious that the Army had finally decided that their quarry weren't going to surrender. As soon as the last of the party had escaped the bar, Gideon quickly reattached the grate and followed everyone else at a dead sprint. Within a few yards of the bar, as expected, the members of the Army who were watching the streets around the bar sent up the call and began to give chase. Shouts as well as arrows flew as the men who were continuing their attempts to arrest the criminals gave chase. All the time they were running toward the docks, they had to duck spears and arrows, as well as those civilians that crowded the streets. The pro-military sentiment was strong in Illimar, and just about everyone tried to do their civic duty by slowing down the wanted fugitives. A long few moments passed, and finally the docks were within view.

The Raging Storm was going to be the only chance of escaping Illimar. The group continued running at as fast a pace as they could manage, and they could see the ramp to the ship with Aryx standing at the top of it. Half way to the dock that berthed the Raging Storm, a group of sailors interceded, cutting off the escape. They were a rag-tag group of men, but they were heavily armed. Skidding to a stop, Logan reached for the sword at his hip.

"We haven't got time for this. Get out of our way, or I won't be held responsible for the consequences."

"I'd rather not get arrested for letting you pass," the leader of the group replied taking a step forward, flashing a toothy grin. "So, drop your weapons kiddies, and don't do anything you may regret later. I have no problem turning your corpses over to the Army."

"Out of our way now," Pike pressed.

The sailors didn't move, and brandished their weapons.

"Enough!"

Talon screamed at the top of his lungs and threw himself toward the sailors. Pike, Lane, and the hobbling Gwydeon followed without a moment's hesitation. As Logan pulled his sword free of its scabbard and lunged forward, a hand took hold of his shoulder and spun him around violently. The next second, the point of a dagger was pressed into his side.

"Drop the sword boy and surrender. My lord may show mercy on you."

A whistling sound and a rush of air darted past Logan's ear as an arrow slammed into the soldier's forehead, giving him his answer. Blood oozed from his mouth and nose. His grip tightened for a moment, and the tip of the dagger threatened to rip open Logan's flesh, but then the thin blade clattered to the ground as the man's body slumped. Logan looked to his left, and the bar maid, whose name they learned was Midarin, was retrieving another arrow from her quiver.

"I hate rude men," she said flatly, fixing her eyes on her next target.

"The Army is upon us Logan," Eldar said after a moment.

When he turned back toward the city, he saw that Eldar was right. A detachment of about twenty-five men had just reached the entrance of the docks, and they were charging the group's position. With sword drawn, Eldar and Logan sprinted side by side toward the advancing force, as Midarin began picking her targets and opening fire. As fast as Eldar and Logan were, Gideon was faster.

He was like a streak of light as he rushed past, his speed bordering on unnatural. There was a glimmer of light from the blades of his twin daggers as they caught the light of day, and within a matter of seconds he was upon the first few members of the detachment. Two of the men in the front rank fell with Gideon's daggers embedded deeply in their throats. After the first two daggers were released, Gideon leapt into the air and continued into a full flip, landing behind the final group of men. It was almost as if he had flown. With daggers flying in every direction, he took out five more of the soldiers before Eldar and Logan had reached their front lines.

Eldar and Logan hacked their way into the group, arrows buzzing past as Midarin was thinning their ranks even more. The first soldier in front of Logan hefted his ax to strike, but he had no time to react as the tip of Logan's sword flew with deadly accuracy to his gut, running him through quickly. With over half of their number slaughtered in a matter of moments, the rest broke and ran, obviously sending up the call for reinforcements. They had been taken by surprise, not prepared for the deadly accuracy of Midarin's bow, or the sheer feral lethality of Gideon's skill. It would only be a matter of time before three times the number of soldiers would be flooding the docks, and no matter of luck would win that engagement. Turning back toward the Raging Storm, Logan saw that the battle with the motley group of sailors continued. Eldar led the charge back toward the docks, in the direction of escape, and with every intention of assisting their compatriots.

* * * * * * * * * * * *

Talon's charge took him right into the largest of the sailors blocking his path. His muscles bulged, and he looked more like a living wall than a man. The thrust of Talon's blade was parried quickly by a crashing blow from the sailor's huge claymore. Using his size and strength to full advantage, the sailor forced Talon nearly to his knees with the power of his blow. Talon quickly changed his tactics, rolling out from under the pinning strike and slashed wildly at his opponent's legs. The sailor jumped backwards to avoid the slash, but was slow to find his balance again. Charging again, Talon used the moment of hesitation to strike. A long broad slash opened a large cut across the sailor's chest. Unfazed, the sailor lashed out again, sending Talon staggering backwards from another powerful blow. Talon regained his wits quickly enough to see the sailor closing in for the kill. Talon rolled through another strike and his blade found the back of the sailor's knee.

The sailor cried out in pain as the strength left his legs and he toppled to his hands and knee, the sword skidding across the pier. A heartbeat later, Talon's blade struck though the heart of his opponent, ending the battle. Recovering his sword quickly, Talon turned to look for Pike.

* * * * * * * * * * * *

Pike found competition in the form of a small sailor with a long sword in one hand and a dagger in the other. He looked lean and very fast, something that would prove to be a challenge for Pike's slow moving ax. Trying to use something he was never known for, tactics, Pike stood straight and motioned for the smaller man to attack. His wounded arm ached, and he would need every advantage possible if he was going to come out of the batter alive. Smiling widely, the small sailor slashed with his sword and followed up quickly with his dagger, neither attack meeting their mark. Though slower of foot than his opponent, Pike had no trouble dodging either of the attacks, and took one of his own. The sailor sidestepped the broad downward slash and stepped into Pike, burying the full blade of his dagger into Pike's exposed thigh. Instinctively; Pike brought the haft of the ax crashing down on the back of the sailor's neck, flattening him to the ground. Without full balance, the follow-up attack was slow, and when the blade of Pike's ax came crashing to the ground, the sailor had already rolled away and had scrambled back to his feet.

Taking a moment, Pike looked at his wounded leg and frowned. Blood trickled down the front of his pants, and the fabric soaked with blood began to stick to the wound. Not having the time to deal with the pain or the wretched blade in this thigh, Pike screamed and charged again, the blood fury beginning to take him. Swinging wildly, Pike rushed the sailor, but the smaller man was too quick, and dodged the intended blow and dove straight for the hilt of the dagger protruding from Pike's leg. With is free hand, the sailor took hold of the dagger and twisted it deeper into Pike's flesh and jerked it free. But Pike could not feel the pain; he couldn't feel anything except the hate and anger that had seized his thoughts. Kicking with the injured leg, Pike's foot found the stomach of the sailor, stunning him long enough for Pike to bring the blade of his ax crashing down into the middle of the sailor's back. The blow split the sailor's spine, killing him instantly. The sailor crumbled to the ground, blood flowing from his mouth and nose and forming little pools beside him. However, the rage still holding him, Pike was not satisfied with the quick kill.

Cursing and screaming, Pike continued to rain down strikes upon his fallen foe, blood flying everywhere. When the energy to raise his ax finally fled from his exhausted arms, Pike fell to his knees in a growing pool of blood. His breath slow and erratic, Pike looked at the remains of the sailor, now in too many pieces to count. Pike's clothes were covered with blood and gore, and though the necessity of the kill was in his mind, the horror of what he had done began to enter his heart. Forcing his way to his feet, he caught motion out of the corner of his eyes, and though his muscles screamed and protested, he raised his ax and turned on his would-be attacked. Seeing his friend Talon there, he lowered his blade. Suddenly a cry went up, and Pike turned just in time to watch as both Gwydeon and his opponent fell.

* * * * * * * * * * * *

Gwydeon looked at the sailor he had matched up against and was haunted for a moment. It was almost as if he had stepped into his nightmare. He had fought this man before many times, and each time he was cut to ribbons but fought on past the point of death. It had been one of the Tarnae's riddles that had begun the battle, and Gwydeon had thought for a long time that the man did not exist, and that he was just a figment of the Tarnae's twisted imagination. But now, Gwydeon was face to face with the nemesis that the Tarnae had created for him. This time, there would be an end to the battle, and Gwydeon could see nothing other than his victory,

Gwydeon's sword was drawn in a heartbeat, and he eased forward into a strike to test his opponent's defenses. The sailor whirled his sword in front of him and parried the blow before Gwydeon's blade was half way to its intended target. Gwydeon reset himself and attacked again. The two blades struck each other and the two men pushed into each other, trying to gain the leverage advantage. Pushing with all his might, Gwydeon could feel that he was no match for his opponent. Before he could react, the sailor pushed Gwydeon away, and slashed him cleanly across the shoulder. The pain caused Gwydeon to shrink back for a moment, but then he recovered and flew at the sailor. The sailor was shocked at Gwydeon's speed and was unable to parry the slash that ripped at the flesh of his leg.

Gwydeon stopped and turned quickly after the passing blow and tried to retain the element of surprise, however the sailor was not one to be caught unaware twice by the same opponent. He parried the quick blow and was able to land a blow square on Gwydeon's sword arm. Gwydeon's fingers tingled, and he tried with all his might not to lose the grip on the hilt of his blade. The sailor saw his hesitation and cracked the flat of his blade across the back of Gwydeon's hand, and a similar incident in Dreamscape ran quickly through Gwydeon's mind. The blade fell harmlessly from Gwydeon's hand, and it was accompanied by the sharp stinging pain of the sailor's sword ripping through the flesh of Gwydeon's side. While the pain slowly faded, it was replaced by the heat of the blood flowing from the gaping wound. As if by instinct, Gwydeon dropped to his knees to recover his sword, and then brought the blade up quick enough to block a blow that would have sent his head flying. Gwydeon flailed with his sword and struck the sailor hard on the wrist of the hand that held his sword. The slash severed the man's hand, leaving the man defenseless. Gwydeon stood slowly, feeling the pain that wracked his body.

He wanted to fall and fade away into the protection of his dreams, but he knew that he would surely die if he did. Gwydeon looked at his adversary and raised his sword over his head. This would be the strike that would finish the battle. Before Gwydeon could bring the sword crashing down, the sailor drew a dagger from a concealed sheath on his belt and threw it with a backhand motion toward Gwydeon. Had his aim been better, the dagger could have pierced Gwydeon's heart, but lodged in his shoulder, it did enough damage to send Gwydeon reeling. Dropping his sword, Gwydeon staggered backwards and then fell to the ground. The sailor was not on his hand and knees, crawling toward his fallen victim. The sailor had the taste of blood, and was ready to end the battle. Crawling slowly over to where Gwydeon lay, the sailor recovered his sword and held it tightly in his remaining hand. Pushing himself to his knees, the sailor pressed the blade to Gwydeon's neck. The point of the blade pierced Gwydeon's flesh, and he could feel the moments of his life slipping away. However, in that fateful moment, Gwydeon could feel strength returning to his injured shoulder. He would not, could not die here. Taking hold of his sword, Gwydeon swung with all his might, and the sailor was forced to recoil to prevent his own demise. The sailor recovered and slashed Gwydeon across the chest, but pain no longer touched the young swordsman. The next blow was parried by Gwydeon's faster blade, and the parry flowed directly into a strike that buried the blade of Gwydeon's sword between the sailor's ribs. Pulling the blade back and up, Gwydeon continued the strike across the sailor' chest. Quickly, Gwydeon reset himself and launched the attack that would prove to be the fatal one. The sailor thrust his blade meekly, and Gwydeon parried the blow and thrust the point of his blade deep into the heart of the sailor. Blood flowed quickly from the man's mouth as he slipped from the now blood-soaked blade of Gwydeon's sword and sank to the ground. Gwydeon stood for a moment, looking down at his fallen adversary, and then fell to his knees. All strength fled from his body, and he felt the sensation of sleep begin to fill him. The next thing Gwydeon knew, he was face down on the ground.

Moments later, Talon and Pile grabbed Gwydeon by the arms and hoisted him to his feet. Gwydeon was covered in blood from head to toe, most of it his own, and looked to be in as bad of shape as the man he had killed. Talon and Pike didn't say a word as they helped Gwydeon to where the rest of the party had regrouped.

* * * * * * * * * * * *

Elwyne began tending to Gwydeon as soon as Pike and Talon dragged him up the ramp and onto the deck of the Raging Storm. Satisfied that he was being well cared for, Logan continued his brief conversation with the captain of the Raging Storm. With the danger of the Army of Illimar still looming, he had a couple of his crew help Pike and Talon get Gwydeon aboard the vessel. Within a matter of moments, they were clear of the dock and headed out to sea. Aryx and the captain were confident that the Army of Illimar would waste their resources chasing down a few stubborn brawlers, especially with the greater threats looming; though no one relaxed until the ship was over an hour away from Illimar.

Standing out on the top deck, Logan gazed out over the clear blue sea. The majestic masts of the Raging Storm towered above, giving an odd sense of comfort. The massive white sails reflected the sun and warmed the deck pleasantly. According to the captain, the Raging Storm was the most heavily used ship in the area, except for the military vessels of Askronilka. After a moment, Aryx approached.

"I thought you would like to know that there are no signs of pursuit coming from Illimar."

Logan took a deep breath and smiled.

"We'll make port in Falke within four days. You know that what you did was reckless. You should have stayed at the cottage where it was safe. It was a needless and foolish risk."

Aryx did not wait for Logan's answer before turning to walk to meet the captain at the stern of the ship. Logan, feeling dejected returned to the cabin where he found Elwyne and Eldar fussing over Gwydeon, who despite being bandaged heavily enough to be confused with a corpse, was trying to get out of bed to walk around. Naturally, Elwyne was not going to stand for such a whimsical and foolish notion, and was threatening to tie him to the bed if he didn't stay put. Of course, Pike and Talon being the sensitive fiends that they were, made sure to taunt and tease Gwydeon as much as possible, though Pike was obviously hampered by his own wounds. As Logan laid down on one of the empty bunks and tried to relax, he heard a conversation that piqued his interest.

"Somethin' occurred ta me," Gideon said slowly, "we got dis lassie with us and we don' know who she is or where she's from. So how 'bout it lass?"

"My name is Midarin Rice," she said coldly. "Once I was Princess Midarin Rice of the Kingdom of Brea."

Pike and Talon both laughed and were going to poke fun until they saw the serious look on Midarin's face. Both Elwyne and Eldar's attention shifted to the woman, but Logan was sure that there was something sour in Elwyne's glare.

"If you're a princess," Eldar asked, "then why were you waiting tables in Illimar, especially in that outfit."

Eldar was always the diplomat of the group, but her patience with other women, especially those that were to be considered her betters, always had seemed to be lacking. In times that she had dealt with the women of the

City Council back in Aradon, her manners resembled Pike's more than they did Elwyne's.

"That's a long story," Midarin replied trying to evade the question.

"I don't know about you," Gwydeon said from his forced position, "but there appears to be plenty of time."

Laughter all around seemed to break whatever walls were holding back Midarin's story, and she smiled brightly through her own polite laugh and began to tell her story.

"In Brea, it is the woman who has full control over the courtship process. All of the young ladies have many suitors and have many torrid affairs. However, if you are of royal blood, and especially if you are the Princess and heir to the throne, things are very much different. When I reached the age of twenty-five, my parents would abdicate the throne to my husband and I. However, my parents would choose a suitor for me on my eighteenth birthday, and we would be married on my twenty-first. At first, I didn't see the problem, and I didn't long for the complicated lives of the other girls my age. But, as I got older, things changed. I didn't want to be the high and mighty princess stored away in her tower waiting for the day that her parents chose her groom. I wanted to be a normal girl, doing whatever I pleased.

"Well, on my eighteenth birthday, my suitor was brought to me by my parents. He was not the most handsome of men to say the least. He was a fat man with a very ugly face. The only reason my parents chose him for me was the fact that he was the Queen of Trelon's cousin. If we were to marry, it would end the disease and mistrust that had been raging on for over a hundred years. But, I was a silly girl caught up in my own whims. One night just before my twentieth birthday, I met a man that served as one of the personal guards to my suitor. I fell in lust with him the minute I laid eyes on him, and I knew that he had to be mine. Well, I lured him into my room. Before anything could happen between us, one of my guards burst into the room and placed us both under arrest. My suitor's guard claimed that he was innocent in the whole affair, but he was executed the next day. I was found guilty of high treason against the crown for disobeying the laws of tradition and of succession. The punishment for my crime was banishment from the kingdom,

"After I left Brae, I wandered around for a while, looking for a place to stay. I eventually made my way to Illimar where I was hired as a bar maid. I worked there for almost a year without any trouble. And you know the rest of the story."

"That's awful," Elwyne said softly, "how could your parents just throw you out like that?"

"It is common law," Midarin replied, "everyone in Brae follows the law, regardless of the personal connection, or they suffer the punishment that goes along with breaking it. For my parents, they could have been executed for not banishing me. And while I am still angry with them for letting it go as far as they did, I understand their reasons."

That moment a large wave crashed against the hull of the ship. Everyone was tossed from their bunks and sent scrambling. Logan made his way to his feet and ran toward the top deck. There was already water in the short passage that led to the deck, and the set of five stairs that ended the passage were covered with sea water. Most of the top deck itself was in shambles. The large main mast was broken in two, and the upper half was in the sea. Sailors were running around the deck trying to hold the ship together. Rain poured down, and large black clouds were rolling in on top of the ship. The moon had been completely obscured. Clouds pulsated with lightning and made their power known with the sounds of crashing thunder. Lightning struck the top deck not five feet ahead from Logan, and while he was able to get clear, three sailors in that area were not so lucky. Debris and bodies flew in different directions, most of which ended up in the churning sea below. The ship moaned from deep below deck as the ship's hull was being tormented by the fury of the storm. A huge gust of wind picked up, ripping the remaining sails to shreds with its power. Logan raced back below deck and joined the rest of the party. Without hesitation Logan threw Gwydeon over his shoulder and returned to the chaotic scene above. The rest of the group was only a few steps behind, with Talon and Lane helping to support Pike. For the moment, it seemed as though the wind had calmed, but there was a feeling that it was just the prelude to a more powerful assault. To the west the jagged rocks of the shore seemed dangerously close.

"The ship is being pushed toward the rocks, Logan," Aryx said quickly, "and it won't survive,"

"Jump," Logan yelled to everyone who could hear me, "it's our only chance."

The rolling waves and constant motion of the water below made Logan hesitate, but finally he held Gwydeon tight and leapt into the black sea below. Talon and Aryx pulled Gwydeon and Logan above the surface of the water mere seconds after entry, and with the help of a piece of a broken mast, everyone made it to shore.

* * * * * * * * * * * *

Once they had all made it onto the shore, the only thing they could all do was watch in horror as the Raging Storm was battered against the jagged rocks until the last bits of its majestic frame were reduced to kindling. Their brief salvation and means of transportation had fallen, and though they had escaped with their lives, there was the chilling question that lingered as to how many more times they could cheat death. The remains of what had once been a road stretched on to the south, and alongside was a simple hand-written sign, battered by weather and age.

'You are now entering Sarmeel.'

Illusions

From a distance, Sarmeel seemed like an average small town. It had some tall buildings that were spread out through the whole of the town, and no great concentrations of buildings. There were wide pathways and wide open spaces that were very reminiscent of Aradon. This veneer of normality was shattered as one approached the town proper. The quiet comfort that could be found in Aradon was conspicuous by its absence in the barren and desolate Sarmeel. It seemed as though a dark pall had stretched over the entire town, bathing it in dread. Many years ago, when the group from Aradon was barely out of diapers, it was Sarmeel and not Illimar that was the largest and most often used port in the world. However, once Shau-ling began to take over areas of the world, Sarmeel fell into a shroud of mystery. There was a disaster of some kind that befell the town, and very few knew exactly what. Survivors of Sarmeel were few and far between, and those that claimed Sarmeel as their home that still drew breath had not been in Sarmeel when the disaster happened.

The few stories that circulated about the last days of Sarmeel came from bards and traveling merchants that were on the edge of the city. What the stories agreed upon was it started with a storm that sprang up out of nothing; one that created a massive waterspout that collided with the docks. Every ship in port was destroyed, as well as the docks themselves. After that, the stories became more varied, and many too fantastic and disturbing to be believed. Many wild tales flew around about the walking dead, and a dark plague that spread through the whole population. People seemed to die at random and what remained was only a horrid visage of the stricken. One of the most credible stories that Logan had ever heard was from a very old bard, one whom he had known from childhood. The bard always contended that he was on a ship that had just left the port of Sarmeel just before the waterspout struck. Though he shuddered when speaking about it, he recounted seeing a single black spire that rose in the center of town. It wasn't there before the waterspout struck, but once the storm had cleared; there it was, rising out of the mist like a demonic finger that had pushed its way through from the underworld. Perhaps the strangest part of the story was the fact that Sarmeel was half-way across the world from Old Lakestone, where Shau-ling's forces made their first appearance.

When the first stories began to circulate about the horrors of Sarmeel, the King of Trelon went to Sarmeel with four legions of his troops in an effort to discover the true fate of the town. Only one soldier returned alive, and he had been driven mad by the experience. The only information that could be extracted from the soldier's broken mind was that not a single person who had been in Sarmeel after the storm were to be found, not even their bodies. Since that point, no one entered Sarmeel. It still stood as a monument to the madness of the last war, and the ultimate proof that fate had a truly wicked sense of humor.

As Logan looked skyward, the dark clouds that accompanied the storm that had caused the destruction of their ship were still hanging over the sea, and they extended as far as the eye could see. Everyone else stood in the clearing outside the sign that denoted the town limits. Though everyone was skeptical at best about traveling through Sarmeel, the dangerous storm gave them little choice. If it struck again with the type of ferocity that had forced them from the sea, it would be foolish to be caught in the open when there was shelter available. Unfortunately, Sarmeel seemed to be the most logical place to find such shelter until the storm blew over. And it was anyone's best guess when that would happen. Not only that, it was quicker to go through Sarmeel to make it to Falke, as to by-pass Sarmeel would add at least two days to the journey because of the dangerous mountain passes at the southern edge of Sarmeel. It was either Sarmeel, or go back to face the Army of Illimar.

"Well," Logan said turning toward his friends, "this looks like where we are going to be staying tonight. Or, at least until the storm rolls out."

Everyone looked at him and had no choice but to agree. However, the concern showed on many faces, no more than on Gideon and Aryx. It was clear to Logan that they knew more than they were saying, and perhaps that was for the betterment of the group. Better to keep silent that to sew fear that could not be mitigated. As though thinking he needed to say something, Aryx spoke.

"Though we must stay here, we must be sure that we remain together. There have been many wild stories about the fate of Sarmeel. Unfortunately we must also scout the city and be sure that there is no hidden threat waiting for us as there was in the Mithacarthian Woods. I fear that the storm was not a natural event, and Shau-ling may have a surprise waiting for us." Aryx suggested calmly.

"I concur," Logan added. "We will stay together, but also stay alert."

Again there were nods all around, and the group began to gather what little had survived the shipwreck. Luckily everyone had managed to recover their weapons, but it looked as though at least half of Midarin's quiver of arrows had not survived the swim to shore. The wounds to many members of the party aside, there was a wave of uncertainty and shock that resonated through everyone. Even Aryx seemed to share the apprehension, but he hid it under the practiced façade of duty and detachment. It was clear that Aryx was ready for anything that Sarmeel was going to throw at him, but as for the rest of the group, there were no such concrete declarations of confidence. So much had happened in just a matter of days. First the attack on Aradon, the Tarnae, the misunderstandings in Illimar, and now the destruction of the Raging Storm right underneath their feet. Nerves all around were pretty frayed. Logan's mind went back to the conversation with Aryx at Logan's table. He remembered Aryx mentioning terrible creatures that served Shau-ling, creatures that were far more dangerous than the Shadowwalkers or even the Tarnae. They were all battered and bruised and they had not even begun to face the true horrors at Shau-ling's disposal. Then, as though a fog had lifted from Logan's mind, he realized what Aryx had said.

"Aryx, do you think that Shau-ling could in any way be behind this storm?"

Aryx took a moment to think and then responded.

"With all of my experience with Shau-ling, I have found that he is not able to directly control the forces of nature. For some reason, it seems to be out of his sphere of ability. The phasia, as well as Shau-ling can manipulate the primal forces of nature, just as the *Erieal* and the *Coromor* can. But there is a large chasm between controlling wind and creating a hurricane with rain and lightning. However, there are some of Shau-ling's beasts that do have the ability to create and manipulate such forces. It is not so much a direct application of power, but more enhancing conditions that already exist. These creatures could not create a storm out of nothingness, but with their power they could increase a simple shower into a deadly typhoon, if there were enough of the creatures focused on the task."

"Do you think these beasts could be behind this storm?" Pike asked quickly.

"No one beast has the ability to conjure such a storm. However a large enough group could combine their abilities and theoretically could create this storm. Unfortunately, magical theory was never one of my strengths. That was Mailock's area of expertise."

Lane took that as his queue to intervene.

"It is very likely, if I am interpreting Aryx's description of these beasts correctly, that in order for the storm to have been created by these beasts, they would have to be very close to the point where the storm struck."

"That is very true," Aryx nodded seeming impressed with Lane," If we use where the Raging Strom was struck as a reference point, we can determine that the beasts would have to be either here in Sarmeel, Rana, or Rama."

"So I suppose we should be on our guard while searching Sarmeel," Eldar offered.

"I agree. We should search Sarmeel, but with great care. We don't know how many of these things may be in Sarmeel, and we don't know what we're up against. Don't forget, whatever it was that wiped out the entire population of Sarmeel as well as killed the old King of Trelon and four legions of his men may still be here. I for one don't want to be its next meal."

"Ain't nothin' makin' a meal o' me," Gideon added finally.

Gideon's words brought some levity to the group, but it only lifted the clouds for a moment. With Gideon in the lead and Aryx at his heels, it took only a few minutes before the group had crossed into town proper of Sarmeel. Darkness seemed to pulsate all around the deeper they ventured into Sarmeel, as though the darkness was a living thing that slowly drew breath and undulated with want. The buildings seemed to be there in form, but not in substance, like a great shadow. The soul of the town, if such a thing existed, had been torn away leaving only a hollow and shattered husk, one that knew only hunger. Fear welled up inside of Logan as the wind whipped about with the screams of banshees riding upon it. With all of the phantoms about, fear was the only tangible enemy to fight. When he was a boy, Logan's father had always told him about fear killing more quickly than the sharpest of swords. How many battles had been decided before a single sword was drawn because one side gave into fear? While unconsciously Logan prayed for a sign of life, he feared that yet again, it would be fate's cruel humor that answered.

On the way through Sarmeel, they moved down the main road, everyone keeping a sharp eye for any movement. However, the darkness and the occasional lightning flashes made it difficult. Aryx tapped Gideon on the shoulder and pointed to an opening in the wall of a nearby building. At first, there was nothing, just a hole. The whole group came to a stop, and Midarin went to one knee, her bow in hand and an arrow trained on the doorway that Aryx had indicated. To the naked eyes, there was nothing more than an old building crumbling from old age. There was something in the darkness of the doorway, a faint light that could only be perceived at the closer inspection urged by the most experienced member of the party. Under normal circumstances they would have continued walking and perhaps placed themselves at greater risk. Logan motioned for Pike, Talon, and Gwydeon to move around the front of the building and for them to enter through the front door. Then, he motioned for Midarin, Eldar, and Lane to go in through the back. Aryx, Elwyne, Gideon, and Logan then slowly worked their way through the opening in the side wall.

As they entered the opening, it was apparent that the damage to the building was not the work of time and simple disrepair. Someone or something had burrowed several hundreds of passageways into the ground as well as the walls of the building. The maze of tunnels that had been created was very elaborate and just large enough for a person of average height and weight to crawl through. Though it was against their better judgment, it seemed that there would be no answers found without taking on some additional risk. The choice of action was clear, and one after another each member of the group crawled into the tunnels.

There were several places that the passages narrowed, forcing a change in direction, and some that required complete backtracking. It would have been easy to get lost in the maze and never find your way out, but after a few minutes of crawling, it became apparent that the tunnels were all contenting to something deep beneath Sarmeel. Sure enough, the group eventually emerged into a large central chamber. Logan's group was the first to emerge from the tunnels into the chamber, but only a few seconds later, Eldar's group also appeared. The chamber itself had smooth blue walls, similar to those in the tunnels. The chamber itself was massive, easily large enough to contain the whole of the *Traveling Bard* with quite a bit of room to spare. After only a few minutes of exploring, Pike emerged into the chamber.

"Hey," Logan's voice echoed across the chamber, "where are Talon and the others?"

"I'm here," Talon replied crawling out of a passage to the west of Logan, "Lane will be here in a minute. He wanted to try to fit through one of the smaller passages to see if there was anything hidden there."

Eldar spoke up next.

"It's simply amazing Logan. Whatever made these took a lot of time to finish."

"I don't like it," the cautious tone of Aryx rang out, "Whatever made these tunnels wouldn't leave them unprotected."

"Maybe these are storage areas," Midarin said walking towards Aryx, "We used to have caverns like this in Brae to store grain. They were hardly ever guarded, because guards brought attention to the caverns. Maybe the people in Sarmeel did the same thing. They could have used the warehouses to store the materials and shipments that were leaving via ship or cart while using the caverns for the items that would be used by the city itself. That way there would be no confusion as to what belonged where."

Elwyne's voice rang out in opposition to Midarin's thought.

"If the tunnels were only in the ground or from cellars, that might make sense," her cold voice countered. "These tunnels are also in the walls of the buildings and in some cases look like they've cracked the foundations."

"I agree with Elwyne," Pike commented. "Whatever dug these tunnels didn't care what they were digging through. I bet a lot of the collapsed buildings we saw were because these tunnels made them unstable."

Logan nodded absently and took another look around. The light was stronger there in the central chamber, but there was no obvious source for the light. By then, Lane had emerged from a tunnel near where Eldar stood, on the other side of the central chamber from where Talon emerged.

"Lane, do you have any theories?" Logan asked.

"None whatsoever, I'm afraid. There are no markings in the tunnels, not even the smaller ones. What I can tell you though is that whatever cut these tunnels cut through solid stone while leaving a smooth surface. There are only a handful of stone smiths in the whole of Mithacarthia that could do that, and it would take them several lifetimes to carve all these tunnels with that kind of quality."

Taking a long deep breath, Logan's eyes wandered from tunnel opening to tunnel opening.

I don't like it. There's something here just waiting for use to make a wrong move and then it'll be right on top of us. Maybe Midarin is right after all, maybe this is just a storage area, and once the city became abandoned, whatever had carved the tunnels in the first place ran amuck. But if something carved these tunnels, where is it? Where's that light coming from? Is the light stronger up there?

"Gideon," Logan said pointing up at one of the higher passages, "does the light look like it's stronger up there?"

Everyone turned their attention to the place where Logan was pointing, and it was Aryx and not Gideon that answered.

"Good eye, Logan. It does in fact look stronger there."

"You're the only one of us that has a chance to get up there in one piece, Gideon. Do you think you can do it?"

Gideon grumbled.

"Not getting' paid enough fer dis."

He said something else that was unintelligible in his thick accent before ducking down and propelling himself upward in a long standing jump. He was just able to grab a rock outcropping that projected from the wall roughly two feet below the passageway. Skillfully he climbed the steep wall and within a few minutes made it to the top. He looked down the tunnel for a quick minute and then shouted down.

"Dere's nothin' dere. Da light seems ta be comin' from da end of da passage. Hold on, dere's somtin' movin' back dere."

Gideon pulled himself fully into the passageway and then disappeared from view. It was a few moments later that he reemerged. His feet emerged from the passage and he pushed himself back hard until his feet slid down the edge of the wall onto the outcropping. He pushed himself backwards at a quickening pace, and as soon as his head and shoulders had cleared the opening, he sprang backwards off the wall, flipping through the air. He was able to control his fall and landed roughly on the hard ground near the center of the chamber. The next second his hands were clenched around daggers, and he was looking back up at the passage. Before any other member of the party could take any action, all hell broke loose.

From the opening, what looked like little balls of fluff began springing out. The balls themselves were different colors, though most of them were either white or gray, and they were of varying sizes. The hair or fur that they were coated with most reminded Logan of a long-haired cat. They hit the ground everywhere, and as more and more poured from not only the opening with the brighter light, but also some of the other passages high in the room, they began to fill the floor of the chamber. After some time, it became clear that the balls of fur were keeping their distance from the members of the group. They creatures were leaving a perimeter around each of the members of the group about three feet across. When the last few balls of fur trickled out of the passages, the floor was completely covered except for the fully formed and defined areas around the party. Gideon remained crouched and was about to lash out at one of the closest balls of fur when Elwyne's voice restrained him.

"What are you doing Gideon," Elwyne said shocked, "those are just sweet innocent little purring balls of fur?"

For the first time there was a sound that came from the balls of fur. At first Logan thought that it was a low hum, but the more he concentrated on it, but more it sounded like purring. The little balls of hair laid there motionless, but sure enough, there was a distinctive purring noise coming from them.

"Aye lassie," Gideon replied, "dey may look like sweet lil' balls o' fur, but dese furballs 'ave teeth!"

Sweat rolled down Gideon's face, and it was clear that whatever he had seen up in that tunnel, he wasn't willing to go through it again. How the little balls of fur had put such a fright into him was beyond understanding, but if the Alimidarian thief thought that the balls of fur were a threat, then it was clear they were. Logan had formed enough of an impression to know not to doubt him. Just then, one of the balls of fur began to move. Gideon tensed and started to move toward the thing. Logan raised his hand, attempting to restrain Gideon's advance, and then he drew his sword.

"Just a minute, Gideon. Maybe you frightened them, and they were just trying to protect themselves."

"Ach, frightened dem? By da Light! If ye call tryin' ta rip me arm off wt' nine inch fangs protectin' demselves, den give me a trumpet da next time ya want a hole checked out."

The one ball of fur that began to move was then joined by another, and then another. In a matter of seconds, the whole floor was a moving mass, and the little puff balls began to edge their way closer and closer to the feet of each of the members of the party. Then it happened. In the very back of the cavern a large black ball of hair emerged from the rest of the undulating mass. It was much different from the rest. It was easily three times the size of its compatriots and seemed to be purring in a much deeper tone and much louder than the others. It was almost as if this creature's purr was setting the tone for the rest. After several more moments, the purr from the large black ball increased in volume and lowered almost another octave. As if the change in harmony was a signal, all of the balls stopped purring at once. All eyes went to the large black ball, and Elwyne barely stifled a gasp as the creature began to change.

Within a matter of seconds, a pair of eyes appeared. The eyes themselves didn't appear to have any color, but when the light began to reflect off the blue walls, the eyes took on an eerie bluish hue. The ball puffed up, becoming larger and larger until it stopped growing once it had reached the size of roughly two feet in diameter. A tail then became visible and it began to wave around behind the creature. For some reason, the light reflected off the tip of the tail, as if it were a piece of metal caught in the morning sunlight. Looking straight at the creature revealed a horrid smile of nine inch fangs. The fangs glowed impossibly bright, a testament to their sharpness. Sensing an impending threat, Logan brought his blade up and took a defensive position. Gwydeon, Pike, Talon, Eldar, and Aryx followed suit. The rest of the party was still in shock at the transformation of the larger ball of fur. In fact, the party was so transfixed by the large black ball that they failed to notice the smaller balls of fur as they began to open and reveal the same hideous features. As the ones closest to the large black ball finished opening, they began hopping in place. The almost rhythmic and hypnotic motion began to lull everyone into a state of distraction. There was something incredibly soothing about the motion.

"Stay sharp."

Aryx's voice cut through the haze and brought everyone back to sharp focus. Sensing that the distraction had failed, several of the balls of fur launched themselves at members of the party. Because everyone was surrounded, it made it difficult to effectively dodge the attacks. They came rapidly, their tails whirling and their teeth chomping at anything that might get in their way. Logan ducked one of the creatures jumping at him, and struck another in mid-flight. The stroke of his blade split one of the creatures in two, and putrid green blood was sent splattering everywhere. A drop of blood fell on the sleeve of his shirt and it immediately began to burn. Not hesitating, Logan ripped off the burning sleeve and cast it to the ground.

"Watch out," Logan yelled to his companions, "their blood is some kind of acid. It'll eat whatever it touches."

There was a flash of recognition that came from everyone in the party; some were audible while some were just a nod or jerk of the head. Logan's concern then immediately shifted to the blade of his sword. The blood from the vicious creature dripped down the sword and slid off without leaving a mark on the forged steel.

"Get ready," Gwydeon shouted. "Here they come."

CHAPTER 4

Chapter V

Malice

Tension filled the room as the group of young warriors prepared for the inevitable wave of assaults from the small yet deadly balls of fur that coated the floor. Then, as if on cue, the first dozen of the creatures launched themselves forward. Elwyne barely ducked the two that flew at her, and Gideon leapt from where he stood and crossed the distance to where Elwyne crouched. While passing through the air, he loosed two daggers toward the airborne creatures, connecting with one but not the second. The one that was struck flew out of control and hit the wall, its smoking blood splattering against the wall. Even the stone did not seem to be immune from the blood's acidic effects, and the rock began to slowly melt away. Standing over Elwyne, Gideon threw more and more daggers at the innumerable targets. Gwydeon and Eldar were also holding their own, but for every one that they were able to strike down another three replaced it. Talon was the first to miss a strike, and one of the creatures latched onto his arm with its razor-sharp teeth and began to gnaw and rip. The muscles in his arm began twitching uncontrollably and his hand seized, causing him to drop his sword. Blood flowed down his arm, but Midarin was able to end the creature before it could do permanent damage with a well-placed arrow that no only killed the creature but also kept the blood splatter away from Talon's exposed skin. However, when the creature fell away, it ripped a large chunk of Talon's skin away with it. Aryx's golden gauntlet glowed bright red, and he slammed the gauntlet into the ground at his feet, and a stream of lightning cut across the floor, disintegrating a mass of the creatures, and clearing a path from where he stood to where Talon had fallen.

"Everyone to me!" Aryx yelled as he moved across the newly opened path.

Gideon helped Elwyne to her feet and pulled her along behind him as he traversed the distance to Talon. Instead of using his daggers, Gideon kicked at several of the creatures, narrowly avoiding his foot being bitten on several occasions. Aryx and Gideon stood back to back, fending off the advancing waves and opening gaps for the rest of the members of the party as Elwyne knelt beside Talon tending to his wounds. Once Eldar and Gwydeon added their blades to the growing defensive circle, Lane and Midarin were able to join without much difficulty. Though the close quarters lowered the effectiveness of her bow, Midarin was still shooting as she could, picking off several of the creatures as they flew in the direction of the now massing party. Once everyone was gathered, the creatures seemed to change their tactics, and instead of coming in groups of six or eight, they now swarmed in groups of twenty or more. Though there were more blades brought to bear in the small area, the creatures' attacks proved to be far more effective. While the amount of bites was lessened, the tails were vicious and potent. The tips of the tails were not only sharp, but they also seemed to be super-heated. As the tail ripped through the skin, it also burned the exposed edges cauterizing the wound immediately. While the wounds inflicted incredible pain, there was no blood. There wouldn't be a member of the group that would escape the battle without a permanent scar. The larger danger of the close quarters was that each of the creatures that died had a better chance of splattering the caustic green blood and causing collateral damage. It seemed that Aryx's patience with the conflict ended. He brought the gauntlet to his chest, and a moment later, a dome of lightning covered the group. Several of the creatures leapt at the dome, but were incinerated as soon as they contacted the sparking exterior. The line of creatures retreated from the boundary of the shield, but Aryx was not content to simply create a stalemate. He closed his eyes and concentrated. For a moment nothing happened, but sweat began to bead on the man's forehead. Moments later the barrier began to expand, pushing the line of creatures back even further. The advance sped up, and the creatures were unable to escape. Those who were not able to bound away were vaporized. Then the gauntlet flared again, and the barrier exploded outward filling the rest of the chamber. When the flash receded, the barrier was gone, and so too were the creatures.

Logan immediately turned his attention to Talon, and the other members of the party also were tending to each other's wounds. Elwyne was doing her best to stop the bleeding, but as soon as Logan saw the wound, it was obvious that the creature's teeth only inflicted part of the damage to Talon's arm. There must have been ducts in the teeth that secreted the acid that was in the blood, because the skin around the tooth marks was bubbling and steaming. Elwyne was using water to try to wash away as much of the acid as possible, but had to do it slowly to prevent the acid from spreading to other pieces of Talon's skin. Once the wound was cleaned, she ripped a piece of Talon shirt and wrapped it around the wound. It was then that Logan became aware that the low purring had returned to the chamber, and as he stood and looked around, he saw that the larger black ball had somehow survived Aryx's attack. It was sitting where it had been before the battle started, and it seemed that the larger creature was nothing but a general, waiting to see if its talents were going to be needed in battle. It made no move and took no action but just sat, its tail waiving behind it. Midarin raised her bow, drew an arrow, and looked in Logan's direction.

"Shall I?"

Logan looked first at the black ball of fur. It made no motion at the threat, and if Logan didn't know better, he would have sworn that the creature was grinning. When Logan looked back at Midarin, he nodded.

"By all means."

Midarin flashed a brief smile and then took very careful aim. She drew her bowstring back farther and farther, and then released the arrow. In a split second, the arrow was upon the creature. In an all but unseen motion of its tail, it split Midarin's arrow lengthwise, saving itself from certain death. The arrow dropped to either side of the beast harmlessly. Again, the thing just sat there, its wide toothy smile mocking in its malice. Looks of shock and disbelief were the common expressions.

"Suggestions?" Logan asked softly.

"A good suggestion would be ta get the hell outta 'ere," Gideon replied.

"Gideon may be right." Aryx added. "This may not be a time for bravery."

"Okay then, nice and slow."

Gideon and Midarin kept their sights trained on the creature as everyone backed slowly through one of the larger passages. The large black ball had no reaction to the retreat, and while it was not a rapid retreat because of the hampered members of the part, the black ball seemed to be completely disinterested. Pike and Gwydeon hobbled through the passages, the battle straining their slowly mending wounds. Once the group had emerged from the passages back into one of the crumbling buildings, Gwydeon collapsed in a corner and took a long deep breath. It seemed that the consummate warrior was finally feeling the exhaustion of nearly constant fighting. Everyone took the cue and the building became a makeshift camp. Eldar fixed her eyes on Midarin and pointed at her bow.

"How did that thing do that with your arrow?" Eldar asked.

"I don't know," Midarin replied. "I've never seen anything like that in my life. The speed and accuracy that it would have to have to split an arrow lengthwise is beyond anything I thought possible. I don't even think that Gwydeon or Aryx could have diverted that arrow, let alone split it."

"Agreed," Aryx said cleaning his blade.

"Well," Pike said wiping the sweat off his brow, "those were interesting little creatures, weren't they? Are those Shau-ling's friends, or were they just having fun?"

"I doubt if those things serve Shau-ling," Lane said after a moment. "And I don't think those were the creatures that caused the storm."

"How do you figure?" Talon asked holding his wounded arm. "Those things seem mean enough to me to be working for Shau-ling."

"For one thing, if they were Shau-ling's servants, why didn't they finish us off? And for another thing, if they did have the power to affect the weather, or any other abilities at all for that matter, why didn't they use them against us?"

"Point well taken," Logan said catching his breath. "Aryx, have you ever seen or heard of those things before? I mean, I'd like to have a name so I know what to avoid in the future."

"There was a story of creatures matching that description, and they were called Snags."

"How long have you known about those things?" Gwydeon asked.

"All I knew was that they were supposed to exist, nothing more. Myths and legends. And just like the rest of you, I hope that is the last time I ever have the pleasure of seeing one. Even during the journey with Lord Cedric, we didn't meet all of the creatures that served Shau-ling. The legends I've heard was that the Snag were created to be shock troops, a fast-moving ground attack force that would act similarly to the Shadowwalkers in terms of sheer devastation. But legend has it that they were too difficult to control, and that is why Shau-ling simply banished them and they fell into the shroud of myth."

Logan rose from where he crouched.

"It's late," he said after a moment. "After everything we've been through, we need to try to get what rest we can. We're going to be on foot for a while before we get to Falke, and it's anyone's best guess how much good night's sleep we're going to get between now and then. Sarmeel may not be the safest place, but I think we can be sure that these Snags or whatever they are will be coming after us. It seemed like the big black one was content to just leave well enough alone. I think we can safely camp here. I'll go out and try to find some wood for a fire. Gideon, why don't you see if there is any wildlife crazy enough to call this place home that could make dinner for us? All our supplies are gone so we're going to have to rough it. Lane, I thought I saw a small stream back at the entrance to the town, take Eldar with you and see if there is any fresh water to replenish our water skins. Everyone understand?"

Aryx stood.

"I'll come with you, Logan. None of us should travel alone."

Logan bristled.

"Very well. Who will go with Gideon?"

Midarin stood.

"Everyone else is injured, and Elwyne is needed here to treat their wounds. I'll go with Gideon."

There were nods all around.

The party split up and everyone went in separate directions, with Elwyne staying to tend to the wounded. Gwydeon and Pike would be the last to admit that they were relieved and happy for the rest, but if the group were going to continue to prosper, everyone needed to be as close to full strength as possible. Logan started his search in the immediate area of the house where the tunnels had first been discovered. He kept his sword drawn and in his hand, and could not help nervously tightening his grip on the hilt of his sword. As he continued to search, there was a flash of motion that he barely caught out of the corner of his eye. He turned sharply, expecting to see one of the small balls of fur, but instead found nothing. Whatever it was, if it were anything at all, had only been there for a fraction of a second. While normally he would have chided himself for jumping at shadows, with the current state of things, every shadow was a threat. Within a few minutes Logan had come across a larger building that looked as though it had been used as a storehouse for supplies. It was possible that there would still be something that could be useful. After a cursory inspection, there didn't appear to be any holes or outward signs of Snags. The large wooden door to the building creaked open with a single push. Entering the front room, a flash of motion in the back of the room made Logan tighten the grip on the hilt of his sword again. Continuing into the room slowly, Logan found himself face to face with yet another unfamiliar beast.

Unlike the Snags, this creature was nearly Logan's height, and was generally human in build and appearance. The only difference was easily noticeable pointed ears, round pointed horns, and dark red skin. Additionally, the creature's features were incredibly sharp without any rounded edges. It wore a smile on its face that screamed cunning and malevolence. Brandishing his sword, ready to defend himself, Logan addressed the creature.

"Can you speak?" he asked, trying to keep strength in his tone.

"Yes," it said in perfect, non-accented speech, "I am very capable of conversing with you pitiful little humans. Your language is so limited by the aspect of using your mouths and throats to produce sounds that almost no other breed of creature can understand. Our form of communication is much more efficient and better equipped to be adapted for use with other breeds of creature."

"You remind me of the Tarnae, that same smug superiority," Logan countered. "The only difference is that we aren't in Dreamscape, and that you don't speak in rhyme and riddle."

"Dreamscape," it scoffed, "such a dreadful place. Why Master even lets that horrible place remain in existence is beyond me. And those Tarnae, such wasteful creatures. Always with their games and their schemes. I could never understand what Master saw in them."

"So, you are one of Shau-ling's creatures. I should have known."

"Why yes, isn't everyone? Oh, silly questions. You humans, always stating the obvious with such genuine surprise. Because you are unwilling to accept the truth doesn't make you able to change it. Don't tell me that you are in league with that petty little band of adventurers that think the *Coromor* will be able to kill Shau-ling, now are you? How can they possibly destroy the Lord of Shadows, when they can't even sail from place to place without sinking?"

Anger boiled inside of Logan, but before he could say anything in response, the creature put up its hand and smelled the air.

"You have the stench of the *Coromor* all over you! Be a smart lad and walk away from that miserable thing. It's not like the rest of you humans. It's dangerous."

"You mean it's dangerous to your master," Logan countered.

"So you are a fool after all. Don't you even know what the *Coromor* is? In order to save the world, it must first destroy everything that is important to it. That is where the Lion failed. He cared too much about saving his human friends and not enough about his own existence. He wasn't ready to sacrifice a few petty lives to save hundreds of thousands of others. Now, because of his oversight, he is dying. And so shall the Dragon, because his flesh will fail just as Cedric's did."

The hatred for Shau-ling swelled in Logan, and the hatred for the beast standing before him was overwhelming. Logan took a step back and tightened the grip on his sword bringing it up into a defensive position. It laughed loudly, pointing at Logan's sword. The smile widened on the face of the beast, and it began to laugh again.

"What's so funny?" Logan demanded.

"It just occurred to me," the beast said, "you actually think that you can defeat me in battle, don't you?"

"That shouldn't be funny. I could tear you apart right now if I wished to."

The monster threw its head back and laughed as loudly as it could. For a moment, it almost seemed that the sheer force of the laughing would shatter its lithe body. A moment later, the creature straightened itself and took a long stride forward.

"Your *Coromor* has no chance of defeating my lord. Why do you follow something that is just as destructive and just as powerful as Shau-ling itself?"

"Because he is doing what is right," Logan answered without hesitation.

"You follow a monster! Who is the *Coromor* to dictate wrong and right? You don't even know what the *Coromor* really is," it replied scornfully.

"The *Coromor* is the one who brings change. He is the only one who can defeat Shau-ling. He is the one that will save us from the darkness that Shau-ling brings down upon us."

"Spoken like a true puppet. You are more of a fool than I imagined possible. Didn't the question of 'why' ever enter that tiny brain of yours? Why is the *Coromor* the only one who can defeat Shau-ling? Did it? Do you want to know? Do you want to know who the real power in the world is? Shau-ling is the creator of darkness. And Shau-ling was created out of the nightmares of man. He is the true embodiment of all evil. The *Coromor* is as much kin to Shau-ling as light is to dark. Without each other, both will die. That is why the Lion is dying. If this so-called *Coromor* wants to live another day, he will turn himself over to the forces of the Shadow, and rule the world at Shau-ling's side."

Logan shook his head in disbelief. He couldn't believe what he was hearing. However, before he could make a move or craft a response, the door burst open behind him, and he spun around in time to see Aryx coming through the door with his sword drawn.

"You should work on your rhetoric, Jeresei, its beginning to sound stale."

"So, Aryx Terian, we meet again."

"I thought the Lord Lion and I had the pleasure of exterminating the last of your kind when we took down the walls of Shau-ling's palace."

"Surely you exaggerate, White Lightning, but you will never see the end of my kind. We are the proud soldiers of Shau-ling and his children the phasia."

"I take it you know this thing, Aryx," Logan asked quickly.

"In form, yes. Maybe not this particular one, but I have met its kind in battle many times. This is one of the Jeresei, Shau-ling's personal guard and foot soldiers."

"At your service," the Jeresei said going into a deep and feigned bow. "What is it White Lightning? Couldn't stand to be leashed to a lame master? Or was it perhaps that the thrill of adventure finally went to your head, and you latched onto some boy claiming to serve the *Coromor*?"

"How many of you are here, beast?" Aryx challenged, tired of the banter.

"Enough to kill the two of you a hundred times over."

"Very well then. Tell your master, if you survive the day, that the *Coromor* is ready, willing, and able to fight him at any time."

The Jeresei laughed harder.

"Your delusions of grandeur worsen with your age, White Lightning. You are as much the *Coromor* as I am Shau-ling himself."

"No," Logan interjected, "Aryx is not the *Coromor*. I am."

For a short moment, the beast stood there in shock. Then suddenly, it let out a hellish call that made Logan's skin crawl and his hair stand on end. It crouched down with its hands extended to either side of its body, its mouth open, revealing sharp teeth that it hid behind its thin lips. Ever so slowly, razor-sharp claws began to extend from its outstretched fingers. Aryx took a step toward the Jeresei, but Logan took hold of his shoulder and pulled him back.

"The Shadowwalkers were yours;" Logan said coldly, "this one is mine."

He nodded and stepped back to the open door. Sure that Aryx would not interfere with the battle, Logan advanced toward the crouching monster. Its eyes stared up at the advancing human with a hateful fire. The eyes had now taken on a reddish tint, and were filled with a palpable lust for blood. The claws on its fingers were now fully extended. Logan advanced slowly toward the monster his guard up, looking for an open to exploit. He never got the chance as the creature suddenly leapt at him. It leapt high in the air, and started to fall from the ceiling. A flash of reflected light from its claws could be seen as it swooped down from the top of the building. Quickly Logan maneuvered his blade over his head and parried the blow from the falling Jeresei. Taking the offensive, Logan thrust at the creature several times, but the beast was too nimble darting in and out, avoiding the blade. They began to circle each other, each waiting for the other to make a mistake. The first mistake was made by the Jeresei. Its eyes were focused solely upon its prey, and it stumbled over a large rock that lay on the floor. The Jeresei stumbled to the ground, and with a quick downward stroke of his blade, Logan drew first blood. Had he intended to kill the beast at that moment, he could have, but his anger had gotten the better of him, obstructing his clarity of thought, and he fell into the trap of wanting his opponent to suffer. After Logan's long cut across the back of the Jeresei's neck, it leapt away but jumped back instantly. It flailed with arms and legs, and Logan was able to easily parry each of the attacks. After a few failed attempts to score a hit, it retreated back to the back wall of the house. Its chest was covered with small wounds from the Logan's sharp blade. Logan lowered his sword and took a step closer to the beast.

"Had enough?" the young warrior taunted.

"Fool, don't you know to never lower your defenses against an enemy?"

Even before it uttered those final words, the Jeresei leapt again. This time however, it took a more direct path. Logan barely saw one of the clawed hand extend, and then the pain came. The long blades of its fingers dig into the flesh on the left side of Logan's face, easily ripping through the tender flesh. Hot blood dripped from the wound, each drop wetting the already sweat drenched shirt that clung to his shoulders. The Jeresei landed on the other side of the room, near to where Aryx had taken position to guard the door. Aryx made no aggressive move toward the Jeresei, letting Logan fight his battle, though Logan was sure that if Aryx though the Jeresei was about to end Logan's life, he would have interjected. Calming his nerves and his anger, Logan raised his sword and sliced at the beast. The strike missed the mark badly, his vision impaired by the wound. The Jeresei's counterattack caught Logan's shoulder, leaving another bloody wound. However, the attack had not struck Logan's sword arm, so he was still nearly at full fighting strength. Slowly, they began to circle each other again. The thought of the missed opportunity to end the duel early began to weigh heavily on Logan's mind, and he knew it was a lesson that he would carry with him for the rest of his days. Then, the opening that would end the battle suddenly presented itself. Feeling confident, the beast began to strike wildly, hoping to catch Logan with a glancing blow that would provide an opening for the fatal strike. However, its pattern of motion soon became predictable. The Jeresei brought its right arm up for another strike, and acting quickly Logan ducked the blow and buried the tip of his sword into its side. Again the creature howled in pain, and not giving it time to regroup, Logan lunged at the wounded beast. He feinted low as Gwydeon had taught him, forcing the beast to commit a defense as and then immediately lunged upward, severing its head from the rest of its body. The head of the Jeresei rolled along the ground and came to rest near Aryx's foot, and the rest of its body first fell to its knees before toppling forward and spilling its essence onto the floor. Wiping the combination of blood and sweat from his brow, Logan approached Aryx who still stood at the door. Aryx looked Logan over, judging the severity of the wounds.

"Overconfidence is a death that no one, no matter how skilled, can escape forever," Aryx cautioned. "Shau-ling's servants always believed they were superior and invulnerable. In many battles that was the only edge we had to exploit."

Logan nodded.

"I'll remember that."

Aryx looked back out the door.

"We need to get back to the others as quickly as possible," Aryx said coldly, "your friend was not alone."

Logan looked out the door and saw a mass of shadows moving on the far side of town. They could be seen ducking from alley to alley, but enough were massed on the main road that ran through Sarmeel that they could not hide their advance. The army of Jeresei would be upon them in a matter of moments, with numbers that made their victory seem assured. With nowhere to run, there was only one option left...to fight.

Overwhelming Force

At such a long distance, it was impossible to make out exactly how many Jeresei were advancing on their position, and to make the situation more difficult, the creatures moved in and out of ranks and between the buildings in order to further disguise their numbers. However many of them there were, a sea of red-skinned, human-like Jeresei was coming. Logan looked back at the decapitated body of the Jeresei that was still lying on the floor. Even with his mistakes in the battle, the Jeresei was a difficult opponent. Its tactics, while manageable in a duel, en masse would have been extremely difficult to manage. A dozen of the creatures darting in and out, striking with their long claws; they would be able to easily keep an opponent off-balance. Their combat style favored hunting and attacking in packs, and with the numbers that were coming, they would overwhelm the group like waves crashing against the shore.

Looking again at the oncoming Jeresei, Logan wiped the colorless blood off his blade and hurried out the door with Aryx at his heels. By the time they returned to the encampment, both Midarin and Gideon had returned from their camping expedition, and was positioned to protect the wounded until Logan and Aryx returned. Obviously they had seen the oncoming force of Jeresei, and were ready to fight. Logan ducked quickly into the house and found Gwydeon and Pike on their feet, preparing their weapons. Eldar brushed past Logan without a word, her sword drawn. Talon was still getting to his feet, and seemed very unsteady. Elwyne had fashioned a makeshift sling with the fabric from his shirt, but with only one arm against the Jeresei, he would not stand a chance. As it was, Gwydeon and Pike's mobility was hampered. In close quarters that would not have mattered, but in the wide open streets of Sarmeel, the Jeresei would take advantage of their superior mobility. However, Gwydeon's skill and Pike's strength and tenacity could nullify that advantage, if all their luck held. Lane was preparing the components to summon the arcane forces that would be needed in the battle to come. Logan moved the Talon and put his hand on the man's good shoulder.

"Don't worry, Logan," Talon reassured, "I can still fight."

Logan nodded.

"I know you can, Talon. But the creatures that are coming, they're vicious and quick. I need you to stay here, protect Elwyne. In the house here you can use your reach and keep the creatures from overwhelming you."

He opened his mouth to argue, but stopped short, finally nodding his head. Logan moved to Elwyne and brushed the back of his hand along her cheek briefly. She produced the dagger that Eldar had given her many years ago, and taught her to use. She was not as adept with the weapon as Gideon was with his daggers, but in close, as she would be with the Jeresei, she would at least be able to defend herself. Logan turned away and started out the door. However, once he stepped out of the house, Pike intercepted Logan, and put his hand on his friend's chest.

"Get back inside the building, Logan."

Pike's tone caught Logan by surprise. While he was usually boisterous and loud, he was not known for using his voice in a commanding manner, or taking the kind of responsibility that would require such a tone. Pike was considered many things, from a troublemaker, to a letch, to a talented blacksmith and carpenter. However, Pike wasn't the kind to take initiative at least not for anything serious. Sure, he could plan a petty theft or a practical joke, but for the really important decisions in his life, Pike relied on the guidance of others. More often than not he took that lead from either Logan or Talon, and for a time it seemed like he was taking his queues from Eldar. But regardless of his motivations or his joviality, he was a man that could always be counted on in any circumstance, and he was fiercely loyal to his friends and to the people he loved. Moreover, his loyalty knew no bounds, and the more reckless the action, the more likely Pike would be there. Logan tried to move past Pike, but his larger and broader friend blocked every advance, and when he became frustrated with the game brought his axe to bear, and frowned, shaking his head.

"Listen to me, Logan;" Pike said in a gruff tone, "sometimes you are as stupid as Elwyne says you are. When we were kids we could get into all kinds of trouble together, but we're a long way from that. This is not a time to be brave. Remember that you're the one that has to go up against Shau-ling. But you haven't acted like that, not at all. Aryx told us about the Shadowwalkers. He tried to keep you safe, keep you out of the fighting, but you wouldn't stay away. You were standing right there, just feet away from something that would have killed you. Then again, in Dreamscape, you were the one putting yourself in danger. Yes, you saved us, and we're all eternally grateful for that. But if you would have failed, trying to save us, then we all would have been lost, forever. Then in Illimar, when we should have stayed safe in the cottage, you let Talon and I talk you into going out. Then you're right there in the thick of the fight. By the Light Logan, you even took on a dozen soldiers from the Army of Illimar! Where is your head? Shadowwalkers, soldiers, Snags, Tarnae, and now Jeresei? We're not even a week out of Aradon, and how many times do we have to stare in the face of death with you right in the thick of it?"

Pike's face was flushed, and frustration was thick in his voice. Finally, Pike lowered his axe and forced a smile.

"We have to get you out of here alive, and I can't guarantee your safety if you're here in the thick of it with us. Look, you're a good fighter, and I'd gladly wade into hell with you, you know that. But right now we have to think about bigger things. So, you're going to get out of here and let us cover your escape. And before you think this is an argument, it's not. This is the way it's going to be. If you fight me on this, I'll knock you out and I'll have you carried to safety."

For a long moment, Logan just stood there looking at Pike. As much as he didn't like what his old friend was saying, he had no choice but to admit that there was logic in his words. Logan was envious of his friend, never before had Logan had the courage of his convictions to stand up to any situation in the way that Pike had. Pike's forcefulness also brought doubt into Logan's mind as to how fit he truly was for the role that fate had chosen him to play. When the situation called for it, Logan knew that he would fight, but that was the true problem. His role was not to be a warrior like Pike and Gwydeon were. Or even like Aryx was. His role was to do what was necessary, no matter the cost, and no matter the sacrifice needed. That was the decision that Logan wasn't sure he would ever be able to make. Could he sacrifice one of his friends, or leave them to fight his battles while he made an escape. Pike's head was clear and he knew exactly what needed to be done. Logan hoped that the next time, if there was a next time, he would be able to must the courage to do what Pike had done.

Pike's eyes were full of fire, and Logan knew very well that whatever he said, he meant. But there was something else. There was another layer behind the fury, something that Logan had never seen before from Pike. Fear. When they were children there were plenty of times that they had been afraid, waiting for the reprisals by their parents for their misdeeds, but this was different. This was the kind of fear that comes when a person realizes that they can no longer see anything past the next few moments. When there is no complete confidence in the mind that they will be a tomorrow. It was a fear of death, but more than that, it was an expectation that death was real and close. With a small shake of Logan's head, the point was conceded.

"Alright Pike, you're right. You're in command."

There was a brief wave of relief that passed over his face, but it was short-lived. The grim look and cold eyes returned; a quiet confidence. The fear seemed to recede for the moment.

"Good. Elwyne, Midarin, Aryx, get Logan out of Sarmeel as quick as you can. Stick to the alleys and head back out the way we came. Don't stop at the city limits, just keep going. I know we weren't very popular in Illimar, but at least there we have men to worry about and not monsters. No matter what, get Logan out alive, so do whatever you have to. If we're lucky, you can lose these things in the alleys while we hold here. We'll by you as much time as we can."

There was a look of uncertainty in Elwyne's eyes as she moved to stand my Logan's side. Pike forced a smile.

"Don't worry, Elwyne. We'll buy you as much time as we can, but this won't be the end of us. I don't fight hopeless battles. Our best chance is to get them to split their forces and come after you. If we can hold them off long enough, hopefully, when they realize you're out of the city, we can make our escape."

Pike turned away and left the building. Logan could see him move up beside Gwydeon as he focused his attention on the on-coming Jeresei. Despite his speech and the valor that he was trying to show, it was clear that Pike was not holding out much hope of his own survival. But no matter the trial ahead, Logan had to admit to himself there was no one else he would rather have at his back. Without any further delay, Elwyne, Midarin, and Aryx followed as Logan headed toward the back of the building. There was a secondary opening that led out to an alley, one that hopefully would keep them out of the line of sight of the enemy and out of combat. Without a word, Midarin took the lead, her bow ready. Elwyne never strayed from Logan's side, as much for her own protection as for his, and Aryx brought up the rear, watching everyone's flanks. As quickly as they could, the small group moved through the maze of buildings and alleys until a grassy glade was in sight. It was still quite a ways away, but it was a significant first step to safety. After another few steps, it became painfully clear that the glade was not salvation; it was a trap waiting to be sprung.

It was clear in a moment, that the group had severely underestimated the abilities of their Jeresei adversaries. The creatures had carefully planned out their plan of attack, and had stationed a significant amount of troops in the glade outside the city to prevent exactly what Logan and his group were attempting to do. Because of the size of the frontal assault, it had never occurred to Logan or to any of the others that the Jeresei would attempt any kind of strategic assault, like the pincer movement that they had apparently implemented. The group on the glade was not as large as the group advancing on Pike's position, but if they were to move to meet up with the larger force, they would easily overwhelm Pike and the others. If Logan was able to sneak passed the ambushing group, then they would move to block Pike's retreat. If Logan moved to engage the ambush, then it was possible that they would be overwhelmed. There was no right answer in the situation, and Logan had little time to come up with a plan. If they fought separately, there was a chance that everyone would fall. The best option was to make their stand together.

After stopping in an alley for several moments to make sure that the assault group had not detected their presence, Logan and the others turned back and made their way as quickly as possible back to the abandoned building where the others were making their stand. By the time Logan and the others made it back to the abandoned building where they had first encountered the Snags, Pike was starting to lead a reckless charge into the front ranks of the oncoming Jeresei. It was a bold move, one that the Jeresei would not have expected, but it was also bordering on insanity. A call went up from behind their position, and it was clear that the ambush group had tired of waiting, and was advancing.

"We make our stand here," Aryx called. "Give no quarter as none will be given. The Jeresei do not believe in mercy."

The rear force of Jeresei was nearly upon them, and everyone held their weapons, ready for combat. The moment was filled with so many emotions, fear, uncertainty, anxiety; but it all changed the next moment when first blood was drawn.

From somewhere behind Logan, there came the sound of a bowstring being drawn. An arrow leapt though the air seconds later, flying high into the darkened sky. In the advancing twilight Midarin wouldn't have been able to make out a single target in the sea of red, but there were plenty of targets in the area to be struck, and her skill as a marksman was apparent. In a matter of seconds the deadly arrow struck true. The tip of the arrow found its target, splitting the skull of one of the Jeresei. Flailing uncontrollably, the Jeresei dropped to the ground, leaving a small hole in the oncoming ranks. The nearly unnoticeable break in ranks lasted only a few moments before another of the Jeresei stepped forward and filled the gap. Rapidly, arrows flew from Midarin's bow, taking Jeresei after Jeresei in the head, throat, or some other vital organ. Usually the tip of the arrows struck true in the heart or brain, but even the ones that were evaded caused damage as they found their way into arms or legs. No matter how many of them fell, another always stepped up to take its place. There seemed to be no change in the amount of Jeresei that were quickly crashing down upon them. They just kept coming.

Hoping to seize the opportunity that Midarin's strikes had caused, Logan motioned for Elwyne to Elwyne to take shelter in the building while he motioned for Aryx to follow him. Together they broke into a sprint towards the ranks of Jeresei, Aryx's gauntlet again beginning to glow a brilliant red. Arrows still flew over their heads, striking down Jeresei, but Midarin had altered her targeting to the rear ranks of the red-skinned beasts. Logan's first target was mere feet in front of him, and the Jeresei had its claws fully extended, ready to destroy any in its path. Beside the Jeresei were a dozen more, each as blood-thirsty as the first. Aryx slowed, and let loose a volley of lightning that leapt from Jeresei to Jeresei leaving scorch marks on the chests or heads of the creatures struck. Midarin and Aryx's attacks had thinned the ranks somewhat, but there were still too many to be managed in close combat.

As soon as he closed to combat range, Logan's sword swung freely from his side, and followed a path straight toward the head of the Jeresei. It blocked the blow with its claws, and began to deliver a strike of its own. However, the Jeresei was wild and it blood lust caused it to over-extend. The Jeresei flashed its claws and slashed at Logan's head. Dropping to one knee, Logan slashed back across the chest of the beast, nearly ripping it in two. It fell to the ground, but Logan's attack pushed him into the face of another of the beasts. Pulling his blade down, Logan's steel found one of the creature's exposed knees, severing its leg there. The Jeresei flailed about as it fell, trying in vain to inflict some type of wound on its attacker. The Jeresei obviously were efficient killers for Shau-ling, they kept trying to win even after the fatal blow had been struck. This Jeresei was not yet ready to concede its trip to meet the Great Dark One. It managed to fight its way back onto its remaining leg and lunged at Logan. The wild, off-balance slash of its claws was far off the mark, and a quick upward slash sent its snarling head flying in another direction.

When another Jeresei lunged at Logan, it was only the instinctive reaction that forced his sword forward to run the vile creature through. Gwydeon had trained Logan well, and his reactions and instincts had been enough to keep him alive in the face of overwhelming odds. Logan twisted the blade deeper into the body of the Jeresei, forcing death down upon it. After he was sure that the creature was dead, Logan kicked the corpse away from his blade, gore still dripping from the blade and the smell of death hanging thick in the air. The smell of lightning also permeated the air, a lingering smell of burning unmistakable. Aryx had closed into close combat range as well, striking as many creatures down with his powers as he did with his sword.

All around them, Jeresei lay with arrows stuck in them, while others were still had smoking craters in their chests where Aryx's strikes had claimed them. Many others showed wounds consistent with a sword, while many more had their heads completely ripped off by the ferocity of Aryx's abilities. The Jeresei had fallen back from the combat, regrouping from the significant losses. Logan glanced over his shoulder and saw Midarin running toward the battle with a short sword held high in the air. At first Logan thought that the woman had run out of ammunition, but then he saw the other figures that were close behind her. The battle must have taken a turn for either good or ill, because Pike and Elwyne were only a few steps behind Midarin. However, the pause in the combat was short-lived, and Logan's attention was only able to be diverted for a moment as a sharp pain rocketed through his shoulder. The pain caused him to turn back, and Logan could see the cruel sharp features of a Jeresei smiling down at him, the claws of one of its hands still buried deeply into Logan's tender flesh.

Hot blood flowed from the wound in his shoulder, and his right arm fell limp at his side. The pain from the injury caused Logan's hand to fall limp and his sword to slide harmlessly out of his grip and to the ground. Unconsciously Logan reached for the dagger at his right hip with his left hand, and drew it quickly. He was not as adept in combat with his left hand, but given the circumstances, he didn't have much of a choice. The motion was clumsy and alerted the Jeresei to his intended strike. It leapt backward, but the claws had struck bone in Logan's shoulder, and the vicious instruments would not pull free so easily. Though there was incredible wrenching pain, and Logan flirted with unconsciousness, he took the opportunity to act against his attacker. The advantage would last for only another few seconds. Trying his best to ignore the pain coursing through his body, Logan plunged the dagger deep into the belly of the Jeresei. All he saw after that moment was a haze of red followed by darkness. Shaking away the deep desire to give into the pain, Logan's senses returned from the veil of pain, and he found his arm still stabbing the fallen Jeresei. Its chest had long since risen and fell with its last breath, but Logan could not stop the dagger from spraying more blood everywhere. Finally, as though the haze had relinquished its control on is reflexes, Logan regained control of his body.

Regardless of the return of control, the pain was almost too much for Logan to bear, and he slowly fell to both knees. The pain in his arm kept me from moving, and though he knew that staying where he was would mean his death, no matter how hard Logan tried, the pain thwarted every attempt to move from that spot. He even doubted his ability to defend himself should another of the Jeresei try to take advantage of his weakened state. Luckily, the Jeresei had suffered so many losses that their ranks were broken and Aryx was keeping them off-balance. Finally some sensation returned to his hand. He was able to move my fingers, but there was still not enough strength left to pick up his sword from where it lay beside me, let alone be able to wield it in combat. However, without his blade, the Jeresei would overwhelm him. With every ounce of strength that was left in his arm, Logan picked up his sword and slowly fought his way back to his feet. It was then that Logan realized he was completely surrounded. None of his companions were in sight, even though he could hear the explosions from Aryx's attacks in the distance. More of the Jeresei gathered as the seconds passed, massing like wolves around wounded prey. Suddenly a dark veil passed over his sight, pain from the wound on his shoulder bursting through him as he tried to take a defensive position. In his weakened state, he could not resist the pain or keep his eyes open any longer. Logan thought he was dead, and in his heart he knew he was dead.

Behind Logan's closed eyes there was nothing but darkness, and he braced for the inevitable pain that would come. However, the next moment it seemed as though he could see without opening his eyes. There were wisps of color and light floating across his line of sight, and though there was still pain, his mind was strangely at ease, and then suddenly all the pain that he was feeling was simply gone. In the new calm, Logan could feel every part of his body, down to the last hair. Even though the impression of danger was still outside the small island of calm in his mind, Logan began to feel as though he was no longer in control of his actions.

Whatever the island of calm was, and whatever force had created it, it seemed to be holding him. He could not force his way back to consciousness or open his eyes to return to the waking world. The place was so tranquil, and it seemed as if nothing could harm him there. Within no more than a few seconds, the thought of danger returned and the calm was shattered. At that moment, his eyes shot open.

Along with the consciousness of danger came the reemergence of the pain in Logan's shoulder. On the ground all around him were the bodies of dozens of Jeresei. None of them had any visible wounds, but they were dead just the same. Whatever it was that had happened, it had been while the island of calm held him, and there was no time to unravel the mystery. Before all of his senses had returned to normal, a new pain shot through his left leg. Logan fell forward, and by the time he rolled onto his back, he saw another cruel Jeresei smiling down at him. It yelled a few words in some guttural alien tongue and glared back down at Logan again. It then spoke in a low growling voice that Logan could understand.

"Your life is over, Dragon. Shau-ling will be pleased."

It laughed menacingly and spat in Logan's face. Shortly thereafter, he found himself bound in some sort of chain and surrounded by Jeresei. Two of the beasts picked me Logan up and carried him toward the building where the group had encountered the Snags. Apparently it had been designated as a holding area. The Jeresei were not gentle in their handling of their prisoner, and Logan felt as though he was being tossed around like a sack of potatoes until finally he was thrown down on a low stone table. When Logan chanced a look around, he saw a wooden cage housed the rest of my friends, and all of them were similarly chained. Aryx had been bound, gagged, and knocked unconscious. A small stream of blood flowed from his forehead, and his breathing appeared labored. After scanning the faces, Logan realized that someone was missing. It was Pike. Either he was going to be their last hope, or he was already dead. Fearing there was no other option, Logan closed his eyes and tried to replicate what had happened to on the battlefield, tried to find the island of calm that had been there in his mind. However, this time nothing awaited his closed eyes but darkness. Pain shot through Logan again, and his eyes opened to the sight of a large sword perched above him, ready to strike. There wasn't much time left.

Hidden Power

Pike screamed at the top of his voice and led the charge into the front ranks of the Jeresei. He hoped that the size of their army was nothing more than an illusion, but deep down in his heart, he knew better. Gwydeon and Gideon were far ahead of him, wading into the waves of Jeresei like they were possessed by the Great Dark One himself. Even though Gwydeon was hampered by injury, he still moved as though he was at full strength. Pike started to run as fast as he could, but he was unable to shrug off the injuries as easily as Gwydeon had. Before Pike knew what hit him, he was lying flat on his back looking up at the sky. He didn't even see a blur of motion, but it felt as though a brick wall hit him. There was a tremendous pain that flared across his chest, and he had trouble getting his breath. It felt as though every one of his ribs and his sternum had been broken. While the attacker was not apparent, Pike knew that he wouldn't have much time to get back to his feet before one of the Jeresei was on top of him. Looking for his ax, he finally found the haft, and flung his arm outward to grab it. His hand touched the wood of the haft, and just then a Jeresei stomped down on his arm at the elbow. The pain in his arm made his fingers extend, breaking his grip on his ax. Pike looked away from his ax and looked up at the face of the Jeresei.

The Jeresei's cruel and hateful smile beamed down at Pike, gleaming white teeth displaying startling malice. The rage built up inside of Pike every second that he looked at the cruel inhuman face. The desire to see the Jeresei's broken body lying at his feet coursed through his veins. The rage inside of Pike made him more powerful than a dozen Jeresei. He grabbed the Jeresei's leg with his free arm and pulled the creature off its feet. The Jeresei's head crashed to the ground with such force that its skull shattered, sending blood and brains out a wound in the back of its head. Pike jumped to his feet, all of the pain in his body forgotten, and recovered his axe where it still lay on the now blood-soaked ground. The bloodlust was upon him, and his only thought was of the accursed Jeresei and watching as many of them die as possible. He was still at the edge of the battle that had been raging on, but for the forces of the Light, the battle was looking grim. Everyone except for Pike had been captured by the Jeresei, and somehow, during the scuffle with the now dead creature, Pike had escaped the greater force's notice. Pike ran to the shadows of one of the buildings and waited. Rushing in now would only result in his capture and the death of everyone else in the group. What puzzled Pike was why the Jeresei even bothered taking prisoners to begin with. What was there to gain? He looked around and saw Logan's force charging another phalanx of Jeresei. He had to warn Logan. Pike grasped his axe tightly and ran as fast as his feet would carry him toward Logan. The ranks of Jeresei closed around Logan like a fog, and then suddenly there was a burst of light, and dozens of Jeresei had fallen. Whatever time the outburst had given him, Logan seemed frozen, and it only took a few seconds for more of the red-skinned beasts to surround and restrain him. Then the purpose of the capture became clear. Watching from the seclusion of the shadows again, Pike watched as Logan was carried to a low slab of stone and the Jeresei prepared to execute the would-be savior of the world. The Jeresei were about to win the battle once and for all for their master. This execution would shatter the faith of the other captives, proving once and for all that the forces of the Shadows were stronger.

Rage grew within Pike hotter and hotter, as if there was a fire that burned within him, and the brighter it burned, the more it threatened to consume him. The burning rage begged to be released, and it pulled at the last strings of his control and fought for its freedom. Pike suddenly felt his whole body go numb, as if the rage was wrestling with his conscious mind for control of his body. His hands throbbed, gripping tight around the haft of the axe. Whatever was fighting against him then caused his hands to relax, causing the axe to slip from his hands. Feeling light-headed, Pike felt his eyes close, and the whole world as he knew it began to change. Behind the veil of darkness, he felt his arms extend out in front of him, and he knew that something was happening outside the dark world. The white hot violent rage that held him suddenly melted away, replaced by a striking cold. The wave of numbness penetrated every part of Pike's body, down to the bone. The wave of cold brought new sensations, not the least of which was uncertainty and fear. Pike fought against his eyelids, trying to break the void that held his vision. Whether he won the battle, or he was released, Pike didn't know, but when his eyes opened, he was greeted by an astounding sight.

Pike's hands moved wildly in front of him, but he had no control over the seemingly useless movements. Then, water began to spew from his outstretched fingertips. From the shores of the ocean, a large tidal wave began to form. The small leading waves crashed against the shore, sending sand and rock flying in all directions. As the seconds passed, the waves grew in size and strength, penetrating further inland with each iteration. Finally, Pike could see the largest of the waves, one that towered high into the sky, and one that would easily cover the entire city of Sarmeel when it struck. This final wave built, Pike regained control of his body.

"What the hell?"

Knowing what was coming, Pike ran toward the ranks of confused and awestruck Jeresei. Their impending doom obvious, the Jeresei began to break and run. With the Jeresei distracted, Pike was able to make his way into the building and release the party who were chained and caged. Once everyone was freed, including Logan who had been chained to the stone slab, the party fled toward one of the larger and more intact nearby buildings.

* * * * * * * * * * * *

"Everyone," Pike yelled over the sound of the approaching wave, "get inside that building and make your way to the cellar."

There were shocked looks all around as the group fled the confinement of the Jeresei and out into the streets of Sarmeel. There were gasps of disbelief at the sight of the huge cresting wave. Once the wave came into view, it was clear why the Jeresei were running. Without a word, the group made their way to the large building that Pike had indicated. Near the center of a small room off the entrance to the building was a trap door that led to a cellar. Pike was the last down the stairs, and he slammed the trap door shut behind him. Somehow Pike had known that the cellar was there, and somehow he knew that it would offer the protection they needed from the massive wave. Once in the cellar, Pike continued to hold the door shut, and there was an air of uncertainty that filled the small dark room. Lane managed to mumble a quiet incantation and conjured a small light that sat in the palm of his outstretched hand. Above them, Logan could hear the shuffling of feet, as it was obvious that some of the Jeresei had followed the group into the building in an attempt to find shelter from the impending disaster. Something jerked at the cellar door, nearly pulling Pike off his feet. Logan and Aryx joined Pike at the cellar door, Logan holding the handle along with Pike while Aryx took hold of Pike's belt and pulled downward. They could hear curses above them, but there was another sound. A terrible din was growing, a rumbling that rivaled the hungriest stomach. The wave was coming, and it was hungry to devour Sarmeel.

"Everyone down, cover up," Pike yelled above the growing din.

Eldar pulled Elwyne down, and Talon threw himself over both of the women. Midarin pushed herself back into a corner and Gwydeon shielded her with his body. Gideon also pushed himself into an incredibly tight corner, and all waited for what was coming. Then it happened. There was a thunderous crash, and it felt as though the ground above and below them rolled as though they were on a ship being buffeted by an angry ocean. Screams of pain and horror barely rose above the sound of shattering wood and glass, and then were gone. All that was left was a strange, eerie creaking sound that emitted from the house, and the walls themselves seemed to be swaying from side to side like hanging clothes in a strong wind. Some water spilled down through the cracks in the cellar door, while still more tried to flood in from a crack in the foundation above them. At first the flow of water being forced into the cellar was strong, and then it began to slow to only a trickle. In a matter of minutes, the horrible sound of groaning stone and twisting metal was gone. Pike let go of the handle of the cellar door and wiped his brow.

"Okay everyone," Pike said softly, "everything is fine now. We're safe."

After a few moments of confusion and some disbelief, Pike pushed the cellar door opened, and another flood of water rushed in from above, but the torrent was short-lived. Brushing his soaked hair out of his eyes, Pike pulled himself up through the opening, and helped each member of the group back to the surface. The tall building that had once been above the cellar was simply gone. There were pieces of walls still standing, and piles of debris could be seen everywhere. The most shocking sight was the broken bodies of Jeresei that had been slammed into walls and rocks, spines and necks snapped, faces contorted into eternal monuments to the horror that they had experienced in the last moments of their existence. All around them, the scene was the same. Buildings lay, broken shells of their former selves, and new streams of water ran through the streets around the flotsam. The ground floors of some of the buildings looked more like lakes with irregular stone outcroppings surrounding their borders. The massive wave had wiped away what once had been the city of Sarmeel. Now it was nothing more than a flooded ruin, and a den of painful memory. There were no living Jeresei anywhere to be seen, and Logan inwardly wondered how many of the creatures had been able to escape the devastation.

Despite the cover that they were able to find in the cellar, enough water had flooded in that most of the members of the group were soaked, and the advancing night brought a cold wind that chilled them to the bone. Luckily Talon and Gideon had been able to recover some bundles of kindling and firewood from the cellar where they had taken shelter, and after some looking, the group was able to find a dry enough spot to set up a camp. One of the buildings close to the center of town had apparently been built on a very small hill, but it was enough of an elevation change that the gathering water flowed away from the broken foundation. The ground was moist, but it was not holding water, which allowed for their small fire to flourish. Everyone was exhausted and wounded to some degree; however the worst of the wounds was to Logan's shoulder. Elwyne did her best to mend the wound, but it would be several days before it was mended enough for Logan to fight at full strength. It seemed that none of them had escaped being wounded in some way or another, and as Logan looked around the faces of his friends, he could see the exhaustion and the pain on their faces. The confrontation with the Jeresei had taken a toll on everyone.

Everyone's clothes had been stained with blood, and while the greatest majority of it had come from the Jeresei, some of it was also their own. Eldar's shirt had been ripped at the stomach where one of the Jeresei had cleanly raked its claws. The bloody wounds were not sharp, but they were clearly there. Even Lane and Elwyne had not been above the fray. Lane had a deep gash in his forehead, and Elwyne's lip and nose had been bloodied. Logan felt as though he could have slept for a week, and from the looks on the faces of his companions, the sentiment was shared. There had been some bandages and some sort of medicinal herbs down in the cellar as well, and Elwyne was trying to ration them to ensure that the most serious injuries were treated first. Whatever the herbs were, Logan could feel them have an immediate effect on his shoulder. The pain was almost completely gone in a matter of minutes, and a cool soothing feeling spread down through his arm. He was even able to close his hand tightly without feeling like he was going to pass out. One thought that Logan could not shake was the fact that it was incredibly convenient that everything they had needed seemed to be waiting for them in the cellar that Pike led them to, right down to some dried fruit and trail rations. Pike stayed away from the group for a while, making the excuse of needing to scout for surviving Jeresei, to ensure that they would not be surprised in the deepening night. Once he finally returned to the camp and sat, Talon offered him a bottle of old wine that had also been secreted away in the cellar. Pike took a long drink and relaxed back. Midarin was the one to break the silence.

"Would someone mind telling me what just happened?"

"The powers of the *Erieal* are mysterious indeed," Lane commented.

"The what?" Midarin asked.

"*Erieal*," Talon replied, "old legends that obviously aren't so legendary."

"Whatever it was," Midarin said looking at Pike, "thank you."

Pike balked.

"I wish I could take credit. Whatever happened, wherever that wave came from, I know that it came from me, but I didn't do it."

"That's how it is at first," Aryx replied. "The power is part of you, but no matter how strong you think you are, the power is stronger. It starts as a reflex, coming in times of danger or when death is imminent. In time though, you will be able to understand it, and to summon it. The power wants to be controlled, but it's so overwhelmingly strong that it can sometimes take every ounce of will you have just to summon the smallest fragment of it."

"Aryx," Logan asked his own flirtation with unexplained power fresh in his mind, "I've seen a sample of the powers of the *Erieal* through you, but I wasn't aware that the *Erieal* had the kind of power that Pike just demonstrated."

"That's because of this."

Aryx took the brilliant golden gauntlet off his hand and laid it on the ground beside Logan. The golden light faded the second it left his hand.

"Pick it up, Logan," Aryx said coolly.

Reaching down, Logan took hold of the gauntlet. The harder he pulled, the heavier the gauntlet seemed to become. Again and again his attempts to lift the seemingly light piece of metal were met with failure.

"This is what Lord Cedric calls a *Debuisa*, or a controller. It's the metal that is special, and it was fashioned into the form of a gauntlet to make it more functional for me. It was fashioned similarly for Lord Arathorn, but was made into a less cumbersome form for Mailock and Diana. The metal has what have been described to me as divine power that thrives on the natural abilities of the *Erieal*. Before you can understand how it works, you have to understand the power itself," Aryx replied.

"It's about time," Pike grumbled.

Aryx stared a Pike coldly for a moment and then smiled.

"As I've told you before, the powers of the *Erieal* revolve around the four main forces of nature; Earth, Fire, Wind, and Water. I have found that in my generation of *Erieal*, my powers over the sphere of Fire tend to be more powerful than the others. However, in all of our travels, I never saw

Mailock do anything like Pike just did. I would imagine that from generation to generation, the level of power in each of the *Erieal* would change, so no one sphere would have more power than any of the others."

"Before you go on," Pike said slowly, "I'd like to know what it felt like when you first used your powers without the *Debuisa*."

"Well, I actually had no control over what was happening to me. Everything went black and I felt a strange sensation move through my arms. My eyes flew open and I was shocked to see bolts of lightning flying from my outstretch fingers. It happened a few more times when I had no control. Soon enough, I learned to work with what was happening to me, and I could actually control it partially. Then, when I met Lord Cedric, I could control my powers better than I ever could before."

"That must mean that the *Coromor* is in some way a focal point for the powers of the *Erieal*," Lane commented.

"As Mailock has also come to believe over the years. Then, during one of our many journeys, Lord Cedric discovered an armory filled with magical items, and within it was a smithy that defied description. Living within the smelting pots was a red, worm-like creature that possessed an incredible intelligence, capable of crafting any items imaginable. They were aware of whom and what we were and they gave each of us a *Debuisa*. These allow us to control our powers and release them with just a thought. The way it has been explained to me, the *Coromor* helps to act as a lens which focuses the power of the *Erieal* and makes it easier to establish control. The *Debuisa* has a similar effect, allowing powers to be used more like a needle and less like a sledgehammer. It's the difference between creating a wave that can destroy a city, and channeling just enough water to fill a cup. The latter is not possible for an *Erieal* without some kind of assistance."

"Why does the *Debuisa* change color when you're angry," Talon asked.

"Yes, the powers of the *Erieal* feed off of the emotions of the person. Usually the stronger the hate and anger in an *Erieal*, the easier it is to release their power. However, other emotions can trigger the release as well. That is why the color of the *Debuisa* changes when the power is triggered. You see, mine glows red because my power is that of Fire. Mailock's turns blue,

Arathorn's green, and Diana's becomes as colorless as the wind. The color of the metal is usually gold or silver, in order for the wearer to be sure of the color change."

"So you're telling me that I won't be able to control my powers until I get one of these *Debuisa* things?" Pike said disgusted.

"Not necessarily," Aryx replied. "As long as you are around Logan, you should have a fairly good degree of control. I will help the three of you learn some basics on your own. However, until the fourth of the *Erieal* is in our midst, we cannot even begin the assault on Shau-ling's palace. Some of the most potent powers that can be used by the *Erieal* are cast by all four at the same time. In those moments, the power wielded by the *Coromor* is more than Shau-ling could possibly sustain."

"Dat be all well an' good, Aryx," Gideon remarked, "but what say ye if we dinnae find da fourth?"

"I hadn't thought about that possibility," Aryx replied slowly, "Mailock always believed that..."

"Mailock dis, Mailock dat," Gideon interrupted, "Who da 'ell is dis flintin' Mailock?"

"He is a very wise man, and you would be a fool to question him."

"Wise man, eh? Well den, Light forbid a wise man be insulted by da like o' me."

"You are trying my patience, Gideon," Aryx bellowed, "do not make me show you my true power."

Gideon rose and pulled his shirt quickly over his head and dropped several knife sheaths to the ground.

"Been wantin' ta try ye old man. White Lighnin' da great an' powerful. We know better, don't we, Aryx. Yer nothin' but a fraud. A coward."

Aryx rose in a fit of anger. This was no game to him. His sword fell to the ground quickly, and the golden gauntlet was back on his hand in a heartbeat. The instant the metal touched his skin, its color changed to a deep red. Everything in Aryx's manner said that he fully intended to kill Gideon. There was no way that Gideon stood a chance against Aryx's awesome powers. A scream of rage burst from Aryx's chest, and he thrust his hand toward the heavens. Storm clouds began to roll in from the sea. Fearing the worst, Logan rose, about to intervene, but Pike held him back.

"This is their fight, Logan," he said, "let them finish it. I want to see what Gideon can do. Something tells me there is more to him than what he's been telling us."

Logan nodded and stepped back, watching the two men move away from the rest of the group to give room for their battle. When Logan looked over at Gideon again, his eyes were closed and his hands were extended to the ground. Suddenly, columns of rock began to shoot up all around him. Seconds later, Aryx's lightning attack struck. The vicious white lightning shot from the heavens and sped toward their intended target. However, the lightning struck the raised towers of rock instead of Gideon. The thief had been prepared for the assault that Aryx had planned, and the fact that Gideon was able to summon the columns so quickly made Logan believe that it was not the first time Gideon had done so. But the battle was not to end there; Gideon still had something to prove. Moments later Gideon launched an attack of his own. The earth began to shake and groan at the intense power exerted upon it. Out of the ground, a large boulder grew. Gideon raised his hands into the air, and the boulder was lifted off the ground. The large piece of rock sped toward its target until it hovered over Aryx's head. Despite the apparent danger, Aryx did not move a muscle. He moved the glowing red gauntlet to his chest and closed his eyes. The boulder fell upon its target a moment later. A foot from Aryx's head, the boulder disintegrated with a flash of lightning. After the expulsion of power Gideon needed to create the columns and the boulder, he fell to his knees in complete exhaustion. Aryx went to one knee and let his now-golden gauntlet fall to the ground. The battle between the *Erieal* had ended in a stalemate. Gideon crawled over to where Aryx sat and extended his hand. Aryx regarded Gideon for a moment and then took his hand, completing the truce. It took them a few moments to get back to their feet, but with the other's help they soon made their way back to the fire.

"So," Gideon asked sitting and taking along drink, "what do ya think?"

"If the fourth *Erieal* is as powerful as you and Pike are, Shau-ling won't know what hit him. I don't want to challenge Talon, not even when I recover from this one. In fact with his power, I doubt I would survive."

Talon cocked his head and a wide smile spread across his face.

"From each generation to the next, as I said, there must be balance. In my generation, while my power was the strongest, the powers of my wife, Diana, was the weakest. So, in order to maintain the necessary balance in this generation, the Fire *Erieal* in this generation will be the weakest, and the Wind *Erieal*, you Talon, will be the strongest. Even as the weakest, using Pike and Gideon as an example, it's quite possible that the Fire *Erieal* of this generation will be stronger than me."

"First we have to find him," Logan commented.

"Yes," Aryx answered, "but for now we should sleep. Tomorrow we should make for Falke. It will be many days travel on foot, but once there, the first half of our journey shall be complete. We should move at first light."

It didn't seem that sleeping was going to be difficult for any member of the group, even with the amount of pain that so many were in. Aryx chose to keep watch during the night. Logan lay on his back near the fire. A few moments after he closed my eyes, Logan felt Elwyne snuggle up beside him and rest her head upon my chest. Stroking her hair, he looked up at the full moon in the cloudless sky above them. The tumultuous time in Sarmeel had ended, and for the first time since they arrived, the eeriness and foreboding was gone. For the rest of the night, Logan faded in and out of sleep, spending most of his waking moments stroking Elwyne's hair and taking comfort in the fact that she was close to him. The night wind was cold, and Logan could feel Elwyne try to snuggle closer to him every time the wind blew. Though hours passed, part of Logan wished that night would last forever. When first light broke over the hills to the east, the party slowly roused from their slumber and beheld the beautiful sunrise over the ruins of Sarmeel. Whatever evil pall had once shrouded the place was gone, and only valiant memories remained. While there was still a long road ahead, hope was becoming their strongest ally.

Chapter VI

Myth and Legend

A cold wind blew across the plain as the wayward and exhausted company made their way out of the ruins of Sarmeel. The shipwreck of the Raging Storm had robbed them of any chance of a fast trip to Falke, and there were no safe places to stop to acquire horses for the rest of the travel, at least none that the party was aware of. Now that they were confined to travel on foot, the trip to Falke would take over three times as long, and the most troubling part of the upcoming journey was the fact that most of the trip would be across vast plains. Wide-open areas, especially when a possible adversary could fly great distances and blanket an area with liquid fire, were not appealing. A group of Shadowwalkers would have no problem picking the group off one by one, and moreover, a mass of Jeresei would be able to overwhelm them. Of course, any threat would be able to be seen coming, but without cover, the creatures that served Shau-ling would have a distinct advantage. Even with the power of the *Erieal* at their disposal, there were no were no guarantees of the kind of success that Aryx had at Aradon, or that Pike had at Sarmeel.

The morning sun did little to fend off the incredible biting cold of the early morning wind, but the sun's rays were a welcome respite from the long nightmarish storm. Remnants of the storm could still be seen on the horizon, a mass of blackness hanging over the ocean to the north. The group could have followed the coast to Falke, but that path was far too difficult to be handled on foot. However, there were several paths that wound their way across plains, and over small hills. Making their way slowly down the dirt road out of Sarmeel, Logan turned to regard the city once more that had been the site of so much destruction. The once great towers of Sarmeel were now nothing more than a few scattered pieces of wood, broken foundations, and crumbled ruins. After scanning the horizon for a moment, Logan returned his attention to the road. The wide-open plain and gentle rolling hills made the road seem like it stretched on forever. All clouds, except for those hanging over the coast had been burned away by the bright and hot sun. Traveling down the dirt road was long, monotonous, and exhausting. Many of the group had suffered wounds from the battle in Sarmeel, and even with the medicinal herbs that had been discovered in the cellar that had served as a refuge during the tidal wave's strike; the injuries were slowing their journey considerably. Gwydeon's wounds by far were the most severe, and were affecting the group's pace. However, Talon still seemed to be in the most pain, and he winced with nearly every footfall. Pike too was worse for his experiences, but he carried himself as though he did not feel the weight of his injuries. Aryx on the other hand appeared to be more annoyed with the situation than concerned for their predicament. In his time in the service of Lord Cedric he had been called upon to do many unpleasant things, and war and death were simply unavoidable realities. What was clear was that Aryx had dedicated himself to his duty, and his sense of duty was driving him forward. His duty was to his Lord, and to the mission that the Lion had sent him on. That mission, and the fate of the world were driving the party forward, at least most of them.

Aside from Midarin and Gideon, the whole of the party knew what was at stake. All of the heartache and loss, all of the pain that they had experienced, weighed heavily on Logan's mind. Long ago, when Logan was just a boy, he had always dreamed of being a knight. It was a shared dream among several members of the group; Gwydeon, Pike, Talon, David, and Logan. Out of the lot of them, Gwydeon always seemed the most deserving. He practiced with the sword so many hours every day that it began to seem the piece of metal was permanently affixed to his hand. Pike and Talon never showed that same kind of dedication, and neither did David, but for completely different reasons. David was a smart and dedicated young man, but his dedication was to his job, as well as to his family. David's father never would have allowed David to be a soldier. He would bide his time working as an apprentice blacksmith until such time as David's father wanted him to begin interjecting himself into the political arena. David's path was set from the moment he was born. Logan's on the other hand was not. He grew up in a quiet household with his father, and they both worked the fields for most the day every day. Once he entered his teenage years, Logan's thoughts turned away from the farm to other priorities. And as much as he tried, one of those priorities was not the sword. He was more interested in winning Elwyne's favor than in perfecting his sword techniques. Gwydeon was a solid enough teacher, having learned much from his own father and Logan's father Arin. While Logan didn't know much about his father's military background, his skill was clear, and now that Logan understood how much favor the Lord Lion showed for him carried a lot of weight in the backward little farm town that they had all grown up in.

Pike and Talon were never interested in the sword. Talon eventually started training with Gwydeon, more because the girls of Aradon would linger around the training grounds than because he wanted to become a master swordsman. Pike fell in love with his ax when he worked in the forests with his father in the summer helping the town stock up on firewood for the winter. Logan had asked Pike once about the axe, and he told Logan that Gwydeon had always said that when you find the weapon that is right for you, it talks to you. Pike told Logan that every time he held that axe in his hands, he felt like a different person, as though there was something inside him wanting to get out. Sometimes, it almost seemed to scare him, and the fear was apparent in his eyes. Logan could remember a time just before Logan left Aradon. He had wanted to tell Pike what he had been planning, but something had happened with Pike, and he was far angrier than he usually was. Logan eventually found him just inside the boundary of the Mithacarthian Woods, swinging his axe as hard as he could at one of the largest trees that Logan had ever seen. If Logan could have stood in the center of the tree with his arms outstretched, he doubted he would have been able to touch both sides with his fingertips. Logan watched him for a long time, just chopping away at the tree, for what seemed like hours. There was a moment when the gigantic tree shuddered, and Logan couldn't believe what he was seeing. Finally, there was groaning and cracking sound from deep within the tree and there was a moment when Logan found he was holding his breath. Then the tree began to fall.

It crashed to the ground, bringing limbs and leaves falling from other trees, and Pike stood there, the axe still in his hands. Though he was exhausted and could barely lift his arms, Logan could tell from the fire and pain in his eyes that Pike could have willed himself to do it all over again. When he finally dropped his axe, all of that power flooded from his body and Pike fell to the ground laughing. Now that it had been revealed that Pike was a member of the *Erieal* he had more power at his disposal, and after the demonstration at Sarmeel, it was a power that seemed to rival even Aryx's control over lightning. And if what Aryx said was true, that the powers of the *Erieal* were fueled by strong emotion, Logan was sure that Pike would be able to create enough tidal waves to drown the world before all of his rage was expended.

By the time the sun began to sink low on the horizon, the group was more than ready to set up camp for the night. After several hours of travel, a small grove of trees entered the field of view, and seemed as though it would make a suitable camp site for the night. It would give them a small measure of cover, as well as provide material for a fire. What they didn't know until they had actually broken the tree line was that there was a small pond in the center of the wood that seemed to be a favorite spot of the local wildlife, judging from the tracks. While Gideon hunted down a few rabbits for their dinner, Aryx's experience as a woodsman allowed him to identify some edible plants and berries to complement their meal. Aryx had told them of his time as a hunter and wanderer before he entered the service of Lord Cedric, and apparently there were many more facets to the man than he let be known. Aryx Terian was a hero of the greatest war the world had ever known, and for most people, that is where their knowledge stopped. Getting to know the man, as Logan and the others were getting the opportunity to do on this journey, a rare glimpse into the reality behind the legend.

Before Logan's father had died, he had regaled Logan and his friends with tales about the war. Though his tales were always filled with wonder and bloodshed, sometimes he would tell about the great heroes of the war. What Logan didn't know then, but had discovered from Aryx was that Arin's stories weren't gleaned from traders, bards, and other soldiers as he had always claimed. The stories had instead come from Arin's own experiences as a member of the Lion's Mane. Most of the time, all Logan wanted to hear about was the Lord Lion or Arathorn Geoffry, the greatest of the heroes of the War of the Lion. However, for every story of Cedric or Arathorn, there was a story about the mysterious White Lightning, Aryx Terian. His background was shrouded in mystery, and Arin only said once that Aryx had joined the quest against Shau-ling under dubious circumstances. But regardless of the cautions of Lord Cedric's inner circle, Cedric never outwardly doubted the man who would carve a legacy for himself. After a while, it seemed that the name White Lightning was everywhere. Arin had always told Logan that if there was an important mission that had to be done, Cedric would always send Aryx. That was the kind of trust that Cedric had for Aryx. The man had the reputation for getting things done, no matter the cost, and no matter the trial. Obviously that was why he was tasked with extracting Logan from Aradon, and not a full detachment of the Lion's Mane. It was clear though that the position as the problem-solver for the great Lord Lion was not at all an enviable position.

Then again, Logan was starting to not envy his own position. Growing up, Logan and the others had all dreamed of adventures, fighting dragons, searching for buried treasure, killing an evil wizard. Even with all the war stories, we only saw the glamour of fame, never the cost. It wasn't until David became a victim of something they couldn't understand that the price of their arrogance began to sink in. They had learned that there was a price to be paid for success in their cause, and they still didn't know the full extent of that price. They could see the end of the road, but as Logan began to add up the cost in his mind, and projected that forward, it further clouded their destination. The fact that the powers of the *Erieal* as well as the powers that Logan himself possessed were starting to reveal themselves were a small ray of hope in the dismal night, but it barely pierced the growing darkness. But Sarmeel had also taught Logan something, something that could not be denied. They were still alive, and as long as they were willing to fight, they could prevail.

Within an hour of stopping for the night, the moon and the stars had begun to take over the sky. There was a little underbrush that easily served as a cushion to lie upon, and there was no need to sacrifice trees for shelter with the cloudless sky. Almost everyone found a spot to lay there head almost immediately, trying to leave enough space for some privacy. Despite the cold winds that had buffeted them for the majority of the day, the temperature that night was moderate enough that the party chose not to build a fire. Elwyne and Logan lay down together, and she snuggled up to him as she had the previous night and nearly instantly had fallen asleep. As with the previous night, however, Logan could not succumb to sleep easily. As soon as he was sure he could move without disturbing Elwyne, Logan got up and walked slowly through the grove to the small pond.

The full silver moon shone brightly in the sky, and the beams of light reflected off the placid water, giving that part of the grove an almost silvery glow. There were many of the small animals that Aryx had indicated earlier scurrying about. For the most part though, it seemed that the grove was refuge for some, home for no one. After a few moments, Logan began to feel that it was too quiet, but he shook his head and scolded himself for jumping at shadows. There were enough real threats waiting for them out in the world, there was no need to invent more. There was a large hollow log near the back of the pond that looked like a good place to sit down and think. Admittedly, the rough bark was not comfortable at first, but Logan got used to it after a few moments. Logan sat for a long time reflecting, most of his thoughts having nothing to do with their journey. No matter where his thoughts started, they eventually always took him back to Elwyne. His feelings for her ran deep. There was a sound from behind him that shook him away from his distraction, and when he turned, he was not expecting the face that he found.

The fallen princess, Midarin Rice, moved wordlessly to the log where Logan sat, and sat on the other end, looking over the water.

"What are you doing out here?" Logan asked.

"I suppose I could ask you the same question, Logan. But from what I've been able to gather from the conversations I've been privy to, you have a lot on your mind."

Logan nodded.

"I just needed some time to think."

"Would you like me to leave you alone?" she asked.

"No," Logan said after a moment. "But you still haven't answered my question. What are you doing out here?"

"Looking for you."

"Really?" Logan replied, confused.

She drew a small dagger from her belt and began to slowly digging its point into the log. She looked back out on the lake and sighed.

"I think you owe me an explanation."

Logan frowned and nodded his head. He had wondered when this question would be coming. Obviously it had been in Midarin's interests to tag along during the escape from Illimar, but Logan was sure that once they reached Falke, the she would have gone her own way. But now, after Sarmeel, after what she had seen, and heard, she had to have a million questions running through her mind.

"You're right. You've put your life at risk for us, and the least I can do is be straight with you about why," Logan said softly.

"I take it that this has something to do with the fact that Aryx Terian is with you," Midarin posed.

Logan smiled.

"Did you know who he was before you heard one of us mention his name?"

Midarin nodded.

"Back in Brea," Midarin replied, "the major dignitaries of all kingdoms would come through periodically. Especially when my parents were searching for suitors for my hand. I remember the day that Lord Cedric came to Brea. My parents were so excited. They thought for a moment that perhaps he would welcome marrying me. An alliance like that would have combined the kingdoms of Marcwell and Brea into a single entity. Of course, that wasn't the reason for his visit. He was there for the military pacts to defend against another war. Aryx Terian was with him then, but I doubt he would remember me. I was still just a girl then."

Logan smiled.

"I'm sure he remembers you, he seems to remember everything, but he doesn't seem like the kind to bring things up unless absolutely necessary."

Midarin laughed at the thought.

"So," Logan continued. "You know what Lord Cedric was; you know why he was important?"

Midarin stared at Logan.

"I would know better than most. My parents involved me with all discussions with heads of state, so I got to hear it from Lord Cedric's own mouth. He talked about the prophecies, and he talked about the new war with the Shadows that was coming. I remember him talking about the coming of the Dragon, his successor."

Logan's glance fell to the ground. Suddenly his throat was impossibly tight.

"Is that you?" Midarin asked.

He could tell she was trying to be delicate and respectful. Logan tried to speak, tried to give voice to his thoughts, but his throat would not cooperate. Finally he could do nothing else but nod. Midarin regarded Logan for a long moment, no expression on her face. Then she reached out and put her hand on his shoulder, for only a moment.

"So we're going to have people trying to kill us every step of the way."

It wasn't a question; it was a statement of fact. It was more than that though. With that one comment, Midarin had thrown her support behind the quest, and was going to accompany the group for as long as it was possible.

"Is Elwyne your wife?"

Midarin's question took him completely by surprise.

"No," he managed to answer, "but I love her very much, and I hope one day she will be."

Midarin smiled, but then her features suddenly went cold.

"Love is your way of shielding yourself for everything that's going on around you. You will be fighting to protect your loved ones, protect your friends that you love, avenging the dead that you loved. But if you aren't careful love is what is going to get you killed. You don't have that luxury, just as I had to think about duty over love, so do you. Love is a burden, and it is a weakness. With the type of adversaries that lay ahead, do you think that the forces of the Shadow will hesitate for a moment to use Elwyne against you if they have the chance?"

Logan was dumbfounded, but he could not shake the fact that everything she was saying was absolutely true.

"You have to admit to yourself that your attachment to anyone in the group, even your friends, Pike and Talon, are a risk. There is going to be a point where you are going to have to leave everyone behind and walk on your own, not only to protect yourself, but to protect them."

Logan began to get angry. He wasn't angry at Midarin, or himself, he was angry at the cruel twist of fate that had saddled him with the mantle of the *Coromor*, and put so many people that he loved at risk.

"You're right Midarin. Even if I survive the battle with Shau-ling, I probably will not live long enough to enjoy the victory. Lord Cedric, the last *Coromor*, developed a sickness that is slowly killing him. This sickness was directly related with him defeating Shau-ling. There is a good chance that this will happen to me."

She nodded somberly.

"I appreciate that you care enough to bring this information to my attention, and I'm going to do everything I can to protect both you and my friends from the thorns of fate that I will have to walk through. Elwyne has chosen to stay by my side, regardless of the difficulties ahead, and regardless of whether it is love or loyalty, I have to respect that devotion. I feel the same about the rest of my friends, just as I do about you and Gideon and Aryx."

She thought for a moment and then smiled.

"You're a good man, Logan," she replied. "We're lucky you were the one chosen."

She disappeared into the night and Logan was left with his thoughts again. Eventually he returned to Elwyne's sleeping form and held her through the rest of the night. As Logan expected, no sleep found him yet again, and when Aryx's call came the next morning, he was ready for the journey to continue, but was still unable to shake the exhaustion.

Continuing down the road, Logan noticed that Gideon was no longer with the party. The revelation was a concern until Aryx informed everyone that Gideon had left at the crack of dawn to scout the road ahead. Gideon didn't seem the type to wait around, nor was he a great lover of company. There was no sign of Gideon, or his track, until about mid-day, and Logan saw his familiar form coming over a hill just ahead of them. He was running very fast, and by a gleam of light coming from one of his hands, it was obvious that his weapons were drawn. He made his way back to where the group had come to a halt and dropped to his knees in exhaustion. The words that came out of his mouth were broken by heavy gasps for air.

"Over…next ridge…two towns….huge…battle…"

There were dumbfounded looks all around.

"Hold on a minute," Logan said brushing away the barrage of questions that came the next moment, "give the man a chance to catch his breath."

Everyone backed off and allowed Gideon to regain his composure. He caught his breath and then stood straight again. Then, he sheathed his daggers and began to speak.

"Thanks," he replied finally in his thickly accented voice. "Dere's a huge battle goin' on over da next ridge. Dere be two towns on either side o' a river. Armies be marching on each other, and dey looked about ta charge on me way back."

"Opinions?" Logan asked looking at Aryx.

"Well," Pike said scratching his head with the haft of his ax, "I don't see a reason for getting ourselves caught up in a battle that doesn't concern us. We have enough people trying to kill us already, I don't want to make any more enemies."

"I know it's not like me to disagree with Pike," Talon asserted, "but I gotta say this seems like an opportunity. If we help one of the sides win, then maybe we'll have an ally for once that is here with us instead of sitting in some tower in Marcwell. It'd be nice to have a couple dozen soldiers with us for the trip to Falke."

"I don't know, Talon," Logan said slowly, "but I have to admit, you do have a point."

Pike smacked Talon on the back of the head.

"And who says you're brainless?"

Eldar and Elwyne couldn't help but laugh.

"What do you think, Aryx?" Logan asked, turning his attention back toward the more experienced soldier.

"The decision has to be yours, Logan. Remember, if you take a risk this far away from Shau-ling's palace, and so early in the journey, there is a good chance that you will not see its completion."

"We'll have to deal with that when the time comes," Logan replied, dismissing Aryx's warning. "Gideon, lead the way, let's see if we can find some allies."

With Gideon leading the way, the group quickened their pace, and before too long, were standing on the very hilltop where Gideon had made his discovery. There, in the valley below were two of the most beautiful towns that many of the group had seen in all of their travels.

The buildings of the towns seemed to be made of solid gold. Brilliant beams from the mid-day sun reflected off the metallic buildings and lit the whole valley with its splendor. The light was nearly blinding if a beam of it hit your eyes, but from the angle high on the ridge, the light was breathtaking, not harmful. In between the two towns, there was what appeared to be a large plain bisected by a dry riverbed. There were three bridges that crossed over the chasm, and an mysterious, albeit scintillating light coming from the structure of the bridges themselves. The valley surrounding and separating the towns was a lush green that moved softly in the breeze, and off to the north of the towns was a huge grove of Seluiyn trees. Scanning the lush valley, Logan quickly found the reason for a lack of wildlife. Near the foot of the hill were two armies of men. One of the armies was dressed in brilliant white, while the other in green. Both armies bore the symbol of a lion on their standards, shields, and armor, obviously in reference to Lord Cedric. At first Logan thought it was a training exercise until the first killing blow was struck. Whatever the difference between these two peoples, they both seemed to be killing in the name of the Lion. Suddenly, Logan felt a stinging pain in his neck, and everything went black.

Conscripted

Logan awoke in a dark cell his head throbbing and his neck feeling as though it had been bent in several unnatural directions. He tried to sit up, but the feeling of faintness overwhelmed him and all he could see were stars in his field of vision. He laid his head back down on the thin pillow, closing his eyes and trying to will away the pain. When he opened his eyes again, his field of vision was clear. The stone-walled room he was in was made up of cold dark-gray stones, and he lay upon what felt like a wooden plank. When Logan moved his feet to try to take some of the pressure off his lower back, one of his feet hit the thick chain that held the far corner of the plank that Logan lay upon. It was clear that the wooden plank was bolted into the wall on one side and was supported on the other side by large thick chains. The bed would have easily supported several hundred pounds, but was certainly not designed for any level of comfort. When Logan sat up again, he did so slowly enough that he was able to avoid the wave of nausea and disquiet that had waited for him on his first attempt. There was a small amount of light coming from a window just above where he was lying. Sensing an opportunity to escape his imprisonment, Logan slowly and carefully stood on the bed and found his way to the break in the wall where the light was coming from. However, his hopes for escape were immediately dashed. The light did cascade through the opening, but the open led not to the outside, but to a narrow shaft that led several feet upward to a mirror that reflected the sunlight down into the cell. Though

Logan tried not to be heartbroken by the discovery, it certainly brought heaviness to his heart and mind. Sitting back down on the wooden plank of a bed, Logan locked his eyes on the large wooden door in the far wall of the cell. He could only sit up for so long before the pain in his head and neck would begin to throb, and it would force him back into a lying position. There was no way to mark time, and he wasn't sure how long he lay there before a sound came from the other side of the door.

The sound of a bolt lock being drawn back came from the other side of the door. The door slowly creaked open and a warm white light flooded into the room, and it was so bright that Logan had to shield his eyes as they were so accustomed to the darkness. Before his eyes could adjust to the new level of light, there was an indistinguishable form in front of him. Logan was desperately blinking his eyes, trying to make a better identification of the creature. It appeared to be human, but the water that was streaming from his eyes continued to hinder his vision. The form raised one of its hands and something struck Logan in the stomach. The pain from the strike was intense and caused Logan to immediately double over. From where Logan was seated on the edge of the bed, he lost his balance and fell hard to the cold stone floor. Logan wasn't sure if his head struck the hard floor or not, but his vision began to blur once more and the stars started to return. Two other sets of footsteps entered the room, and then the sensation of a set of hands grabbing each of his arms became apparent. As the assailants dragged Logan up off the floor, the wave of nausea assaulted him and he felt his stomach lurch. The feeling of being sick, caused a spark of panic deep inside of Logan, and as the thugs started to carry him in the direction of the door, Logan unconsciously began to struggle. Under normal circumstances he wouldn't have given into the panic or the lack of control, but his body was rebellious to the demands of his mind. The strong grip didn't relent, and in fact the large hands tightened around his arms. Logan was sure that when all was said and done, there would be large bruises on each of his arms. Finally the assailants must have tired of his struggling, and it was put to an abrupt end by the clubbing blow over the back of his head. It took only a moment before the veil of darkness fell over his eyes again.

* * * * * * * * * * * *

The next time Logan awoke, it was not because he wanted to. As the veil of unconsciousness began to be pieced, Logan was aware that someone was shaking him. Somewhere in Logan's mind he realized that the actions were not malicious and that someone was trying to get him to wake up. When Logan finally opened his eyes, all he could see was darkness. But the darkness faded quickly and a familiar form hovered at the edge of his vision. It didn't take long to recognize Pike looking down at him. At first it was hard to make out his face in the low light, but somehow Logan knew it was Pike. Logan could still feel the blows that the guards landed to my stomach and head, and as Pike helped Logan to sit up, it was hard to keep from vomiting. Finally back in an upright position, Logan took a long deep breath despite the pain it caused.

"Are you alright?" Pike asked, his voice barely above a whisper

"Yes," Logan said his voice more a groan than he intended, "except for the knot in the back of my head, I'm fine."

"I know what you mean. These people aren't exactly the welcoming kind. It seems that force is the only language they understand. I look forward to showing them some of my own."

Pike clenched his fists and looked over his shoulder for a moment at the door before turning his attention back to Logan.

"Where are we, Pike? The last thing I remember is looking down at those two armies, and then waking up in a cell."

"Well," he replied softly and slowly, "from what I know, we were taken prisoner shortly after they knocked you out. There was a force of about three hundred on the ledge just below us, and a group of about fifty behind us."

"How could they be behind us, Pike?"

"They were expecting us," he said, his jaw tight and his anger barely restrained. "They knew we were coming and they were lying in wait for us. You know what that means don't you?"

Logan sat silent for a moment and then realized what Pike was trying to say.

"No, Pike. I don't want to hear any accusations made against any member of the group. Maybe they saw Gideon when he was scouting and figured he would be coming back."

"I wasn't accusing Gideon of anything, Logan, at least not yet." Pike answered the anger barely restrained. "Right now though, I'm worried about where we are, and how we get out of here. I don't like being in anyone's cage."

Immediately Logan's thoughts shifted to the rest of the group, concern blossoming in him.

"Have you seen anyone else?"

"She's fine, Logan," Pike replied forcing a smile. "The only people I haven't seen are Talon, Gideon, and Eldar."

The pain was starting to subside in his stomach, and with Pike's help, Logan was able to get back to his feet.

"Well, that doesn't help our cause much, does it? Who do these people work for? What do they want? Are they going to kill us, or are they going to ransom us to Shau-ling or his followers?"

Pike shook his head.

"I don't have any answers for you Logan. All I've managed to see are simple guards. They don't talk much, and they don't seem interested in having any kinds of conversation. But at least they aren't trying to knock us out like they did with you. I guess they figured that once we saw what they were willing to do to you, it would lessen our will to resist."

Logan frowned. He certainly didn't like the idea of being the object lesson for acceptable violence. Finally, he shook his head.

"We still don't know who our illustrious captor is, and we are no closer to Shau-ling sitting in here."

Pike opened his mouth as if he was going to answer, but then he shut it quickly and put a finger to his lips. Logan took Pike's direction and didn't say another word. Pike pointed to the door and then motioned in the direction of the darkest corner of the cell. Logan nodded and moved into the shadows while Pike made his way to the door. Pike stood in the shadows, by the large wooden door waiting for it to open. Logan heard the bolt click, and the door swung open violently. A large burly man's silhouette stood in the hallway, his features obscured by a bright light source. Before Pike could act, another form was thrown into the room, quickly followed by another. The first form was on its feet and stumbled into the room under its own power. The second form on the other hand just slumped to the ground, barely clear of the doorway. The burly man kicked the second form's feet out of the way and then slammed the door shut. As soon as Logan emerged from the shadows the first from ran quickly across the room, and wrapped her arms around Logan. Pike moved to the form laying on the ground and slowly turned him over on to his back.

"Oh, Logan," Elwyne said through tears. "I thought you were dead. That man hit you over the head, and you fell, and I thought it was all over."

Logan held her tightly in my arms, and while she couldn't stop crying, he knew that they were tears of joy not sorrow. As he looked over at the other figure lying on the floor, Pike looked up and shook his head.

"It's, Talon, Logan. He's hurt pretty bad. Help me get him onto the bed."

Talon's shirt had been ripped off and there were what appeared to be whip marks all over his back and legs. Talon was still unconscious, so Logan and Pike carefully lifted him off the ground and carried him over to the wooden plank of a bed on the far side of the cell. While they were as gentle as possible, it was difficult to move him without causing a grunt of pain from escaping Talon's lips. In order to cause the least amount of damage, Pike helped Logan to roll Talon onto his stomach so that the wounds on his back and legs would not be irritated further.

"What happened to him, Elwyne?" Logan asked as tenderly as he could.

It was obvious that she was severely shaken by what she had witnessed, but without all the information, Logan wouldn't be able to make the right decision in the circumstance. There would be time enough for tenderness and for grieving, but now was a time to be pragmatic and attempt to save everyone from further torture.

"These men, I think they were part of one of the armies we saw earlier, took Talon, Gideon, Eldar, and I to another part of the dungeon. I don't know what happened to Gideon and Eldar, but they strapped Talon to the wall and started whipping him. Then they would ask him all kinds of questions about the *Coromor* and other questions I didn't understand. No matter what he said they just kept whipping him and asking him the same questions over and over again. When they would stop, one of them would turn to me and threaten me. He would tell me that he wasn't above hitting a woman, and if I wasn't truthful with them, I would get the same if not worse than Talon did. Then he just went back to beating Talon, without asking him any questions at all. Talon took it for a long time, and then he just passed out. I thought for sure that I would be strapped to the wall next, but the men just took Talon down from where he was bound and they threw us in here."

Pike grimaced before he asked a question that Logan himself was dreading.

"Did he say anything?" Pike asked.

"What?" she said puzzled.

"Did he answer any of the questions?"

"I don't think so," she replied finally, "at least not with any information that would be useful."

"Good," Logan said, partially relieved but still dreading the possible implications of the torture and questioning. "Now all we have to figure out is why they are still holding us. If Aryx were here I could ask him some things about these towns."

"I think it's pretty obvious why we're being held here," Pike said calmly. "They want the *Coromor*, and information about the *Erieal* and Shau-ling."

"If they wanted that information, why didn't they take us?" Logan replied.

"Good question. Maybe they don't know what they have down here."

"They may not know exactly," Talon said trying to sit up, "but they aren't taking any chances."

He sat up slowly and tried to shake all the cobwebs out. A few times he faltered, but eventually made it to a sitting position.

"How do you feel?" Elwyne asked softly.

"About the same way I did when father switched me for getting into old man Terran's ale stash. Of course it didn't hurt at the time, because I was too drunk to see straight. But father made sure I couldn't get out of bed the next morning."

"Can you remember any of what they asked you?" Logan asked ignoring Talon's attempts at levity.

"Not much. No matter what I said, they would still whip me, and then they would whip me if I said nothing. I do remember what they said right before I passed out. They said something about a battle, and finally putting an end to a war."

Before Logan could react or ask any more questions, the sound of the door bolt being pulled back came again. This time though, neither Pike nor Logan moved from their position. Obviously escape was the preferable solution, but under the circumstances it was not the responsible one. With Talon injured and with so many of their group unaccounted for, Logan though it best to stay where they were until more questions had answers. Once the door had fully slid open, it was apparent that the bright light source that had been in the hallway earlier had been extinguished. Now the light in the hallway was much softer and calmer. After several moments two large armored guards strode into the room, stopping just inside the doorway. Each brandished large swords and carried shields. The stood like a wall between the members of the party and the hallway. Several moments later, the guards took a step in each direction, opening a path. Between the guards stepped a man dressed in very rich green garments, and on the front of his green tunic was the symbol of a lion embroidered in gold. Following the unarmed man were two more guards who remained in the hallway. For several long moments the unarmed man simply looked across the four confused faces in the cell. Finally he took a step past the two guards who were already in the cell and cleared his throat before speaking.

"Lord Merric, Elwyne Tamerlane, Pike Rhuiden, and Talon Aielin, your presence is requested in the great audience hall of his highness Lord Elouix of Rama."

Logan's puzzlement was apparent on his face for only a moment before he shoved the feeling deep down inside. So much was finally beginning to make sense, especially why none of the members of this Lord Elouix's interrogation group had questioned him. Aryx had kept up his guise as Lan and had apparently reminded everyone, especially Gideon and Midarin, that Logan's identity was changed to Lord Merric in Illimar. It was a stroke of genius, and a bit of good fortune. Lord Merric would have been considered above the rudimentary humiliation of torture because of his status as royalty. Though there were obviously some perks to the ruse, it had not however benefitted his companions. Logan pulled himself up to full height, shifting his shoulders back and keeping his chin high, as was expected of someone in his adopted position.

"Very well, sir," Logan said calmly and proudly, "lead us to your Lord Elouix. And I hope he has an explanation for this outrage."

As they were being led out of the cell, the rest of the members of their company were being led out of other cells in the hallway. Once the group had been reunited, Logan made his way over to Aryx and spoke to him in a soft voice. There were many answers that Logan needed before meeting with Lord Elouix, but he didn't want the guards hearing their conversation.

"It was a brilliant plan to keep my identity as Lord Merric, Lan, I never would have thought of it."

Aryx stared straight ahead, his eyes never leaving the back of the guards that lead them through the hallways.

"I don't know what you're talking about," he replied shortly.

Logan was dumbfounded.

"You didn't tell everyone to continue the use of the ruse we used in Illimar?"

Finally Aryx tilted his head slightly in Logan's direction.

"No," he replied. "If these people think you are Lord Merric, then there is only one conclusion that can be drawn. This Lord Elouix must have spies in Illimar that have reported back recently. That could either be to our advantage or our detriment."

Logan nodded and sighed. There was no telling what side this Lord Elouix was on, or what he intended to do with 'Lord Merric', but Logan was sure that he wasn't going to enjoy the result. The guards led them down a long hall and then up a flight of stairs and out of the dungeon. Of the group, only Gideon was still restrained, a set of manacles on his wrists. The guards led everyone down another hall and through a set of doors until they were standing in front of a large dining table set in the middle of a huge audience chamber. Sitting at the head of the table was a fat man, dressed in bright green with a white lion on the chest. It finally dawned on Logan at that moment that the lion was the crest of Rama, meaning the green lion on the crest of white belonged to Rana. At the right of this fat man was a man that Logan recognized as soon as he came into view. The man was the same man who allowed the group to use his cottage in Illimar. After he arranged the meeting with the dock master he must have left to report in to his masters in Rama. He was obviously the Raman spy.

As soon as the doors closed, the man who could only have been Lord Elouix stood and began to address his guests.

"Greetings. As you have probably been able to surmise by now, my name is Zar Elouix. I am the lord and protector of Rama. And you, my young friend, are Lord Merric of Baldazar. You travel with strange company, Lord Merric."

"The company I keep is my own affair, Lord Elouix," Logan responded keeping his voice as even and confident as possible.

"You travel with three women, none of which share your name, and one of which has been exiled for her well-known dalliances. You travel with mere boys, not bodyguards, including a thief who is wanted in more cities than I care to list, and lastly you travel with this warrior named Lan. He seems familiar to me, but I do not know where I can place the face. I have heard rumors of the great and powerful Aryx Terian traveling with a group of adventurers, but none of you could be Aryx Terian, none of you are old enough."

"But lord," the other man chimed in, "I heard him reveal himself as Sir Aryx Terian, White Lightning himself. I am sure of it."

"Fool," Lord Elouix replied, "he was just trying to scare you into doing what he said."

"I hate to interrupt," Logan said crassly, "but do you always treat your guests so roughly, and with so little regard for their well-being?"

"Bad form, Lord Merric," Elouix replied. "A lord of your stature and reputation should know that speaking out of turn would never get you anywhere. However, I will answer the question. I have a proposition for you, Lord Merric, one that could be beneficial to both of us."

That smile on Lord Elouix's face is what would stick in Logan's mind the longest. His yellowing teeth showed between his thin lips, a clear indication of how pleased he was with himself. However, that haughty smile seemed to somehow fit his round face. Lord Elouix was a fat man, one who did not look as if he had missed many royal feasts. He seemed to be so pleased with himself as he laid out the groundwork for his little 'idea'.

"Rana and Rama have been at war for centuries, in one form or another, Lord Merric, but we have come to a breaking point in the war. Our supplies, our numbers, and our will to fight have ground down to this opportunity for either total victory or total defeat. As I'm sure you saw on our approach, armies are massing for one final decisive battle, the winner of which will be able to set the course for a combined government for hundreds of years to come. I do not wish to allow such an opportunity to pass me by. However, I do not have generals with the experience or the drive to do what must be done. But then my little birdie told me about your run in with the Army of Illimar. He said that you single-handedly took on a whole detachment and made your escape without so much as a scratch."

Logan frowned at the folktale that their suffering had been turned into. Now, the recklessness that they showed in Illimar had come back to haunt them.

"As I see it, we can help each other. You need horses and supplies and all manner of other provisions for the rest of your journey. Those things, Rana and Rama have in great supply. I need a general to engineer a lasting victory for my people. If you give me what I want, Lord Merric, then I will ensure that you have what you want."

He went on to detail all of the troops and military might that he had at his disposal, as well as detailed intelligence about the enemy. He would provide us anything that we needed for the assault, and we would be treated with respect for the rest of our stay.

"And the questions, and the torture?" Pike interjected.

Elouix frowned.

"We hear stories, you understand, Lord Merric. We had to be sure that you weren't in league with some dark force whose purpose was to plunge everything further into shadow. We've seen the dispatches about what is going on in Lakestone. We cannot allow such darkness to take root here. I apologize for our methods of course, but not for the reason behind them."

Elouix held himself very tall, but Logan could feel something coming off the man. For all of his smug assurance, there was doubt and fear behind his eyes. There was more to all of this than he was letting on. Some shadow that was lingering.

"So, as you can see," Lord Elouix said smugly, "it is a simple operation for a man of your statue and reputation."

You have no idea, Logan thought to himself.

"If I were in a different position," Logan replied shortly, "I would have a choice in the matter. However, since you have the upper hand, we seem to have little other choice but to go along with your plan."

"That is very wise of you, Lord Merric. My guards will escort you to rooms where you can bathe and change clothes. The first strike party will leave at first light tomorrow morning. Please, do not think about trying to escape. The members of the army that you are going to lead have explicit orders to kill every one of you that tries to leave ranks before the battle begins."

The Tides of War

As Lord Elouix had promised, the group was shown to rooms on the far end of the palace. By this time even Gideon had been freed from his bonds, but the presence of the guards had not lessened. When he was ushered into one of the rooms, Logan saw a large copper basin filled with steaming water in the middle of the floor waiting for him. On the small palate of a bed in the corner of the room were laid three sets of clothes, as well as his sword and a new set of armor. The armor was simple at best, a light chain shirt, but it was more than he had been protected by to that point. At that sight Logan sighed. He wasn't sure if he was more relieved at having his sword back or about being alone for once. After a moment of reflection, he was sure that it was the latter.

Only one thing could make this better, he thought to himself as he stood there, *if only Elwyne were here with me. I wonder if I'll get to see her before the battle starts.*

It took only a few moments before Logan found himself sliding into the still very warm bath water. The heat from the water relaxed every muscle in his body almost immediately upon contact. It was the first bath and more importantly the first time he could truly relax since he had left Aradon.

I imagine that Elwyne is simply in heaven, Logan thought as he began to wash the dry blood off of himself. *I remember how much she enjoys a warm bath. It seems like forever since I've had a bath. Any longer, I don't think anyone could have tolerated being around me.*

Logan lingered in the bath longer than he normally would, trying to hold on to the moments of relaxation and what passed for safety. He dried and dressed, and as he turned back toward the door to the room, he started to pull the sword belt around his waist. It was in the middle of the motion that he stopped and sighed. He didn't like what he was becoming. At least for the moment he had foregone putting on the armor. Logan walked to the door of the room and knocked softly. As he had expected, one of the Raman guards opened the door and stood there barring the way. He was a large man who had the look of a lifetime soldier.

"What do you want?" he grumbled.

"I would like to see other members of my party so that we can plan out the assault tomorrow."

"You and your companions are allowed free run of this part of the palace, so long as you leave all of your weapons in your rooms. That is why there are guards at every door. Now, if you mean to leave your room, I should warn you that we all have instructions to kill anyone who leaves their quarters armed. No questions asked, yourself included."

Logan reflexively swallowed hard at the edict which could have come from none other than their host, Lord Elouix. Ceding to the demand, Logan unfastened the belt that held his sword, leaving it on the bed. After the guard was satisfied that his charge was unarmed, he allowed Logan to leave the room and enter the large hall. In was obvious once Logan was in the hall as to which rooms contained members of the party. Three of the doors on the left side of the hall were guarded by women, an obvious indication of where Elwyne, Eldar, and Midarin were. The other side of the hall was dominated by male guards. However, down at the far end of the hall, on the left side was a reinforced door guarded by three male guards. When Logan walked in the direction of the heavily guarded door, he was immediately greeted with three drawn swords.

"No one is allowed to have contact with this one," the guard said quickly, "under orders of Lord Elouix."

"May I ask who is being held in this room?"

"The traitor, Sir Aryx Terian."

The words caused Logan to shudder. If Lord Elouix knew the true identity of the man called Lan, then there was a chance that the ruse of Lord Merric had been, or would quickly be pierced. The guards eyed Logan for only a moment, and were satisfied when he walked in the opposite direction. Logan then went to one of the doors guarded by a young woman who looked barely old enough to hold a sword let alone be a trained soldier. She didn't draw a weapon, but simply smiled and opened the door. Stepping into the room, Logan wasn't surprised to find that it was nearly identical to the one that he had been housed in. The door closed behind him, and his eyes soon found Eldar sitting on the bed in the corner of the room. Logan was slightly annoyed at the sight of the bed. It appeared that Elouix had a soft spot for the female members of the company and had given them significantly better accommodations in terms of an actual mattress.

"Logan," she said, clearly surprised at Logan's appearance. "How are you?"

"I'm fine, Eldar. Are you alright?"

"Yes. Have you seen Elwyne yet? She was looking forward to talking to you as soon as she could."

"No. Have you talked to her?"

"Briefly," Eldar responded. "Go see her, Logan. She's worried about how you have been getting along. Believe me; you've changed a lot since you came back to Aradon."

"How so?" Logan asked with genuine concern, his earlier thoughts about his sword coming back to his mind.

"Well, you're much deeper and darker. One could almost see death hanging like a shroud over you. It's very odd, but you also seem more caring and are more concerned about us. I mean all of your friends."

She fell silent for a moment, her glance going back to the ground.

"I know we've never been the best of friends," she said between sobs, "but thank you for being there for all of us, including…David."

"I'm sorry Eldar; I know how much he meant to you."

Eldar nodded absently before raising her head and forcing a smile. Everything that had happened on this quest had been weighing heavily on everyone, but Logan had not yet allowed himself to put it all into perspective. That was the danger of time and silence. In those moments, memories and demons are plentiful, and it is often difficult to find true perspective. Logan had taken David's death hard, and he had almost lost the rest of his friends that very next day. He had sworn to himself that he would never be helpless again when it came to their safety, but once again he found that he was placed in a situation in which he had no control. They could have forced small talk, but Logan decided that it was better to follow Eldar's advice and find Elwyne. He excused himself and left the room. When he returned to the hallway, he stopped to speak to the young woman who was guarding Eldar's door.

"Hello, my name is…"

"Lord Merric, I know," she replied lightly.

"Could you tell me where…"

"Elwyne Tamerlane is next door, Logan," the guard replied.

Logan's blood ran cold. Had she been listening at the door when he and Eldar were talking, or were his fears realized that Lord Elouix had discovered their true identities?

"You needn't fear, Logan," the guard said in almost a whisper, interpreting his wide-eyed reaction. "The guards at these three doors were originally in the service of Lady Rice in Brea. We were banished when she was, and it seems that we found better places to start new lives than she did. We know all about you and the rest of your group. We have once again pledged our loyalties to Princess Midarin, as well as your friends and your true identities. Watch your tongue around the men who guard your doors though, they are still loyal to Lord Elouix."

"It's nice to know we have friends," Logan said relieved.

"You have friends everywhere in this palace, Logan. Never forget that."

The female guard at the next door winked at him with the hidden message as she opened the door to admit him to Elwyne's room. The door had not even fully closed before she had crossed the room and thrown her arms around him.

"Logan," Elwyne said with obvious relief, "I'm so glad you're safe."

She held him tighter and laid her head on his shoulder. He was content to just stand there and hold her, and it couldn't have lasted long enough. How many nights had he dreamed of a time when he could hold Elwyne in his arms once more?

"I need you with me, Logan," she said with a strange look in her eyes, "I don't think I can stand being without you. I don't care what father says, Logan. I want you to be my husband."

Elwyne pulled away from him and pulled loose the bow that held her hair up. With a gentle shake of her head, her hair fell and covered her shoulders. At that moment Logan didn't think that she could have done anything to make her more beautiful in his eyes, but he was wrong. She pulled him to her, and once her lips met his, all thought about death and pain and the uncertain future were gone. All that existed was that moment, and he wanted that moment to last forever. At some point they tumbled together onto the bed, the rest of the world ceasing to exist. All he could feel, and all he wanted to feel, was her silken skin gliding against his. They were joined together in the bonds of love, and as night fell, they lay together in each other's loving arms. When Logan's eyes closed and he drifted off to sleep his ears were filled with the gentle rhythm of Elwyne's soft breath and her calming heartbeat. The morning came too quickly, and they were roused just before first light by a knock at the door. Logan slipped softly out of bed and pulled on his pants. Elwyne did not stir as he walked over and answered the door. The same guard that held Elwyne's door earlier that evening was standing there looking past him at Elwyne's waking form.

"Yes," Logan said trying to stifle a yawn.

"You are to go back to your room and prepare to leave in an hour," she replied.

"Thank you," he said to the guard before closing the door and returning to Elwyne.

By this time Elwyne was awake, and she had rolled on her side and was smiling at Logan. He slowly went to his knees and kissed her softly.

"Lord Elouix is ready for his pound of flesh."

Elwyne frowned, but finally nodded and kissed him again.

"I love you, Logan."

"I love you," he replied wrapping his arms around her and pulling her close, "more than I have words for."

Finally, after a few more aborted attempts to leave, Logan managed to leave Elwyne's room and return to his own. He hurriedly put on one of the other sets of clothes that still lay on his undisturbed bed, pulled the chain shirt on over his tunic, and then strapped the sword onto his hip. Once Logan returned to the hallway, he was led to Aryx's heavily guarded room. The door opened to reveal that everyone had gathered with the exception of Gideon and Elwyne who entered the room mere moments later. There were looks of acknowledgement around the room, and Logan felt all eyes moving to him.

"So," he said calmly, "are we all ready?"

"Logan," Aryx said in a serious and professional tone, "I have already gone over the troop deployments with Lord Elouix. You and Pike are to lead the first infantry division. Gideon and Talon will lead second infantry, while Gwydeon and I will lead first cavalry. Lane and the women will be in charge of the three archer units. The deployment and movements of these units are completely up to you."

"Six units," Logan said softly, mostly to himself. "Aryx, tell the troops to adopt their typical deployment alignment."

"Is that wise, Logan," Lane asked shortly.

It was obvious that he was nervous, as was everyone else. None of them, with the exception of Aryx had seen any type of military engagement on this scale. However, there was something in Gideon's mannerisms that told Logan that their plain and simple thief had also seen his share of conflict.

"Logan is correct in his planning, Lane," Aryx said calmly. "Without a familiarity with the enemy, his own troops, and the terrain, to plan anything would be haphazard and most likely foolish."

"Well," Logan said glumly, "I suppose we should meet our army."

After leaving Aryx's quarters, Logan's thoughts were focused on the battle ahead, a battle that could very well be their last. The war between Rana and Rama was legendary for its brutality. Pike kept pace with Logan, and after several long moments of silence, Logan shared a risky plan with his old friend. Pike was shocked by the idea, but eventually agreed that it was worth considering. When everyone arrived at the muster, several thousand men stood in their units, waiting for their orders. Logan had never seen such an assemblage of fighting men, except for the processional that had accompanied the Lord Lion on his official visit to Aradon after the war. That group though was ceremonial, even though Logan knew that they would have easily held their own in battle. The army of Rama however was well maintained, well-armed, and had the look of men who had seen more combat and death and peace. If there was fear to be found anywhere in that courtyard, it was in Logan's eyes and not theirs. Logan was sure that could expect the same cold fury in their opponents. The man who appeared to be the highest-ranking member of the army stepped forward and saluted.

"Lord Merric. My name is Captain Antrobus. I am the First Infantry section leader under you and your associate Pike Rhuiden. My seconds and their men are at your disposal," he recited with a mixture of pride and disgust in his voice.

He's got every right to be angry, I suppose. If I had any choice in the matter, I would let him and his seconds lead the invasion and I would stay here and be quite content. However, his lord would surely frown on that, and the chances of us getting out of here alive would be greatly reduced.

"Separate your men into their units, and have them gather behind their appointed commanders. My unit will follow me to the gate for instructions. The other units will be given orders as soon as they are assembled. Understood?"

"Yes, sir," he responded proudly, if not a little irritated.

"Carry on."

He turned and relayed the orders to his seconds and the courtyard came alive with movement. As if they were all being pursued by Shau-ling himself, the men ran to their appointed commanders and listened intently as they received their instructions. Logan was not as quick to relay his instructions to the men. They gathered around as quickly as the other units had, but Logan kept on walking toward the outer gate. The men to their credit kept in step, and in formation, and if they seemed at all disturbed by their leader's enigmatic behavior, they did not give any outward show of it. Pike walked slowly beside Logan, a half step behind. He kept his eyes trained to the ground as he walked, matching his friend's stride. Then Logan heard it, the soldiers behind them had matched their strides to their commanders', and it felt to Logan as though he had instantly become a hundred feet tall with foot-falls that shook the ground. For that brief moment, he began to feel like the champion he was fated to be.

"Are you ready, Lord Merric," Pike asked, "or have you reconsidered what we spoke about a few minutes ago?"

"No," Logan replied, his pace steady. "I plan to go on as we discussed. Have you spoken with Aryx, Talon, and Lane about my little scheme?"

"Yes. Needless to say, Aryx was a bit skeptical of our chances of surviving if you go on as planned, but he never thought we would survive in the first place if you ask me."

"What about you, Pike? Do you think it's a good idea?"

"Look, Logan, you and I have been friends for a long time. We have all been through a lot since we left Aradon, and personally, I think that your plan has a better chance of getting us out of here alive than sticking to this hare-brained invasion of Lord Elouix's. The only downside is that there is a chance instead of fighting men we could be fighting Shadowwalkers and Jeresei. I don't think I need to remind you that six or seven Shadowwalkers destroyed our home, and an army of Jeresei very nearly had you on Shauling's dessert plate."

"No," Logan said glumly, "You don't have to remind me. But then again, I have you to bail me out again if I get in too deep."

Pike just glared.

"You have to admit," Logan continued, "this is the best chance we have to get out of this alive, and not have to kill anyone or anything to accomplish it."

For the first time, Logan realized that they were standing in the glade just inside of the gate. The men had fanned out into more formal battle lines. Captain Antrobus was beginning to approach, and Pike put his hand on Logan's shoulder.

"Whenever you're ready, Logan, I put it in your pack," Pike said as he straightened and drew his ax from the loop on his belt. "I don't want to know how you got it."

Logan drew the sword from the scabbard on his hip and clutched the pack in his other hand tightly. This was a gamble. With a quick turn he was facing the men that he would lead into battle. All of the men immediately turned their attention to their commander, but a moment later the gaze turned from one of practiced respect to one of wonder. Logan could see Aryx out of the corner of his eye, and he was surprised to see that the knight had left his unit and was approaching quickly. As soon as he was close enough to speak without shouting, Aryx's voice filled Logan's ears. At first Logan didn't understand what the man was saying, but then as though the voice had echoed down a tunnel, Logan's mind was able to make sense of the sounds.

"Logan, you're glowing."

As Logan looked down at his hands, he was incased in a brilliant red glow. As he had in Sarmeel, Logan closed his eyes and emptied his mind of all thoughts. This time however, there was no release of power that snapped him back to reality. Logan stood there, alone in the emptiness of my mind, connected to nature and every part of the world at the same time. The power was incredible, but somewhere deep, Logan knew that he had no control of it. Somewhere outside of the peaceful and placid island of power, Logan was vaguely aware of the sound of hundreds of gasps fill the void, and then he slowly opened his eyes.

* * * * * * * * * * * *

Logan was alone; there was nothing around him but sky. Looking down at himself, the body that once was so familiar to his vision had been replaced by one so alien that it caused Logan's breath to catch in his throat. The long human arm that sported five lean digits had been replaced by a red scaled leg with three, talon-laden claws at the end. In that moment, no longer than a blink, he had been transformed into his new namesake; he had become the Dragon.

The exhilaration of flight was amazing, and as land finally came into view, Rana and Rama were nowhere to be seen. Suddenly, Logan realized that he was not alone in the sky. An immense black form flowed in his direction, buffeted by winds that Logan could not feel. As it came closer, the shape of the dragon was apparent. There was something about the beast that made filled Logan's heart with fear and anger. The blackness of the other dragon's skin was dark enough to rival even the shroud of death. Only the golden glow of the creature's talons pierced the blackness. Logan knew at once that he was looking at Shau-ling. A million thoughts crossed his mind before the black form was actually hovering just feet away from him, but most of them were thoughts of death or escape. The dragon's mouth opened and a ball of green fire erupted from its open jaws. There was no time to flee. The ball of flame engulfed Logan, and the reflexive roar of pain bellowed from his jaws, but a moment later Logan realized that there was no pain. A roar of laughter burst from Shau-ling, and then the most horrible and cruel voice Logan had ever heard rang true in his ears.

"So, Dragon, we finally meet. However, this is the only way I can see you because you are hiding from me. Are you afraid to reveal yourself,

Dragon? Are you afraid to admit who and what you really are? Are you afraid that once I know, I will take everything that you hold dear and crush the life out of it? Your home was only the beginning, Dragon. Soon, your friends, your family, your loved-ones, every innocent man, woman, and child on this pathetic ball of dirt will be crushed. You and I are blood, Dragon. You are the one who brings destruction, and I am the destroyer of worlds, the nightmare of men."

Shau-ling laughed again, a laugh that shook Logan to the core. Then a burning rose in the pit of his stomach. The sensation was a mixture of searing pain and intense pleasure, but for some reason, Logan found himself enjoying the pain more and more every moment that passed. Then, without any control, Logan's jaws flew open, and a ball of red fire leapt from his mouth and hurtled toward the unsuspecting form in front of him. Shau-ling dodged away from the attack at the last moment, and it laughed again, a cruel smile showing razor-sharp teeth.

"I see you will be more fun than your predecessor. We will meet again Dragon, and the next time, the advantage will be mine."

* * * * * * * * * * * *

Logan suddenly found himself standing in front of his troops once again. No one said anything for a long time. Finally, Pike and Gwydeon walked up to their friend together with a mixture of wonder and concern on their faces. Before they could speak, Logan motioned for them not to. After a look at his arms to confirm that his humanity had returned, Logan addressed the men.

"Warriors of Rama. The sights you have just witnessed have left you with many questions, questions for which there are no answers. Captain Antrobus?"

"Yes sir?" he answered in a relatively calm voice.

"Summon your standard bearer."

The call went up a moment later. The raised banner of Rama could be seen moving through the ranks of men until a boy appeared from the throng. He didn't seem afraid at all, and no matter what he had seen that morning, he still had the wonder of innocence in his eyes.

"Standard bearer Alexander Mealon reporting as ordered, sir."

"You shall raise my banner, Alexander," Logan said drawing his shoulders back, "and you shall ride at my side in battle."

"Yes, sir," he said proudly.

Logan knelt down and recovered the large white parcel from his pack. It was a white banner that Midarin had commissioned from one of her allies in the palace. Apparently Pike had seen this moment coming as well, and once he learned of the underground loyalty to Midarin in the palace, he had hatched this elaborate plan. Pike too had seen too much death, and this was the opportunity to end the bloodshed. As he unfolded the banner and helped Alexander attach it to the standard, the form of a flying red dragon became apparent. At the sight of the raised banner, the men of Rama all went to one knee and bowed their heads.

"Arise, men of Rama. You are now the Army of the Dragon. Rana, prepare to fall under the might of the *Coromor!*"

Pike's call led to a cry of 'long live the *Coromor*' echoing through the ranks. The men rose and reformed quickly, sending up cheers that reverberated through the valley. Pike, Alexander, Captain Antrobus, and Logan each mounted our horses and led the first infantry out of the front gates of Rama. The newly named Army of the Dragon marched proudly across the vast plain between the Twin Towns, ready to die in the name of their new lord and master. Once the Ranan army was in sight, the pace quickened. It looked as though they were greatly outnumbered; a tribute to the inaccuracy of Lord Elouix's intelligence, but the troops had been galvanized with a courage granted by what they perceived to be a god. The commanders of the Army of Rana rode out from the vanguard, a sign that they wished to parlay before the battle. Captain Antrobus sounded the order to halt, while Pike, Alexander, and Logan rode to meet the three men in the center of what would become the battlefield. The man that appeared to be the leader of the Ranan army did not appear to be much older than Logan, but his face was marred by two great scars that were visible from quite some distance. The other two people with him were a boy that served as standard-bearer, and an old man with a long white beard. The old man was wiry, but there was a great wisdom in his eyes.

"What right does the Army of Rama claim to show the banner of the Dragon? Your claim over these towns is not ordained by the Dragon any more than ours is ordained by the Lion."

Logan moved closer to the trio so that his words would be heard clearly, and Pike remained no more than a foot behind him.

"The Army of Rama is no more. You now look at the Army of the Dragon, led by the Dragon himself. By the right granted to me under the decree of Lord Cedric, the Lion, all hostilities between the Twin Towns will end, and the unnecessary bloodshed shall cease."

"No bloodshed is unnecessary," the young general replied. "It is the mark of a true warrior to accept death as the way to end a war. Your Lord Cedric understood that, and anyone who claims to act in his name would know that."

"Even a fool knows that death begets death, and war begets war. Lord Cedric understood that no war should be fought, but there are times that in order to prevent war, one must make war," Pike countered.

"Enough bickering," the old man said roughly, "the Lord Dragon's presence demands our attention."

"It would be in the best interests of the Twin Towns to end this war here and now under the name of the Dragon. The bloodshed must end, and we must have a united front as Lord Cedric did against the Shadows in the last generation."

"He speaks wisely, Klarre," the old man said. "Lord Dragon, my name is Talos. I am the last surviving member of the Moridon tribe, whose duty is to serve the *Coromor* in all ways. I renounce my ties to Rana and dedicate myself to my ancestral charge."

"You are welcome, Talos of the Moridon. What is the decision of the forces of Rama?"

"The war ends here," Klarre said gritting his teeth, "under the name of the Dragon."

As Logan turned toward Rama, cheers went up from the men on both sides. The war was over. But inside Logan, the full weight of what he was becoming came crashing down upon his shoulders. Just by displaying his banner and using his title, he had ended a war that had raged on for generations. However, the shadowy and mysterious confrontation with Shau-ling in those unknown skies still left him with a sense of puzzlement. Logan still did not fully understand what he was, nor did he understand all of the powers at his command. What was clear was that he had the power to stop the wars and the constant killing that filled the world. But was that power achieved through respect or fear? What was it that the men of the Raman army as well as his friends had seen during his confrontation with Shau-ling? He tried to shake away the uncertainty and focus on the positive of the moment, but the lingering doubt grew in his mind, and as he saw the brilliant white banner billowing overhead, he knew he should have felt hopeful, but all he could feel was cold.

CHAPTER 6

Chapter VII

Parting Ways

The streets of Rama were no longer crowded with the movement of soldiers and equipment. The War of the Light that had been raging on for as long as the people of Rana and Rama could remember was now over. However, the people had come out from their homes, lining the streets to see the small processional of the heroes of the war, and the man rumored to be the Lord Dragon. The white banner could be seen flowing about the small group as they made their way to Lord Elouix's palace in the middle of the city. For so long, these towns had been hidden in a shroud of mystery and fantasy, but now, their splendor and mystery would be known by the people of the world, and they would now be staunch allies for the forces of the Light in the second war against the Shadows. The processional continued down the main street of town and walked up the flights of stairs that led to the door of Lord Elouix's palace. The path to the palace was lined with guards in full armor. The red carpet had been laid out, and the conquering heroes were shown in by one of the many guards standing by the door. Before long Logan found himself standing in the same dining room as they had been the day before, only this time, the situation was much different. After a few moments a trumpet fanfare came from an adjoining anteroom. The doors then burst open and Lord Elouix, followed by his entourage, entered. There were trumpet players, flower girls, other highly honored guests, as well as many other people whose whole purpose in life seemed to be to serve Lord Elouix. Elouix sat down at the head of the table and bid one of his many servants to fetch the dinner the cooks had prepared. Within a matter of seconds, a dozen cooks and servers walked into the room with trays laden with food and drink. After the food had been set out, and the drinks poured, Lord Elouix stood up and began to speak.

"Good friends, and faithful associates, welcome to my humble house. I stand here in front of you as a man grateful for the blessings that have been awarded him by the Creator. If it were not for these fine people sitting here at my table, the War of the Light would still be raging on, and would continue to do so for generations to come. The forces of Rana and Rama have reached an agreement of mutual peace and cooperation because of our victory in this last decisive battle. Now is a time for great celebration. And I have one man to thank for all of this. And that man is none other than Lord Merric of Baldazar. Please, Lord Merric, stand and say a few words."

"Thank you, Lord Elouix," Logan said flatly, "however; this charade has gone on long enough."

There were a few gasps from those in the hall, but Logan continued undisturbed.

"We were brought here to Rama against our will and held prisoner until we agreed to kill for you."

Now the gasps gave way to mumbled conversations and looks of shock traded between the onlookers.

"Now that we have done what you have asked us, you welcome us into your house like we have known each other for years and are the best of friends. Have you even heard of the deeds of the last battle, Lord Elouix?"

"No, Lord Merric," Elouix said after a moment of hesitation, "Captain Antrobus was going to make his triumphant report during the feast."

"Tell you men to fetch him now, as well as a boy named Alexander who served as the standard bearer. When Alexander comes, he is to raise the banner from the battle."

Lord Elouix quickly shooed one of his servants out of the room with the orders. Logan stood in the uneasy silence until he heard the sound of rattling armor outside. Logan knew what was happening, but the tortured look on the face of Lord Elouix helped him to hold his tongue. The people of Rama had been witness to their arrival from the battlefield, but Elouix in his arrogance had been locked away with his advisors. But his ignorance would soon be shattered. Within a few seconds, Captain Antrobus burst through the door follower by Alexander holding the Dragon Banner aloft. Lord Elouix gasped loudly and then stood in a panic.

"What is the meaning of this insult on my house? Who are you to order one of my men to carry this blasphemous banner in the very town that cherishes the memory of the Lion?"

"Sit down ye ole windbag 'fore ye find yer guts on da end o' one o' me daggers," Gideon challenged.

"Allow Captain Antrobus to give his report, Lord Elouix, and all of your questions will be answered," Logan ordered, crossing his arms under his chest.

"Very well Captain," Lord Elouix said, trying to regain the regal tone, "tell us of the great victory on the field of battle. How many of those Ranan bastards did we kill?"

"None, sire," Antrobus answered, his face cold as stone.

"None!" Lord Elouix shouted. "How in the name of the Light could we have won a battle without a single casualty?"

"At the order of Lord Merric, the Banner of the Dragon was carried into battle. At the sight of the banner, the forces of Rana surrendered in the Dragon's name, as did the forces of Rama."

Lord Elouix's face flushed, and it looked as if steam were going to begin pouring from his ears. The rage within him was apparent, and the thought of his prize army surrendering was pushing him past his level of restraint. He stood again and shouted at everyone, but no one in particular.

"My army surrendered! Those traitorous bastards! I'll have the lot of them strung up in the town square for high treason! I don't care what ends came of their surrender, it is a shame on all of the houses of Rama!"

"Sit down and shut up you pompous ass!" Pike shouted, standing and reaching for his ax.

Elouix's face was a patchwork of embarrassment, anger, and frustration. The red sank quickly away from his face, and he forced himself to sit down. He kept his eyes trained on Logan the whole time, but his gaze was little more than daggers of hate.

"Lord Elouix," Logan said calmly, "my name is not Merric, and I am not from the town of Baldazar. In fact, I had never even heard of a town called Baldazar until Sir Aryx told me of it briefly in Illimar. My name is Logan Ranthall, and I am here from the town of Aradon."

"By what right do you raise the Dragon Banner?"

Aryx stood at the question and bowed slightly. However, to Lord Elouix's surprise, Aryx bowed to Logan.

"Under the authority given me by Lord Cedric Binosear, the Lion, as the second in command of the Lion's Mane, may I present the Lord Dragon, the second *Coromor* of the prophecies, Logan Ranthall."

Elouix stood stunned for a moment, the truth of his situation finally sinking in. Finally, Elouix bowed slightly, and the rest of the assembled servants and guests bowed to Logan as well. When Elouix finally straightened, he smiled widely.

"Lord Dragon, for you to grace my home with your presence is a great honor, and anything that is mine is yours for the asking. We greatly thank you for ending the war that has held us for generations, and in the name of the Light and in the name of the Dragon, the peace shall reign so long as the Creator allows."

Elouix's change of position was greeted with the applause of everyone in the room, and though Logan could hear Pike grumbling something unkind, Logan was happy that there would be no more battle, at least in the Twin Towns.

"We appreciate your hospitality, no matter how late it may be. We shall require provisions, supplies, and horses. We will remain in Rama for three more days in order to mend our wounds, and then we will continue on our journey."

"I'm afraid, Lord Dragon, that is quite impossible."

Logan stopped, and turned to face Lord Elouix. Talon spoke before Logan could.

"Do you presume to tell the Lord Dragon what to do?"

There was a frown on Talon's face, but Logan knew that inside he was smiling. Talon was the kind of person who pushed any advantage to the edge, and most of the time didn't stop until he was well over the cliff.

"The Lord Dragon is now the ruler of the Twin Towns," Elouix responded smiling. "Upon the surrender of the armies of Rama and Rana in the name of the Dragon, Lord Logan became the sovereign lord of all lands and territories under the rule of these towns. As such, the Lord Dragon must dictate law to his people."

Turning, Logan felt his hand fall to the hilt of his sword; a motion that did not go unnoticed.

"Lord Elouix," Logan said calmly. "What I did was for the people of Rana and Rama, not for my own glorification. I have no intention of dictating law to men who would know the needs of the people far better than I. The title of the Dragon requires more from me than to sit upon a throne. Therefore I leave the position to you and your counterpart from Rana. You may have the rule of your kingdoms with my blessing and my thanks."

Lord Elouix seemed equal parts surprised and relieved.

"You are as wise as you are bold, Lord Dragon. My counterpart and I will graciously rule Rana and Rama in your name for the rest of our days."

"But I do leave two conditions that you will cede to. Otherwise, I shall remove you from power and appoint those who will cede to my will."

Some fear could be seen behind Elouix's eyes, but he simply inclined his head and waited for Logan to continue speaking.

"First, there will be no record of my name in any texts or correspondence, only my title. That should be easy enough to accomplish. The second is that when the war with the Shadow begins again, the forces of Rana and Rama will answer any request for aid, and shall mobilize in the name of the Lord Dragon without question."

Lord Elouix bowed, more formally this time.

"As you command, my lord, so shall it be done."

He bowed low again and then ordered one of his guards to show the group to their new accommodations in the lord's suites on the other end of the palace. Captain Antrobus and Alexander were asked to meet with Logan in his quarters within two hours. Then, Logan had Lord Elouix send a courier to Rana, in order to procure the services of the one named Talos. The group followed the guard to their new rooms. Elwyne told the guard that she and Logan would share a room, and that her belongings were to be moved as soon as possible, additionally the guard was ordered to arrange for a private meal for the Lord Dragon and his companions, as they had no desire to share in Lord Elouix's victory celebration.

The new suite that had been given to them was three times larger than the one Logan had stayed in previously, and it was painted in the fabulous hues of an evening skyline just after the sun begins to set. There was a large feather bed, as well as an easement outside the large window in the back wall. From the easement, all of the city could be seen, as well as most of Rana. Elwyne was also very impressed with the view, and together they stood for a long time looking at the immaculate skyline and holding each other's hand. What seemed like minutes later, there was a knock at the door. Walking back into the room, Logan reached for the sword and scabbard that lay on the bed, but thought better of it. As he opened the door the shadows of a small boy and two larger men was visible. It became obvious to Logan at that point that Elwyne could easily make him loose track of time.

"Come in, Alexander. You too, Captain Antrobus and Talos of the Moridon. Welcome."

They each entered the room and sat down on the wooden chairs that surrounded a large round dining table that sat in the center of the room. Elwyne joined the gathering as Logan began to address the guests. However, before any words came out of Logan's mouth, Captain Antrobus spoke.

"Is it necessary to trouble my lady with this discussion? Surely the Lady Dragon could find much more interesting things than standing here listening to us speak about war."

Elwyne countered quickly.

"The *Lady Dragon* is interested in anything that concerns Shau-ling and more importantly, my fiancé. I remember reading once that humility was a treasured virtue in Rama, and that speaking out of turn was frowned upon. Surely, I wouldn't have to remind you of that."

"You do not have to remind me of that, my lady," Antrobus replied, his eyes lowered. "No one who has served in Lord Elouix's army could ever forget."

Elwyne smiled.

"It's good that you are loyal. It may serve to be your saving grace; I wouldn't want to have to call for Pike or Gideon."

Logan tried hard not to smile, but it was clear that Elwyne was truly enjoying her new-found power.

"Now, if you will excuse me."

Elwyne turned away from him sharply and strode towards the door. Logan followed closely behind her, trying to give the impression that he was unaffected by the whole exchange. Before she left the room, however he wanted to say something.

"Do you think you hurt his pride?" he asked softly.

"Pike's ax couldn't hurt his pride, Logan. "

Again Logan stifled a laugh.

"I'll be talking to Eldar if you need the opinion of the Lady Dragon in your boring talk about war."

She smiled quickly and made her way out of the room, after leaning in to give him a soft kiss on the cheek. Logan smiled to himself and made his way back to the table and sat.

"Well, gentlemen, this is an interesting situation that you have all been placed in. I wish to tell you now that none of you have any obligation to me after you leave this room, and you are all entitled to stay on if you wish."

"With all due respect, Lord Dragon," Captain Antrobus answered, "I know very little about what will happen after you leave Rama, but I am sworn to serve you until I die. I gave you that oath the minute you took command of my forces, and unless you release me of that oath, that bond will continue as long as my body holds breath."

Though Logan was surprised by the words, he nodded and looked at the one named Talos. Though he looked like a simple old man, no different than the elderly farmers who lived on the dell back in Aradon, it seemed that inside him was hiding a secret power.

"I will follow you all the way to Shau-ling's throne room, Lord Dragon. I am the last of my kind, and the people of the Lion died with the greatest glory and honor. I wish to become one of the people of the Dragon, with the hope that I can serve to protect you and see the fall of the master of all evil."

"I accept Talos of the Moridon, and I hope you find the same honor as the others of your kind."

Logan gaze then fell to the boy who sat quietly. He was so young, and so full of hope and energy. Alexander had grown up in war, and that was all he knew.

"It would be an honor to carry your banner in battle my Lord Dragon," Alexander said proudly. "Please allow me the honor of being your standard bearer."

"I accept, Alexander. You shall carry my banner wherever my quest takes me."

He said nothing else, but the large smile that even the most dedicated of military men couldn't have held back told Logan exactly how he felt.

"I need your decision, Captain Antrobus," Logan said after a moment, "but before you decide, let me present you with another option. Rana and Rama are in deep need of an extension of my will here to control both of the armies. I would give you complete control of the Twin Towns, and you would rule in my name. Lord Elouix and his counterpart would make up a law council, but ultimately you would be in control."

If he was affected by the temptation of power, Captain Antrobus didn't show it. What was obvious was that he was mulling over his options. Finally, he nodded to himself and then spoke.

"Lord Dragon, if I may, thank you for the chance to prove myself to you. I would gladly rule in your name; however that would be the only thing I could do. There would be no way I could have your insight and compassion in the matters of state. If you ever need the Army of the Dragon again, we will be ready. I accept you offer for the charge of the Twin Towns."

Upon the end of his gracious and flattering speech, he bowed deeply and then stood and left the room. Talos then stood and left the room followed quickly by Alexander. Before Logan could go to look for Elwyne, there was a knock at the door.

"Logan!" Pike yelled from the other side of the door. "Get up off your papered royal ass and open this door! There's a letter for you!"

Always one for subtlety, Logan thought to himself.

Logan opened the door and was greeted by Pike and Talon rushing into the room and pouring themselves a drink from one of the bottles that sat on the table.

"Make yourselves at home," I said laughing. "Now, where is this letter?"

Pike took a drink from one of the older bottles of wine and then handed Logan a sealed envelope. On the front of the envelope was printed, 'Lord Dragon, from Queen Camille, Trelon.' On the back of the letter was the familiar seal of Trelon; a lion sitting on a wide field. After a moment of reflection, Logan broke the seal on the envelope and then pulled out the letter. As he looked at it, he noticed that it was written in a brilliant golden ink, and that the handwriting was clearly a woman's. Obviously Queen Camille had heard of the existence of the new *Coromor*.

Lord Dragon,

The people of Trelon hope this message finds you well. We received news from Lord Cedric that you had survived an engagement in Sarmeel and that you were slowly making your way to Falke. We were advised to send this letter to Rama. I am very well aware of your ultimate mission; however, the people of Trelon would greatly appreciate your presence in our court. This is both the wish of myself as well as that of Lord Cedric. However Lord Cedric also requested that some of your group remain on the path to Flake, for reasons that will become evident soon enough. I look forward to your presence in Trelon in a matter of days.

Regards,

Camille Talaat, Queen of Trelon

Just as with the letter Aryx delivered in Aradon, Lord Cedric had charted out Logan's next moves with a letter to Queen Camille. There was resentment building within Logan, but he continued to hold on to the trust and reverence for his predecessor.

"What does the letter say, Logan?" Pike asked.

"You'll find out shortly. Gather everyone here in my quarters in ten minutes. I need to speak with Lord Elouix for a moment, and then I will join you all."

Pike nodded and left the room, followed quickly by Talon. As strong-willed as Pike had always been, he seemed to have no issue following Logan's orders, no matter how strange they may have seemed to him at the time. In more ways than one, Logan believed that Pike was better suited for the part Logan was playing than he was. Logan strapped his sword around his waist and walked out of the room, where he found the halls were empty except for a few chambermaids and other servants who were doing the odd tasks that were demanded of them. Upon reaching the chambers of Lord Elouix, one of the lord's servants opened the door and motioned for Logan to enter. Lord Elouix was sitting in a decorated wooden chair behind a large table. He had papers scattered all over the table and appeared to be hard at work.

"Well, Lord Logan, to what do I owe the unexpected pleasure of your company? Care for a drink?"

"No. I wanted to inform you that my party and I will be leaving early tomorrow morning."

"So soon?" he commented. "We were expecting you to stay several more days."

"As was I," Logan responded. "However, something has arisen that demands my immediate attention. Also, there is a matter of command of my army. I have placed Captain Antrobus in charge of the garrisons here, as well as an Overseer position of both towns. However you and Lord Trebor will still retain law-making positions, but must have Overseer Antrobus approve all legislative decisions."

"As you command, Lord Dragon."

If he had been affected by the orders, he didn't show it. After Elouix bowed slightly from his seated position, Logan turned and made his my way back to my quarters. As he entered the room, Logan immediately noticed that everyone was there, including Captain Antrobus. Pike, Talon, Eldar, Gideon, and Captain Antrobus were having a drink and talking at one table, while Talos and Lane were talking about the realms of magic in front of an eager yet quiet Alexander. Elwyne and Gwydeon were speaking about something, while Midarin was talking to Aryx. As soon as Logan stepped into the room, all of the conversation stopped, and attention was turned to him.

"I have received another letter containing Lord Cedric's wishes, and just as we did in Aradon, I am compelled to obey these wishes."

A few, especially Pike and Talon, grumbled a little at the mention of Lord Cedric's wishes.

"Some of us are to make our way to Trelon to meet with Queen Camille."

"What do you mean, 'some of us'," Lane asked.

"Lord Cedric thought it best if we split our forces and send a diversion force on to Falke. It might be dangerous, but I can see the Cedric's logic."

"Logan," Pike spoke up, "if it's all the same to you, I would like to lead the group to Falke. I would rather travel with you, but from what we've been told about the *Coromor* and the *Erieal*, it may be safer if I go with the diversion."

"Thanks Pike, you made this a lot easier. I have already divided our force up taking into consideration all of the factors involved. Alexander, Aryx, and Elwyne will come with me for obvious reasons. In case you were not aware of it, Talos of the Moridon has joined our ranks, and he will also go with me to Trelon. Though I agree with Pike's estimation of the sensitivity of this mission, and the chance that the connection of *Erieal* and *Coromor* may serve to be dangerous, I would like to take Gideon along. What do you say, Gideon?"

"Well," he started, "dinnae suppose Aryx'll be offerin' ta pay me again, but it don't look like der's many better places ta be."

"My team is set then. Best of luck to you Pike, and I hope that Cedric's wrong about this. I have planned for all of us to leave tomorrow morning at first light. Once our errand in Trelon is done, we'll meet back up in Falke."

Pike scratched his chin and sighed.

"My group should leave now. Give us a good head start to draw off whoever might be watching."

"If that is what you think is best," Logan replied.

"Besides," Pike added smiling, "there aren't any good taverns here. Everyone get your things together and meet me at the front gate. We'll head out as soon as everyone is ready."

Pike led the members of his group out of the room. Elwyne and Eldar shared a quick moment and then left the room together. Everyone else filed out of the room as well, with the exception of Captain Antrobus. He did not speak until he was sure everyone else was gone.

"What of me, Lord Dragon?"

"You are to take command of the garrison here tomorrow morning as soon as I am out of sight. I have already informed Lord Elouix of the situation, and you should meet with him after you leave here. I may or may not relay orders from the road. If I do, they are to be followed to the letter, if I do not, you are to rule this province in my name. These are my orders. You are dismissed."

Captain Antrobus did not hide the look of dismay well, but snapped a salute nonetheless and strode out of the room with his head held high. As he left the room, he passed Elwyne and greeted her.

"Don't you think you could have found a better way to take out your anger?"

"Does it show that much?"

"No, not really. I just know you a lot better than some of these other people do. Though Pike and Eldar noticed, and I think Gwydeon did too. We are all worried about you, Logan."

"I'm the same man that you fell in love with Elwyne," Logan answered putting his arms around her. "It's just that this quest is weighing on me heavily, and I can't be myself because that isn't what's expected of me."

She kissed him gently on the forehead, and then pulled away, taking his hand and leading him to the window. The night sky was laced with hues of fire and ocean meeting somewhere in the middle of the sky, and the sun had already hidden itself behind the mountain range. The peaceful war of night and day was beginning to ease, and the moon would again gain prominence in the sky. In that soft and still night, the two sat, wrapped in each other's arms, leaving the world of troubles behind. She fell asleep in Logan's arms, and as soon as he was sure he could move without disturbing her, he carried Elwyne to the bed, and slipped her under the covers. Opening the door without making a sound was no easy task for the large wooden door creaked when opening. Pike was still in the courtyard when Logan arrived, though the others had apparently just departed.

"I didn't expect to see you, Logan. Where's Elwyne?" Pike asked.

"Upstairs, asleep. I didn't see a need to wake her."

"Well, it's good of you to see us off."

"Keep your eyes open, Pike. This doesn't feel right."

"You know I will, old friend. There's more to this than we know, but there's nothing new about that, is there? Give my regards to Elwyne, and Eldar says to keep your head down."

Logan laughed at the old joke.

"And don't worry," he said turning his horse toward the gate, "Talon and I will try to save some ale for you in Falke."

His mind full of unclear thoughts, Logan walked aimlessly for a while and eventually found his way back to the room, and slipped quietly into bed with Elwyne. She rolled over and laid her head on his chest. A few hours later, the expected knock came at the door. Aryx was on the other side.

"It is near first light, my lord. It is time."

Secrets

Clouds began to gather over the twin towns of Rana and Rama as a small party of adventurers made their way out of the front gates. As the group turned their horses toward Trelon one rider stopped and turned back to face Rama. He didn't know why he was turning back, but there was a feeling as if something was wrong, something was being forgotten. But so much was still lingering in the air from the battles in Rana and Rama, the misunderstandings and the near losses. In the end they had been victorious, but what the cost could have been.

In one of the royal palace windows, a form stirred. To the man on the horse below, the form was indistinguishable due to the unusually dark morning. The clouds had blocked out the rising sun, and the golden towers of Rana and Rama were denied their breathtaking glow. The form in the window moved out farther onto the easement and looked down at the party of adventurers. He knew two of the people in the company well, and hate for them swelled inside of him. He soon became aware that one of the horses had stopped and that one of the people he knew was aware of his presence. For a scant few moments he stood there staring at the man below and trembled with violent hatred. Then, after the initial feeling of anger had passed, he ducked quickly back into his chambers and walked over to the table that stood beside the large bed.

On the bed lay a long sword. Its naked blade shimmered in the soft candlelight of the room. His eyes moved down the blade and locked on the golden brilliance of the symbol just above the cold iron hilt. Into the flawless blade, the shape of a striking viper had been etched. The crevices of the artwork were filled with the slightest hint of gold, making the viper stand out from the rest of the gleaming blade. The man picked up the sword and slid it gently into the plain scabbard attached to his belt. In all of his travels, the sword had been without a doubt his most precious possession, the only thing that he trusted, sometimes even more than his chaotic thoughts. As he fastened the sword belt around his waist, his eyes fell to an open letter that lay on the table. That letter had been the reason for his trip to Rama. Yet, he still had no idea why he had been summoned, or for what purpose. He looked at the flowing golden script on the page and shuddered inwardly at the words written there.

Korrd,

The next phase of your life is about to begin my son. Travel to the city of Rama near the borders of Old Sarmeel. There you will seek out a man called Captain Antrobus. You should be very aware of who he is if you are what I believe you to be. You will be given room and board, and there is nothing to fear from His forces. Take care, the world is yet too light for us, yet we shall soon control all.

A Friend

It didn't really matter how the words 'phase' and 'control' were fit into the message. What did matter was that he knew exactly what those words meant. Korrd knew that he had cast his lot in with the forces of the Shadow many years ago, and that he was now at Shau-ling's beck and call. The letter had been signed 'a friend' to keep others from suspecting what he actually was, but Korrd knew that it had to have been sent by a phase. The phase had been right, he did know who Captain Antrobus was, but he did not remember ever meeting or hearing about him, but still the memory of the man stood out in his mind.

This had been the first time in seven years that Shau-ling had called on him for any kind of service, and Korrd was not even sure that Shau-ling knew he was alive. However, Korrd had dreamed of the day when he would be called to Shau-ling's palace and led down through the Hall of

Terrors to the Throne of Power. The thought of being brother to the likes of the Jeresei and the Shadowwalkers filled him with a sense of elation and horror. How it was that there were so few humans used had always puzzled him, but he knew that there was something about him that was different than most other mortals, and that was why Shau-ling wanted him. In his heart he felt that the honor to serve was more than any one man should ever be blessed with, but he also knew that it was countered by the ever-present fear of failure. The mortal world had turned its back on him long ago, and now that he was being accepted into the ranks of the Shadow, he would gladly repay the slight with blood and fire. With letter clutched tightly in hand, Korrd made his way to the presence of the one known as Captain Antrobus.

* * * * * * * * * * * *

Captain Antrobus sat at the table in the middle of what used to be the palace war room and sighed. He took a long hard look at the stacks of papers that were strewn over the table and longed for the days of simple battles before Lord Logan, the Dragon, had come and made everything so complicated.

Troop deployments, food rationing, advancements, training regiments, law violations, army strengths, thousands of reports from faceless soldiers, and countless others I wish had never learned to write. What did I get myself into?

As he glanced across a page of one of the many reports from his newly named Army of the Dragon, there came a knock at the door.

"Enter," he said quite annoyed at the interruption.

The door cracked open and one of the many palace serving girls stepped into the room.

"Sorry to disturb you, my lord," she said with sincere apology, "but there is someone here to see you."

"Who is it? If it is Lord Elouix, tell him that I am too busy to trifle with matters of the law council."

"It is not Lord Elouix, sir."

"Then who is it? Speak up, girl."

"He wouldn't say, lord. He only said that I was to tell you that he was sent because you were the only one who could help him to gain control of the next phase of his life."

The words caught Antrobus somewhere in the pit of his stomach. Part of him wanted to ask the girl if she had gotten the message right, but he knew that she would not have made a mistake with something that simple. It had been a long time since those key words had announced the coming of one of his master's servants to Rama. But now, someone was there in the very town that the Dragon had just departed from. In that moment he regretted everything he had ever done before setting eyes on Logan Ranthall. The miserable creature he had once been was almost completely swept away, only now to be forcibly dragged back into the burning light of day. Antrobus took a deep breath and then replied.

"Show him in. Make sure that we are not disturbed. If I hear so much as a knock at the door, I'll..." it was then that he caught himself and realized he was shouting.

The girl looked startled to see her master in such an uproar. Before he could apologize or express any regret at his raised voice, she fled the room as quickly as she could and found the man on the other side of the large wooden door. She returned to the room mere seconds later followed by the young man. As soon as he was fully into the room, the girl left again and closed the door behind her, not willing to insight her master's anger again.

As soon as he caught sight of the young man, Antrobus began to size him up. He was proud and strong, shoulders pulled back and arms hanging strongly at his sides. His light brown hair was cut short enough to reveal the tops of his ears, and his dark eyes flickered with a cold fire fueled by anger and aggression. There was something familiar about the young man, but Antrobus was unable to put his finger on exactly what it was. Antrobus studied the man from head to toe, until he noticed the sword that hung from his left hip. The sheath of the sword was cut short enough to reveal the part of the blade just above the hilt. Carved into the blade was the shape of a viper striking from its coil. The brilliant work of art was inlaid with chips of gild, making it sparkle like all of the stars in the heavens. Only this had not been the first time that Antrobus had seen that symbol.

Lord Elouix had always demanded that the members of his army be educated in the strategies of past warlords. When Antrobus was young, he had been the perfect general from the start. He memorized the troop deployment strategies of Cedric Binosear, Arathorn Geoffry, Aryx Terian, Aralias Imstra, and many others. However, after his encounter with the forces of the Shadow, Antrobus had sought out the information on the battle strategies of the phasia, as well as the attacks planned out by Shau-ling himself. This is where he had first encountered the symbol of the striking viper. This symbol came from the Time of Conquest, before Aralias Imstra and the Hand of the Light gave the prophecies to the world.

When the phasia were first brought into the world by Shau-ling, they began to carve up the world into their own kingdoms. Jeroch built his kingdom into what was now Brae, and his was often the most powerful. However, all of the phasia feared the one called the Viper. He was the most evil and diabolical of all of the phasia. He enjoyed inflicting pain on the people of his kingdom, and would not rest until he crushed the life out of all of his enemies in battle. Of all the phasia, Saurn had been the worst, and until Aralias Imstra appeared, the banner of the Viper had flown unabated over the towers of Trelon. But that symbol had disappeared after the Hand of the Light had been extinguished and Imstra slain. The phasia began to quarrel amongst themselves, and the world was caught in the War for Power. This was the first time since then that the Viper had ever been displayed with pride.

"You are Captain Antrobus, I presume," the young man said as he sat down across from Antrobus.

"I am, sir," he replied coldly, "you look very familiar to me, have we met before?"

The young man smiled and then shook his head.

"No, Antrobus, we have never laid eyes on each other before now. Regardless of that, I know all that anyone needs to know about you."

"Do tell," Antrobus said sitting back in his chair.

"You are Captain Antrobus, former leader of the first infantry of the forces of Rama during the War of the Light. Just recently however, you have taken on a new role in the government thanks to the Dragon. You are now the Overlord of Rama and Rana, as well as the commander of the Army of the Dragon. However, there are a few things about your past that are much more interesting."

An evil glimmer flashed in the young man's eyes, and when he spoke the words dripped from his lips like venom.

"About three years ago, you were leading an expedition out to the city of Sarmeel. There you encountered a force of Jeresei and Shadowwalkers. You and your soldiers tried to escape, but you were too greatly overmatched. All of the men under your command were killed, but you managed to escape without a scratch."

"Everyone who has any connection with the forces of Rama is aware of that battle," Antrobus replied defensively. "I have been cleared of all suspicion for that event."

"But that suspicion was well-placed wasn't it, Antrobus? What no one realized was that you were taken prisoner by the forces of the Shadow, and taken back to the Island of Mist. There Shau-ling placed you into his service, and you were brought back here and ordered to wait until someone came and gave you your orders."

Captain Antrobus' jaw fell open. He tried to find words to defend himself, but they were too far out of his reach to be effective. Finally, he managed a question of his own.

"Are you the one who bears my new orders?"

"No, Captain Antrobus, but I am here to find out a few things about the *Coromor*."

"I know nothing," Antrobus replied.

"You are the worst liar I have ever seen, Antrobus. The problem is that you sweat too much to be believable."

Captain Antrobus suddenly became aware of the huge beads of sweat that ran down the sides of his face. He wiped his brow quickly and leaned forward to get a closer look at the young man. There was something about his face that seemed so familiar. It was the way his jaws slimmed down to the bottom of his chin. The look in his eyes was familiar too. He was sure that he had seen that look of power and confidence somewhere before, he just couldn't remember where.

"You know as well as I do, that Lord Logan, the Dragon, is none other than Logan Ranthall, a backwards farm boy from Aradon."

Antrobus' heart dropped from where it had been in his throat mere moments before to somewhere near his toes. If a servant of Shau-ling knew the identity of the *Coromor*...

"You know the identity of the *Coromor*?" Antrobus said in a combination of shock and horror.

"It is clear that I do, Antrobus," the young man replied in that proud tone that had rung clear even in his first words.

"Have you informed Master of this development?"

"Why should I?" the young man replied. "If Shau-ling knew the identity of the *Coromor*, the war would be over too quickly. And what's more, if a phase or one of the Jeresei found him before I did, that would rob me of my bit of personal revenge against our friend Lord Logan."

Antrobus wiped his brow again, and took a long drink from the glass of water that sat on the table.

"If the *Coromor* is unmasked, the Master must surely know about it just as soon as one of his servants learns of his identity."

"Ah, but that's the trick isn't it?" the young man replied leaning forward. "How could Shau-ling learn such information from one who has not been Bonded into his service?"

That caught Antrobus completely by surprise. If this was not one of the Master's Bonded servants, than he was not subject to the Master's rules.

He was free to do whatever pleased him, at least until the time he was taken down to the Hall of Terrors and into Shau-ling's throne room. It was there that Bonding took place. After that time, every beast was sworn to serve, and then was always pulled back to the Master, no matter where it was or what it was doing. That was why escape from Shau-ling's clutches was impossible. Antrobus had tried for three years to find a way to reverse the Bonding, but it seemed all but impossible. However, Antrobus did have one advantage over the rest of the beasts in Shau-ling's service. For some reason, human thoughts and the thoughts of the monsters worked in different patterns. One wise man that Antrobus had spoken to said that it was possible that Shau-ling could only read the thoughts of the beasts he created, and that was why he could never read the thoughts of humans, or the phasia for that matter. The phasia…

"What about your sword?" Antrobus asked quickly.

For the first time the young man appeared to be taken aback by Antrobus' words. He had been in total control of the conversation, and of Antrobus from the first words that left his mouth. This time though, he appeared to be on the defensive.

"What about it?" he asked, setting back into the cold, sly posture.

"Of all the things that you have said and done since you walked into these chambers, only one thing about you puzzles me. You speak like the high and mighty lord of all, serving evil yet exacting your measure of revenge against whom and what you please. However, you wear the symbol of the Viper on your hip."

The young man took a step back and then reset himself. He had obviously not expected for anyone to recognize the symbol on the sword, let alone ask why he wore it. Sensing his opponent's hesitation, Antrobus moved in for the kill.

"That symbol has not been raised since the Time of Conquest, and the Lord Saurn has not been seen since as well. So since all of this has occurred, and here you stand with the Viper on your hip, I must ask. Are you Saurn?"

"No, you fool," the young man replied with little hesitation. "Do you think that I would trifle with the likes of you if I were the mighty Saurn?"

Antrobus was a bit surprised by the young man's defensiveness at his question. He then realized that talking about Saurn must be a soft spot with the boy, so he pricked it again.

"You would be wise to rid yourself of that worthless symbol then. If anyone who knew the Viper saw you with that on your hip, you would be dead long before you felt the blade."

The young man's hand began to tighten around the hilt of his sword, and his haughty grin changed to a deeply etched frown. Regardless of this, Antrobus continued to prod away at the young man.

"That symbol holds no more power in this world you mindless whelp. Saurn abandoned his kingdom and fled when the prophecies were announced. He is as weak and powerless now as you are."

Before the last few words were out of Antrobus' mouth, the young man drew his sword and leapt over the table. He seized Antrobus by a tuft of hair on the back of his head, and pulled him out of his chair. Antrobus flailed at the youth until he felt the cold steel of a sword digging into the flesh of his neck. The young man was breathing heavily, trying to find a release for all the anger that had been placed inside of him by his adversary's comments.

"You know nothing of power, Antrobus," the youth roared. "You sit here over your piles of papers, and then you dole out orders like a king sitting high and mighty on his throne. Do you feel this blade? Do you feel it shortening your life by minutes and seconds? Do you feel your power slowly slipping away?"

Antrobus swallowed hard and locked his fearful gaze back on the fiery eyes of his attacker.

"Good. Keep those thoughts in mind Antrobus, because those fears will be realized if I hear one more word about the Lord Saurn escape your lips. If one word does go by unguarded, you shall surely lose your lying tongue as well as your pitiful life."

With that the young man released his hold on Antrobus and sheathed his sword as he walked back to his chair on the other side of the table, but his eyes never left Antrobus' fallen form. He sat down slowly, his hand still clutching the hilt of his sword. Antrobus rose from the floor, and made his way back to his chair. He rubbed his neck thankfully and sat back down in his chair.

"This symbol still holds power in this world. It does not command the respect that it deserves, but it is powerful enough to be respected by the likes of you. As you say, the Lord Saurn did leave his kingdom of Trelon, but he left it for his own purposes. He was not afraid of Aralias Imstra, nor was he afraid of the prophecies."

Antrobus nodded absently, still rubbing his neck and looking around nervously, trying to locate his blade.

"Do you not believe me, Antrobus? Saurn the Mighty was the only one of the phasia who could have stood up to the Hand of the Light."

"What about Jeroch?" Antrobus asked, trying to buy himself some time.

"The Shadow is a coward in the eyes of the servants of Shau-ling. You should know that as well as anyone, Antrobus. Jeroch has always been Shau-ling's favorite, and he could not chance losing his most valuable of the phasia to fighting Imstra. Surely Jeroch was happy that Shau-ling held him back from the battle. However, Saurn had no such leash holding him to the side of his Master. He met Aralias Imstra and all two hundred of the Hand of the Light in the fields outside of Aradon. It did not take long for those people to overpower the army of Jeresei and Kalbraks, but Saurn would not be so easily vanquished. He stood in the center of the battlefield drawing all of his strength to overwhelm the Hand. He eventually released his power in a strike that obliterated the Hand and robbed Imstra of his life. Saurn stood there and laughed as he watched every last one of them die. He took pleasure in their pain and suffering. He was truly the greatest and most feared of all the phasia."

"But then what happened?" Antrobus asked, still looking for his blade. "Why did Saurn leave?"

"He left because his time was over. He knew what he had to do, and it was done. No one should question the actions of a phase."

"So, what are we to do now?"

"You are going to tell me where the Dragon was headed, and then you will die."

Antrobus looked at him quickly and then started searching for his blade again, only this time he was much more blatant about it.

"After I finish cleaning my blade, I shall set forth to end the War of the Dragon by severing my good friend's head from his body and delivering it to Shau-ling. Surely then I shall be able to conquer the city of Trelon and beckon for Lord Saurn's return."

"You are a fool," Antrobus shot back as he stood, "what makes you think that you are powerful enough to defeat the *Coromor* and the *Erieal* by yourself? Surely you must have taken their powers into account before you launched this harebrained scheme. You could no more hurt the *Coromor* than a flea could hurt a stone."

"Have you been thinking about challenging me, Captain Antrobus? Do you think for a moment that you stand a chance against me?" the young man questioned, not making any move.

"Ever since the moment you walked through the door."

"What do you think your chances are?" the youth asked slyly.

"Ever since the day I could lift a sword and swing it without throwing myself across the glade, I have been training to become a warrior. I have bested everyone in my army at least once, and had it not been for my extraordinary skill as a swordsman, I never would have survived the siege by Shau-ling's forces outside of Sarmeel. There is only one man that I have ever seen in my life who has trained harder to be the best. He is traveling with Lord Logan's forces, and I know well that you could not defeat me, let alone him. So, again I tell you that your chances on revenging yourself against Lord Logan are slimmer than you could ever imagine."

"Gwydeon Sandar is the man that you speak of," the young man replied. "He is not the one that I would be concerned about. You may have trained for your lifetime, but you did not defend Trelis on the shores of Almadicia. You did not fight for seven days without sleep in the hills of Kandor. "

"What are you talking about?" Antrobus asked stunned. "Those battles took place over three hundred years ago. Some of the places and wars you are talking about happened during and even before the Time of Conquest."

Another lifetime, another set of memories. How can I remember things that I never did? How is it that I can remember other men's lives? Those are not my memories. Those memories did not come from my head. I could not have been there.

"So," Antrobus continued as he read the shocked look on the face of the youth across from him, "how do you explain this?"

"I owe you no explanations, worm. But if you want to try to get answers out of me, test your pathetic skills against mine. You will only serve to test your own embarrassment. You will fall to me as surely as the Lord Dragon will."

Antrobus looked around again for his blade. He had not seen it since he walked into the room earlier that morning, and he had not thought it necessary on this day. With the Army of the Dragon around him, he never would have thought it possible that an agent of the Shadows could have made his way into that room.

"Looking for something, Antrobus? Can't find your sword, or is it that you lost your pride somewhere on the floor?"

Antrobus looked up from the table and saw that the youth was holding his sword. Suddenly, the young man threw the sword across the table at Antrobus and drew his own sword.

"Now that you have your weapon," the youth said smugly, "prepare to defend yourself."

The youth leapt up on the table and slashed down at Antrobus. He successfully blocked the strike and slashed at the man's legs. The young man jumped to avoid the strike and then jumped off the table, connecting with an elbow to the side of Antrobus' head as he came down. Antrobus reeled from the strike and staggered backwards. The younger man slashed at Antrobus' knee, and severed his lower leg from the rest of his body. Antrobus fell to the floor and floundered for a moment. He forced himself back onto his one good leg with the help of his sword and a nearby chair. As he leaned on the chair, the young man struck mercilessly with his sword. Antrobus blocked most of the strikes, but after the young man stepped back from his opponent, he left a bloody mess. There were slashes and deep cuts all over Antrobus' chest, and his sword arm hung limp.

"Ha," the youth laughed tightly, "you look worse than Carassis did after we stormed the royal palace at Dalx."

Those aren't my thoughts. I have never been to Dalx, let alone in the royal palace. Who is Carassis? And when was I ever in an army that had a force enough to storm anything?

He kept his eyes trained on Antrobus, and was only met by a blank, stunned stare.

"Do you want to know who has beaten you before I send you to your grave, Captain Antrobus? I wouldn't want you to go kicking and screaming to the gates of hell without knowing who it was who defeated you. I am Korrd."

"Korrd?" Antrobus choked. "You're Korrd?"

Korrd went into a deep feigned bow and then replied.

"The one and only. Have you yet to figure out why I look familiar to you, Antrobus? Have you? Is there anyone you know who shares these features?"

Suddenly Captain Antrobus' eyes widened and he opened his mouth wide. Before he could force any words out of his throat, Korrd buried the blade of his sword into Antrobus' skull. His eyes rolled back in his head, and he fell from the chair that had served as the only means he had to support his weight. Korrd pulled his blade free, and wiped the oozing remains of Antrobus' head onto the clothes of the corpse.

CHAPTER 7

"That's right, Antrobus. I do look very much like my younger brother. However, Logan never did know what to do with such marvelous features."

Shadows and Reality

At Aryx's call, Logan and Elwyne dressed quickly and gathered their belongings before heading down to the stables to meet the rest of their small group. Only Aryx waited for them, but the others followed quickly. Horses had been made available for every member of the group, and once saddled and mounted, the group moved quickly through the gates in the direction of Trelon. Though Gideon grumbled about traveling by horse, he seemed an expert enough horseman and opted to scout ahead of the party. Alexander, Talos, and Alexander rode out together at a medium pace, one that would not put stress on either the horses or the riders. Just after passing through the gates, Logan felt something turn in the pit of his stomach. It was a feeling he had before, one that made him feel that he was forgetting something. Pulling up on the reins, Logan turned back toward the palace of Rama and looked up, his eyes scanning the windows of the upper floor. He caught just a glimpse of a figure standing on one of the easements of one of the palace windows, but the form was gone as quickly as he saw it. However, just the form's appearance sent a cold shiver through Logan's heart, and it wasn't until Elwyne rode up beside him and put her hand on his arm that he realized he was holding his breath.

"What's wrong, Logan?" Elwyne asked with concern in her voice.

Logan looked over to her and tried for force a reassuring smile, before shaking his head. When he turned to look back at the form in the window, it was gone. Reaching out, Logan took Elwyne's hand, squeezed it tightly, and together they turned and rode toward the path that led out of the city. It was still early in the morning, and the sun had just broken through the clouds on the horizon and was rising over the high mountain ranges to the east. It was very cool that morning, but the fires in the sky seemed to take a bit of the chill out of the air. Throughout that day of travel, there was little conversation among the members of the group, except for small snatches of conversation between Aryx and Talos. Logan found himself speaking to Elwyne very little, though her presence often made it feel like they were always wrapped in conversation, even without a word said between them. Logan's mind was still on the form he saw for that split second in Rama. When his mind wasn't wandering to the events of Rama, he focused on the road ahead, often surprised at how smooth the road was. He wasn't sure what he had expected from the road between Rama and Trelon, but it was clear that unlike the road between Aradon and Illimar, that this road was not a heavily traveled route. In the road out of Illimar, there were deep furrows carved where heavily-laden carts had packed down the dirt. There were no such furrows on the road out of Rama. It would make for a pleasant ride so long as the condition of the path held, and it would prove to be much easier on the horses should any kind of threat present itself and the group was force to flee. Just before the sun began to sink low in the western sky, the group found a place to camp for the night. The quiet day gave way to a quiet night, and for once Logan actually felt as though he were relaxed enough to sleep. But just as the nights before, his mind was plagued with thoughts of the past and the future that waited for them, and even Elwyne's heartbeat against his chest could not quiet his mind.

The second day of travel mirrored the first, in both form a fashion. Logan though began to be troubled by Aryx's evasiveness. On several occasions, Elwyne had tried to ask Aryx about what would be waiting for them in Trelon, and if he in his travels had come across any information that would be helpful to them. Aryx said little, and would only confirm that Trelon was a staunch ally of Marcwell, and that no matter the troubles they were there to combat, that the group was sure to find safe places to rest and would have to worry little about attacks from the darkness. Though Logan was sure that the statements were designed to allay their fears, the words had little to no effect on Logan's anxiety. For all of his talents, Aryx was not adept at lying or hiding the fact that he knew more than he was letting on. But Logan eventually had to cede that if there was a danger, Aryx would have brought it to their attention, and that his vagueness had to be indicative of something other than wanting to keep them in the dark.

By the second night, they had reached a small town that was on the outskirts of Trelon's realm of control. They were still about a day's travel from the capitol, but they had made good time thus far. Much like Aradon, the town seemed to be built around the inn, which was easily the largest building in the town. However, unlike the inns at Aradon and Illimar, it was obvious that the little town did not expect many travelers with the fine inns of Trelon close by. There were only a handful of rooms, and from the appearance of the common room, the inn was nowhere near capacity. Gideon and Alexander stabled the horses and then met the rest of the group in the sitting room off the main common room. It didn't take long for the innkeeper's wife to make her way over and make them feel welcome. However, the woman spoke so quickly that it made her words blur together. Logan could only make out about half of what she said, but he smiled more in reaction to the friendly tone than anything else.

"Oh welcome, welcome. You fine Lords and Lady are welcome in our little manor. Could I perhaps get any of you a drink? Maybe you would like something to eat after your journey? Is there anything at all that I can get for you? You know it's been so long since any lords of your obvious stature passed through this little town. I think the last time was…"

Aryx put his hand up and cut the woman off mid-sentence.

"We would just like some rooms," Aryx interrupted.

If the woman was perturbed by Aryx's rudeness, she didn't let it show on her face. Her smile still beamed, and she brushed her hands down the front of her dress wiping them on her apron.

"Of course, of course. You're probably tired after your travels, and I stand here jabbering on like some old crazy fool. Now, how many rooms will you need? Are you expecting more people? If you are, we could have their rooms made up for them proper for when they arrive."

"It will just be the six of us tonight, thank you," Logan responded. "We will need four rooms."

"Make dat three," Gideon remarked, "Trelon's close enough fer me to scout ahead."

"Very well then, Alexander can have his own room. We'll still take the four rooms."

"As you wish, my lord," the woman said smiling. "The rooms are at the end of the hall. Take any ones you want, we have no other guests at this time. The price is twenty gold pieces per night, per room, and that is payable when you leave."

"I'll pay it now," Aryx replied, reaching for his coin purse, "we may leave before first light, and there is no reason to disturb you."

She nodded with that same cheerful smile on her face. Aryx opened the coin purse and looked briefly at it before pressing the whole bag into the woman's hand. There was a brief look of confusion on her face as Aryx held tight to the bag and the woman's hand for several seconds before release both. She bowed slightly to him, and then smiled once more before walking the other direction.

"I'll have some food and drink sent to your rooms," she said shooing some of the bar maids into action.

"Aryx," Elwyne asked conspiratorially, "how much was in that bag?"

"Money encourages silence, my lady," Aryx answered. "The peace and lack of questions a few extra pieces of gold can buy is worth far more than the coins themselves."

Logan said nothing and just smiled. Aryx consistently surprised him with his awareness of the situation, and inwardly Logan wondered if Cedric had to worry about such things during his quest. Even Elwyne seemed to appreciate the gesture, and it was the first time that Logan began to see the change in the way they were leaving their lives. For most of their lives, they had been sheltered by the utter simplicity and straight-forwardness of Aradon. There was a way of speaking, a way of being, and a way of dealing with people that was expected, no matter who one dealt with. There was an honest that came with familiarity, and a kind of communication that developed where not everything had to be spelled out. But as comforting as that kind of life was, it was also insulating. Now that they were out in the greater world, there were more things moving than they could understand. They would have to adapt to more than just the constant danger. Perhaps that was the easier part of the adjustment. People with no nefarious motives still had had to be dealt with, and there was no telling how they could either help or impede progress. This new dynamic that Aryx had introduced them to would be the new constant, and if Logan and Elwyne didn't adapt, they would find themselves in more difficult situations than they were prepared to handle.

As they made their way to their rooms, Logan asked Gideon to stop for a brief conversation before he left on his scouting trip to Trelon. He returned to the stables to arrange for his horse before returning to the inn and knocking at Logan's door. Elwyne answered the door and showed Gideon in while Logan was just pulling his boots off.

"I'm glad you came," Logan said, motioning to the chair on the opposite side of the table from where he sat. Gideon stood behind the chair rather than sitting down.

"Why did ye wish ta see me, Logan?" he asked shortly.

Elwyne sat on the edge of the bed, and Logan sat forward, resting his elbows on the table.

"I was curious why you felt it was necessary to scout the road to Trelon tonight."

"Well, ya see, in me younger days, da Prince of Alimidar was a friends o' mine, and my place was at his side as a squire. Life was not dat fun. But, a few t'ings stuck with me. If yer goin' somewhere, Lord or Lady, ye need ta be properly announced."

"I never thought of that," Logan commented.

"How does me lady wish ta be announced?" Gideon asked raising a brow.

"Announce her as the Lady Dragon. I heard Captain Antrobus call her that, and I think it would be appropriate for this little gathering. Don't you think so, Elwyne?"

"Yes, if you can call anything that cretin said or did appropriate. But if you think that it would be to our advantage, Logan, so be it. Though I'm sure with Queen Camille expecting us, they would be understanding of a slight breech in protocol. Is this announcement really necessary?"

Logan picked up on Elwyne's train of thought.

"That can't be the only reason you want to go ahead of us."

"Ye be right dere, Logan. Listenin' ta Aryx on da road, made me nervous. People don' avoid questions unless dey got somethin' ta hide. Or somethin' dere ashamed of. Dis whole ting stinks. And ff ye don't mind me sayin' so, dis letter from da queen be a little too convenient."

"How so?" Elwyne asked.

"Well, dere's not much 'bout dis quest dat makes sense, but how did anyone know we'd be in Rama? Weren't dese towns supposed to be a myth? How did a courier find da way dere? Another t'ing, da letter was marked too well. Do ye t'ink dat anyone who would send a letter marked 'Lord Dragon' would ave any success gettin' da letter to ye? And it get dere just as we're dere? "

"Good point. But the fact that it included orders from Lord Cedric…"

"Don't ye t'ink dat anyone else who wanted ta lead ye into a trap wouldn't do da same t'ing? Lord Cedric may be da savior of da world an' all, but unless Aryx be leavin' out a lot o' details, den how could he know where we were?"

Gideon's words certainly made Logan think. Everyone knew what Lord Cedric was, and anyone who knew about the prophecies would know that the next *Coromor* would be called the Dragon. Now that the forces of the Shadow had re-emerged, there were more people looking for the signs of the emergence of the Dragon, and more individuals with vested interests on both sides of the war. For those who wished the Shadows to gain power, it would be an easy matter to bait a trap by dangling the name of the Lion and waiting to see who appeared. For all the time that Logan had spent dwelling on the terrible things that waited on the road to Shau-ling, he had not thought about the potential dangers of following the supposed orders coming from Marcwell. All they had faced to that point had been direct threats, whether it had been the Shadowwalkers, or the Tarnae, or the Jeresei. Logan hadn't thought laterally enough to envision treachery that could rear its ugly head around any corner.

"Dis is all wrong. So ye be needin' a lay o' the land, and ye got me fer dat."

"Thank you, Gideon. You may have just saved all our lives. Meet us back here in two days at sunrise. If you aren't here…"

"Den I'd be dead."

With that, he walked out of the room. Elwyne followed him to the door and locked it behind Gideon before returning to the bed. She sat for several long moments, obviously turning thoughts over in her mind before she looked back at Logan. She couldn't stop the frown from coming to her lips.

"I don't like him, Logan," Elwyne said shortly.

"Why?"

"He seems like he had no respect for anyone or anything. He interrupts, inserts his opinion where it wasn't wanted, and it seems like he always finds a way to get into trouble."

"That sounds vaguely familiar. If I remember correctly, that was part of the same speech your father game me when I told him that I wanted to marry you."

She laughed softly, but her thoughts were obviously still troubled. Logan moved from where he sat to the bed. For several moments they sat in silence, Elwyne holding Logan's hand in hers. Still looking at the floor, she started to speak again.

"But more than his lacking manners, it's clear that there is a lot more to him than he's letting on. Did you see him go toe to toe with Aryx? Sure Pike created that wave in Sarmeel, but he didn't have any control of what he was doing. Gideon, he knew exactly what he could do, like he had done it before. He may have even had the same level of control that Aryx did."

Logan frowned.

"Aryx has his share of secrets too. But if I had to choose between them, I'd sooner trust Gideon. He's cagey, true, but so far everything he's done seems to have been done for our benefit. I can't say the same for Aryx."

"Remember what your father always said, Logan," Elwyne cautioned. "Men who are more comfortable fighting alone will be the last to come to your aid when you need it the most. Not because they don't care, but because they won't see until it's too late."

"When did you start quoting my father?"

Putting her arms around Logan, she spoke in a hushed voice.

"He was always more sensible than my father gave him credit for. Then again, so are you."

"Just like I told your father," Logan countered smiling, "I knew you would be mine. I don't think he thought that was too sensible."

"Shut up and kiss me."

* * * * * * * * * * * *

At Aryx's behest, the group spent most of the next day in seclusion, emerging from their rooms only for a quiet dinner in the common room. Talos had chosen to regale the group with the tale of how he had come to be in Rana, having followed a small tribe of Moridon from the mountain in an effort to learn more about the coming war. They were best upon in Sarmeel, and only Talos and his brother survived the assault. Wounded and unsure, they, like Logan and his group had stumbled upon Rana. Though Talos' wounds could be mended, his brother's injuries were too severe.

Feeling indebted to his saviors, Talos had elected to stay on as advisor to the ruler of Rana. In that capacity, Talos had taken the opportunity to educate his new lord about the coming war with the Shadows, and the need to prepare for the time of the Dragon. In some ways, had it not been for Talos, Logan's gambit on the battlefield would not have worked. Logan had hoped to learn more about the Moridon, but Aryx made sure that the tales did not become anything that would have compromised their identity. This close to Trelon, there were many that would have recognized Aryx, or any talk that touched upon the coming war. Elwyne and Logan retired early after dinner, and Logan expected to be awake before dawn, hoping that Gideon would be good to his word and return with tales of Trelon.

Early the next morning, as expected, Logan awoke long before dawn. He hadn't slept much, but he had managed at least a few peaceful hours with his arms wrapped around Elwyne's lithe form. She always slept peacefully next to him, but she seemed to sleep the deepest when her head was resting on his chest, one arm draped over him, her hand resting on his shoulder. That morning though, Elwyne had started tossing and turning before Logan decided to roll out of bed. There was something wrong, and even Elwyne in her unconscious state could feel it. For once Logan felt that his paranoia was warranted and that perhaps he wasn't simply jumping at shadows. He slipped out of the room as quietly as he could manage, his sword firmly strapped to his hip. He was no more than half way down the hall when a form ducked out of the shadows and blocked his path. Logan's hand went to the hilt of his sword, but a split second later, he recognized the form as Gideon. Before Logan could say anything, Gideon put his finger to his lips and pulled Logan back down the hall to the room where Elwyne still lay sleeping. Once in the room and the door shut fully behind them, Gideon seemed to relax. Elwyne had heard them enter the room, and she sat up in bed, the covers pulled up around her to protect her modesty.

"I take it that the news out of Trelon isn't good?" Logan said softly.

"It's hard ta explain," he said scratching his head. "On da surface, everyt'ing looks like its supposed ta. People goin' about dere business, bein all good citizens. But it feels like dere turnin' a blind eye ta what's really goin' on. Dere be soldiers in da streets all da time. And somthin' funny is happenin' in the palace dat's got everyone on edge."

"How so?"

"Can't be sure," he said finally turning one of the chairs around and sitting, straddling the back of the chair, "but dere be some kind o' power struggle 'twixt da queen and da prince. He's secretly massing a force fer a takeover. Da situation be close ta explodin'."

"Surely the queen knows it's coming if you were able to find out so quickly," Elwyne interjected.

"Maybe," Gideon answered. "But if she knows, she ain't makin' a show of it."

If there was going to be an all-out war in Trelon, then there was a good chance that it would occur when a symbol as powerful as the *Coromor* would be present. The winner would obviously be seen as chosen by the *Coromor* to reign in his name. For some reason, it all seemed so logical; albeit strange. Given Trelon's ties to Marcwell, perhaps the queen was counting on Logan to ferret out the prince's scheme and confirm her power in the region. Either way, the possibility of danger was clear.

"What do you think the danger is to us?" Logan asked.

"Dere's no way ta know if ye'd be in danger, Logan," he replied in earnest, "but dere be a chance dat someone wouldn't t'ink twice 'bout killin' ye if ye got in da way o' da power play. If da prince tinks dat ye be supportin' the queen, he may want ta take ye out o' da picture before ye can cause him trouble. Da prince is a smart one. Not movin' too quick, and lettin' his people do da dirty work, and keepin' above it all. When he makes his move, it'll be quick an' brutal. Maybe Aryx would know more 'bout thing in Trelon. May want ta ask him how da people reacted ta da Lion."

"That sounds like a good course of action. I'll see what Aryx has to say, though he hasn't been very forthright about Trelon so far."

Elwyne steered the conversation back to the matter at hand.

"Did you have a chance to speak to the queen before you came back?"

"Aye. She said dat she would expect ye before mid-day, day after tomorrow. Not sure she liked hearin' from me an' not from Aryx or someone like dat. Don' think she trusts dat my words were from ye."

By this time Elwyne had pulled on one of Logan's shirts and had gotten out of bed. The shirt fell to the middle of her thighs, and for the moment she didn't appear that the uncharacteristic exposure bothered her.

"Sometimes I wonder if we should trust you either, Gideon," Elwyne said with little to no emotion in her voice, "but I have to admit that you do a fine job."

Gideon seemed genuinely taken aback by Elwyne's words, but there was more to it than just a reaction to what could have been perceived as an insult. He seemed surprised that she was questioning him.

"If dere be anyt'ing dat was done ta deserve yer mistrust, lady…"

"No, Gideon, it's not that you've done anything to upset me. You're a thief, and a professional liar."

His expression changed very little. Then he went into a quick yet deep bow and came up smiling.

"A thief, I be, but an honest thief."

Elwyne laughed.

"A true contradiction if there ever was one."

Gideon straightened and smiled.

"If dere be a way to prove myself, lady, give it ta me, and da proof will be in me actions."

Elwyne stood there for a moment, unquestionable in deep thought. Then she smiled.

"As a matter of fact, there is a way. But it can wait until after breakfast, and after I have had a chance to put on something more befitting my station. We'll talk again before leaving."

Gideon bowed again and started toward the door. Before he could open the door, Elwyne spoke once more.

"You may have made a mistake trying to prove yourself to me, Gideon," Elwyne said lightly. "Logan is still regretting it."

The Price of Failure

Beasts in the Pen stirred nervously as rumors of the failures of the Tarnae and the Jeresei circulated through the crowds. All of the beasts shook nervously except for the Stone who had no emotions. Suddenly, a group of Jeresei burst into the Pen dragging others of their kind. Some of the captive Jeresei were horrible disfigured, while still others were dead, and their broken bodies hung limply from the grasps of their captors. It was not usual that one clan of the Jeresei would dishonor the memory of another, but this was the price of failure that all beasts had to endure. In a way, robbing the honor of another clan was like robbing the honor of all Jeresei. Such was the punishment that the Master chose this time. Next time though, the rest of the Jeresei might not be so lucky. Only now the beasts of the Pen were beginning to realize that the Shadowwalkers had suffered the same fate that the Kalbraks had so many years ago, total annihilation.

Shau-ling did not hesitate at times to destroy one of his creations. This he thought served as an example of the punishment that was possible for failing him. However, failure had been occurring more and more often lately. Everyone in the pen and all of Shau-ling's servants around the world knew that the *Coromor* lived, and that their fates were directly related to his. If the Master bid that one breed destroy the *Coromor*, and they failed, the punishment was liable to be light. However, if one of the breeds continually failed in tasks or made a foolish decision as the Shadowwalkers had, that breed could possibly be exterminated. The beasts of the Pen watched as Jeresei after Jeresei were dragged by others of their kind toward the Hall of Terrors. Finally, two humans walked into the Pen flanking a Jeresei.

The first of the humans had midnight black hair, and mysterious glowing yellow eyes. He was dressed in black and trailed a gray cloak behind him. On his right hip he wore a long sword, and on his left hung a sheathed dagger. The man walked proudly with his shoulders pulled back and his head held high, as if he were a lord entering his own palace. His thin legs looked like willow branches through his black silk pants, but the appearance of his appendages were deceiving. With these light limbs, and thin, streamlined body, the man was capable of aerial feats that would make a falcon or an eagle envious. His hair was slicked back away from his face and hung long down the back of his neck. One of his strong hands held a firm grip on the arm of the Jeresei as his long, sharp fingernails dug deeply into the imitation human flesh of his captive. The haughty and cruel smile he wore on his face mirrored the picture of his personality; hateful, devious, cunning.

The man to the left of the Jeresei was shaped more like a terrible crag of rock than a man. His chest was broad and powerful, and his arms were as big around as his companion's waist. This hulk was shorter in stature than his companion, but what he lacked in height, he more than made up for in bulk. The man wore a gray tunic from which he had cut off the sleeves in order to display his massive shoulders. Muscles rippled down his arms, indicating to everyone that his power was more than just imagined. The man's dark gray hair was cut short, and he ran his chubby digits through it every so often to make sure that it was exactly the way he wanted it. His mouth was drawn into a massive frown, and his cobalt blue eyes flickered with disdain and jealousy. The hulk stepped lightly enough for his size, and squeezed his captive's arm tightly, reminding him of the predicament that he had been trapped in.

The three walked slowly through the Pen, but none of the beasts even thought about impeding their progress. It was not unusual to have humans in the Pen. It seemed that more and more humans were being placed into service every day. The danger of the *Coromor* and the *Erieal* was real and called for Shau-ling to take whatever measures were necessary to ensure his success, even if it meant enslaving humans. However, these two were not ordinary humans. These men had been servants to the Master longer than any of the other beasts, and it had even been theorized by the Wise Ones that they were born shortly after, if not at the same time, as Shau-ling. These humans were two of the phasia.

The one of the left of the captive Jeresei was called Basille. Basille had been Shau-ling's warlord in the realms of Thardus and Taren for many years before the Time of Conquest. He had been known as the Raven longer than anyone could remember. Basille was the only one of the phasia save Saurn who had ever had an open conflict with Jeroch, and that conflict many times led to colossal battles and trading of territories during the Time of Conquest. However, during the War of the Lion, Basille had seen his role limited to merely gathering information on the Lion's movements, and was forbidden to attack until the time had been right. Be that as it may, the time never did come for Basille. He had always blamed Jeroch for the failures of that war, even to the point of accusing him of attacking other phasia and rendering them unable to fight. This had been the reason for Basille's inner hatred of Jeroch. The day before Basille's and Jeroch's armies were to stop the Army of the Lion outside of Lakestone, Jeroch had attacked Basille and sent his army into the depths of the forest outside of Lakestone while they were all under his hypnotic power. Before they were aware that the battle was over and the Lion had triumphed, they were pursued and exterminated by parts of the Lion's army. Basille himself had also found ignominious defeat at the hands of the Army of the Lion, but took no greater pleasure than to hear the details of Jeroch's ultimate defeat at the hands of the Lion himself.

The man on the other side of the Jeresei had been Basille's ally for many years. They were always part of the same confederation of kingdoms during the Time of Conquest. He was called Warron. Because of the shape of his body and his tendency to be set wild by the littlest things, Shau-ling and the other phasia called Warron the Boar. Warron despised the nickname that he had been given, because whenever he heard it, he conjured up the image of a slovenly beast that was ugly and never respected for its power. However, that had never been the case with Warron. Kandor shook under the power of the Boar for many years during the Time of Conquest and the War for Power. However, Warron had found that allying himself with one of his own kind often became necessary, so he found friends in Basille and Zarsi. Of all the phasia that Warron had ever been at war with; Jeroch, Aldridge, and Saurn had been his least favorites, and he often found that Jeroch was the most troublesome and hateful of all of the phasia. Warron had taken great pride when he allied with Basille to defeat Jeroch at the Crags of Power outside of Sarmeel, and they would have held that ground had not Farax, the Vulture, been lying in wait to destroy the remaining forces of this victor. But, in these times when the *Coromor* roamed free, all of the phasia had to put aside their mutual hate for each other and fight to destroy the *Coromor* and the *Erieal*. However, some of the phasia seemed to forget that fact more often than not.

Basille and Warron led the Jeresei down the corridors and passages, following the dead and deformed bodies of the members of his clan, as they made their way toward the Hall of Terrors. As they entered the Hall, only the Jeresei showed any hint of fear. Warron and Basille had been there far too many times to be affected by the sight of the whirling fire and the flame spurts anymore. The beasts in the cages screamed obscenities in their native languages, at least until one of the phasia shot them a look of disgust or replied in the same dialect. That was one of the advantages of being at Shau-ling's right hand. All of the phasia had the power to instantly understand any language spoken by any of the beasts that served the Shadow. This was one way that the phasia could command armies that were mixed with different breeds of monsters. It was never easy for the beasts to work together, but after factoring fear into the equation, the army held together under a phase's power.

The Flame stood beside the door that led to Shau-ling's throne room and laughed as each of the captive Jeresei was led into the presence of the Master. Warron shot the Flame a look of disgust, but the Flame continued to laugh in the same booming voice.

"Bite your flaming tongue *Relspein*," Warron said in disgust, "you may be the next to be dragged into the Master's presence."

The Flame stopped laughing after the ancient insult had been uttered, but replied in a spiteful tone spitting fire at the phase.

"I could only hope that the skin on your hands is as thick as your Boar head, Warron," the Flame responded. "For if it is not, I will set you to burn if you ever tried to drag me around as you do this *Valtamine*."

After he had finished his insult, the Flame boomed out his laugh again, this time though it was much more intense. Warron's face began to redden with anger, and had it not been for Basille's calm and even temper, there surely would have been one of them falling to the floor dead, and it would not have been the Flame.

Warron turned his face away from the Flame and walked proudly into the throne room beside the Jeresei. As soon as the three had entered the room, the door slammed shut behind them and the lights flickered. Suddenly the room went black, and all of the dead bodies of the Jeresei were surrounded with a green glow. The bodies levitated out of the hands of their captors and floated towards the black dragon symbol that was marked in the exact center of the throne room. The bodies formed a funeral pyre that once formed set to blaze by an unseen torch. As the Jeresei burned in the center of the room, the natural light came up, and another human form stepped forward from the back of the room. In an instant all of the Jeresei went to one knee and bowed their heads. Only Warron and Basille remained standing.

The man was tall and muscular. He wore a combination of gray and black, but his face was shrouded by the hood of the cloak that had been pulled over his head. His hands were not normal human hands. The fingers were longer and slimmer, and ended in a golden talon rather than a human's fingernail. The man wore no shoes, and his feet were similar to his hands, except that they were broader and the talons were a darker gold. As soon as the man reached the two phasia, he removed the hood from his head. The face was similar to that of a human's except for the eyes and the mouth. The eyes were those of a serpent, and they glowed with a yellow fire that made Basille's look calm and dim. The man's mouth was full of razor sharp teeth, and a snake's whip-like tongue lashed around as he breathed.

"Have you forgotten that you are still my servants," the man said to the phasia, "or will I have to teach you two the same lesson that I taught Zarsi at Frontgate?"

The two phasia shivered at the thought of that punishment. Zarsi once thought that he was powerful enough to combat Shau-ling during the high point of the War for Power. He challenged Shau-ling at Frontgate, which was now a field outside of Askronilka. Their battle raged on for what seemed like weeks, but all those who witnessed the battle knew that Shau-ling was merely toying with Zarsi. On the seventh day of the battle, Shau-ling grew tired of playing with his opponent, and created a magical shield around Zarsi that robbed him of all of his abilities. Then Shau-ling created a blade of pure white flame and used it to carve vicious scars into the body of his servant. The worst of these wounds was inflicted upon his face. From that time on, in every lifetime, Zarsi bore a scar that ran from the top of the right side of his face, down his cheek, and diagonally across his neck. No one of the phasia had dared to oppose Shau-ling after that, at least, not directly.

After the thoughts of Zarsi ran through their minds, Warron and Basille quickly went to one knee and bowed their heads to their lord. Shau-ling laughed loudly and then turned back toward his throne. He walked slowly down the center of the room, making sure that each of his servants was well aware that he was in total control. Leisurely he set himself into his golden throne and then commanded his subjects to rise.

"Warron, Basille, what have you brought me?" Shau-ling asked softly.

The two phasia approached quickly, with the surviving Jeresei in tow. As soon as the Jeresei reached the foot of the steps that led to the throne, he fell to his knees and then began to beg and plead for forgiveness in his native tongue.

"Get that groveling lackey to his feet Warron, my servants do not beg for forgiveness unless I wish them too," Shau-ling said coldly.

"Yes, my lord," Warron answered.

He seized the Jeresei's arm again and then dragged him to his feet. The Jeresei kept his head down, and mumbled something under his breath that was inaudible even to the ears of Shau-ling.

"Now," Shau-ling continued, "report."

"As you commanded my liege," Basille responded in a flowing, heavily accented voice, "we searched Sarmeel for word as to the fate of our army that was to attack the people of the Dragon."

"As you had expected, lord," Warron continued, "these pitiful creatures…"

Shau-ling cut him off with a raised fist. Warron could feel the collapsing pressure of an invisible hand on his throat. The phase went to his knees gasping for air.

"Mark me well, Warron Ysamaran, you may have been second-born of the phasia, but you do not have the right to insult the creations of your father. I made them to be the perfect warriors, and for centuries they have proven time and time again that my craftsmanship has been more than perfect. You would be well to remember that they are your kin, and thus deserve to be treated as such. Not even Jeroch, the first-born, dare insult my children. If you wish to continue this slander, I would make sure that you do so in my larder."

Suddenly the grip of the invisible hand loosened, and sweet air rushed in to fill Warron's lungs.

"My brother Warron apologizes for his ignorance my liege, but I…"

Basille's words were cut off as a ball of wind and fire burst from Shau-ling's outstretched hand and slammed hard into his chest. The force of the blow propelled him across the room, and he slammed hard into the wall of the chamber. He fell to the floor gripping his chest in agony and spitting blood out of his mouth into a small pool.

"Do not make excuses for the insolence of another Basille. If you wish to say anything in your brother's defense, you may only do so if I ask you to. Never interrupt me when I am conditioning one of my subjects."

"Yes, my lord," Basille groaned.

"Now, get yourself up off the floor and come here. I am awaiting your report from Sarmeel."

Basille dragged himself back up to both feet and walked slowly back over to the throne. By this time Warron had managed to get back to his feet, and was staring at Basille with a hateful, yet fearful fire in his eyes. This was not the first time that Shau-ling had been in this kind of mood. When the Kalbraks had failed to kill White Lightning, he had been this angry. After he finished destroying the remaining Kalbraks one by one, which took more than a week, he threw Aldridge up to the ceiling with a ball of wind and let him hang there for the better part of the next month when he asked if killing all of the Kalbraks was necessary.

"Now, continue your report."

"As you command, my lord," Warron answered. "As we were searching the remains of Sarmeel, we found several of the Jeresei in the basements of the destroyed houses. The survivors were few, and those that did survive were horribly disfigured. All save this one suffered from the battle my lord."

Shau-ling leaned forward to take in the sight of the Jeresei. The beast met his gaze fearfully for less than a second and then turned his attention back to the floor of the chamber. This time Shau-ling did not laugh at the intimidation of his prey.

"You are the leader and elder of the clan Hoemsai, are you not?"

"I am, my lord," the Jeresei answered fearfully.

"You were the leader of the greatest and most powerful of any of the clans that serve me. Warron, the Hoemsai was the clan that was at your side that day in Frontgate, and Basille, they were at your side when you battled the forces of Farax at Caris' tomb."

Both phasia sparked a quick recognition of anger. They knew what Shau-ling was doing. He was stripping the clan's honor with his biting sarcasm. In the battle at Frontgate, Warron had been defeated by superior numbers of Stone and Kalbraks when half of the Jeresei in his army fled the impending battle. Basille had not triumphed at Caris' tom either. When the phase Caris had been killed by Saurn during the Time of Conquest, Basille and Farax began to fight over the lands that Caris had controlled. Basille's army of Jeresei was defeated by an inferior number of the same breed, but those Jeresei had been from another clan. The Jeresei bowed its head again, this time the weight on his shoulders had been magnified by more than he could handle. The Jeresei's knees buckled, and he fell to all fours at the feet of his lord.

"For the leader of such an honorable tribe, we should leave the punishment to only the best," Shau-ling said maliciously.

He pointed to the door with a long, scaly finger, and it opened slowly. As soon as the door opened fully, the Flame appeared.

"Bring me the Friuseon," Shau-ling commanded.

The Flame bowed its fiery head and then disappeared. Moments later it reappeared with a horrible beast at its side. The beast looked as though Shau-ling had taken a human and mixed it with a dog. It stood up on its back paws, and its tail hung down behind it and dragged across the floor as it walked. The fur was matted all over, except for a few tufts that stuck up here and there. The color of the fur was generally brown, but it was covered in many places with dry, flaking remains of where it had gotten the blood of its victims on its fur. It stood taller than all of the Jeresei in the room, but was not as tall as the Flame. One of the arms of the beast ended in a large, scaly red claw. The other arm was the stranger of the two. The skin of the arm thinned as it passed the elbow, and then came to a complete end near the middle of the forearm. From that point, the bone of the arm continued, and at the end it hooked down to a razor sharp point. The Friuseon held a wicked smile on its twisted and cruel face, and it licked its fat lips in anticipation of its meal. Shau-ling smiled to himself as he looked at his creation, and then found laughter again as he saw the Jeresei tremble at the sight of his fate.

"Do you wish to beg now?" Shau-ling asked coldly.

The Jeresei looked up at his master, and for the first time, hatred swelled inside of it. The Jeresei soon found the strength to make it to his feet, but as he rose, he was greeted by the large arm of Warron pounding him on the back. The Jeresei fell back to the ground, to the enjoyment of Warron.

"Beg you insolent creature," Warron said laughing, "if you do, Master may show pity."

The Jeresei began to rise again, and Warron was about to strike, but something held his arm back. Not something, someone.

"Do not damage my pet's meal, Warron," Shau-ling remarked playfully. "Besides, he looks as if he has something to say."

The Jeresei stood and looked at his master with the fires of hell burning in his eyes. The only other time he remembered this sensation was when he was young, and before Shau-ling Bonded him into service. Now, it appeared that the Bond had been broken, and the will had returned from where Shau-ling had exiled it.

"Well," Shau-ling urged.

"I suppose that since there is no way that anything I say will have any impact on your decision, I would like to be given leave to say what I wish," the Jeresei responded strongly.

"What? Has the animal finally found a bit of spine in that entire body of his? Perhaps the threat and inevitability of death has put a spark in him," Warron prodded.

"Be still Warron," Basille laughed, "let the condemned beast have his last words in peace. You were one of those who always wanted to make your words clear in death, so do not mock another of the same mold."

This time Shau-ling laughed, and Warron was still.

"Leave for your words are granted," Shau-ling replied shortly.

The Jeresei looked at his master and inhaled slowly. It had never felt these words in his brain, nor had he ever had a need to.

"I have served you for many years now Master and I have fought personally along the side of all of the phasia, save only Saurn. I defended your throne when the Lion crashed down upon you in Lakestone, and I was fortunate enough to survive to serve you again in this time. I have never doubted my orders from the beginning of my service, and I have never disobeyed. Your price for failure is high, and I had hoped that I could die at the hands of an enemy rather than at the hands of my master."

"You have served well in the past, but this last failure is inexcusable. Your words of defense are noted, and my praise should carry you well through your death," Shau-ling said turning from the captive.

"I am not finished!" the Jeresei screamed.

Shau-ling turned and locked his fiery yellow gaze on the Jeresei. Basille and Warron both took a step back in reaction to their lord's anger, but the Jeresei remained firm. Fear no longer touched him.

"Through all my service, as you call it, I have lived with the wrongs that you have made me do. The last mission, I saw our enemy. I expected to see a great warrior like the Lion, or at the very least one kindred to White Lightning. However, the one whom you fear…"

"I fear nothing, weakling!" Shau-ling boomed.

"The one that you fear, and the one that you wish dead more than anything else in this world, is merely a boy. He is nothing more than a child ripped out of his safe world by the hand of a fearful yet vengeful god. He does not realize what he is capable of, and his skills will never match your own. Yet you still fear, and you badger him along, taking great pride and pleasure in killing whoever or whatever is necessary to ensure that you will win the game and spite the prophecies. Aralias Imstra was the first to have beaten you. He did not beat you with a sword, nor could his army overtake your palace, but he beat you with the words that will hound you and bite you in every lifetime until he exacts his revenge for the rest of eternity. He will beat you with his prophecies, and watch you as the Great Dark One drags you kicking and screaming to the gates of hell."

Shau-ling beamed at his child with fury burning in his eyes. The words stabbed at him, prodding him farther and farther down the road to losing control and loosing his fury. The Jeresei continued, undaunted by his master's ire.

"So, you will be defeated, and you hear it first from the mouth of one of your own children. Your reign is over, and as I am about to die, with my last breath I will shout LONG LIVE THE *COROMOR!*"

Then Shau-ling's restraint snapped. The room exploded in a torrent of fire and light. All of the Jeresei in the room fell to the ground clutching their stomachs. They felt the pain growing inside of them, and they howled in agony. Suddenly, one by one, the skin of their stomachs ruptured, and fire leaped from their exposed entrails. Every Jeresei, save the captive, died a long, painful, fiery death. As Shau-ling watched his creations die, he turned his fury back to the one who had released it. He thrust both hands at the Jeresei and seized it with his magical grip. The Jeresei rose into the air, and hung there suspended over the destruction below. As he hung there, he shattered. Shattered is the only way to describe the way that the Jeresei was ripped apart by the forces that Shau-ling imposed upon it. Pieces of the Jeresei flew in hundreds of directions, adding to the strewn piles of charred bodies and flowing pools of blood. Only the whimper of the Friuseon came from the survivors.

"Flame, take it to the Pen," Shau-ling said angrily.

"Yes, my master."

"Friuseon, there you may choose any one of my beasts to work your deeds upon. A substitute meal is a meal nonetheless."

The beast barked a response that needed no translation. Shau-ling then looked to his phasia and sighed inwardly. He turned back to his throne and beckoned for them to follow. The two phasia looked at each other quickly and then followed their master. As they approached the throne, a portal of blue light appeared. In the open air between the steps of the platform and the throne, a whirling blue form appeared. This portal was the first ability that all of the phasia had been taught. This was a way that they could travel from one place to another in mere moments, rather than the days and weeks that it would take normal creatures. This portal however was different from the rest. This portal did not lead to a place, it led to nothingness. It led to the Council.

As the three stepped through the portal, the throne room disappeared. Instantly, they found themselves standing in a familiar black room. In the center of the room were three concentric circles, the first of which was only large enough for one to stand in. Around the perimeter of the second circle were ten circles similar to the one in the center of the room. Unlike the circle in the center, each of the ten circles contained the silhouettes of different animals. These symbols gave the phasia their places for the Council. Basille and Warron took their places, and as they stepped on their appointed symbol, the circle below them filled with a bright yellow light. Shau-ling strode to the center circle, and stepped inside of it. The instant his foot entered the circle, it filled with a brilliant crimson light. The light changed color several times, and as each color faded into the other, a ball of that color launched into the air above them and arched into the nothingness. The color gray brightened and then faded below Shau-ling, and as the ball lurched into the air, it immediately changed its course and slammed into Warron's chest. Rather than bouncing off or dropping to the ground, it penetrated his skin and the color of the circle below him changed its color to gray nearly instantly. The same happened when blackness flashed blow Shau-ling. The ball melded with Basille, and the color beneath him changed back to the blackness of the nothingness around them. As each of the ten balls launched into the blackness, one of the other phasia appeared, standing firmly on their appointed spot. Then suddenly a white light flashed into the room, and the only blackness remained under Basille's feet. Only the violet circle remained empty.

"It is good to have all of my children back home again," Shau-ling said proudly.

"Not all father," the only female member of the phasia said slowly, "Saurn has not decided to grace us with his appearance as of yet."

"Patience, Caris," Shau-ling replied. "He will come to us in due time."

Caris nodded, but she was not settled by the comment. Caris was a lovely woman. Shau-ling was right to call his only daughter the Wolf. She was as cunning as she was beautiful, and her greatest weapon was the deceit of those who trusted her in their beds.

"Caris speaks truth, father," the scarred Zarsi continued, "Saurn has not been heard from for many years, and he could be doing anything. He could even be in league with the *Coromor*."

"Zarsi, you are more of a fool than I once believed you to be," Jeroch scolded. "Do you really believe that one of us would really go to the other side and betray our own creator?"

"Bite your tongue, Jeroch," Basille berated, "you know that he is not welcome here, or in the presence of any of those who fight for the shadows."

"You honor me and degrade me at the same time brother," Jeroch mocked. "I do not know whether to thank you or kill you."

Jeroch was the only phase not named for an animal. Because he was first-born, Shau-ling believed that he would fight hardest for the shadows, so he was dubbed the First of the Shadow, commonly called only the Shadow.

"Enough of this useless quibbling," Warron interjected, "Master has summoned us for a reason."

"Yes," Shau-ling hissed. "I want you to be wary of the things around you. My spies tell me that the *Coromor* has united three of the *Erieal,* and he is learning more of his abilities. He is moving again, so you are not safe in your kingdoms no matter what you think. All of you are to retain your positions, and I will reconvene the Council when I feel it necessary. Now, all but Basille must leave me. Live for the Shadows!"

"Live for the Shadows!" all repeated.

"Death to the *Coromor*!" Jeroch added.

"Long live Shau-ling!" all answered.

Each vanished one by one, leaving only Basille to face his master.

"What of me, Master?"

"The circle must be complete, Raven," Shau-ling replied. "I want you to find Saurn and bring him back to me. Do this at any cost, and do not fail me. Now, be on your way."

"Long live the Shadow," Basille commented.

"Death to the *Coromor*," Shau-ling replied.

CHAPTER 7

Chapter VIII

The Weight of a Name

A few minutes after Gideon's departure, the innkeeper's wife arrived with breakfast. Elwyne had barely had enough time to dress, and was annoyed at the state of her hair upon the woman's arrival. However, as soon as the woman arrived and delivered the meals, she smiled and departed, leaving Logan and Elwyne to sit and enjoy their breakfast in peace. They had just barely finished their meal, when a knock came again at the door. Elwyne retreated from the table mumbling something about a hairbrush while Logan answered the door. As Logan expected, Gideon was waiting on the other side of the door, and Logan ushered him in quickly. By the time both Gideon and Logan sat down at the table, Elwyne joined them, quickly running the brush through her hair. Before Gideon could speak, Elwyne began again where she had left off, her tone gruff.

"I have no trouble saying that I neither like nor trust Aryx. But no matter how I feel about Aryx, his value to Logan is undeniable. He has been at the right hand of Lord Cedric for over twenty years, and in that time he has seen the best and the worst that this world has to offer and wonders that we have never seen. Whatever information he chooses to share, is valuable to us, even if it doesn't come in the way that we want or in the volume that we want."

Here Elwyne paused, and then she locked her eyes on Gideon.

"So, Gideon, here is your opportunity. You're more than you say you are, and if you want me to trust you, if you truly want to prove yourself, then you are going to answer one question for me."

Gideon frowned, but finally nodded.

"You've known you had powers long before you met us in the woods, haven't you? Someone taught you how to use them."

Gideon looked down at the table and suddenly a dagger was in his hand and he twirled it through his fingers and across the back of his hand before thrusting the tip of the blade down into the table.

"Had powers fer a long time," he said finally, his voice calm and slow. "Been learnin' how ta use dem fer years. Some in Alimidar, some lot o' places. Started small at first. Feelin' tremors when people walked. Makin' me own footfalls silent. Makin' caves when it stormed. Makin' tunnels ta sneak inta places. But nothin' like wit' Aryx. An' now, wit' Logan, dere's so much more power. Like da flood gates been opened."

Logan was shocked at the admission, but Elwyne simply nodded.

"If it is alright with you, Logan, I would like to have Gideon as my protector."

Gideon looked mildly shocked for a moment, but he appeared to recover quickly.

"What do you say, Gideon?" Logan asked.

"As ye wish, me lady," he replied softly.

Elwyne let her smile open wider this time, and then took my Logan's hand. Gideon laughed softly to himself, and after a few moments excused himself and said that he would meet them at the stables. It took only a few moment for Logan and Elwyne to gather their belongings, and together they made their way off to the stables. In the common room, Logan found Talos and Alexander waiting for them. Talos quickly mentioned that Aryx had started early that morning and was out at the stables ensuring that everything was ready for their journey. Together the four walked the short distance from the inn to the stables and were surprised when they arrived to find Aryx and Gideon sitting on the ground at the side of the stables. They were facing each other, sitting cross-legged with their eyes closed and their hands resting on their knees.

"Hello Logan," Gideon said softly, "The horses have been prepared, and the stable boys have been given adequate compensation to ensure that they will not disclose whose horses were quartered here and for how long."

All at once Logan realized that his eyes had remained closed, and that somehow his voice was different. Gideon no longer spoke with his thick accent, and his voice had lowered almost an entire octave. Then, without another word, he stood and opened his eyes. When he spoke this time though, his voice had returned to normal.

"Are ye ready ta leave, lord?"

"In a moment, Gideon. What were you two doing?"

"Aryx 'ere was showing me a few tricks dat we *Erieal* can do. It's very strange ta say da least, but figured any pointers White Lightnin' had 'ere ta share, would be foolish not ta listen."

By this time, Aryx was on his feet and adjusting his clothes, brushing the dirt from them.

"All power comes from controlling the mind. I was simply helping Gideon to learn how to quiet his mind and feel the powers that are lying under the surface. When we fought, it was clear that Gideon had raw power. However, with time and practice, he will be able to develop the fine control necessary to make that raw power difficult for his opponents to deal with."

"I'm sure that every advantage we can get will be needed," Elwyne added quickly.

"You should sit in on our next training session, Logan," Aryx said moving to take the reins of his horse. "I'm sure that you could use the help with your powers."

"My powers?"

"Lord Cedric will have to explain it, for I know little of the powers of the *Coromor*. All I know is that the *Coromor* somehow feeds off the powers of the *Erieal*. However, any groundwork that I can help you to establish will make the training that Lord Cedric will give you progress that much faster. Also, it's clear you have already stumbled onto some measure of your powers. Just understand that there is a depth there that you will discover in times of stress and tension. In those moments where you feel the most out of control, that is when you will need to seize the power inside of you and let it rise to the surface."

The conversation faded as energy shifted toward mounting the horses and starting their journey. There was a day's worth of riding ahead, and Gideon had ensured that lodgings in one of the inns on the outskirts of Trelon waited for them. If all went well, they would be in a comfortable bed just after nightfall. While the ride was uneventful, the closer that the group got to Trelon, the more traffic they found on the roads. Just after the sun disappeared below the horizon, the group had arrived at the small inn. A hot meal and a comfortable bed waited for them, but early the next morning, the group was back up and preparing for their meeting with the Queen of Trelon. Baths were prepared for everyone, and just before mid-day, the group was riding through the city of Trelon, headed for the palace that rose in the center of the city.

Trelon was just the way Logan remembered it, granted that he had not been to the city since he was a boy. The tall spires of the many churches dominated the skyline. There were also the large billows of smoke rolling out of the many smokestacks. Just outside the inner wall that separated the palace grounds from the rest of the city, the group stopped at the small stables that was reserved for those visiting the palace on official business. Gideon retrieved some papers from his pack showing that they had been given leave to use the stables, and the stable boys went quickly to work. A squire then led Logan and the others to the palace gates. Two guards stood firm at the entrance in their full dress armor, gleaming partisans in hand, with broadswords strapped to each hip and a massive tower shield in their off-hands that stood easily five feet in height. In ceremonial fashion, they moved their shields and crossed their spears to block the path.

"State your business."

"Lord Logan Ranthall an' company ta see da Queen of Trelon," Gideon. "We're expected."

"Papers?" the veteran guard challenged.

Gideon quickly produced the papers that had been given to him by the Queen of Trelon, and as soon as the guard inspected them, both guards snapped to attention and cleared the path into the palace grounds.

"Follow the squire."

The squire led the group through the beautifully landscaped palace grounds. There were gardens as far as the eye could see with sculpted hedges and topiaries. The entire path was lined with abstract sculptures and small fountains. In the center of each of the gardens were larger fountains that were brightly lit even in the glaring morning sunlight. The squire came to a stop pair of double doors that stood between two massive columns and under a white stone arch. The guards that held the door opened both after a curt nod, and the squire hesitated only a moment before continuing into the palace itself. A short walk from the main doors of the palace were another set of doors that were also guarded by a duo of guards, but before the squire could say anything to them, the doors opened and a young woman in a light blue dress appeared. The young woman said something quickly to the squire, and the squire bowed in response.

"Follow me please," the lady in waiting said with a clipped tone, "Queen Camille shall receive you now."

The guards opened the door and the group followed the lady in waiting into the room. A large throne sat on a raised platform at the back of the large audience hall that had a small set of five stairs leading up to it. Behind the throne was a large circular window that had a stained-glass lion in the center of it. The parts of glass that made up the lion were stained gold, and when the sunlight hit the window at a certain angle, the room was encased in a brilliant golden glow. On the throne sat a young looking woman. She did not seem to be much older than Elwyne or Midarin, but she had the sense of maturity about her. She was shorter than Elwyne, but the way she presented herself more than made up for what she lacked in size. Her thin figure was wrapped in rich garments, and she wore a small yet elaborate crystal crown on her head. We stood there for a moment just inside the entrance to the throne room, and then Queen Camille bade them approach. Once they reached the base of the steps, Aryx dropped to one knee, and Logan and the others quickly followed, with the exception of Elwyne who lowered herself into her best curtsy.

"Arise, my distinguished guests."

She then turned to one of the ladies in waiting and spoke.

"Leave us."

The women bowed and quickly left the room. As soon as the last member of her entourage left the room, Queen Camille stood and began to speak in a rich and regal tone.

"Sir Aryx Terian, it is nice to see you again, but I wish that it was under better circumstances. Your appearance here does not bode well for the future of this kingdom. But there are many kingdoms that know you as Doombringer. How is Cedric?"

Aryx rose, but kept his head bowed.

"He is the same, my lady; however, his condition worsens by the hour it seems."

She signed softly, and then nodded.

"I was hoping for better tidings from you, Aryx, but I would only be deluding myself to believe anything other than the fact that he is slowly dying. Now, which of you is Logan Ranthall?"

Logan rose and took a step forward.

"I am Logan, Queen Camille. I…"

"Please," she interrupted, "it is time that you knew the truth. If you are going to trust me with your identity, then I shall trust you with mine. I may be the Queen of Trelon, but my name is not Camille. My given name is Anabel Binosear, but you may address me as Lady Anne."

"You mean, you are Lord Cedric's sister?" Elwyne asked, straightening.

"The same. It is a very long story that I do not wish to explain at this time. Aryx is aware of the circumstances, which he can inform you of when there is time. So, you are the one who is prophesied to save our world. Lord Cedric has a good successor," she said.

"Thank you my lady," Logan responded bowing, "you are too kind."

"Now," she said looking over my party, "introduce me to your companions."

"First, this is my fiancé, Elwyne Tamerlane."

Elwyne walked forward a step and then bowed. Logan saw a barely perceptible flinch come from Lady Anne, but he wasn't sure why. Aryx had almost the same reaction the first time he saw Elwyne. Her eyes looked very sad, but as soon as her eyes met Elwyne's, she began to smile.

"Next is Talos of the Moridon."

Talos stepped forward quickly. Lady Anne raised a closed fist to her heart and bowed her head. Talos returned the salute in kind, and then stepped back.

"It is good to see that one of the Moridon survived the battle with Shauling. It would be a shame to see such a brave people wiped out."

"It is enough to know that they died while serving the *Coromor*," Talos replied proudly. "I hope that they are serving him on the Other Side. I only hope that my end comes with the same honor and peace that theirs did."

Lady Anne nodded, and her gaze fell upon Alexander.

"And who is this charming boy?"

"This is Alexander Mealon, my standard bearer."

Alexander stepped forward quickly, and bowed.

"Tis a pleasure to meet you, my lady," he said proudly and eloquently.

"And I you," Lady Anne replied in a mixture of pleasure and surprise.

"Of course you have already met Gideon Viruci."

"Yes," she replied, "he does make an impression."

Lady Anne then sat back onto her throne, and recovered a parchment that sat on a low table to her right. She untied the string that was wrapped around it and then opened the letter. She scanned it quickly and then put it away.

"This letter arrived from my brother only a day after I sent my letter to Rama. In this letter there is some shocking information about your quest. If what is in this letter is true, and both my brother and I believe it is, Shau-ling's forces are massing outside Castleer and are preparing to attack."

Aryx's words interrupted Logan's thoughts.

"What is in Castleer?" he asked.

"Lord Cedric believes that the Jeweled Dragon's Flame is being kept there by the forces of the Light. You see, the Jeweled Dragon's Flame exists much as Shau-ling doe. It is in all times, and in all planes of existence at once. However, it is never in the same place for long. It moves around at will, moving from Keeper to Keeper until it is in the hands of one of the forces. "

"If it is the only thing that can hurt Shau-ling," Logan replied, "then how is it possible that the forces of the Shau can possess it? It's a weapon of the Light, isn't not?"

"It may be a weapon of the Light, Logan, but the Flame has a mind of its own. The Flame itself is a neutral thing. When the *Coromor* and Shau-ling arrive in the same time frame, the cosmos is in balance. In order to perpetuate this balance, the Flame must be neutral. Whoever controls the Flame will ultimately destroy the other, and that side will win. Think of the Flame as the key to a door. Whosoever holds the key controls whatever lies behind the door. In this case, the door holds dominating power and the fates of generations to come."

Those thoughts sent chills down Logan's spine. He couldn't help but shiver, and he knew that everyone had to feel the same way. Logan looked up at Lady Anne for a moment, and then spoke.

"Then there is no other option, we ride for Castleer in the morning."

"I believe that is the only course of action that is possible. Since all of the Watchtower forces have been activated, there are no troops that can be mobilized to defend Castleer without compromising the forces that protect Trelon."

Aryx took the opportunity to step forward and speak.

"Is all well here in Trelon, Lady Anne? There have been rumors circulating throughout the palace that there is to be a coup attempt," Aryx chimed in quickly.

"And who is plotting this coup?" Anne asked slyly.

"Prince Allan, me lady," Gideon replied.

"I have heard similar rumors, I must say," she said running her fingers through her hair, "though I put very little trust in them. Why would my own son try to take over my seat? He must know that if he were to kill me, my daughter Cairyn would rule. Trelon has always been ruled by women, and it will continue to be so long as the Binosear family holds breath."

With that, she smiled.

"I have rooms for all of you here in the palace. However, you must promise me that you will do one thing for me before you leave."

"Anything, my lady," Aryx replied.

"I want you to have dinner with myself and my daughter tonight. My ladies in waiting will show you to your rooms so that you can clean up. If you want, I can have the court tailor provide you with some new clothes this afternoon.

"That would be wonderful, my lady," Alexander replied.

Anne smiled.

"Elwyne," she continued, "I suppose that you will share a room with Logan?"

"Yes, my lady," Elwyne responded almost blushing.

"Very well then. I will have my servants prepare a suite for you on the other side of the palace. Very few people stay there, and you will have all the privacy you could ever ask for."

"Thank you, Lady Anne," Elwyne said bowing.

Lady Anne nodded and clapped her hands loudly twice. All of the doors of the chamber opened suddenly, and tens of women streamed into the room. Anne relayed her wishes to the women, and we were ushered quickly out of the room.

Elwyne and Logan followed two women down an extremely colorful yet empty corridor, and then were led into an enormous room. The walls of the room were painted in gleaming white, and there were large windows all over the room, covered with red draperies. As they looked around, the two women backed out of the room, giving the couple some well-deserved privacy. Moments later, there was another knock at the door, and two men wheeled in two large basins filled with steaming water.

* * * * * * * * * * * *

After rather lengthy baths, Logan and Elwyne found themselves in the strange and new sensation of being fawned over by the court tailor. He and his assistants took a series of measurements and then laid out a series of garments to help determine style and color. Elwyne selected a regal looking sapphire dress with a white sheer piece of material across the chest that ran all the way to the throat. Logan picked what was closest to a common black tunic with bronze accents and a dark gray set of front ties. Many of the other choices were much less conservative, and it seemed like Elwyne was tempted by some of the more revealing options. An hour before dinner, the tailor returned with the fitted garments. They dressed quickly, and as they started to leave the room, Logan instinctively reached for his belt and sword. Elwyne slapped his hand away and scolded him for even thinking about taking his blade to a dinner with the Queen of Trelon. He frowned, mostly at himself, and then laughed. Elwyne kissed him on the cheek and they walked out of the room and down the hall. They were intercepted by one of the ladies in waiting and led through a series of halls before stopping before another set of double wooden doors. The woman bowed slightly and then turned, opening the door.

The dining room that they were led to was not the formal palace dining room as Logan had expected, but the smaller private dining room that Lady Anne used to entertain special guests to Trelon. The table in the center of the room seated roughly ten people, and had three gleaming silver candelabras sitting on it. The light from the candles was the only light in the room aside from the fireplace and the two torches mounted on either side of the room. The rest of the group had already arrived and were seated, with the exception of Aryx. The ladies in waiting that were stationed in the room led Elwyne and Logan to their seats, and there wasn't much time for conversation with the others before the doors on the far end of the room opened and the Queen and a young woman who was presumably her daughter were led into the room by Aryx.

As soon as they entered the room, everyone at the table stood. Aryx showed Lady Anne to her seat, and then in turn pulled the chair out for Princess Cairyn. The princess stood slightly taller than her mother, but had the same youthful appearance and soft features. Cairyn however had light green eyes unlike the brown eyes of her mother. Where Anne dressed conservatively, Cairyn was much more daring her wardrobe, with a plunging neckline and high slit up to the middle of her right thigh. Anne wore little to no jewelry, but Cairyn seemed to enjoy her position, wearing a long string of pearls and golden bracelets on each wrist. Once the Queen and Princess were seated, everyone else sat, and Anne immediately reached for a small crystal bell that sat next to the plate in front of her. Mere moments later, servers flooded into the room carrying trays overflowing with food of all kinds.

"Lord Logan," Anne said, with a wide smile, "I would like to introduce you to my daughter Princess Cairyn Binosear, the heir to the throne of Trelon."

"It's a pleasure to meet you, Princess," Logan said trying to keep his tone regal, "we appreciate the hospitality that you and your mother have shown us. It has been a difficult road for my friends and I thus far. In fact, in order to ensure that we were not followed here, half of my group went on to Falke ahead of us. I'm sure they would have appreciated the welcome."

Anne smiled and raised her glass. Cairyn folded her hands on the table and fixed her gaze on Logan.

"So, Lord Logan," Cairyn said casually, "you seem to travel with a rather eclectic group; though I'm sure given the circumstance that was to be expected."

Logan could feel Elwyne tense at the princess's words. She had obviously taken the comment as an insult.

"Most of our party is made up by those that I grew up with in Aradon. Alexander and Talos joined us in Rama, Gideon joined us just outside Aradon, and Midarin Rice joined us in Illimar"

Cairyn nodded.

"Midarin Rice," she said as if trying to place the name. "Ah, yes, the tramp. I would be wary of her if I were you; she has more ways to bed a man than any woman I have ever met in my life. She also has a terrible temper that is fueled by her ambition. Given your position, she may try to bed you to recover her lost title."

Anne cleared her throat, but Cairyn ignored her and continued speaking.

"But it seems like someone may have already staked their claim on you. Does this lovely girl hold the key to your heart, or are you still looking for a woman who could rule beside you?"

Logan felt Elwyne balling her fists, but he tried to ignore the more obvious insult.

"Princess Cairyn, may I present my fiancé, Elwyne Tamerlane."

The princess looked Elwyne over, then inclined her head and frowned.

"Pity. But, I supposed everyone has their standards."

Elwyne was furious. But before the arguments could escalate, Cairyn rose from the table and started toward the door. Anne put her hand on her daughter's arm as she passed. Cairyn pulled her mother's hand away.

"You'll forgive me, mother," Cairyn said looking back over her shoulder, "but I am needed elsewhere, some matter for my brother. Besides, I've lost my appetite. You know how finicky I am about company."

Anne waited for her daughter to leave the room before lifting her glass and tilting it in Elwyne's direction.

"You'll have to forgive Cairyn," Anne said smiling. "She is her father's daughter. And I believe he may have dropped her on her head as a baby."

Elwyne laughed and raised her glass in answer to Anne's apology. The rest of the dinner conversation was much lighter and stretched on late into the night.

Sador

Pike Rhuiden looked up at the sun and sighed. He knew from looking at the maps that his group had made good time over the night. Traveling at night was not something that Pike wanted to do, but it seemed necessary to keep the diversion as realistic as possible. Something else was eating at him inside, though. Some of his fears had been quelled when Logan had spoken to him before his group departed, but more were placed in him by his friend's mysterious words.

Well, he thought to himself, *I can think of a lot worse places that I could be in at this moment. I mean, it isn't like Logan told me to lead my friends down to the gates of hell and spit in the Great Dark One's eye. I suppose that I would be a little more secure with the idea of splitting up if it had been Logan's idea in the first place. But of course, it hadn't. Lord Cedric is sitting up in the tower of his palace back in Marcwell, controlling Logan's every move. According to him, he sent that Aryx character to help us find the Jeweled Dragon's Flame, as well as keeping us from getting killed. Then, he keeps sending letters to Logan through his different associates all over the world, and is quietly pulling Logan's strings. I wonder if Lord Cedric realizes that more lives are hanging on Logan's strings than just his own.*

Quit thinking about yourself man, another set of thoughts interjected, *Logan is the one you should be worried about. The way that Lord Cedric is controlling his every move is really starting to destroy the confidence he has in himself, and he is starting to doubt that he will survive the trials of this quest long enough to do what he has to do. I can't believe that I didn't see it at first though. I was so blinded by my faith and loyalty to my friend and to what he had become that I refused to see the truth. Then Elwyne approached me and told me that she was concerned about Logan. He and I are close, and I would have thought that I would have been the first to notice any change in him, no matter how small. Then again, Elwyne and Logan seem to have reconciled their differences caused by his absence over the last few years. I suppose that a lover would realize things like that a bit quicker than a friend.*

Pike smiled to himself and began to wipe his brow. It was extremely hot for as early as it was, but when he started to realize that he was looking around for a supernatural cause, he scolded himself. He looked up at the sun again, and then reached for the canteen that hung from his saddle. As he took a long drink of the cold water, a new set of thoughts rushed into his mind.

I suppose that I would get discouraged too if I allowed someone to run my life like Logan is allowing Lord Cedric. The difference in my situation is that I know, and am able to see my superior on a regular basis. Logan has never really known Lord Cedric. We all met Lord Cedric, back when we were younger. The difference is that we didn't really know what he was, nor did we really care. Things were different back then. We didn't have to worry about battles, nor did we think about invisible terrors that only invaded our minds when we slept. I guess that's why I can't sleep well anymore. If I lower my defenses for a second and sink deep into sleep, the dreams come. Logan has it much worse. And I wonder if there is any choice left for him. It seems like a hundred years since I worked with my father in the fields as a boy. At least I still have my freedom.

As Pike's thoughts rambled, he shivered uncontrollably. He looked ahead at the rest of his group. The large limbs that sank low onto the path obscured his vision a little, but he could make out every member of his party clearly. Lane, Eldar, and Midarin rode together at the front of the group, and they appeared to be engaging in very limited conversation. Gwydeon and Talon rode about five yards ahead of him, and were talking and laughing most of the time. No doubt, Talon was telling Gwydeon some of the jokes and stories he heard while frequenting the inns and taverns in Rama. Pike rode by himself, bringing up the rear of the force.

A fine leader I turned out to be, he thought to himself as he looked around. *In my first command back in Sarmeel, I nearly got the whole group killed, as well as almost winning the war for Shau-ling. If it weren't for the fact that my powers made themselves known when they did, we would all be dead, and the world would be in Shau-ling's clutches for the rest of eternity. I certainly don't envy Logan's position being the Coromor; I don't think I would be able to handle the weight he has to bear. I find it hard to believe that one life can hold the key to the fates of so many other lives, but from what I hear, that is what is written in the prophecies. I wish I had the strength that it must take for him to handle all of this.*

He turned his thoughts away from those subjects and tried hard to think about something else. For some reason, his thoughts always seemed to turn back to his friend. It was as if he could feel Logan, and he found himself looking back toward Rama, wondering how he was. And even then, he could hear Logan's words ringing true in his ears as if he were there beside him shouting in his ear. Something about this certainly didn't feel right.

Pike's thoughts trailed off as a new idea came into his head. He dug his heels softly into the flank of his horse and rode quickly up to Talon and Gwydeon. Talon patted him on the back as he came into arm's reach of his friend, and as soon as Talon saw his friend's face, he knew that something was wrong.

"What's on your mind Pike?" he asked.

"A lot of things Talon, but some of them weigh more heavily than others," Pike answered.

"Such as?" Gwydeon inquired.

"Well, I'm not sure if either of you are aware of it or not, but Logan came down to the stables before we left and wanted to talk to me," Pike replied.

"I noticed that something had delayed you when we stopped just outside the gates, but at the time we didn't think that it was important enough to ask you about," Gwydeon remarked.

"There wasn't much to the conversation. At the time it seemed like nothing, but now that I have thought a little more about it, it makes a lot of sense."

"Was it that bad?" Gwydeon asked somberly.

"Why does it have to be bad news?" Talon demanded gruffly. "It seems that no matter what we do and no matter where we go there is always bad news following us."

"Really, Talon," Gwydeon replied coldly, "can you actually believe in your heart that there could be any good news in the world with Shau-ling and the phasia running loose, making grand nuisances of themselves all over the world?"

Talon had no choice but to concede the point.

"I guess you're right Gwydeon. Well, Pike, out with it."

"Logan told me to keep my eyes open, that something about all of this didn't feel right. But I think there is more to it than that. I think maybe that is why he sent Midarin with us rather than taking her with him. I think he expects us to see combat."

"Maybe her past would have just complicated things in Trelon," was Talon's short reply, "but Logan's right. This stinks. Just don't like the idea that he's getting premonitions or something."

"I agree," Gwydeon added, "but the way that Logan has been acting lately, I'm starting to believe that he is capable of anything. He hasn't exactly been the carefree old Logan that we grew up with."

"At the very least, I would think that Logan would have given a reason for anything that he said. Even when he was young, he was able to justify even the most trivial and stupid thing that he did. It isn't like him to just say something and not back it up," Talon contended.

"He didn't have to give a reason," Pike responded earnestly. "We all feel it. There's something going on in the shadows, something we're just aware enough of to be uneasy. It's like when we were kids. Anytime we were doing something we knew we shouldn't you could almost feel one of our parents looking over our shoulders just waiting to catch us. Like we always said, the worst beating…"

"...was the beating you thought you were going to get. I know, I know," Talon concluded.

They all laughed a tight guarded laugh at the old yet true axiom. It seemed that more and more of these axioms were proving true, and it was only time before some of the dark and sinister ones that they learned as children proved to be true as well. For a few minutes, an uneasy silence held between the three friends, and it seemed as if they were all thinking about the same subject. However, after a time, Gwydeon cleared his throat, announcing that he was ready to break the silence.

"Have either of you ever talked to Elwyne about Logan?" he asked softly.

Pike and Talon looked at each other for an instant and then turned back to Gwydeon.

"As a matter of fact..." Pike started.

"Yeah," Talon cut in.

"Why do you ask?" Pike continued.

"Just wondering," Gwydeon balked.

"There is more to this Gwydeon," Pike prodded. "You've never been able to keep any secrets from us, and I don't want to have to beat the information out of you like I used to when we were children."

"I suppose you're right," Gwydeon conceded. "If I can't talk to two of my oldest and best friends, then who can I talk to?"

"Damn right!" Talon retorted.

"Anyway, all these strange things going on have caused me to do some serious thinking about Logan and all that he is going through. He's been acting differently lately, and I didn't notice it for the longest time. Elwyne decided to pull me back into the reality of the situation just after Dreamscape."

"She did that to all of us, Gwydeon," Pike replied, "I suppose that she had the worst of it in there."

"I would tend to agree with you, but she seemed more worried about Logan than about what had happened. Granted that she was really shaken up, but there was more to it than that."

"A lot of things have happened between them since Logan returned from Trelon, Gwydeon. Most of all, they seem to have rekindled their relationship since the quest started," Talon commented. "Her father will not find that very pleasing to his ears. Mayor Tamerlane has never liked Logan, and he forbade Elwyne from seeing him. Had it not been for David..."

"Don't rehash old wounds, Talon," Pike said shaking his head. "Let the dead rest."

"Sorry, Pike."

"Getting back to what I was saying," Gwydeon interjected, "that was the first of two times that she found me to talk to me about Logan. She asked me if I thought Logan was changing, and she wondered aloud about the things that were different about him."

"What did you tell her?" Pike said in a tone that barely masked the twinge of concern inside him.

"I told her that I didn't notice too much of a change. However, if there was one that I had overlooked, because of what we went through in Dreamscape, I told her that it would be understandable. I told her that the weight that had been placed on him because he was the *Coromor* must be tremendous, and it would make it impossible for him to be the same man that he was. In some ways I think he is a better man. Darker, but better. And to top everything off, having to save our skins in Dreamscape would bring about a lot of change. It changed all of us, and I told her that she couldn't expect him to be immune to it."

"In a roundabout way, I told her the same thing, only I was a bit more direct about it. I don't have the vocabulary or expertise with words and phrases that you do," Pike replied.

"Thank you."

For the first time in a long time, the three friends shared a smile at Gwydeon's dry wit. Smiles were not on the faces of the adventurers often, but when a smile did grace a face, even for an instant, it was a cherished return to the life before Shau-ling's appearance.

"You said that was the first time that Elwyne pulled you aside?" Talon asked.

"Yes, that's right."

"What about the second?" Pike inquired.

"Well, we were in Rama, and it was just after we had returned from the battlefield, after Logan put Elouix in his place of course. She apparently..."

* * * * * * * * * * * *

Elwyne walked quietly down the corridor and stopped just in front of Gwydeon's door. Her conversation with Eldar was shorter than she had anticipated, but she did not feel like returning to her room. As far as she knew, Logan was still in conference with Captain Antrobus, and after their brief run-in a few minutes previous, she did not want to have to face him again so soon. She needed someone else to talk to because she had heard Eldar's opinions so often that she was sure that her old friend never did have anything new to say. It was for this reason that she was standing outside of Gwydeon's door instead of sitting talking to Eldar. Of all the men that she traveled with, she felt closest to Gwydeon, and she knew that if anyone could help her, it would surely be him.

Elwyne and Gwydeon had been friends as far back as she could remember. Gwydeon's father was the most prominent blacksmith in Aradon, and he was also the head of the Village Council. The Village Council would take its concerns to her father the mayor in the person of Torris Sandar. So, whenever Torris would visit her father, he would bring Gwydeon along, for the sake of company. Every time there was a meeting though, it would always turn into a shouting match, and she and Gwydeon would be sent out of the room while the adults would have their 'chat'. This was how she and Gwydeon became such good friends. After Logan left on his adventures, she stayed close to Gwydeon, trying to keep some semblance of her life the way it had been. If there was anyone that she felt comfortable talking to, it would most definitely be him.

As Elwyne approached his door, she noticed that it was slightly open. It was not enough of a crack to see through, and it looked more like carelessness than anything else, but Elwyne knew better than that. Gwydeon had always been a private person, and he never liked to have an audience for anything that he did, even if it were just a few of his friends. For this reason, Elwyne found the open door too suspicious an occurrence to pass up. She pushed the door open slowly, not thinking to announce herself. When the door opened enough for her to see in, she was slightly taken aback by her discovery. After the momentary shock of her discovery passed, she had to put her hand over her mouth to stifle a laugh.

As the door opened, it revealed a host of young women sitting at various places beside the walls of Gwydeon's room. As Elwyne scanned the faces of the women, she recognized some of them as the guards who held her door and the doors of Midarin and Eldar their first night in Rama. Most of them wore wide smiles on their faces, while still others looked on with half stifled gasps of amazement and wonder with glowing eyes. All of the women focused their attention on one thing. Gwydeon.

In the center of the room, Gwydeon stood holding his wooden practice sword. Elwyne had seen this routine many times during the years that she had known Gwydeon, but she had never seen him so public with his practice sessions. This was the same set of forms that Logan's father had taught him, and from the time of his death, Gwydeon had done this practice routine every day. This was done not only to stay in shape, but also to pay homage to his teacher and to the father of his closest friend. As usual, the only thing Gwydeon wore was a short white set of breeches that came to an end just before the caps of his knees.

As Gwydeon moved through those practice forms, his muscles rippled and beads of sweat rolled down his glistening chest. Gasps and sighs came from some of the women as he moved smoothly and effortlessly from one sword form to another. He slashed and parried as if the sword were not just an object that lay in his hand, but an extension of himself. Elwyne recognized the continuity of the forms and knew that the routine was coming to an end. Gwydeon parried and took a long broad slash at the air and then continued into a spin. He then fell to one knee and thrust his sword with such power that he could not help but utter a scream of rage, his battle cry. As he finished, he closed his eyes, bowed his head, and lowered his practice sword slowly to his side. Upon completion of the breathtaking exhibition, the room erupted in laughter, applause, and screams of admiration. He raised his head slowly and smiled at his audience. As he looked around and turned to place his practice sword on the bed behind him, one of the women, who was sitting behind him, rose and took him a carafe of water and a towel. He smiled graciously at her and then gently took the towel that she offered him. He then took a drink of water, and upon wiping his lips, he pressed them to hers. They held the kiss for merely an instant before he turned back to the rest of the women. One of the women then stood and spoke.

"That was wonderful Sir Gwydeon. I have never before seen finer sword play from anyone in my life. Could we perhaps attend your training again tomorrow?"

"If I am here tomorrow, I am at your disposal. But I would remind you that I am not a knight no matter what company I may keep. I am merely a simple farm boy," Gwydeon replied with all possible modesty.

For a few minutes, the women stood around the room, trying to get close enough to Gwydeon to tell him how much they enjoyed watching him practice. After that, the women filtered out of the room quickly, leaving Gwydeon and the woman who had offered him the water alone. He turned back to her and took her into his arms. He kissed her gently and then pulled back to look at her for a moment. She was nearly as tall as he was, and her thin body felt soft against his as she nestled close to him. He put his thumb and forefinger under her chin and raised her face to look at her. Her shimmering blue eyes turned up toward his and they shared an intimate moment that only true lover could ever understand. He ran his fingers through her short brown hair and then kissed her again. As the kiss ended, she looked up at him and smiled.

"You may be a farm boy, Gwydeon Sandar," she said plainly, "but you are far from simple."

He smiled at the joke and kissed her again. She pulled away from him mere moments later and made her way out of the room. Gwydeon turned and he watched her as she left. As his eyes followed her out of the room, he noticed Elwyne for the first time, standing just inside the door to his room. When he saw her, his face immediately reddened, and he reached for the shirt that lay on the bed beside him. He pulled it hurriedly over his head, and then looked back at Elwyne who merely smiled and shook her head. Before she could say anything however, the woman ducked her head back in the door and spoke.

"Gwydeon," she said in a sweet, melodious tone, "I forgot to tell you, I'll bring you your dinner in an hour. If you are still talking to your friend, I'll bring it later. When I do though, you can teach me to 'dance with the sword' as you so elegantly put it. Until then, my love."

She smiled at Gwydeon, blew him a kiss, and then left. Elwyne watched her as she left, and then closed the door. Elwyne turned back toward Gwydeon with a wider smile on her face. Gwydeon could tell that she was enjoying every minute of this strange predicament that he had found himself in. He finished dressing, and then sat back on the bed. Elwyne continued to look at him with that same quizzical gaze as she sat down in a chair across from him.

"My love?" was all that she said.

Gwydeon cleared his throat at the phrase, and then laughed a little. Elwyne could tell that it was a nervous, uncomfortable laugh and that Gwydeon was off-balance. Gwydeon may have been masterful with a sword, but when it came to women, he was just a beginner.

"Yes," he replied, "we've gotten a bit closer since we met the first day of our capture. She is really an incredible soldier, Elwyne. She was the section leader of the force that I commanded in the battle. I have even heard that she is second only to Antrobus in the command structure."

"She was the guard at my door the first night. I even talked to her before the battle a little. She is a charming woman, Gwydeon. I'm surprised that she never said anything to me about you."

"I asked her not to Elwyne."

"Oh, I see. What was her name again?"

"Leane. Leane Torne," he replied.

"Leane," Elwyne repeated, "that is a beautiful name to fit an equally beautiful woman. You're a very lucky man Gwydeon Sandar."

"Thank you Elwyne. For some reason that means a lot coming from you."

"Now," Elwyne continued, "what is this about teaching her to 'dance with the sword'?"

All Gwydeon could do was blush.

"If I remember correctly," Elwyne added, "that was the song that Arin Ranthall used to sing about the princess who was so mesmerized by the talents of a young swordsman that she gave up everything and went to his room one night to give herself to him. After that, the swordsman devoted his life to her, and they ruled together in her kingdom."

Gwydeon's face reddened a little, and he tried to speak. Elwyne stopped him and they shared a laugh.

"Stop squirming Gwydeon. I understand completely."

Gwydeon took a long deep breath and decided to launch a question of his own.

"So, what was it that you wanted to see me about, or did word also reach you about my little practice session?"

"I've seen you practice in less than that white pair of breeches Gwydeon Sandar, and unlike these women, I was never that impressed. However, I must say that you are a lot bigger than you were back then."

Gwydeon laughed and took his sword from the scabbard that lay on the floor beside the bed. As he took out a cloth to polish his blade, Elwyne continued.

"Gwydeon, I wanted to talk to you about Logan."

"What about?" he asked softly, concentrating on his blade.

"Have you talked to him lately?"

"Not really, at least, not since the quest started. There really hasn't been that much time to sit down and have a civil conversation since we left Aradon."

"What about when we first got our rooms here in Rama? There must have been time for you two to talk."

"I spent most of my time here in my room talking to the guards and the servants that stopped by for various reasons. That was when I took the time to get to know Leane. Besides," he said looking up from his blade directly at her, "from what I've heard, he wouldn't have had much time to visit with me anyway."

This time it was Elwyne who blushed.

"I suppose you're right."

"What's this all about Elwyne, if you don't mind my asking?"

"I'm just worried about him Gwydeon. He seems so different since the quest started, and I can't figure out why. I know why he changed, I'm not that blind, but I just don't know what to do about it."

"I can't say that I completely understand what you mean Elwyne, but since you came to me for help, I'll do my best. Logan is really a very special man. Putting aside the fact that he is the *Coromor*, he is still special. He cares about us all, and I think he would gladly give his life to protect us. I think in a way, this quest is his way of proving that same conviction that he has always contended to have. He loves each and every one of us as if we were a part of his family, and I'm sure that it won't be long until you two are married."

Elwyne smiled a little at that, but continued to listen to Gwydeon as he continued.

"It is this powerful love that makes him so special Elwyne. That is why there has been a change in his attitude. After David died, he realized how precious and fragile life can be, and just how much we all mean to him. He's trying his best to show us how much he cares for us in the time that he has left."

"The time he has left?"

"I don't mean to worry you any more than you already are Elwyne, but this is something that you should know. I've been talking to Aryx recently, and he told me a few things about Lord Cedric that aren't exactly common knowledge."

"What is it, Gwydeon?" Elwyne urged.

"Lord Cedric is dying, Elwyne, and it has everything to do with the fact that he killed Shau-ling in his time. At the most he has a year left, if even that long. It's only been seven or eight years since that final battle with Shau-ling took place, and each year his condition has slowly deteriorated. If the same holds true for Logan, after the battle, he will just wither away. At the most, Aryx and I think that he would have no more than ten years of life left."

* * * * * * * * * * * *

"You really shouldn't have told her that Gwydeon," Pike said softly, "there is no need to worry her any more then she already is."

"That's true Gwydeon," Talon commented, "but I want to hear more about the girl."

"What girl?" Gwydeon asked with mock innocence.

"The girl, Gwydeon," Talon prodded, "this Leane Torne. Who is she?"

"She's Antrobus' second in command in the Army of the Dragon. Her mother and father were both warriors as far as I know, and her father saw action in the War of the Lion."

"I didn't want her family history, Gwydeon. I want to know what she looks like," Talon urged.

"Okay, okay. She has the most gorgeous sparkling blue eyes that I have ever seen in my life. She has short brown hair, and incredible legs. Her body is so thin and strong, she's incredible."

"I think I remember seeing her coming out of your room when I came to tell you that we were leaving for Falke," Pike commented.

"Was she wearing a high necked green gown?"

"Yes," Pike replied.

"That was her all right. She loves the color green. You know, she once told me that green . . ."

"Pike!" Lane yelled from a few feet ahead.

"Saved by the yell," Pike mumbled.

The three friends stopped their conversation and rode up to meet the rest of their companions just at the edge of the forest.

"What is it Lane?" Pike asked.

"There's a town just off to the right there, and I think we could all use a little rest."

"I agree Pike," Eldar chimed in, "some of us could most assuredly use a bath."

Eldar glared at Talon for a moment, and then he flashed a smile and blew her a kiss. Midarin giggled a little at the exchange and then turned her attention back toward the town.

"Anyone know anything about this town?" Talon asked.

"Only a name," Midarin replied, "Sador."

The Viper

Korrd looked at the fallen body of Captain Antrobus again and smiled. He turned toward the large table that was covered with papers and reports from the self-titled Army of the Dragon. He scanned a few lines of a page until he found the information that he wanted. There on the table before him lay both the internal command structure, and the proposed strike plans of the army. The names were unfamiliar to him except for one, Leane Torne. She was the second in command of the first infantry, and once the body of Antrobus was discovered, she would gain command of the Army of the Dragon. Those old words from his father rang true in his head. "Know your enemy," he had always said. From the time he was born, to the day that he left to devote his life to the Shadow and the destruction of all that was deemed light, Korrd had heard those words almost daily. It was either in his training exercises or the stories that his father had always told him about the wars.

Korrd and his father had always gotten along, but mostly in part to his mother's intervention. After Logan was born, that all changed. Korrd found himself cut off from the rest of the family, and became the loner that part of him always felt that he should be. The only reason that he didn't leave was because of his mother's failing health, and the needs of his father and his younger, yet hated brother. After his mother died, there was nothing to hold Korrd back any longer. He left, telling his father that he was no longer a part of that family, and he would never be seen again in Aradon. But that was far from the truth.

After years of searching for a way to be accepted into the forces of the Shadow, Korrd moved into a little house just outside the Gate, on the other side of the glade from the Ranthall house. He watched as his younger brother grew into a man and endeared himself in the hearts of all the people of Aradon, as well as some of the ladies. Logan was too young to understand what he was becoming, but Korrd saw, and it burned in the pit of his stomach. It had always been Korrd who was the favorite. He was always adored and loved by everyone. He was always the sweet little child. Logan had cost him all that. Hatred burned inside of Korrd, and he vowed that he would somehow gain revenge over his little brother. Never would he realize that Logan would become the *Coromor*, the appointed savior of the world, a position that should have been Korrd's as the first-born. Again Logan had denied him what should have rightfully been his. But now, Korrd could have his revenge. He could serve the powers that he had given his soul, and he could kill his brother for those years of torment and pain. Korrd had become the quintessential soldier: alone, unloved, and unfeeling; the perfect killer and it was all thanks to the little brother that should have never been born.

Korrd laughed softly to himself and then walked to the doors on the opposite side of the room. As he turned back around, Korrd was satisfied to see that Antrobus' dead body could not be seen by a mere glance into the room. He opened the door, stepped out, and then closed it quickly behind him. Thoughts from another place and time still filled his head, but he pushed them aside as best he could. He could not afford any distraction now. He had to have a clear mind in order to keep his alibi straight. If he were to let those fragmented thoughts invade his mind and cloud his judgment, there would be no escape for him. Antrobus' body still lay where Korrd left him, on the far side of the table, face up on the floor. The broken pieces of the chair still lay under him as it had collapsed under the fatal blow. It would not be long before someone discovered that Captain Antrobus had not emerged from his chambers and went looking for him. Murder was not such a heinous crime, but when it involved the assassination of the Overlord of two towns, or at the very least, the leader of an army, under the command of the *Coromor* or not, it would not take one long to find and kill the culprit.

The same female servant who had greeted him and shown him into Antrobus' chamber minutes earlier stood outside of the large double doors, waiting for one of the two parties to emerge. Her face tightened into the learned response that had become so familiar when being faced with a member of the upper class as Korrd turned to face her. She began to walk past him to see if her master had any desire. As she moved toward the door, Korrd grabbed her arm roughly and turned her back toward him.

"Captain Antrobus does not want to be disturbed," Korrd said as confidently as he could. "He would however like you to arrange for food, water, and supplies enough for a week of travel to be put on my horse. I will be leaving within the hour, and this is to be considered of the utmost importance and top priority."

"As you wish, sir," she answered dejectedly.

Korrd released the girl's arm and then watched her as she turned and walked toward a long and winding staircase. As soon as she was out of sight, a smile flashed onto Korrd's face.

If only it had been this easy in Karnil. We lost over three hundred men and women climbing the walls of that palace. Even Lorill fell from those heights.

That final set of thoughts staggered Korrd. This time, unlike the other times that these strange thoughts drifted though his mind, he retained the knowledge and memories of those places and names. The other thoughts were merely shadows, but this memory was full and rich. This memory was powerful and full of phantom voice and resonant scenes. For the first time since these memories of other people's lives started popping into his head, Korrd was aware of everything connected with that memory, and for a few brief moments, Korrd actually felt like that person.

Get out of my head! Korrd's thought's screamed. *I am Korrd Ranthall. I was never at Karnil, I never fought alongside a man named Lorill, and I was never in an army! I am Korrd Ranthall!*

Yes, a voice said from somewhere in his mind, *but who exactly is Korrd Ranthall? Are you the son of the infamous Arin Ranthall? The brother of the Coromor? Servant of the mighty Shau-ling? Or are you just a common boy trying to be something that you were never met to be?*

That poignant thought was accompanied with an equally powerful image of several faces flashing in and out of view. It was then that Korrd suddenly realized it was imperative that he get out of Rama as quickly as he possibly could. The haughty smile had long since faded from his face, and he turned and ran down a familiar hallway. His errand in Rama had been accomplished, and now he had to leave. Only his thoughts rang out in his head now, and for the first time since he had arrived in Rama, he felt as if he were truly alone. The seldom-used hallway was dark and deserted; nothing could hinder Korrd's progress. He reached the end of the hallway promptly, and opened the door to his temporary quarters.

The dark servants of the phase who had summoned him did a very good job of keeping Korrd away from the mainstream of Raman society. This 'forgotten wing' was once used to house visiting dignitaries and their parties. Once the war of the light started, there were more and more people in the palace, so new wings were built, specifically for this purpose. After the arrival of Shau-ling, Rana and Rama were cut off from the rest of the world, and their existence soon became merely legends and stories told to children. Only the Keepers of Knowledge and other wise men knew of their existence. Now this wing was cold and neglected; the perfect hiding place for an unexpected assassin.

Korrd stepped into the room and began to gather his things into his saddlebags. After a few minutes, he was completely packed and he turned to walk out the door. He threw his saddlebags over his shoulder, took hold of the door handle, pulled on the handle, but the door would not budge. Dropping his saddlebags to the ground, Korrd took hold of the handle with both hands. He pulled hard on the door, but it would not open. He released the handle, rubbed his hands together slowly, and then took another hold. He braced himself with his feet against the wall and then pulled again at the door. Suddenly, the handle broke off in his hands and he was thrown back across the room. His head hit the floor violently and Korrd lay there for a few moments, the pain in his head throbbing down into his neck and arms. As he sat up, he took hold of the corner of the bed and then braced himself as he rose to his feet. As he rose, he glanced around aimlessly as he tried to regain his equilibrium. It was then that something on the bed caught his eye.

He turned toward the bed, and there on the pillow laid a sealed parchment. It looked exactly like the one that summoned him to Rama, but he had disposed of that one shortly after his arrival. This letter was still sealed and had a strange aura to it. He was mesmerized by the mysterious letter, and couldn't help but to pick it up off the bed. The parchment seemed to grow in his hands as he looked at it. The pulsing between his fingers became more and more persistent as the seconds passed. Korrd rolled the parchment in his fingers and soon found the wax seal. He was more than a bit shocked to find the striking viper that was engraved into the blade of his sword. This viper seemed different somehow. It had a tangible quality to it, as if it would leap off the wax seal and strike him dead at any moment. He hesitated for a moment, thinking about the phantom threat, and then he broke the seal and opened the letter.

In an instant, it seemed as if the world around him began to crumble. The wall that stood in front of him deteriorated as he stared in disbelief. Chunks of the wall fell from their previous positions and tumbled down as they faded away completely. Instead of the forest that existed behind the wall becoming evident, all that appeared was a nothingness of bright purple. Korrd spun around several times, seeing the same strange events in every direction he looked. The letter that was the trigger of this transformation had now disappeared and he watched as the reality he knew crumbled and fell into a purple void beneath his feet. Within a handful of seconds, the Palace of Rama was gone, and he was standing in a whirlpool of purple, white, and violet. Part of Korrd felt as though he had been thrown into a lake, except there was no feeling like he was submerged. Another part felt as though he was standing on the top of a mountain close to the clouds. It seemed like there were patches of white, almost insubstantial cloud-like masses moving around in the purple and violet pools.

The cloud masses moved freely around him, and the violet and purple pools churned on, unconcerned with the new visitor. Nothing seemed to be disturbed by Korrd's presence, and he started to feel more and more isolated. There was nothing around him that was at all tangible. There were just wisps and currents, nothing for Korrd to depend on as reality. No matter how Korrd tried to move, it seemed that he remained in the same position. He turned around several times, and then suddenly realized that he could not differentiate between up and down. Within a few more seconds, left and right became just as nonsensical. Korrd now began to feel helpless. In a last fit of rage and torment, he closed his eyes and flung all of his weight and power into a forward surge. He felt himself move, and when he opened his eyes, all he saw were the familiar wisps of purple, violet, and white floating around him. Korrd's heart sank. Never before in all of his life had he ever felt this helpless. There was nothing left for him to do, and he had no other recourse but to just give up. But a part of him screamed curses in his head. It was this warrior's instinct that had kept him alive through years, decades, centuries of battles. All of these memories that floated in his head had the same intangible presence that said to not give up. In so many of those phantom memories, he had been injured almost to the point of death, and this mentality kept him alive. Korrd knew somewhere inside him, that no matter what, he would survive.

He looked around again, desperately trying to find something to orient himself by. Then out of the corner of his eye, he spotted something. It was difficult and almost impossible to see what it was at first, but as soon as he turned himself enough, it became clear. He craned his neck in an effort to examine his new found objective, but as he did, a ring of flames burst into existence around him. He felt the dull heat from the flames, but as he examined the flame more and more closely, he found that they had no source from which they originated, and no fuel to burn, they were just there.

Then Korrd realized that there was in fact a source. The place that the flames appeared to originate from the nothingness was the same in all cases. It was then that Korrd decided to orient himself by these common points. Soon he had righted himself, and when he did, a layer of rock began to form under him. In a matter of seconds, he found himself walking around on a newly discovered floor of stone. The rock continued to stretch out in every direction until everywhere Korrd looked, he saw ground reaching out to infinity.

As he walked around on the newly revealed floor, he began to notice some peculiar things about the ring of flames that surrounded him. The flames themselves did not touch the ground, and actually floated about a foot above ground level. No matter how close Korrd got to the flames, they seemed to radiate the same dull, dry heat. It soon occurred to Korrd that these flames were no more than an illusion, just like the thoughts in his head and the floor that he was walking on. He looked at his hand for a moment, and then after taking a deep breath, thrust his hand into the flames before him. The burning sensation that he had prepared himself for never did materialize, and a soothing cool sensation was all that he found. He pulled his hand away and examined it, half expecting it to be covered with charred flesh. But again, Korrd's expectations proved to be inaccurate. His hand was not covered with charred flesh, but was covered with a thin film of moisture.

Upon further examination of the waxy substance, he found that it was confined merely to the palm of his hand. As he scratched at the film, he uncovered a glowing object on his palm. The more and more of the film he removed, the clearer the shape became. More and more of the wax flaked off, and Korrd was shocked to find that the object on his palm had begun to glow a bright violet. The shape was then clearly visible. Just like the letter on his bed in Rama, and just like the sword he now wore on his side. The striking viper that glowed violet on his palm was not a pleasant sight. Suddenly, he heard a laugh erupt from somewhere inside the circle of flames. He turned toward the point from which the laughter seemed to originate, and then approached the flames slowly. Without warning, a gust of wind slammed hard into Korrd and pushed him into the flames in front of him.

Everything went black for a few moments, and when the light reappeared, and Korrd found himself in a new chamber. The room itself was huge, and he saw that the walls of the chamber were lined with glistening white pillars that extended from the floor to the ceiling. In the very center of the room was a large white fountain with blood red water erupting from the center. As he examined the room, he felt a sharp pain in his hand, and as he looked down, he saw that the light emanating from the violet viper on his palm had begun to pulsate. The laughter that had drawn him to this place began again, and when Korrd looked up, the water had stopped leaping into the air, and behind the fountain, on a huge golden throne, sat a man.

Something inside the years and lifetimes of memories clicked. The flowing white hair, the green eyes, the strong, broad shoulders, the man sitting there was none other than . . .

"Lord Saurn," Korrd said regally.

"Korrd Ranthall. Perhaps I should call you Temaris Balchair, or Serif Tork, of maybe Aerith Seth. You have so many names young one, I have no idea what to call you."

Korrd took a step back and then reset himself. He walked around the fountain and stopped in front of the steps that led to the throne.

"I have only one name Saurn . . ."

"Lord Saurn, young one. Do not make me angry with continued impertinence."

"Lord Saurn, my name is Korrd Ranthall, and I . . ."

"You are here to serve me."

Korrd looked at the man for a moment, not believing the audacity of his host. It was not easy for Korrd to accept the pompous arrogance of this man, but, after all, he was a phase. He was the same kind of man that Korrd had sworn to follow when he became a servant of Shau-ling. A man that no one would question, merely obey.

"I serve no one," Korrd replied boldly.

"Ah. So, you do have some fire in you after all. The more the better. I must say though that I did not expect a challenge out of you. It has been a long time since someone had the courage to challenge me. In fact, the last challenge I had that was worth remembering was with Aralias Imstra, and he fell as quickly as his followers did."

Korrd looked at the phase astonished at the reaction. Korrd couldn't believe that Saurn had taken his words as a challenge. Saurn raised his hand slightly off the throne and balled his fist. The sword that hung on Korrd's side twitched slightly. It then began to pull slowly out of the scabbard and rose in front of him. Korrd sighed inwardly and then grasped the sword. When he looked up again, Saurn was already off the throne and was walking down the steps toward him. Korrd slowly took two steps back and set himself into a fighting position. The doubt was gone in his mind now, and Korrd prepared himself to fight for his life. Saurn laughed again, and upon raising his hand, a beam of white light leapt at Korrd. The light sped toward Korrd, and luckily, Korrd managed to get his sword up in time to block the attack. The bar of light enveloped the sword, and it began to glow red. Korrd's hands began to burn, and he dropped his sword. The onslaught of light continued, and Saurn completely disregarded the dropped sword. Quickly, the burning sensation began to move up Korrd's arms. Suddenly Korrd's eyes closed, and the pain left his body.

The darkness that he saw was peaceful. He felt safe and calm in this place. He seemed to float there in the blackness that he saw, but no matter how much he wanted to stay, he knew he couldn't. He forced his eyelids open, and saw a ball of darkness leap from his hands and engulf Saurn. Saurn cried in agony and the light onslaught ceased. Korrd dropped his hands and the ball of darkness disappeared.

Surprisingly, Saurn did not appear as if he were angry, just the opposite. He looked as if he were ecstatic. Saurn laughed yet again, and then stood.

"Very good young one. I must say that I am very impressed. You are more powerful than I had thought. I must remember to never underestimate you again. It is a wonder that Shau-ling has not yet noticed you."

"What are you talking about?" Korrd asked.

"You, young one. But that can wait. Do you recognize this place? Think before you answer. Search all of your memories."

Korrd thought back, and suddenly a vivid memory snapped into his mind. A picture of a man that he knew, possibly one of the men that spoke in his mind, standing beside Saurn in front of the same throne. On the throne sat a huge man with the face of a serpent. To the right of the throne stood a tall man with a flowing black cape and a weak smile on his lips. The man standing beside Saurn dropped to one knee and bowed his head. The man with the serpent face laughed and handed a sword to the man in the cape. Saurn threw a bar of light at the caped man, but the serpent faced man intervened and encased Saurn in a clear magical box. The caped man recovered from the attack and then severed the kneeling man's head from his body.

Korrd quickly snapped back into reality as the painful memory flooded his mind.

"Yes," Saurn commented, "I remember that time well young one. The man who stood beside me was none other than . . ."

"Aerith Seth," Korrd said slowly. "He was a member of the Hand of the Light. The man in the cape was Jeroch, and the serpent faced man was Shau-ling."

"Very good young one, I am again impressed. So, tell me, what do you remember about that incident?"

Korrd thought hard for a moment and then answered.

"Aerith Seth was one of the commanders of the Hand. In most of their battles he fought beside Aralias Imstra as his protector. In the battles between your army and the Hand, your forces of Kalbraks, Jeresei, and Shadowwalkers were wiped out by the Hand, and you took it upon yourself to finish the job your army had started. I seem to remember you summoning lightning and killing everyone except Imstra and Seth."

"Yes," Saurn responded, "Seth was also more powerful than I had anticipated. His powers proved enough to turn away my attack. Imstra then foolishly challenged me and I crushed him with my bare hands. After that Seth surrendered and I brought him back here."

"The Hall of Punishment, Shau-ling's personal torture chamber," Korrd finished.

"That is correct, in part."

"What do you mean in part?" Korrd asked.

"This room is not the actual Hall of Punishment. It is merely a reflection of the actual Hall. The place you are in now is called the Blight. It is the place from which everything in the world originated, including Shau-ling. But, I have learned that this is the only place that Shau-ling cannot exist in. He cannot see here or dwell here."

"So, you can mold this place into anything you want?"

"Correct. Now, I will show you what really happened to Aerith Seth."

The Hall of Punishment flashed quickly with bright light, and the characters of Shau-ling and Jeroch appeared exactly where Korrd remembered them. Shau-ling on the throne, and Jeroch to his right.

"What are they doing here?!? I thought you said Shau-ling couldn't exist here!" Korrd shouted.

"Quiet!" Saurn thundered. "They are not here, these are merely images. Watch, listen, and learn."

The door to their left opened slowly and an image of Saurn walked through trailed by Aerith Seth. Seth's hands were bound with bars of light, and his head hung low. His tattered shirt hung tightly to his broad chest and shoulders, and his breeches were frayed and holed. As he passed, Korrd could see lash marks on his back from where his Jeresei captors had punished him. Saurn led Aerith to the foot of the steps that led to the throne and then turned to face his lord. From the side of the room, a figure dressed in all black walked to the side of Aerith. The man was wire thin, but he appeared to be very strong. Long black hair flowed past his shoulders, down to about the middle of his back."

"Who is that?" Korrd asked.

"That is Basille, last-born of the phasia. He has to take the orders of all the other phasia, and that has made him the most devious of us all."

Basille stood beside Aerith for a moment, and then kicked the back of his legs, forcing him to fall to his knees.

"What have you brought me, Saurn?" Shau-ling asked.

"This is the one called Aerith Seth. He was at Imstra's right hand when he fell," Saurn answered.

"So," Shau-ling responded with interest, "the mighty Aralias Imstra has fallen at the hands of my children. Imstra's prophecies will now never come true now that he has fallen. The so-called *Coromor* and the *Chosen One* will never rise."

"*Chosen One?*" Korrd questioned.

Saurn looked at Korrd for a moment, put his finger to his lips, and then pointed back toward the unfolding scene.

"The *Chosen One* has already risen lord," the image of Saurn said, "I have seen him."

Shau-ling shifted in his seat uncomfortably. This was certainly not what he had anticipated.

"Where is this *Chosen One*, Saurn?"

"He is here in front of you my lord Shau-ling."

At the answer, Shau-ling and the other two phasia roared with laughter.

"This pitiful human is the great and powerful *Chosen One?*" Basille scoffed. "Allow me to vanquish him my lord."

The scene froze for a moment, and Saurn turned to Korrd.

"Basille has changed over the last twenty or thirty years. He is no longer cocky and arrogant. He is now more cunning and devious."

Saurn turned back toward the scene, and then it resumed. The Saurn-image turned quickly toward Aerith, waived his hand, and then Aerith stood and stretched his shoulders. Basille removed his shirt and prepared himself for the fight. Basille charged Aerith and Aerith side-stepped the attack and tripped Basille in the process. Basille fell to the floor face first, and before he could recover, Aerith turned and attacked. He thrust his hand toward the fallen Basille, and a bar of red flame leapt from his outstretched hand and engulfed Basille. He writhed in agony for a few seconds and then disappeared.

Saurn turned to Korrd again and said, "Now you know why he changed."

Korrd smiled for a moment and then turned his attention back to the scene. Aerith had turned back toward Shau-ling, and he held a bar of white light in his hands. For the first time, Aerith spoke, his voice filled with a tapestry of anger, pain, and power.

"Do you doubt my power as well Jeroch? What about you Shau-ling? Do you still think the prophecies are false?"

"What is it you want human?" Shau-ling asked.

"I want you to die. From what Aralias has told me about the *Chosen One*, I am powerful enough to destroy you myself. It is also possible that I am as powerful as the *Coromor*."

"So, you have come here willingly to challenge me," Shau-ling commented. "You could have killed Saurn with ease, but you chose to let him bring you here so you could try to kill me. I applaud your cunning Aerith; you would have made a good phase."

"Merely the opposite, you short-sighted, arrogant, half-breed. I came here to give myself up. You may do with me what you wish."

"Well, this is a surprise. Kneel Aerith Seth."

Aerith went to one knee and bowed his head. Shau-ling reached for a sword that lay beside the throne and then handed it to Jeroch.

"Stop," the Saurn image said quickly, "don't you see, he's fulfilling a part of the prophecies. 'From a fallen hero, a *Chosen* hero, the *Coromor* will rise.' You fool, if you kill him now, you are putting your lives in danger."

"Step away Saurn," Jeroch said angrily, "this is no longer your affair."

Saurn raised his hand toward Jeroch, and a beam of white light engulfed him. Saurn then turned toward Aerith and tried to move toward him. Something stopped him. Suddenly, the walls of a transparent box appeared around hi, keeping him from interfering. Jeroch, slowly recovering from the attack, walked down the steps to his victim's side, and then ended his life. After that, the scene disappeared.

"Do you understand what I just showed you, Korrd?"

"Am I the *Chosen One*, Lord Saurn?"

"You are indeed, my boy. You are powerful enough to destroy Shau-ling, and his phasia. You and I could rule the world young one. You could prove once and for all that you are more powerful than your brother, and get revenge for all those years of neglect."

Those last statements made Korrd's blood boil. To finally have revenge after all those years. To be able to rule at the side of the man that he had idolized. It was like a dream was finally coming true.

"What must I do?" Korrd asked.

Saurn smiled and then answered.

"You must make Shau-ling vulnerable. To do that, you must cripple his defense and information network. That requires the death of the nine other phasia. I will kill as many as I dare to, but you must do most of the work. The powers of the phasia cancel each other out so that a magical battle is futile. To cripple and kill each phase, you must first infiltrate their kingdom and then battle them. I'll show you how to shield yourself from their magic, as well as where they're vulnerable."

"Who is my first target, master?" Korrd asked with an evil tone.

"My sister Caris is your first target. She is in Illimar. First though, we have much to discuss . . ."

Chapter IX

Treachery

Despite their status as honored guests, Logan and the rest of his group had no further interaction with either the queen or the princess before they left Trelon. Logan felt it was for the best considering the impression that the princess made on Elwyne, and of all the things that were out of control in his life, Logan felt that Elwyne's temper was the one thing he had the least control over. Most of his life he had been accused of being hard-headed and not able to see the big picture. Elwyne was far more hard-headed than Logan would ever be, and she was one of the few people that he could never win an argument with. A small breakfast was prepared for them in the queen's private dining room, after which they were escorted out of the palace to where their horses waited. As the queen promised, their saddles and saddlebags were completely stocked with provisions and everything they would need for their journey to Castleer, including small pouches of gold coins for each member of the party. The queen had been beyond generous, a testament to the importance of the mission they were about to embark upon.

Castleer was a little more than half a day's journey from Trelon. However, most of the miles were spent traveling through the edge of the expansive Mithacarthian woods. That ancient string of forest covered a large portion of the continent from Aradon to Marcwell, with only the Great River breaking the contiguity. The journey may have taken considerably less time had the path been better, and the route less winding, but it was commonly known that the Mithacarthian woods were not kind to travelers. The journey was uneventful, and once it was at its end, the group found themselves looking down from a small hill onto the grassy fields and grazing lands that surrounded Castleer. Like most of the villages and towns under the control of Trelon, Castleer was primarily an agricultural and farming community. It stood on the fringes of an empire that never did worry much about them. If there were any place that was more apt to hold a weapon as powerful as the Jeweled Dragon's Flame, it would be impossible to find.

It's hard to believe that power the like of the Coromor, *the* Erieal, *and the Jeweled Dragon's Flame could all be found in such innocent places.*

The coincidence was too much for Logan to ignore. The *Coromor* and the *Erieal* were all from a small town, and now the Jeweled Dragon's Flame was supposed to be found in a small town as well. Logan wondered if a similar coincidence had occurred in the previous generation. Were all of the *Erieal* as highborn as Lord Cedric? Did the Jeweled Dragon's Flam exist as a symbol of power held in a heavily guarded tower in the capitol of a large empire somewhere? Would the fourth *Erieal* of this generation be found in a small town as well, coming from humble circumstances? Did it really matter?

Just as the group made their way down from the crest of the hill onto the glade, the bells of a nearby church rang out for mid-day. There were several small public stables just outside the town, and after hitching the horses they continued into town on foot, wanting to draw as little attention as possible. If there truly was an army of the Shadows massing on the borders of Castleer, the citizens in the outlying area gave no indication, and certainly nothing could be seen on the approach from Trelon. However, the Jeresei, with the right clothes theoretically could have passed as humans, the Tarnae could mimic anything it wanted, and the Shadowwalkers didn't have to be close to launch a crippling attack.

Castleer was very busy in the early afternoon. Most of the activity was centered on the large open air market near the center of town in which the local farmers and merchants bought and sold their wares. It appeared that some of the merchants were doing a very good business from the look of the crowds. Gideon took Logan by the arm and led everyone to a smaller side street close to the market. After a quick look to make sure that they hadn't drawn attention, Gideon frowned.

"Fer a town dats supposed ta be under attack, dis place is quiet. Let's check out a tavern ta get some local gossip."

"If you wanted a drink, Gideon, you didn't need an excuse," Logan countered, trying to keep a tense situation light.

"And just when I thought we had gotten rid of Pike and Talon's bad habits," Elwyne added.

"Unsophisticated boys…but dey have a good mind for drinking," he laughed.

"You should be taking this situation much more seriously," Aryx countered. "But Gideon's idea is sound. There is something not right here."

Aryx was familiar with the town, and he led the other members of the group down a series of smaller side streets and to the door of a modest-sized building. Over the front door hung a small sign depicting a large mug of ale. Above the mug was painted the words, The Sweet Ale. Gideon pushed open the door quickly and they found themselves at the table near the back of the bar within a few moments. There were very few patrons in the bar that early afternoon, and the serving girls sat at one of the tables occasionally making the rounds to their tables to see if any of the customers wanted anything. Moments after the group was seated, one of the girls sauntered over and smiled pleasantly.

"What can I get you young lords and lady this fine afternoon?" the very young woman asked.

"Well, Gideon, what do you suggest?"

"Ales all 'round me young lass, and don' be 'fraid ta come back an' give us some company," he proffered.

The young girl looked surprised for a moment and then giggled softly. Within a few minutes she returned with a tray full of pints, and she and Gideon exchanged smiles.

After the young girl left the table, Elwyne sighed.

"She's young enough to be your daughter, Gideon."

"Aye, she may look young, but she knows more den women twice her age. An' we 'ave ta get information somewhere."

Aryx was first to agree with the comment, and from the way he smiled, it almost seemed as if he had heard the comment somewhere else before.

"Would you mind telling us a story about one of your adventures, Sir Aryx?" one of the women at one of the tables asked.

Before Aryx could answer, Logan interjected.

"And how do you know this is Sir Aryx Terian?"

"Sir Aryx is famous in Castleer," she answered. "He came through town with the Lord Lion and his companions just after the war was over when he proclaimed the kingdom was going to be protected by Queen Camille of Trelon. They stayed in the inn across the street, and he would come here and tell us stories at night when the bar was full and people were anxious to hear about the war. It takes a while for news to reach us here, and so often the stories we do get are not accurate and are hardly believable. So, whenever we get someone as famous as Sir Aryx Terian in our little tavern, we like to hear stories and news from the world from the people who have experienced it first hand," she replied.

"What story would you like to hear?" Aryx asked smiling.

"Tell us about the first time you met Lord Cedric," one of the other women implored.

"Very well."

Aryx settled back in his chair and began his story.

"You see, after I had rescued Lady Erika Belnosian from the force of Kalbraks, she had insisted that I accompany her to Askronilka and meet Lord Cedric. After we met up with the Wind Sisters, Allahanna and Corin, we made our way to Askronilka. Lady Erika led us to a bar much like this one. The bar itself was packed with warriors. All of them seemed to be surrounding two men locked in a duel. Quickly one of the men fell, and the other started barking orders at the men. After he was finished speaking, Lady Erika ran to him and introduced us all to Lord Cedric of Marcwell. After an explanation from Lady Erika of the battle with the Kalbraks in the desert, Lord Cedric knighted me on the spot. However, that was not the end of the day with him. Later that night, Lady Erika came to my room and told me that Lord Cedric wished to see me. She also told me that I was to be armed. At first I wanted to ask why, but I had learned early in life that you do not question the wishes of those you serve."

"Here, here," the bartender added.

The few male patrons roared with laughter, while others seemed to ignore the statement. The serving ladies at one of the tables scowled quickly and then beckoned for Aryx to continue.

"Well, Lady Erika led me to Lord Cedric's room, and she was also armed. During those days, Lady Erika fought with a very long spear, and she was a quite accomplished warrior for her age. When we got to Lord Cedric's room, he stood in the center of the room with sword drawn. He commanded me to sit on the bed, and as I sat there, he struck at Lady Erika. His first blow easily disarmed her, and as he readied himself for another strike, she had no means to defend herself. I stepped between them and parried Lord Cedric's blow. He sheathed his sword and told me the test was over."

"Test?" Elwyne asked.

"That's exactly what Lady Erika asked. You see, I was in Lakestone before the fall, and Lord Cedric found it suspicious that I escaped. He thought that I might have been one of Shau-ling's agents. However, at the time we did not know that Shau-ling existed, so the best he could do was think that I was a shape-shifter or a servant of the monsters' master. He said that a servant of the beast could never save one that was not of its own kind, and would definitely not interfere with a duel that did not concern it. So, by interfering, it proved that I was what I said I was."

"Did you ever have a similar altercation with the great Lord Arathorn, Terian?" one of the men at another table asked gruffly.

"As a matter of fact, I did. Just after we had arrived in Marcwell with Cedric's army from Askronilka behind us we met up with Arathorn. Unbeknownst to me, Lady Erika and Arathorn had a standing bet as to who would kill the other in a duel. In fact, as I remember the story, Lady Erika had offered to kill Arathorn before the monsters in Lakestone did, so he could save face. As I sat there on my horse listening to the two of them bicker, I through it best, as Lady Erika's protector, to intervene."

* * * * * * * * * * * *

"So, Erika," Arathorn said slyly, "are you ready to fulfill your promise to kill me, or shall we wait to see if I survive Lakestone?"

"I don't need your permission to kill you, Arathorn. If I wanted to, I could have killed you long ago and rid this world of its most arrogant man," she responded angrily.

"Is this *man* bothering you, my lady?" Aryx interjected. "If so, I would be happy to thrash him properly for you."

"This *man* happens to be a good friend of your lord, you twit," Erika scolded.

"No, it's alright, Erika. Let your champion here defend your honor, if he has the bravery for such an act stored in that pathetic carcass of his," Arathorn challenged.

"This should be interesting, Erika," Lord Cedric commented. "Allow Aryx to prove his knighthood."

"Knighthood? Come now Cedric, my friend. You don't mean to tell me that you made this boy a knight?"

"As a matter of fact, I did," Cedric answered. "For bravery in the face of incredible danger, in an effort to protect a stranger. I found it necessary to make him a knight to the Kingdom of Marcwell. However, it was Erika's suggestion that made the difference."

"So, Erika," Arathorn teased, "he *is* your champion. Well, let your *knight* get down off his horse and defend you."

With a nod from Erika, Aryx dismounted and drew his sword. Arathorn walked to him and snapped into a defensive position.

"I must warn you, Aryx," Cedric said coldly, "Arathorn is of great skill, and could easily best you with his sword, for it is made of an indestructible metal and also increases the user's strength tenfold. So, in the interest of fairness, Arathorn shall use my sword. Also, Aryx, I am very well aware of your gift. If you use your powers against Arathorn, and he is harmed in any way, I will put an end to the duel with unfortunate consequences."

"I understand, my lord," Aryx answered.

Lord Cedric dismounted quickly and then unsheathed his sword. He held it out to Arathorn, who took it slowly and bowed. Laying his sword on the ground, still in its scabbard, Arathorn returned to his defensive position. Aryx struck wildly with an upward thrust, and Arathorn easily parried, but did not move from his position. Aryx attacked again and again, each time finding Arathorn's steel blocking his intended target. It was obvious to everyone standing there that Arathorn was simply toying with his adversary, and he was enjoying every moment of it. Aryx was beginning to lose patience with the game, and took a hard slice at Arathorn. Arathorn's block had more power than Aryx expected, and his blade flew across the ground and lay there far out of reach. Aryx fell to his knees and yielded to his stronger opponent.

"Another easy victory!" Arathorn laughed. "I would have thought that your champion would have been more of a challenge, my lady."

"He is far from being my champion, Arathorn. He is merely a knight in the service of Lord Cedric, as well as my protector. Should he fail in his duties to protect me, then my champion would reveal himself and smite my adversary with the greatest of ease," she replied smugly.

"Shall I endeavor to ask if this champion wishes to take up where your knight and protector failed?"

"He would," Cedric answered quickly, "but you're using his sword."

* * * * * * * * * * *

"So, the great Aryx Terian can be defeated in battle," a man at one of the tables laughed. "As far as I'm concerned, Arathorn should have killed you that day."

"As much as I hate to say it," Aryx replied, "I must respect your opinion. If this were any other time, I would ask you to back up your statement with your sword. However, there are other matters that need me far more than a defense of honor."

"You have no honor left. Your lord is in exile, you drift around with a band of children, and your steel hasn't seen action in years. I would wager that you couldn't even best a warrior of Alimidar."

At that, Gideon stood and drew two of his daggers.

"What ye be sayin' 'bout, Alimidar ye flintin' ogre? Aryx may not want ta defend his honor, but dere's no problem wit me doin it."

"So be it," the man answered.

The man stood from the table and picked up a large war hammer that lay beside him on the floor. After he was ready, the large man motioned for Gideon to attack. Quickly, Gideon launched two of his lean and deadly daggers into the air. They hurtled toward their victim, and were jerked out of the air by one of the man's massive hands. Gideon looked shocked and hurt as the man broke the daggers in two and tossed the pieces to the ground laughing.

"I should have expected such a pitiful attack from a man from Alimidar. Don't waste my time weakling. If you intend to attack, you best do it now while you have the chance."

Before the last word had escaped his lips, Gideon leapt over the table and rolled across the floor in a ball. He sprung to his feet just in front of the man and buried one of his daggers deep into his flat stomach. The man was shocked, but he managed to lift his hammer over his head and strike down at Gideon. Gideon moved quickly aside and the head of the hammer connected with nothing but the wooden floor. Pieces of wood flew everywhere as the hammer shattered parts of the floorboards. Gideon struck again, this time plunging the blood soaked tip of the dagger into the man's naked side. The man reeled from the second blow and feel to one knee. Recovering slowly, the man dropped the large hammer, and drew a large knife from his belt. He held the knifepoint down and started stabbing at Gideon wildly. Gideon easily dodged the blows, and struck with pinpoint accuracy at vital parts of the man's anatomy. Pricks from the tip of Gideon's dagger in the arms and legs eventually left the man down on his knees, still trying to land a blow. As soon as he was sure the man could no long hurt him, Gideon stepped away and cleaned his daggers.

"I'm not finished with you yet, Alimidarian. Either finished me or let me kill you like the coward you are."

"Ain't no need ta kill ye. Yer beaten. Take yer friends and go."

The man managed to get back to his feet, and he ran toward Gideon. Reflexively, Gideon ducked under the intended blow and buried one of his clean blades deep into the heart of the man. He reeled from the blow and finally fell.

"You killed him!" one of the other men at the table yelled.

"He left me no choice. Ye heard me try ta save him, but he would not listen."

"You'll be sorry after we finish with you, Alimidarian. Our friend shall be avenged."

The men were already standing with swords drawn and ready for battle. The man who had threatened Gideon stepped up with his rapier and dagger drawn.

"Defend yourself, if you have the gall."

"Enough of this," Logan interjected. "We have no reason to fight here. Your friend challenged Gideon and lost. Do you believe that he would not have killed Gideon if he had the chance? There is no vengeance to be gained here."

"That's what you think. He was the Prince's cousin, and therefore all of the new king's army will want you dead. You and your Alimidarian friends."

"What do you mean, 'the new king'?" Aryx asked. "Trelon has always been ruled by women, and we have just come from the queen's court. If anything has happened to her since we left, her daughter will have taken the throne."

"That's what you think, Terian. The queen and her daughter are alive enough, for now. Now that the prince has you out of the way, the road will be paved for a new order in Trelon. No longer will Trelon be under the boot of Marcwell and Lord Cedric. He is no longer in control of his own kingdom so why should he control ours. Your time has ended Terian, and now I will take your pathetic life after the Alimidarian dies."

"No one is dying this day," Logan countered, "at least not by your hand."

With that Logan drew his sword and leapt from his chair. Elwyne pulled Alexander away from the conflict, but he drew his short sword and stood before her to block anyone who tried to advance on her. Talos took his staff out of the corner and pulled the hood of his gray cloak over his head. The shadow of the hood covered all of his face except his mouth, and he began to mumble incantations under his breath. Aryx's gauntlet glowed an eerie red, and he held his sword ready for attack. Gideon retreated from the opponents and crouched low, waiting for an opportunity. The men stood, each with sword or hammer ready for the fight. The man holding the rapier steeped forward and pointed the tip of his rapier at Aryx. The man with the rapier wasted little time and stabbed at Aryx. Aryx parried the blow from the rapier and dodged the follow up from the dagger. Aryx struck with a downward slash and was blocked by the X of the man's crossed blades. The man struck again, but this time instead of parrying the first blow, Aryx dodged it and severed the man's hand from his arm when he thrust with his dagger. He stumbled back, and pointed at Aryx again. Instead of walking back to the duel, the man motioned for his friends to attack. As they advanced, there was a flash of blinding white light. At first Logan thought Aryx had finally used his power; however, as he glanced at the knight's gauntlet he saw that it was back to its normal golden color. The men who were advancing on Aryx had disappeared leaving only one man with a long sword and the one-handed man. Logan looked back at Talos, and he lowered his staff from over his head. Whatever he had done seemed to be very effective, but it had also taken a toll, as he leaned heavily on the staff and the back wall for support. The man with the long sword stepped up and knelt in front of Aryx. He held his sword in his hands, bowed his head, and lifted the sword up to Aryx. Aryx sheathed his sword and took the blade from the man. The man then stood and left the tavern. Following the gesture, the man with the rapier knelt and offered in kind. When Aryx turned to make his way back to the table, the one-handed man picked up the knife that lay by his severed hand and hurled it at Aryx's turned back. In a blur of motion and steel, one of Gideon's daggers collided with the dagger flying toward Aryx, sheering it off course, while another struck the one-handed man in the throat. As he lay there dying, his last words were still clear, sharp, and terrifying.

"You and your lord are lost, Terian. By the time you make it back to Trelon, the queen will be dead and the prince will sit on her throne. It is so easy to manipulate you and the Lord Dragon, whichever one of you it may be, if he is here at all. The prince knew that you would come, after Lord Cedric sent his letter here. The prince then had to get you out of town long enough to kill the queen and his sister and take the throne. It is your fault Terian; the Kingdoms of the Lion are no more. Now the War for Power can being and rage on as it did before Shau-ling and the Lord Lion were ever born."

After those words, his eyes rolled back and the rest of his life slipped away. Gideon reached down and retrieved his daggers.

"What about the queen and the princess?" Alexander asked worried. "Is there any way that we can help them?"

"From what the one-handed man said, it may already be too late," Aryx said shortly, "but we have to try and get there before the queen and the princess are killed."

"Surely the prince would not walk into the throne room of the royal palace and put the point of his blade through the heart of both the queen and the princess. I don't care how big his army may be, everyone would know who had killed the queen," Talos said. "Also, there has to be someone else who knows the true identity of Queen Camille Talaat. Then they would send a letter to Lord Cedric telling him that her own son had murdered her. After what I have heard from Aryx and from different bards about the mental and physical condition of Lord Cedric, he is likely to take an army and level Trelon."

"Lord Cedric wouldn't need an army to level Trelon," Aryx said shaking his head, "not in the condition he's in now. But Talos is right, Logan. Some of the ladies in waiting in the palace have been servants to the Binosear family for years. They grew up with Anne and Cedric."

"Look," Elwyne interjected, "the longer we stand here talking about this, the more chance there is that Anne and Cairyn will already be dead."

"So, what you are both saying is that the prince would have to find some way to kill them both so that no one would know he was involved," Logan said ignoring Elwyne.

"An accident," Talos said quickly.

"Like what?" Alexander asked. "Not like a riding accident or a misfired bow. That may be convincing for one of them."

"A fire!" Elwyne exclaimed. "I'll bet the bastard is going to burn down the royal palace."

"That would be seen as a convincing accident," Talos commented.

"Or it could be blamed on Shau-ling," Gideon added.

"Then let's get to Trelon," Logan said finally.

CHAPTER 9

Using as much haste as they could, the group made their way back out of town, and rode their horses as fast as they could through the forest trying to make it back to Trelon before the unthinkable actually happened. Luckily the prince had not thought that the group would survive their encounter in Castleer and had not left more impediments on the road. Either that, or it didn't matter if they survived or not, and his trap in Trelon for the queen and the princess had already been sprung. Logan and the others made it back to the gates of Trelon in less than seven hours and the sun was just beginning to sink low on the horizon. From somewhere in the town there were huge billows of black smoke that were beginning to block out parts of the sky. Elwyne had been proven right in her fears, and the prince had intended to set fire to the royal palace in an effort to claim the lives of his mother and sister. The group rode through the gates, but found the streets almost impassible because of the mass of people fleeing the growing inferno. Reduced to making the rest of the journey on foot, they ran as fast as we could until they had reached the front of the palace. Orange flames seemed to come from every window, and the black smoke flowed like water from the tips of the flames. Screaming people ran from different doors in the palace, and made their way as far away from the palace as possible. One of the women ran from the palace spotted Logan and Aryx, and ran to them. She wrapped her arms around Aryx, tears streaming from her eyes.

"The queen and the princess are trapped in the palace. Please, please save them."

Hawk

Sador. For some reason, even the mention of the town's name made Pike shudder. It was as if some horrible evil was just sitting in that town waiting for him. He had no reason to think so, but something inside him said that Sador was not a good town to find yourself in after the sun went down. It was not the same feeling that he had about Sarmeel, but a twinge of fear still dwelled inside him. Fear was not to be taken lightly, especially not now, but this fear seemed more unreasonable than most.

It was a beautiful town, even from a distance. It didn't have the flash or the sparkle of Illimar or Rama, but it did have the beauty of nature that surrounded it. The forest ended just past where Pike and his companions stood. Two rows of trees continued and created a path that led right to the foot of the town that Midarin had called Sador. The trees then surrounded the town, and they could even see some inside the town proper. From what Pike could see, the town contained simple houses, and one large palace that rose in the center of the town, high above the rest of the buildings. The town may have been simple, but it had a natural beauty that made this simple little town more beautiful than most others. It seemed that even Illimar's sparkling towers of glass and wood could not match Sador. The palace was the one part of the town that did not seem to fit. Its white walls gleamed in the sunlight, and the palace seemed to exert this sense of power and prestige. Evidently, the magistrate in Sador wanted everyone to know that he was in total control of his kingdom.

"Who is the ruler here in Sador, Midarin?" Pike asked.

"The last report that I saw in my time in Brea was that Lord Zarsi of Baldazar had taken control of Sador. As a princess of the kingdom I was required to learn the names of the rulers of every kingdom and every vassal of those kingdoms. And yes, it was as tedious as it sounds. This Lord Zarsi built that palace in the center of town just after his forces had destroyed Sador's army twelve or fifteen years ago."

"Why hasn't anyone heard more about Sador or this Lord Zarsi? It seems to me anyone who just marches his soldiers in and conquers a town would draw more attention." Gwydeon asked, his voice filled with concern, and a twinge of fear that only his closest friends could detect.

"No one knows for sure. Lord Zarsi has always been a recluse, and he has never been formally involved with any of the peace initiatives of any other kingdom. It seems that he runs his kingdom quietly. You only hear about him when he has built up enough of a fighting force to take over another town or kingdom. Then he just slips back into hiding again, gathering his forces for another raid. There is never any strategy to any of his attacks, he just picks a target and invades. The only part about it is that he has never been defeated, at least, not to my knowledge. As far as why one of the larger kingdoms doesn't stand against him, it's simply the fact that he targets minor independent lands that hold no connection to the larger kingdoms. Marcwell and Trelon ignore him because they don't consider him a threat to their interests. In time though he may feel bold enough to strike at larger game."

That stopped everyone for a moment. This was the first time in their travels that they had come across a man like this. Before they had always dealt with diplomats, even in Rama, but now they dealt with a man who relied completely on force. Pike knew that they had only really dealt with three or so high ranking officials during their travels. All of them had been kind and helpful after their initial meeting. Pike could not see this next meeting ending so favorably.

"So," Talon remarked, "should we stay here for a while, or should we go straight there?"

"I say we go," Gwydeon answered, "there's no sense in staying out here when there is a town no more than an hour away."

"I have to agree with Gwydeon," Midarin added, "we need rest, and there is no better place for a night of sound sleep than a town with a good inn. From what I've heard about Sador, we'll all get the best sleep we had in a long time."

"That's good," Pike commented, "I need to get some sleep. I don't think I've had a good night's rest since this damn fool quest started."

"So it's settled," Eldar chimed in, "we ride for Sador."

* * * * * * * * * * * *

Two men stood as they watched the strangers ride down the marked path toward Sador. One man raised a bow and pulled the string back quickly. As he released the arrow, the other man bumped him, and the arrow flew in another direction, its aim interrupted.

"You damn fool!" the man said angrily, "I could have killed one of them and made our job easier."

"Pipe down Jasef," the other replied, "you know our orders. We were merely supposed to spot any intruders and report back to Lord Zarsi. There was to be no killing except at his order. Unless you want to end up dead like Refel, I'd keep following orders to the letter."

"Come on Hawk," Jasef pleaded, "at least let me wound one of them while their still in range."

"No! We do nothing to alert them to our presence. There is to be no visible threat. That was Lord Zarsi's order. We were just to find them and report back."

Jasef lowered his bow and cursed several times under his breath. He did not like being under Lord Zarsi's beck and call, and he was much happier when Hawk was in command of Sador's army. Now though he had been reduced to merely a soldier in Zarsi's vast army. They mounted their horses and rode down a well hidden path in the forest. Within minutes they were at their army post, and they dismounted and proceeded to their superior's tent.

As they entered, they became very aware that the camp was preparing to move. Lord Zarsi stood beside General Musei planning out what looked like an invasion. Zarsi looked up at the new arrivals with a fire in his eyes. Hawk and Jasef immediately bowed, and Lord Zarsi's eyes never moved as he watched their fearful obedience.

"Hawk, Jasef," Zarsi said as they straightened, "by your presence here, I trust that you have found the six people that I ordered you to find."

"Yes my liege," Hawk answered. "They stopped for a few moments at the edge of the forest, and then proceeded toward Sador down then long forest road. They are a good hour from town now. They were not riding at a very fast pace, so I would suppose that it will take them longer."

"Good. Was the one called Gwydeon with them?"

"I do believe I heard that name mentioned in connection with the tall slim man," Jasef replied. "I also heard the names Pike and Talon which I remember you said to listen for."

"Ah, so my friends' reports were not wrong after all. Good. Join your ranks men. No, Hawk, you will stay with me. Jasef, you will take Hawk's place in the first infantry."

"Yes, my lord," they answered in unison.

The next few minutes were filled with chaos. Men and horses stirred for the places they had entrenched themselves and began riding toward the edge of the forest. Hawk stood outside General Musei's tent, waiting for Lord Zarsi to emerge. A minute later, he stepped out of the tent with General Musei at his side. Hawk looked over at his two commanders for a few seconds, and then turned back quickly to the attention position when Zarsi turn his gaze toward Hawk. In those few seconds he had seen the huge scar on the side of his lord's face. Zarsi had told him of the battle that had inflicted that scar upon him, but Hawk could still not believe that anyone could have been close enough to inflict that wound and not kill

Zarsi, unless the only purpose of the battle was to scar him for the rest of his life.

"Hawk."

"Yes, my lord Zarsi?" Hawk replied, his eyes still cast forward toward the increasing movement in the camp.

"How are you with the sword?"

"I am the best in the camp sir. I am most likely the best in your army."

Hawk finally turned his attention to Zarsi and looked him dead in the face.

"Suffice it to say that I could probably defeat you in a duel."

"Hawk!" General Musei growled. "Stop that insolence now!"

"It's all right Musei," Zarsi said his eyes not shifting from Hawk's face; "I like a little arrogance in my men, at least to a point. So, you think you're good, do you Hawk?"

"I'm the best, sir."

"I doubt that. But all the same, I have a bit of a challenge for you. How would you like to take on a man who says he's the best with a sword? I've heard that he even bested your friend Antrobus."

"Antrobus was a weak arrogant fool. I could best him with one hand bound behind my back. But in answer to your question, yes, I'd like a bit of a challenge. So, do you want this little upstart killed, or just seriously wounded?"

"I doubt you could manage either against this one Hawk. Do your best, and make the boy Gwydeon Sandar kneel before me."

"By your word."

Hawk bowed and then followed Zarsi as he made his way to the center of the camp. He climbed to the top of the little platform and everything stopped as he began to address his army.

"Men. Your mission this day is a simple one to say the least. There are six intruders on the old forest road that leads to your home. They do not come in peace, and therefore must be taken before they can harm your families. There are four men and two women in this party. The men must be taken alive; the women could be taken or killed. They do not matter. If any member of any unit kills one of these men, the families of that unit will all be killed before the day is over. If you fail, and they reach Sador, all of your families will be killed. Do not underestimate their abilities, men. These are the same people who were able to humiliate the Army of Illimar in the confines of their own home. I will not be at this battle, but be sure that I will be watching, as I have always watched you. Fail and be punished, succeed and live. Hawk will lead your forces into battle. To the front!"

"Long live Lord Zarsi!" the men thundered.

Zarsi turned and stepped down off of the platform. He smiled quickly to Hawk and then began talking to General Musei. Hawk hesitated for a moment and then took the platform himself.

"Hawk!" the men yelled.

"Yes my men, I am to lead you this day. You will all succeed for me. There is no plan for this attack. Take them alive if possible, but kill the women if they cause too much trouble. However, the boy named Gwydeon Sandar is mine. Section commanders, sound the attack."

Horns blasted from everywhere in the camp. Men began to run toward the edge of the forest, not caring to stay with their sections. Hawk mounted his horse and rode over toward Jasef.

"I have a bad feeling about this Hawk," Jasef said as they rode toward their advancing army.

"Keep the faith brother," Hawk replied, "our day is coming soon."

* * * * * * * * * * * *

The six friends rode together down the old, tree lined path that led to Sador. They had been riding at a leisurely pace, not in much of a hurry. Pike was at the back of the pack with Gwydeon and Talon, continuing their conversation about the girl called Leane. It seemed that Gwydeon would never stop talking about her, and then suddenly, right in the middle of a sentence, he just stopped. It wasn't that he just stopped talking, but he stopped his horse as well and turned back toward the way they had just traveled.

"What's wrong Gwydeon?" Talon asked.

"Don't you hear that?"

"Hear what?" Pike asked.

Suddenly he heard it. It was a sound like hard rain falling on dry fields back in Aradon; only it was a hundred times more intense. He could then begin to see a cloud of dust beginning to rise over the hill they had traveled over on their way.

"I think we're about to have company," Pike said quickly.

"That's an understatement," Talon mumbled.

Gwydeon jumped down from his horse and sent it galloping toward Sador. By this time the rest of his friends had stopped and turned back toward the on-rushing hoard.

"We haven't got much time to prepare," Gwydeon said as he stripped off his shirt and unsheathed his sword. Midarin noticed as he moved his sword arm that he winced a little from the injury he had taken only a day or two earlier. His chest was covered with half-healed wounds, and for any other man, the pain should have been unbearable, but this was no other man, this was Gwydeon Sandar.

"What do you want us to do Gwydeon?" Midarin asked as she dismounted.

"As soon as they're in range, I want you to start firing arrows into their ranks, try and cut down their numbers. Lane."

"Yes Gwydeon?"

"I don't know much about your magic, but do whatever you can to keep them from getting the drop on us."

"What about me, Gwydeon?" Eldar asked.

"I know you can hold your own with a sword Eldar, but I've never seen you take on more than one person at a time. I want you to stay with Pike and Talon."

"So, what do we do?" Talon asked.

"You guys are two of the mythical *Erieal*, you do what you can."

"Without Logan around, I don't know how effective our powers will be," Pike said, "but we'll do our best."

The other four members of the party dismounted and stood together waiting for the advancing army. There was nowhere to hide, and no land forms that would give them an advantage in the upcoming battle. They could hide behind the trees, but that could end up hurting them in the long run. The trees.

"Lane, Talon, Pike," Gwydeon said quickly, "can you three use your powers to surround us with fallen trees?"

"Great plan!" Lane yelled. "Consider it done."

Pike and Talon nodded, and for the first time they actually tried to exert their powers. Talon had never before attempted to even use his powers before this moment, and Pike had only touched on his by accident. Gideon was the only member of this generation's *Erieal* who had any modicum of control over his abilities. Talon raised his hands toward the trees to their right and it was as if a hurricane hit suddenly and the six friends stood in the eye of the storm. Branches and leaves began to whip around everywhere, and over the storm's intense winds, Gwydeon could hear the sounds of trees breaking. Gwydeon looked back over his shoulder and saw Pike's hands shoot up toward the sky, and streams of water began to explode from his fingertips. The water cascaded all around them, and it seemed to form a dome. Gwydeon then heard a faint mumbling coming from Lane, and then suddenly Lane jabbed the end of his staff into the dome of water, and it immediately crystallized. The six of them were encased in a shield of ice. The winds still exploded outside, and moments after the ice had formed, it shattered under the weight of the trees. However, the shield had done its job in protecting them. They were surrounded with the fallen limbs and trunks of trees.

"Well done gentlemen. Now, let's turn our attention to halting the advance of our adversaries," Lane said slowly.

"Agreed," Gwydeon responded, "Midarin?"

"Not quite yet Gwydeon," she answered, "I'm good, but even I can't fire that distance."

"Well," Talon said, "why don't we help out the arrows a little?"

"What?" Midarin said puzzled.

"Just start shooting, and I'll take care of the rest," Talon said confidently.

Midarin sighed but hefted her bow after a quick shake of her head. She nocked an arrow onto the bowstring and then fired it into the air. It raced toward the oncoming army, and then after a flash of light, the arrow split into thirty. Then the wind kicked up, and the thirty arrows rained death down upon members of the opposition.

Midarin turned to Talon, a quizzical look on her face.

"How did you do that?"

"That's what I'd like to know," Talon remarked looking at his hands.

"I helped a bit with the arrows," Lane commented, "but we have no time for individual honors. Keep shooting, Talon and I will do all we can."

"Is there anything else you can do Pike?" Gwydeon asked.

"My powers seem to be pretty limited without the help of the other *Erieal*, Gwydeon. I'll have to do most of my damage hand to hand."

CHAPTER 9

Gwydeon turned back toward the on-rushing opponents and watched the continuing carnage from Midarin's strikes. Dozens of men fell at a time, and within minutes Midarin's quiver was empty, and the ranks of the enemy were cut considerably. As Gwydeon watched, it appeared that the charge had stopped and their enemy was just waiting for something. Inwardly Gwydeon wished he knew what the opposing general was thinking.

* * * * * * * * * * * *

"I wish I knew what that bastard Sandar was thinking," Hawk yelled. "There has to be some way to get past their blockade and that cursed shower of arrows."

"I guess Lord Zarsi underestimated our friends out there, Hawk," Jasef commented.

"That is an understatement, Jasef. What is the damage?"

"Second, third, fifth, seventh, and ninth battalions have suffered heavy casualties. Battalions four, six, eight and ten are wiped out. Only unit one remains unscathed."

"That's over four hundred men we've lost Jasef! Reform the units and call the charge. If the arrows start again, we're as good as dead."

"Yes sir."

Jasef turned and rode away from Hawk who still sat there with sword in hand. The battle was not turning out well for his forces, and he inwardly wondered if Lord Zarsi was underestimating this Gwydeon Sandar's sword skill as well. The charge was immediately sounded, and the battle cries from his men went up like thunder from the heavens.

"The charge has been called, sir," Jasef said as he rode back up to Hawk.

"Good. Order unit one to circle behind them using the hidden forest road. I'm hoping that this Sandar is not as good a strategist as I am. The rest of the men with go on with the frontal assault with you in the lead. I will take command of unit one personally."

"By your word, Lord Hawk."

Hawk smiled as Jasef rode back toward his men.

* * * * * * * * * * * *

"Here they come again Gwydeon," Talon said as the men advanced.

Gwydeon turned back toward Lane and gripped the hilt of his sword tightly.

"I wish Gideon was still here, he could split the ground and bury those bastards before they get here."

Pike looked at Gwydeon and smiled.

"We may not have Gideon, but I have a great idea."

"Whatever it is, you better do it quick," Eldar said looking at the advancing army, "because they're getting closer, and they look really mad."

"Right," Pike said. "Lane, when I yell, I want you to do that ice trick with your staff again, but you're going to have to throw it about ten yards out in front of us."

"Not a problem, Pike," Lane said nodding.

"Then, when I give the word, Talon, you use the winds and shatter the ice."

"All right, Pike. I don't really see your plan, but I'll do my part."

"Just trust me Talon," Pike said rubbing his hands together, "and pray this works."

Pike took a deep breath and extended his hands toward their advancing enemy. Gwydeon couldn't see anything as Pike concentrated, but then suddenly he knew what was going on. The ground a few yards ahead of them was filling with water. If a huge stream was aimed at it or enough weight was placed upon it, the ground would give out, and the oncoming soldiers would be buried in a swamp. The enemies' ranks were tight, and as

Pike had hoped, as several ranks crossed the soaked ground, it collapsed left them floundering in the newly created swamp.

"Now, Lane!"

Lane mumbled quickly to himself and hefted the staff into the air and threw it like a spear toward the swamp. A few of the men were beginning to climb out of the water and mud, but the second the staff touched the water, everyone and everything froze.

"Talon!"

The winds picked up not seconds after Pike said his name. The winds swirled around the area of the frozen swamp, and then the pressure of the wind shattered not only the ice, but also the bodies that were frozen within it.

"Good show Pike!" Eldar screamed as soon as she was sure of the success of his plan.

"Wonderful Pike!" Midarin exclaimed.

Everyone gathered around Pike and patted him on the back for the plan that had saved them from danger. Suddenly there was a sound from behind them. It was very much like the sound of two gloved hands being clapped together as if in applause. Gwydeon turned and looked up at the man who was cheering their triumph. He looked past him and noticed that there were about a hundred armed men behind him, waiting for a chance to avenge the deaths of their compatriots; at least that was the impression Gwydeon got from the looks on their faces.

"Good show my troublesome adversaries," the man said in a deep accented voice, "I applaud your efforts to dissuade your capture by the royal army of Sador. Which of you is the man named Gwydeon Sandar?"

Gwydeon stepped forward and sheathed his sword.

"I'm Gwydeon Sandar."

"You are the little upstart that is supposed to be the best swordsman in the world? Please, tell me that this lout is joking," the man laughed.

"He is the best you bastard, but I'll happily gut you for him," Eldar screamed as she advanced and unsheathed her sword.

She moved quickly toward him and before she could even move to attack, his blade was at her throat.

"I would back off if I were you young one. My orders were to take these men alive, but I could kill you and the other tramp over there if I so desired."

Pike leaped forward, and the blade of his axe pinned their assailant's blade to the ground. The man withdrew his blade quickly and looked down at Pike from his position on top of a felled tree.

"This is Eldar Merin, not some insignificant girl. The woman back there is not a tramp, she is a princess, and if you think you can kill them and take the other four of us alive, you've got another thing coming. And by the way, my name is Pike Rhuiden, it case you missed it. If you keep flapping your tongue, mine will be the last face you ever see."

The leader of the soldiers cocked his lips in to a cruel smirk.

"You have gall. My lord will find that amusing, at least for the four or five seconds that you will live after meeting him. And by the way, in case you missed it, my name is Hawk Yetre."

"Why are you doing this Hawk?" Midarin asked strongly.

"Because I'm under orders, my little princess. I never thought it would have been this difficult to take on four whelps and a couple of whores, but you made me miss my guess, and I'm impressed."

"How would you like if I impressed my axe into your forehead, Hawk?" Pike said angrily.

He put his arm in front of Eldar, who was still rubbing her neck after the close call with the blade. Pike pushed her away quickly and stood straight with his axe ready to strike at any moment. All Hawk could do was laugh.

"You think this is some kind of joke, Hawk?" Pike asked, the anger creeping farther into his voice. "Well fine, just stand there and laugh, I like it better when my enemies don't put up much of a fight. It's usually quicker and less painful. For me anyway."

Pike moved to strike at Hawk, but before he could move the foot of distance between he and Hawk, three men ran up to defend him, and four others with bows trained their sights on him. Pike stopped short of Hawk, sharp blades threatening to rip through his skin. Hawk could only laugh louder.

"You see, Pike, you can't possibly win. You are horribly outnumbered, and at this range, there is no way that your little powers could kill us all before we get to you. Now, are we going to do this the easy way, or are we going to have to test my little theory?"

Gwydeon walked up to Hawk and put his hand on Pike's axe. Pike got the message and lowered it slowly, never taking his eyes off of Hawk.

"We'll go Hawk, but the women go with us, unharmed, and unmolested."

"I'll agree to those conditions. But if you make any attempt to escape or I feel so much as a cold breeze on the back of my neck, I'll rip both of their throats out with my bare hands. You will be surrounded as you walk, but I suppose I will trust you enough not to tie you up and carry you all to Sador."

Hawk turned and his men cheered. Gwydeon and the rest of his friends were dragged out of their little bunker and then set to walking down the path to Sador. As they walked Pike and Eldar moved closer to Gwydeon.

"Why did you give up so easily?" Pike insisted, "We could have taken them out with our combined powers."

"I wanted to see who was behind all of this, and letting ourselves be captured seemed the best way to do that. Besides, haven't you seen enough blood shed today Pike?"

"I suppose you're right, but you didn't have to play up to that arrogant Hawk," Eldar chided.

"There is where you're wrong Eldar. That arrogant Hawk may just be our ticket out of this little mess. By the way that he was talking, I think that we have ourselves a new ally."

Pike's dumbfounded look was only eclipsed by the horror in Eldar's eyes.

Into the Fire

People continued to flood out of the royal palace of Trelon as the bright orange flames continued to lick at the white walls of the palace, leaving blackened charred remains. Almost the entire palace still remained standing, but the cracks in the walls were starting to lengthen into spider-web like patterns and there were visual trembling in some of the walls. From where he stood Logan could see part of one of the tall beautiful spires of the palace begin to crumble away in the thick sheets of billowing dark gray smoke. The palace was burning fast, but there were few who were brave enough to rush into the roaring flames to make an attempt to rescue the queen and princess. It hadn't taken long for Logan and the others to discover that the royal family was still trapped inside, but thus far every attempt at intervention had been thwarted. The royal guard had their hands full just trying to keep the civilians from being crushed by the falling debris, and there were many foreign dignitaries to protect. In a matter of minutes the palace would be reduced to nothing more than a smoldering cinder of its former self. There may have been nothing that Logan and his companions could have done to save the palace, but from the moment the saw the situation they had dedicated themselves to saving Queen Anabel and Princess Cairyn from the prince's machinations. Logan drew his sword and dropped his scabbard to the ground as he turned to face the others.

"We don't have much time," Logan said with as much conviction as he could manage.

The smoke was thick in the air, and more than that there was a tension and pressure that was permeating the atmosphere. Logan could not stifle a cough, but it was less about the smoke and more about the incredible pressure that was building in his chest.

"We have to do everything in our power to save Anne and Cairyn. Gideon, you're with me. We'll head for the throne room to get the queen. Unless I miss my guess, that's where she'll be. Aryx, you take Elwyne and try to find Cairyn. Hopefully you won't have to go far into the fires, but if you do, Elwyne, keep as clear as you can. If she isn't in her chambers, get out quick. Don't bother looking anywhere else."

"The same goes for you and Gideon," Elwyne urged.

"Right. Talos, you find that bastard Allan. If he won't come quietly, kill him."

Logan didn't bother to wait for a response. He knew that he wasn't alone in the anger that he felt toward the prince, and that if Talos had the chance, even without orders, he wouldn't hesitate to take revenge for Allan's deeds. Logan turned back toward the flaming palace and began to run as quickly as he could toward the broken doors that led into the palace. The crowd still streamed from the doors and windows of the palace. Logan ran as hard as he could, pushing his way through the on-rushing crowd, within a matter of moments he heard the sound of footsteps behind him. Aryx and Gideon came up beside him, both easing into a longer stride, keeping pace with Logan. It was then that the heavy end of the hammer fell, and Allan played his final card.

The flood of people had slowed to a trickle and then stopped. All of the people who were going to get out of the palace on their own were already out. It was clear that Anne and Cairyn weren't going to be able to escape on their own. Suddenly, five men clad in black armor rushed in from somewhere and cut off the rescue attempt. Once Logan saw that they had drawn their swords, it became obvious that they did not want anyone else interfering with Prince Allan's plans. Reflexively, we stopped a few feet from the men and prepared for a fight. There was no need for words, and Gideon didn't wait for their opponents to make a move.

CHAPTER 9

The ground began to shake violently. As Logan turned his gaze toward Gideon, the thief's eyes were closed tightly and his hands were extended toward the ground, palms and wrists flexed. The ground below bucked and groaned under the pressure that Gideon inflicted upon it. The ground began to swell under the assailants, but as a fissure began to open, it appeared as if it would miss the attackers completely. Sure enough, the fissure opened behind the men instead of under them. One of the men fell backwards due to the continued swelling of the ground, but the rest retained their balance. Without thinking, Logan thrust his hands forward and the wind began to pick up. The strong winds slammed hard into the men clad in black. They stumbled under the attack, and as they lost their balance, each of the other four men fell into the fissure. Gideon and Aryx both looked back at Logan, and he could tell that they were as shocked as he was that he had used his powers. If Logan could have remembered how he had summoned the wind, it would have felt as though he accomplished something, but it was nothing more than a reflex. Gideon's attention shifted back toward the fissure he had created. He raised his hands back up to his chest, and as he brought his hand closer together, the ground began to close. The instant that his hands touched, the fissure closed completely, leaving no trace that it was ever there, except for the absence of the five nameless men. Not a word was spoken and they continued into the palace.

Once through the broken doors, Logan and Gideon headed toward the throne room, while Aryx split off and went another direction. Even in the large entry hall, the flames seemed to burst forth from everywhere on the walls and the high arching ceiling. They broke into a run and headed for the long winding staircase in the west wall of the entry chamber. It was, in theory, the fastest way to the throne room from the entry hall, but as soon as Logan saw it, he knew that either they would reach the top alive, or they would burn to death on the way up. Logan only took a minute to survey the obstacle ahead, but it was enough to see what he needed to see. The staircase had originally been lined with beautiful flowing banners and silk decorations of every kind. It was truly a dedication to the beauty of the entire kingdom. However, now the flames had decimated the thin silk and satin banners, but the heavy cloth of the other banners continued to burn and it created a tunnel of flame that continued to spiral up the length of the staircase. The heat in the hall that led to the staircase was nearly unbearable as it was, and Logan could not even imagine the extremity of the heat from the flames lining the stairs. He could hear the wood crackling around him as it burned. It wouldn't be much longer before the entire palace caved in around them. Gideon was slightly behind as they ran single file down the tunnel of flame.

"Logan!"

It was Gideon's voice. Logan had no time to react in the next few seconds, and had it not been for Gideon's warning and possibly his powers, Logan might have found himself reduced to a smoldering pile of ashes in the middle of the rubble of the former royal palace of Trelon. One of the many wooden beams above gave way, and it fell quickly down towards Logan. It would have struck him on the head had it not been for Gideon. He either saw or heard the beam tear loose, and he sailed through the air, tackled Logan, and dragged him to the ground. The flaming beam seemed to crash to the floor that same instant. The impact would have been enough to easily shatter Logan's skull, or knock his head off. The beam landed at Gideon's feet, and it began to burn the rug that they landed upon. Both scrambled to their feet without a word or a look in each other's direction. That momentary danger had passed by without inflicting more damage than the bruise to Logan's shoulder that resulted from the contact with the floor. There were certainly more dangers that waited, and there was the ever present danger that the entire palace would give way the next time instead of just one beam.

The stairs proved to be much more of an obstacle than Logan had first anticipated. Logan should have been used to the fact that his first impressions had been wrong ever since the quest started, but he would never let it stop him. With the huge flowing tapestries that lined the walls, and the single carpet that flowed down the center of the staircase, the flight of stairs that were once the quickest way to the throne room were now nothing more than a waiting death trap. There was no way to get back down the hallway they came down, and the only way out appeared to be through the flames. Logan took a short deep breath even though the smoke was beginning to make breathing difficult and then charged headlong up the twisting flight of stairs. The instant his foot hit the first step, he could feel the incredible heat of the flames coursing through the fabric of his clothes, and even through the thick leather of his boots. Even in the best conditions, the stairs were a bit treacherous. The steps themselves were barely big enough to set your whole foot down upon, and they were also quite steep. The flames however made the stairs all the more terrifying. As Logan ran, he lost his footing on one of the shorter steps, and brushed up against one of the burning tapestries. The fire burned through his shirt before he even registered that it was on fire, and if it hadn't been for a quick and visceral reaction, he probably would have had a patch of charred skin to compliment the rest of his scars. The shirt would offer little protection and would be a hindrance in the open flames, so Logan ripped off the remainder of the shirt and continued to move as quickly as possible through the conflagration. Tension-filled minutes later, Gideon and Logan found themselves standing at the top of the stairs, staring down the length of the receiving hall that led to the throne room. The double doors that led to the throne were already burning, and black smoke filled the honor hall. A quick sideways look at Gideon revealed that the fires of the staircase had claimed his shirt also, and beads of sweat from the intense heat simply poured down his chest. There were also patches of charred skin on his arms and stomach where he had not dodged as quickly as he intended. Gideon wasted no time and started sprinting down the hallway, his body low to stay out of the rolling clouds of smoke. Logan hesitated for only an instant and then followed. He continued running down the honor hall, and as he reached the doors he leapt, and attempted to smash through the doors shoulder first. The doors held despite the power of the impact, and Gideon sprawled to the ground amidst a tapestry of colorful Alimidarian curses.

"Allan must have barricaded the door," Logan yelled over the increasing sound of the blaze and Gideon's curses.

Logan looked around the room, trying to find some way to get through the flaming doors. Then he found it. Each of the massive suits of armor that lined the honor hall carried a large war ax in its empty gauntlets.

"Gideon! The axes! Start chopping through the doors!"

The enterprise took less time than Logan had first anticipated which was fortunate as the heat and smoke sapped their strength with every blow. The flames had not only weakened the doors themselves, but also the barricade of chairs and table behind. After breaking through the barricade, Logan and Gideon charged through into the throne room.

The throne room looked as if a war had happened inside it. Bodies of the queen's royal guard were strewn around the room, and there were also other men who were dressed in the same black armor as those who had barred the path into the palace. It was a safe assumption that they were members of Prince Allan's faithful. The thickness of the smoke made it difficult to see anything in the room, and the flames seemed to leap up from everywhere. The once white walls were now licked with bright orange and red flames, leaving blackened marks of destruction upon the walls. Logan and Gideon had been screaming for Anne from the minute they hit the top of the stairs, but thus far they hadn't had any kind of response. It didn't take long to determine the reason for the disheartening silence. There on the throne sat Lady Anne. Her head was thrown back, and the diamond studded crystal crown lay in her lap. The jeweled hilt that extended from her chest told the story well enough. Allan had to have been in the throne room when his little civil war erupted. He had to have killed her before she had a chance to react, and even her royal guard was not enough to save her. Allan still lived, and Logan vowed to himself then and there that he would not rest until Allan was dead at Logan's feet with his blood soaking the steel of Logan's blade. It was then that Logan noticed the unopened parchment that Anne still clutched in her hand. It had been protected from the flames, and after taking it Logan threw the crown to Gideon. He held it in his hands, for a moment, but understood the implication. He started back toward the double doors, but suddenly the beams above the entrance collapsed, trapping them inside the throne room. Gideon turned back and then pointed to the stained glass window behind the throne. Logan nodded and then picked up Lady Anne's limp body.

"What are ye doin' Logan? We've got ta get out o' here!" Gideon shouted.

"Take my sword," Logan said as he drew it from the scabbard, "clear out some of the glass in the window. I'm not going to leave her here like this, she deserves better."

"Aye, me lord," he said as he took the sword.

He quickly shattered the glass with the sword. And the rush of air that burst into the room was enough to shatter much of the rest of the glass. The flames surged with the new fuel, but some of the smoke flooded out, improving visibility for the moment. They picked their way through the carnage out onto the narrow ledge outside of the window. Logan hefted Anne's body up onto his shoulder and followed closely behind Gideon. One of the long banners that flowed from the top of the palace had just caught fire near the ground, and was still mostly intact.

"Slide down the banner," Logan yelled through the din of burning wood.

"Let me build a stairway out o' da ground, Logan," Gideon countered, "it'd be easier and safer."

"No time, the palace could collapse at any second. Go!"

Gideon nodded and took hold of the banner. After giving it a good tug to make sure it was secure, he slid down. It was firmly planted above, at least for the moment, and hopefully it would stay that way for a few more minutes. The second he hit the ground, he broke into a sprint toward the clearing. Logan made sure Anne's body was secure on his shoulder and then he grabbed the banner and swung out into the air. At that very moment, the beams around the stained glass window gave way and collapsed the entire window, including the easement. It fell into nothingness below Logan, and eventually the shock wave of the explosion sent pieces of glass and wood flying out and down into the massive courtyard. Logan continued to slide down the banner, dodging flying debris the whole time. Before he knew it, Logan was standing in the courtyard again, and then he ran toward where Gideon was standing. When he got there, Gideon helped Logan lay Anne's body on the ground, and then exhaustion caught up with both of them and they fell to their knees. Gideon was breathing hard, but his eyes were still focused on the palace. Something wasn't right. Logan looked around and then up at Gideon.

"Where are Elwyne and Alexander?"

Gideon got back to his feet and looked around. He pointed in the direction of the gates to the palace grounds and Logan was relieved when he saw familiar forms moving toward them. Suddenly there was a sound like a huge clap of thunder, and then a deep tortured groan resounded from deep inside the palace. Logan looked back and watched in horror as the palace collapsed in upon itself. He felt a hand on his shoulder, and when he saw Elwyne's shocked face, the reality struck him.

"My god, Logan," she said, her had almost covering her mouth, "Aryx is still in there."

Before Logan knew what was happening, he was running toward the flaming ruin.

* * * * * * * * * * * *

Aryx pulled off his cloak and shirt before he entered the palace. He knew they would be more of a hindrance than anything else in the inferno. He didn't hesitate to run into the blaze, and if anyone could have looked calm inside of a burning building, it would have been Aryx. He moved down the twisting halls of the palace as if there were no flames at all, and barely even acknowledged the heat that enveloped him. He knew that the princess's chambers were on the far end of the palace, and it would take all of the control and willpower that he had to make it that far in the intense heat. He strafed down the hallways like a ghost, and he moved even faster than the flames that seemed to pursue him. Suddenly he stopped. Something was wrong. At that very instant, the roof above him collapsed. He had no time to react. The burning wood was upon him even before he could raise his hands.

In the middle of the wide hall lay a pile of fiery rubble. Under this rubble was Aryx Terian. Had it been any other man in the world, he probably would have given up. But surrender was not a word that resided in Aryx's vocabulary. After a minute, one of the larger beams shifted, and then fell from the pile. Aryx emerged from the hole, scratches and blood covering his chest. Parts of his skin were singed, but he didn't let the pain deter him. He climbed through the rubble and continued toward the princess's chambers.

In another minute, he was there. The door was closed tightly, and Aryx could hear her hoarse breathing coming from the other side of the door. No one else could have heard her, but this was not an ordinary man, this was one of the *Erieal*. The impossible was almost common place for him. One kick felled the door, and as he entered, he saw the young princess cowering in the corner, sobbing. Without a word, he took her into his arms, and started toward the door. The *Debuisa* on his hand glowed an eerie color of red, and Aryx stopped just before the door. He held the princess close to him and then held the gauntlet to his chest. Suddenly thunder ripped through the entire palace. Had Aryx not been concentrating on other things, it would have deafened him. Then the palace collapsed around them.

* * * * * * * * * * * *

Logan picked his way through the rubble, and found that as he removed one of the beams, there was a flash of light below it. Logan called for Gideon, and as they removed more and more of the rubble from the area, the lightning shield that Aryx had created came more into view. He apparently had enough time as the palace was collapsing to create the shield and protect both he and the princess. As soon as the rubble was cleared, the shield disappeared, and the exhausted Aryx fell to his knees and then looked up.

"Mission accomplished, my lord."

"I can see that Aryx," Logan responded. "Next time though, try to make it out before the building collapses."

"By your word."

Elwyne snorted and then something about 'pigheaded men and their incredible egos'. Aryx quickly regained his composure and then picked up Princess Cairyn who was still unconscious. The six of them made their way to the nearest inn, and without too many words, we were shown to the finest room in the establishment. A cold bowl of water was brought, and before too long, the Minister of Trelon had entered the room, and two of the royal guards stood watch outside the door. Thanks to Aryx, the

Binosear line still thrived in Trelon, and once Cairyn recovered, she would be crowned queen.

Elwyne took the sponge out of the cold water and rubbed it gently across Cairyn's forehead. She regained consciousness quickly, and as soon as she sat up, everyone but Logan and Gideon dropped to one knee and bowed their heads. Apparently, Logan's mastery of the proper etiquette with royalty was lacking, but he comforted himself in the fact that he wasn't the only one.

"You needn't bow," Cairyn said meekly, "I should be the one bowing to you."

"But the Queen of Trelon bows to no one," the minister chimed in, "not even the bloody *Coromor*. This is the same devil that brought this horrid incident down upon us, and for all we know he could have killed your mother."

"You may leave at any time," Cairyn responded, "and consider your days in the court at an end. I have no need for doubters and proud individuals who speak out of turn in my court."

The minister turned quickly and left the room. Cairyn exhaled slowly and eased herself back against the headboard of the bed.

"I must thank you all for your efforts to save myself and my mother, and I can tell from the reactions of the others that my mother is dead."

"She is my queen," Logan responded.

"Cairyn. If you will not allow me or anyone else to address you as a lord, than you may not address me as a queen."

"As you wish, Cairyn," Logan answered, smiling.

By this time everyone else had risen, and stood around the bed. Aryx was the last to rise, and he looked more sad than anyone in the room, more so even than Cairyn. Logan took the parchment out of his pocket and handed it to Cairyn.

"This was clutched in your mother's hand when we found her. I thought it would be for you to open, not me."

"Very well Logan," she replied.

She opened the parchment and read it quickly.

"This was indeed for you Logan," she said not looking up from the parchment. "This is a report from the Army of the Dragon."

"What does it say?"

"Captain Antrobus has been murdered, and the killer has yet to be found. A force of Jeresei attacked the Army of the Dragon in Rama and they pursued. Last word was that they were headed to Illimar," Cairyn read quickly.

"That is strange Logan," Aryx said looking toward me. "Jeresei are not known for hit and run attacks. I would surmise that they were under the orders of one of the phasia for this attack."

"Dat don't help, Aryx," Gideon countered. "Dese phasia are nothin' but generals, an' wit'out us knowin' who or what dey are, we can't do anythin' 'bout dem."

"Gideon's right," Elwyne added, "if we knew who the phase that directed the attack, maybe it would answer the question where they would go next."

"Pointless discussion," Logan said quickly before Aryx could respond. "Antrobus has been killed, and apparently the Army of the Dragon has appointed a new leader."

"Yes," Cairyn said, "a woman named Leane Torne."

"Torne?" Logan repeated. "Why does that name sound familiar?"

"That was the woman Gwydeon was seeing in Rama," Elwyne answered.

Logan shook his head and the turned toward them.

"No matter. Our next order of business is to find Allan and bring him to justice. That bastard is not getting away with this, at least not while I'm still alive."

"Do you really think that's wise?" Aryx questioned.

"This is not up for a discussion Aryx," Logan returned strongly. "We are going to find Allan. These things about Jeresei and phasia can wait."

"As you wish," Aryx conceded.

That instant the door opened and Talon of the Moridon entered. He bowed first to Logan and then to Cairyn.

"Talos," Logan said slowly, "just the man I wanted to see. What have you to report?"

"Prince Allan made his way to the dock on the far end of the Greater Trelon River and boarded a small ship and set sail. His course down river will take him past the docks of Lesin, and then possibly to the Island of Thardus."

"My family has a small palace on the Isle of Thardus," Cairyn added, "but it's been abandoned for years."

"That would be a good place for him to hide while he plans his next move though. Good work Talos," Logan responded.

"Thank you my Lord Dragon."

"We will ride for the docks of Lesin at first light, and we will find Allan. Is there anything that we can do to help you Queen Cairyn?" I asked.

"I really like the sound of that," she responded, "maybe I shouldn't change my name like mother did."

"What would you have changed it to?" Elwyne asked.

"I have always liked the name Sabrina," she answered, "it was my mother's middle name."

"Queen Cairyn has a regal sound to it my queen, you have made a good choice." Aryx said.

As the group started to leave, Gideon hesitated, and then produced the diamond studded crown from his pack and laid it on the bed next to the future queen of Trelon. He didn't say a word, and neither did Cairyn. She simply nodded at him in thanks, tears welling in her eyes. As Gideon left the room, Elwyne caught up to him and took hold of his arm. She was surprised that he too had tears in his eyes.

"We're all sad about Lady Anne," Elwyne said, trying to console him.

Gideon looked at her for a long moment, and then the walls went back up. He sniffed and then smiled.

"Jus' hard givin' dat crown up. Offends da thief in me."

Elwyne smiled knowingly at the evasion. But Logan could not feel the minor humor of the moment. Rage burned in him, and he would not eat, sleep, or laugh again until the prince was dead.

Epilogue

Confederation

Basille walked toward the portal slowly. This was the first time that he had ever been kept after a session of the Council so that Shau-ling could brief him. He was sure that Jeroch was off somewhere cursing because he was not the one chosen to carry out the Master's mission, but if all of the plans that were revolving around him were to come true, Jeroch had better soon learn to cope with disappointment. Basille still was thinking about his Master's words. Something about the whole mission still bothered him.

Why me? Saurn and I have never really been allies, but then again, we have never really been enemies either. I wonder if Shau-ling knows what is going on behind his back, and that is why he wants me out of the palace. But I could just be jumping to conclusions for no reason. Maybe Master just thinks that because Saurn and I do not have the same violent history that he shares with the rest of the phasia, that he will actually stand and listen to what I have to say.

Usually, Basille was the last to leave the Council, unless there was a special briefing after a session. However, Shau-ling always tended to remain. Sometimes he would stay in the Council chambers for hours, even days at a time in deep meditation. For years, some of the phasia had contended that the Council was the focal point of Shau-ling's power, and if he were kept away from the Council for a long period of time, he would begin to weaken and the phasia would be able to take over. While there was no proof of this, it was still in the back of every phase's mind. There was another part to that contention though that no one ever wanted to believe. There was a contention that the phasia also derived their powers from the Council, and that if they were away for a long period of time, they would begin to weaken as well. However, knowing that Saurn had been away for as long as he had made that theory harder to believe. Still, it was something to think about.

There was yet another point of contention that held every phase's thoughts. Ever since Zarsi challenged Shau-ling to a duel and was horribly scared for the rest of his unnatural existence, all of the phasia realized that a battle with Shau-ling one-on-one would always end badly for that phase. They also all knew that their powers were so closely charged that it was impossible to combine them. If they tried to combine their abilities the way that the *Erieal* did, the powers would cancel each other out, rendering both powerless for a time and easy targets. Again it supported the belief that the phasia were cursed to serve Shau-ling forever. All agreed however, that if a way could be found, something had to be done to end the servitude of the phasia.

There were very few things that a majority of the phasia agreed upon, and there were only two cases in which all of the phasia agreed. The first case was the need to stay alive by killing the *Coromor*. He was the greatest threat imaginable. In the lifetime past when Cedric Binosear began his reign, he had not known the full extent of his powers, or exactly what he was up against. Regardless of this, he and his army wiped out almost the entire breed of Jeresei and he personally killed four of the phasia, Basille included. In that time, the *Erieal* were not even a factor. Yes, they had gathered around Cedric, but they had no concept of their connection to him, nor to what they could do with their powers. The only exception to this of course was the thrice damned Aryx Terian. This new boy, the Dragon, had already gathered three of those mythical brothers together, and he was far in advance of his predecessor in knowledge and power. Unlike Binosear however, this boy had a guide with experience. White Lightning was proving to be more of a thorn in Shau-ling's side than he could have ever foreseen. The *Coromor* was the easy agreement. The other point that all of the phasia agreed upon was one that Basille still could not believe.

With all of the whining and boot licking that Jeroch and Erdric did, they both still agreed that it was time for a new lord of the manor. All of the phasia agreed that Shau-ling had long since outlived his usefulness, and that a new leader should be crowned as soon as a way could be found to overthrow Shau-ling. Of course, no one agreed upon who this new leader should be, but the fact that a new leader was needed was clear.

Basille stepped through the portal and within a few seconds he was standing back in the throne room. The thick smell of burnt flesh and entrails still filled the room. Not thinking, Basille took a breath, and was nearly incapacitated by the strong and unpleasant aroma. He made his way carefully through the room sidestepping exploded pieces of Jeresei and leaping over pools of unknown bodily fluids. As quickly as possible without stepping in anything too disgusting, he made his way across the length of the room and was finally standing at the doorway to the Hall of Terrors. Before he could even put his hand on the door, it opened revealing the Flame.

"It is you last-born. I was expecting to see more of the Valtamine," the flame said slowly.

"I can assure you that no Valtamine will be leaving this throne room for a long time, Flame. I suggest that you release the Octal and have it cleanse this chamber before the master returns from his meditations in the Council Chambers."

"By your word."

The Flame turned and walked quickly down the Hall of Terrors. Not one of the beasts dared to comment as he walked, and most appeared to be cowering in their cells. The phasia may not have seen the Flame as a major threat to their lives, but to the small-minded beasts that resided in the Hall, the Flame was like a vengeful god. The Flame turned to a cell on the right side, dead in the center of the Hall. The Flame opened the cell and then turned back toward Basille. As the Flame walked back toward the throne room, a beast began to make its way very slowly out of the cell.

This huge, worm-like beast was one of the most dangerous, and playful of all of Shau-ling's creations. Its skin was smooth and slimy, almost like the surface of a scum covered pond. The skin itself was a dark red color, and the color brightened and faded as the thing crawled. As the beast turned and its front came into view, Basille noted that the Octal had no eyes, merely a huge mouth. This mouth was ringed with at least foot long, razor sharp teeth. A thick yellow liquid oozed from the tip of each of the Octal's fangs. As the liquid dripped to the ground, it began to burn. Even the indestructible berionite stone was affected by the acid the Octal secreted. The body of any beast that Basille had ever encountered would be dissolved in a matter of seconds in the jaws of this monster. No one could ever bring themselves to consider the Octal that dangerous. When Shau-ling created this beast, he did a masterful job. The skin of the Octal was nearly impenetrable, and the acid would eat anything in a matter of seconds. However, when Shau-ling made the Octal, he did not give it a mind. The Octal did not have the ability to think or to make decisions on its own. It could merely react. Never could it be a serious threat. Without this freedom of thought that most living creature take for granted, the Octal had been delegated to merely cleaning up other people's messes.

Basille stepped aside as the Flame led the Octal to its feast. As usual, Basille walked away before the Octal actually began to devour its meal. He had always found the sight of the Octal's messy eating habits disturbing. As he walked, he could hear the squeals of joy coming from somewhere deep inside the Octal, and he could also hear the Flame roar with laughter as he watched the show. Basille continued out of the Hall of Terrors and took the long way around the palace, by-passing the Pit and all of the normal corridors and receiving areas. No matter what path he took, there were always kneeling Jeresei and other servants who were quick to show their admiration and fealty. Basille had prepared himself a room near the bottom of the palace where the water entrances' receiving areas were. No one else ever stayed down that deep, so Basille's privacy was usually assured. But as Basille rounded the last corner to his room, he found two of his brothers waiting for him just outside his door.

The first face, he had all but expected to see. The phasia did not often make friends of their own kind, especially when it came to battle and position in the Council. Basille found that there sometimes had to be exceptions to the rule, and Warron was definitely that exception. He had stood by Warron many times over the years, and if there was a phase he could trust, he knew it would always be Warron. The other man however, was not as close to him. This man was a part-time ally, and a sometime friend. It seemed that he suffered more of Shau-ling's wrath than any of the other phasia, and perhaps that is what spawned the friendship. The scar on Zarsi's face was all that anyone needed to see that Shau-ling was not at all the forgiving and forgetting master that everyone wished he was.

"Warron, Zarsi. I thought that both of you would have returned to your kingdoms after the Council."

"That was assuredly our intention dear brother," Warron replied, "at least it was until we heard master request your presence for a briefing afterwards. It rather concerned us."

"Is that so?"

"Yes, it is." Zarsi answered. "This is the first time in our many meetings that Shau-ling has ever requested you to stay after a session, you being the last-born. Some of us stayed here in the palace afterwards, talking about the possibilities of the meeting. The only explanation that we could come up with, that even sounded worth exploring, was that Shau-ling insisted upon you finding a certain lost member of our sacred brotherhood."

"What?" Basille asked trying to decipher the often thick double-talk that had quickly become Zarsi's trademark.

"What I'm trying to say is . . ."

"What Zarsi is trying to say, in his own jumbled way," Warron interrupted, "is that we all believe that Shau-ling ordered you to find Saurn."

Basille didn't reply. He looked dead at Warron and smiled.

"Is that your Jeresei impersonation, or am I right?" Zarsi asked quickly.

"Pipe down Zarsi," Warron said angrily. "Just keep smiling Basille. Shau-ling is probably listening to our conversation, or at least your part of it. He does that every so often with some of his orders. If they are spoken of to other phasia, he can listen in once the orders are mentioned. I don't want him to hear this, so keep that trap shut, and don't mention anything about Saurn or your mission."

Basille nodded and his smile widened.

"Good. Zarsi, Caris, and I were discussing the possibilities of this little mission that you have been sent on. I'm not sure if any of the other phasia realize the ramifications of this mission, or if they even suspect the mission, but it is important. After we sat talking for a few moments, Caris and I decided that it was time to put the plan into action."

"What about me?" Zarsi asked quickly.

"Shut up!" Basille scolded. "Fine, now where is our beloved sister Caris?"

"She said that it was very important to the plan that she return to Illimar and oversee the beginning of the civil war there," Zarsi replied undaunted by the flurry of insults.

"Right. Now, will someone please fill me in on this glorious plan? I feel like I'm the last one to know about everything in this palace."

"Well, you are the last-born," Warron replied crassly.

Basille shot Warron a disgusted look and then smiled again.

"The plan?" Basille urged.

"Saurn has openly opposed Shau-ling in the past, and now Shau-ling wants him to come back to the Council and the brotherhood as if nothing ever happened. Now, with Jeroch and Erdric watching the Lion and his cronies in Marcwell, Farax sitting on his thumbs praying that the Dragon doesn't come knocking on his door in Kandor, and Taron doing lord-knows-what in Seren, the five of us should be able to take down Shau-ling with little or no interference."

"What about Aldridge?"

"He's a weakling," Zarsi replied in a hostile tone. "You know that as well as anyone Basille. The five of us could kill him without thinking about it twice, and you can never be sure where that coward's loyalties lie."

"His loyalties lie with himself and whoever seems to be in power at the time," Warron added quickly. "Why do you think he is the only member of the phasia who does not rule his own kingdom? He has been biding his time, trying to figure out how he is going to kill both Queen Camille and the princess without making it look like murder. It was either that or kill off the prince that he was posing to be, slaughter the queen and marry the daughter."

"But even if he did that, he would still be at the mercy of his wife, because Trelon has been ruled by women for a long time," Basille retorted.

"I've heard that he has already taken steps to grab the reins of both the kingdom and Shau-ling's favor," Zarsi said slyly.

"I can't wait to hear this," Basille commented.

"Now, he apparently has the Dragon on some wild goose chase in Castleer. While away, he will kill the queen and the princess, and then burn the palace down, making it look like some glorious accident. When the Lord Dragon returns, if he returns, Aldridge says that he will kill him in a duel."

"What a glorious deranged fool. The first dead of the phasia in this lifetime. Now I'm sure that he will not be a hindrance to our plan," Warron laughed.

"So, Aldridge is out of the way, but I still am wondering why Saurn would even want to join us. The two of you have never gotten along with Saurn very well, and some of the best battles of the War for Power were between the three of you."

"That is true brother Raven, but stop being such a blind damn fool," Warron scolded. "Saurn has been rebelling and fighting Shau-ling every step of the way for years now. He has never issued a direct challenge, but then again, Saurn was never that much of a fool. However, he has been bold in his desertion of the Council and Shau-ling. You can surely convince him to help us."

"I'm pleased that you have such unwavering faith in my persuasive abilities. I hope Saurn does as well."

"It's not faith my old friend, its logic. After what happened to Zarsi all those years ago, do you really think that Saurn would be stupid enough to issue a personal challenge to Shau-ling, and actually go through with it with no assistance? Well, he's not a fool, and he will willingly accept any help he can get."

"Saurn may not be a fool, but the three of you most certainly qualify if you are plotting against Shau-ling."

All three of the phasia turned to face what they expected to be another of the phasia. In reality, the thing that had accosted them and intruded in their conversation was none other than a lowly Jeresei.

"Bite your tongue lowborn," Zarsi scolded, "you have no business meddling in the affairs of those who would command you."

"Ah, but you cannot command me, nor order me to follow you any longer without my agreement," the Jeresei responded.

Basille laughed slightly at the bold comment. Neither of the other two phasia reacted to the comment, but Basille knew that Warron was ready to rip the upstart Valtamine to shreds.

"What gives you this miraculous immunity to Shau-ling's powers that you do not share with your brethren? Why is it you do not follow blindly like the other wretches that are leashed to his side?" Basille scoffed.

"That is a very good question Basille. Notice I did not say Lord Basille like the rest of your lackeys. But I digress. The reason, I believe, is perhaps because I belong to the clan Hoemsai."

"The clan Hoemsai?" Warron remarked with extreme amazement. "Basille, isn't that the clan that we were sent to find in old Sarmeel?"

"The same, my friend. It is also the same clan whose leader proclaimed his allegiance to the *Coromor* before his end came."

All three of the phasia looked at the newcomer again and watched as the trademark wide haughty smile of the Jeresei crept onto his lips.

"That, Basille, should give you all the reason that you need in this matter. Before his death, our clan master did the one thing that would save the members of the clan that were not there in the throne room. When he realized that the Bond had been broken and he was free to do what he wished, he released us from his service. That will soon prove to be Shauling's fatal error. The high and mighty master of all does not feel he has the time to put every single member of every breed into service, so he takes our clan leaders and he Bonds them. Then, he leashes all of the members of that clan to their clan leader in an effort to extend the Bond. Our clan leader was smart enough to realize this error, and he saved us all. When the leash was broken, our Bond was broken."

Zarsi laughed loudly after the Jeresei's explanation and then began speaking with a new light in his eyes.

"Perfect," Zarsi commented gleefully. "Now our plan can move forward for certain. The speed of our strike will be greater and we will literally be able to kill two birds with one stone."

"How so?" Basille asked.

"How many of your clan remain alive lowborn?" Zarsi asked turning toward the Jeresei.

"There are three hundred of us here and in the surrounding hills. There may be more of us in the mountains."

"Wonderful," was all that Zarsi said.

"So," Warron said slowly, "do we get an insight to this glorious new plan of yours Zarsi, or must we guess?"

"Of course you may have some insight dear brother, just give me some time to work out all of the particulars," Zarsi replied. "How quickly could you gather your distended flock *Valtamine*?"

"A few hours, maybe a day."

"Good. Time is of the essence, and there can be no delay. Gather your army as quickly as you possibly can and then march toward Rama. There I want you to launch an attack on the Army of the Dragon."

"That is suicide Zarsi," the Jeresei replied angrily. "I will not take three hundred of the finest Jeresei warriors into a battle in which they will all most certainly be killed. What do you take me for? Even three hundred Jeresei could not defeat a force that size."

"You misunderstand me my dear lowborn friend. I'm not telling you to lead a frontal assault right down their throats, as pleasant as that may sound. Nor am I telling you to start a siege and try and outlast them. No, I want you to hit them hard, and then fade back. Then hit them again, and again, and again."

"You're trying to bait them!" Warron exclaimed.

"Exactly, dear brother. You and your army of proud Jeresei warriors will lead Miss Torne and her army right into the middle of the bloodiest civil war this world has ever seen."

"So, I'm to lead the Army of the Dragon to Illimar?" the Jeresei asked proudly.

"Correct," Zarsi replied. "Now, off with you. Go and gather your clan. If any of you survive the fray, they will report directly to me either here or in Baldazar."

The Jeresei's smile faded away from his face, and he bowed to his new commander. As a soldier he had learned how to take orders from anyone, including the phasia, whether he liked it or not. The Jeresei straightened, turned, and walked away. As soon as he was out of sight, the conversation began anew.

"Exquisite plan dear brother," Warron said, "and after the detailed analysis of the workings of the plan, I have but one question to put to you."

"Ask."

"Who, exactly, is Miss Torne?"

"Miss Leane Torne is the new leader of the forces of the Army of the Dragon."

"What about Antrobus?" Basille asked.

"I received word from my agents in Rama a day or two ago that Captain Antrobus had been murdered. No one as of yet has figured out who the murderer is, but the fact that Antrobus is dead is certain."

"I don't see what this has to do with the plan. It doesn't matter whether Captain Antrobus or the Torne woman is leading the Army of the Dragon. They will be lead to their slaughter nonetheless," Basille commented.

"You are correct when you say it does not matter who leads, but the murder itself is important."

"How so?" Basille asked.

"My spies in Rama did a little digging into the murder, and my spies were very thorough. They did some checking into the shady past of our illustrious query, and found out some very interesting things. Everywhere that my spies and I checked, we found the mark of the Viper there waiting for us. I haven't seen Saurn's mark flashed around this much since the incident with Aerith Seth and Aralias Imstra."

"And . . ." Basille urged.

"And, I think that Saurn has uncovered the identity of the *Chosen One*."

Warron looked at Zarsi with a worried look on his face. Basille's reaction came out only in anger.

"I don't think, in light of this new development, that we should continue with the plan," Warron stammered.

"Don't tell me that the great and powerful Warron, the Boar, is losing his gall!" Zarsi prodded.

"No Zarsi, but I am starting to gain a little of the common sense that you appear to be desperately losing. The only time that the *Chosen One* was ever found resulted in the deaths of more than one phase. Last time, Aerith Seth killed four members of the brotherhood without knowing half of his potential. You know that if Saurn has found the *Chosen One* he has taught him more than Seth ever knew. It is certainly a good thing that Binosear never learned the identity of his time's *Chosen One*, or the prophecies could have come true then."

"That's impossible," scoffed Basille.

"Is it Basille? Everyone is very aware of the prophecy about the seven *Coromor*s uniting to vanquish Shau-ling, but the prophecy that always seems to be left out is the one about the *Chosen One*. It is said in the prophecies that if the *Coromor*, the *Chosen One*, and the *Erieal* were to ever unite against Shau-ling, their combined power would be enough to vanquish our damnable master for the rest of eternity."

"Fine," Zarsi said confidently, "Saurn has control of the *Chosen One*, and all we have to do is wait for the *Coromor* and the *Erieal* to storm the palace, and then we slaughter them and take control."

"Idiot! If we were to let the *Coromor* and the *Chosen One* unite, they would not only destroy Shau-ling, but they would also destroy us. What would stop them from slaughtering us as quickly as they would Shau-ling?"

"Nothing," Basille replied. "However, if we were in control of the *Chosen One*, knowing what we know about the potential of his powers, what would we order him to do?"

"I would order him to go after the other phasia. The old divide and conquer routine. After I was sure they were all dead, I would go after Shau-ling with him at my side, and with very little competition," Zarsi replied.

"As would I," Warron agreed.

"Exactly. That's what we would all do. That is exactly my point brothers. How do I know that if I go to Saurn to talk about our plan, this *Chosen One* won't jump out of the shadows and slit my throat," Basille asked with genuine concern.

"I'm sorry to say you won't. It is something that has to be done though. We have to know if Saurn intends to stand with us or against us," Zarsi said quickly. "We also have to know if he truly does have control of the *Chosen One.*"

"Very well," Basille conceded, "I'll go."

"I truly hope that it is not a trap old friend," Warron said slowly, "I would not like to see you come to the same end Saurn and Aerith Seth brought to you all those years ago."

"Nor would I," Zarsi added.

"Thank you both for your concern, but I think you should both return to your kingdoms. They definitely need your leadership, and we also don't want any of the other phasia finding out about our little plan," Basille said confidently.

"Very well," Warron answered, "we will leave. We expect you to notify us when you return though."

"If you return," Zarsi mumbled under his breath.

"And if you don't," Warron added, "we'll have our answer anyway."

Just then, two blue portals appeared behind Warron and Zarsi. They both nodded to Basille and then stepped through their respective portals. As soon as the portals had closed, Basille opened the door to his chambers and stepped inside. The door closed behind him leaving the hallway empty.

Suddenly a figure began to appear near where the conference between the three phasia had taken place. The man had to have been close to eight feet in height, and his body was defiantly not thin for his size. His heavily muscled chest shown through the tight-fitting red shirt that he constantly wore. This was by far the most physically powerful of all the phasia. He was even considered to be more powerful than Warron. This man was the Cougar, Taron.

"So," Taron said to himself, "my brothers are plotting against Shau-ling. That in itself is not so unusual, but to throw a group of traitorous Jeresei, Saurn and the *Chosen One* into the works makes such a plan worth reporting. Shau-ling may even reward me for this news."

With that, he turned and walked toward the throne room.

* * * * * * * * * * * *

As the door closed behind Basille, he took a deep breath. Never before had a conversation between the phasia taken such a drastic turn. There had been hundreds of plans to overthrow Shau-ling, but plans have never been acted upon like this before. Basille took a long look around the room for a moment and then sighed. He walked over to the little palate of a bed that he kept in that room and picked up his sword.

Years ago, almost two hundred, he had been traveling through a minute town out in the middle of nowhere. He was drawn there by the legend of a mythical blacksmith who could forge a sword out of any material for the right price. Years earlier, Basille had found a metal that was light as a feather, but almost as strong as a diamond. He took this metal with him and hired this legendary blacksmith to make him a sword. The metal was black in color, and when the sword was finished, it was the sleekest, lightest sword in the world. The three hundred gold pieces that he had paid for the sword was well worth it, and the minute weight of the sword had saved his life many times over the years.

Basille sheathed his sword and then buckled the sword belt around his waist. After he was sure the belt was securely fastened, he closed his eyes, raised his right hand, and a blue portal appeared before him. Basille opened his eyes and then stepped through the portal. Within a matter of seconds, he was standing in his own throne room.

Going straight to Saurn from Shau-ling's palace would be stupid. I know that the other phasia are watching my every move, hoping that I'll slip up and lead them right to the Viper. It would be easy for them to trace the ripples of power I make when I create those portals. My brothers are fools to think that Saurn will help them. Besides, Saurn and I have already decided to finish Shau-ling ourselves and split the world right down the middle. What I didn't know was that the Chosen One was involved. The War for Power will begin anew, Coromor and Erieal aside. Now, to work.

Basille looked up from the throne he had seated himself upon and then raised both of his hands. All around him, portals began appearing. When Basille finally stood, he was surrounded by ten portals, each identical in form and color. Basille closed his eyes and mumbled a few words under his breath. When he opened his eyes, an image of himself had appeared in front of every portal except the one that stood directly in front of him. Basille smiled to himself and stepped through the portal. He knew that none of the other phasia could track his movements, and none of the other phasia had figured out his special little trick. Every one of the phasia had a special trick all their own, and the ability to split his body was Basille's.

Moments later, Basille emerged in the place where he had agreed to meet Saurn. No one dared to come to the Blight anymore, and there were only a few who still remembered that it existed. Of those, only two or three remembered exactly where the Blight was. Basille himself would have never known that this was where Saurn was hiding had it not been for an accident. He found himself in the middle of a losing battle years earlier, and when he created a portal without naming the destination, he ended up in the Blight.

"Welcome brother Raven," Saurn's voice echoed from everywhere.

"I am here as we agreed Saurn."

"What have you learned?"

"As you and I had expected, there is most certainly a rift in the phasia. Naturally, Jeroch, Erdric, and Aldridge stand with Shau-ling. Caris, Warron, and Zarsi are willing to side with you, and I have no idea where the loyalties of Farax and Taron lie. There has also been word of the Chosen . . ."

"Speak not of that Raven. You have done very well. You must now return to your kingdom, it is not safe here. When you receive word of Caris' death, you will return to Shau-ling and demand that he reconvene the Council. Tell him that is the only way I will return."

"Caris?" Basille asked deeply concerned.

"She is merely another step in our path to conquest brother, as are the rest of the phasia. Think not of it."

"A group of Jeresei is leading the Army of the Dragon into Illimar under the orders of Zarsi. If that is how you intend to kill Caris, I would not be so confident in their abilities."

"What?" Saurn thundered. "The Army of the Dragon is being taken to Illimar?!? That fool! Korrd is in danger! Be off Basille, I will see you when the Council is convened."

There stood Basille, alone. His head was filled with questions, but very few answers. Only the Council and the ravings of his brother Saurn could answer them all.

EPILOGUE

Appendicies

Dramatis Personae

Cedric Binosear
The Lord Lion
First *Coromor* of the Prophecies
Lord of the Kingdom of Marcwell
Twin Brother of Anabel Binosear

Erika Belnosian
Daughter of Arthur Belnosian
Sister of Erdric Belnosian
Betrothed of Cedric Binosear

Aryx Terian
White Lightning
General in the Lion's Mane
Fire *Erieal* of the Prophecies
Knight of the Kingdom of Marcwell
Husband of Diana Geoffry Terian

David Tamerlane
Blacksmith's Apprentice
Son of the Mayor of Aradon
Brother of Elwyne Tamerlane

Logan Ranthall
The Lord Dragon
Second *Coromor* of the Prophecies
Son of Arin Ranthall and Victoria Rhuiden
First Cousin of Pike Rhuiden
Relationship with Elwyne Tamerlane

Pike Rhuiden
Former Blacksmith's Apprentice
Apprentice Carpenter
Son of Tam Rhuiden
Best Friend of Talon Aielin
First Cousin of Logan Ranthall
Elder Merin's Former Lover

Talon Aielin
Apprentice Carpenter
Best Friend of Pike Rhuiden
Professional Carouser

Lane Toridon
Apprentice Magician
Orphan
Adopted by the Town of Aradon

Gwydeon Sandar
Apprentice Blacksmith
Sword Master
Son of Torris Sandar
Brother of Bella Sandar

Eldar Merin
Daughter of Noble Family of Trelon
Sword Master
Champion Duelist
Best Friend of Elwyne Tamerlane
Pike Rhuiden's Former Lover

Elwyne Tamerlane

Daughter of the Mayor of Aradon
Sister of David Tamerlane
Relationship with Logan Ranthall

Arin Ranthall

Member of the Lion's Mane
First *Chosen One* of the Prophecies
Husband of Victoria Rhuiden
Father of Logan Ranthall

Victoria Rhuiden

Member of the Lion's Mane
Sister of Tam Rhuiden
Wife of Arin Ranthall
Mother of Logan Ranthall

Tam Rhuiden

Master Carpenter
Aradon City Council Member
Brother of Victoria Rhuiden
Father of Pike Rhuiden

Torris Sandar

Master Blacksmith
Aradon City Council Member
Father of Gwydeon Sandar
Father of Bella Sandar

Arathorn Geoffry

Leader of the Lion's Mane
Earth *Erieal* of the Prophecies
Brother of Diana Geoffry Terian

Mailock

Member of the Moridon Tribe
Water *Erieal* of the Prophecies

Diana Terian Geoffry

Member of the Lion's Mane
Wind *Erieal* of the Prophecies
Sister of Arathorn Geoffry
Wife of Aryx Terian

Gideon Viruci

Professional Thief
Member of Alimidar Thief's Guild

Ren Manderis

Former Member of the Lion's Mane
Former Pirate
Dock Master of Illimar
Alias: Seelious Monk

Midarin Rice

Former Princess of the Kingdom of Brea
Banished for High Treason
Master Archer

Zar Elouix

Lord of Rama

Captain Antrobus

General of the Army of Rama

Alexander Mealon

Standard Bearer
Squire in the Army of Rama

Talos Berder

Member of the Moridon Tribe
Advisor to the Kingdom of Rana

Anabel Binosear

Sister of Cedric Binosear
Queen of the Kingdom of Trelon
Mother of Cairyn Binosear
Mother of Allan Binosear
Alias: Camille Talaat

Cairyn Binosear

Daughter of Anabel Binosear
Niece of Cedric Binosear
Heir to the Kingdom of Trelon

Allan Binosear

Son of Anabel Binosear
Nephew of Cedric Binosear
Crown Prince of Trelon
Second in Line of Succession

Leane Torne

General in the Army of Rama
Former Member of the Army of
Brea

Aerith Seth

General of the Hand of the Light
The *Chosen One*

Hawk Yetre

General of the Army of Sador

Shau-ling
Master of the Shadows
Father of the Phasia

Jeroch Yetre
The Lord Shadow
First Born of the Phasia

Warron Ysamaran
The Lord Boar
Member of the Brotherhood of
Phasia

Basille Mystic
The Lord Raven
Member of the Brotherhood of
Phasia

Farax Soar
The Lord Vulture
Member of the Brotherhood of
Phasia

The Flame
Personal Guardian of Shau-ling
Keeper of the Hall of Terrors

Zarsi Aeron
The Lord Cobra
Member of the Brotherhood of
Phasia

Aldridge Farran
The Lord Hawk
Member of the Brotherhood of
Phasia

Saurn Macco
The Lord Viper
Member of the Brotherhood of
Phasia

Caris Vale
The Lady Wolf
Member of the Brotherhood of
Phasia

Erdric Yarrow
The Lord Scorpion
Member of the Brotherhood of
Phasia

Taron Steen
The Lord Jackal
Member of the Brotherhood of
Phasia

About the Author

Brian Kershner is a life-long dreamer, writer, and problem-solver. He grew up absorbing anything and everything he could get his hands on, and as a child of the Star Wars era he constantly wanted to see the worlds beyond the little Indiana town he grew up in. There was no adventure too far, and no problem too big.

Emboldened by parents who always supported his curiosity and his thoughtfulness, Brian found himself bounding from Space Camp to Laser Summer Camp to Athletic Training Camp to Piano Lessons to Football Practice to Basketball Practice to Choir Practice and back again. Despite all of the roaming and traveling, his family remained close-knit and supportive.

Though he flirted with the idea of becoming a doctor, Brian's attentions always fell back to the computer world. He got his first computer when he was six, and not long after found his way into a word processing program and began crafting his own fantastic worlds and even more fantastic characters.

As he has grown and changed and experienced life, so too have his characters. He continues to write, craft, and create; whether it is websites for his customers, or characters and worlds for his audience.